SPEEDING OVERDRIVE

FULL THROTTLE
BOOK THREE

KANITHA P.

Speeding Into Overdrive

Full Throttle Series Book 3

Copyright © 2025 by Kanitha P.

All rights reserved.

No part of this book may be reproduced in any form or by any electronic or mechanical means, including information storage and retrieval systems, without written permission from the author, except for the use of brief quotations in a book review.

This book is a work of fiction. Names, characters, organisations, places, events, and incidents are either products of the author's imagination or are used fictitiously.

Editing by Hannah G. Scheffer-Wentz, English Proper Editing Services.

Proofreading by Nyla Lillie.

Cover design by Ivy N. Isles.

For anyone who's ever feared not being able to reach the mountain's peak; you can do it. Prove them wrong. Look over your shoulder — at all your achievements and all the steps you've taken so far — and be proud of yourself. You made it.

And to Celia, you would have loved Indy and Huxley so much. Keep on shining brightly and dancing happily across the galaxy.

CONTENT WARNINGS

This books contains mature language, explicit sexual content (includes use of toys and anal play), anxiety representation, parental neglect, mentions of drug use (substance use leading to death (off-page)), mentions of bipolar disorder and depression, emotional and physical abuse from a parent (off-page), death of a parent (off-page), and on-page alcohol consumption.

PLAYLIST

The Alchemy | Taylor Swift
Cedar | Gracie Abrams
The Only Exception | Paramore
The Climb | Miley Cyrus
Say Don't Go (Taylor's Version) | Taylor Swift
December Days | Tim Hanauer
Pushing Daisies | Ryan Mack
Soulmate | Chanin
Better Half Of Me | Ryan Mack
What Are You Listening To? | Chris Stapleton
Dreams From Bunker Hill | Cigarettes After Sex
Take Care | Beach House
ocean eyes | Billie Eilish
With Or Without You | U2
Fade Into You | Mazzy Star
So High School | Taylor Swift
feelslikeimfallinginlove | Coldplay
Wanna Be Loved | The Red Clay Strays
this is how you fall in love | Jeremy Zucker, Chelsea Cutler
Guilty as Sin? | Taylor Swift
Stay | Rihanna, Mikey Ekko

CHAPTER ONE

ABU DHABI, UNITED ARAB EMIRATES

December 2021

"You can do this, Miles."

Could he, though?

Could he break the record and win?

Could he prove them wrong? All that suffocating pressure, that torturous doubt—could he cross the finish line and show the world how mistaken they'd been about him?

One mistake, one wrong move, and he would lose it all.

Tightly gripping the steering wheel, Miles listened to the engine roar as it vibrated with a desperate need to release its energy. Foot lightly pressing on the throttle, he ignored his racing heart, needing to put an end to his misery and win the Grand Prix. He glanced in his rear-view mirror, the nineteen other cars following the invisible line he'd created by zig-zagging to keep the tyres warm.

Miles was focused on the safety car leading the queue of fast cars, the adrenaline pumping through his veins burning further with every second passing by. The yellow flag would be over soon, he supposed, and these next ten laps would determine his entire future.

For the first time since the nineties, he and his biggest on-track rival, Thiago Valencia, held the exact same amount of points in the drivers' ranking, setting them at the same level—at the top of the championship. They'd battled brilliantly for the entire season, fighting for the first place during each race, but whoever won this Grand Prix would be crowned World Champion.

If Valencia won, he'd be champion for two consecutive years. Miles wouldn't allow this. This was *his* moment of glory.

Perspiration clammed his entire body, created by the heat coming off the circuit and the high temperatures of the warm air. His heart thrummed with anticipation, fast and loud, on the brink of coming to a halt just at the thought of making a mistake.

"Safety car is going in on the next lap," AJ, his race engineer, announced on the radio.

With his thumb, Miles hit the radio button on his steering wheel. "Appreciate the heads up."

The Aston Martin drifted into the pit lane, and that was his cue to accelerate as he saw the green flag being waved in the air. The tip of his foot lightly pressed on the throttle and the car roared off through the straight line.

Thiago was following closely, but Miles' car was faster and swifter in turns, rendering the acceleration easier after taking the chicane.

"Come on, man," AJ said. "Just watch out for track limits. Emerson has a five-second penalty because he keeps crossing them in turn nine."

Miles didn't reply as he shifted his entire focus on the route ahead. If there was one thing he truly hated during races, it was AJ talking to him when it wasn't necessary. If AJ wanted a good chat, he could wait until they hit the pub later.

"What's the gap?" he asked, breathless, on lap fifty. Eight more to go.

"You're already three seconds ahead of Valencia. Keep your pace."

He checked the rear-view mirror. "He looks like he's got good pace, too."

"He does, but you're faster. He's also on a set of fresh tyres. Soft."

Miles only took a breath, letting the smell of burnt rubber invade his senses, his surroundings a complete blur.

"Keep a check on tyre management," AJ continued. "You can win this, Miles. You really can."

"Just let me fucking drive."

※

THE LOUD BASS of the music thrummed through his veins as Miles grinned at his teammate who'd stood up on a table to chug a beer before being chased away by a bouncer.

Arm draped over the back of the sofa he'd been lounging on, Miles adjusted the paper crown atop his hair and took a small sip of water, watching Charlie argue with security.

"Here's our champion!"

Malakai came to plop in the seat beside Miles, wrapping his free arm around the latter's shoulders. His other hand was holding a half-consumed glass of beer—Miles had already lost count of his friend's drinks for the evening.

"Holy freaking hell," Malakai mumbled before slightly backing away, his fingers digging into Miles' shoulder. Even in the dim light, his bright eyes were glowing with pride. "You are the World Champion, man. This is crazy. Absolutely bat-shit crazy! I thought I was going to die from stress during the last few laps. My heart, I swear, it stopped beating, dude."

This was, probably, the fourth time Kai was telling this story to Miles.

Kai was the hugging type when drunk. And bubbly. And slightly emotional. Engulfing Miles in a tight embrace, he sniffled and repeated how proud he was of him and his incredible achievements.

Only twenty-four years old and one of the youngest World Champions to break a record.

Miles patted his friend's back. "Okay, don't get all emotional on me."

"I'm not." Kai stood up, lifting his glass. "I'm going to go and get shit-faced. I hope you're having a blast!"

Of course, he was. Miles didn't need a single drop of liquor in his veins to have the time of his life. "I am."

Dramatically, Kai put a hand above his heart and sighed. "So damn proud."

Miles shook his head in exasperation and watched his friend disappear in the mass of people gathered on the dance floor.

People kept trying to steal his attention, his time, by inviting him over to their booth or asking for a dance. But Miles needed a moment to sit down, breathe, and seize it all in.

He'd won a championship. Had proved anyone who had deemed him unable to beat Valencia wrong. Even he still couldn't believe it—it was like a fever dream that made his mind spin in a constant frenzy.

He'd already danced (albeit against his will) and talked to an awful amount of people. He was sweating, the desperate need to get some fresh air becoming more and more urgent as minutes passed by.

Miles straightened himself, not caring if he was alone. Not caring of his image—the World Champion celebrating on his own and not letting one single person close to him. He took one more sip of water before deciding to head out but...

His stare halted on a blonde dancing in the middle of the crowd. The way she moved beneath the spotlight—it looked like a movie sequence shot in slow motion, all the sounds around him muted as he watched Indigo Bailey dance and dance and dance, uncaring of the whole world around her. She smiled, and laughed, and sang along with the lyrics, making this entire moment one of the most valuable of her existence.

She was utterly captivating. Mesmerising. She had stolen the entire room's attention, rightfully so.

Miles smiled behind the rim of his glass and glanced away. But out of his control, he looked back to Indy—Malakai's younger sister. A fierce, loyal, passionate woman who embodied danger so gracefully that he could get burned if he stared at her for too long.

But, as though she could sense his gaze despite all the other pairs of eyes set on her, she turned around and smiled beautifully. The sight of it fed his soul, felt akin to a breath of fresh air he'd been craving after spending hours in this crowded place. She pushed past bodies pressed together, and he braced himself for the upcoming encounter.

Miles rubbed the back of his neck, holding Indy's gaze as she marched towards him. Confidence emanated from her demeanour, and if Miles didn't feel hot enough, he felt like combusting at the sight of this enchantress entering his orbit.

"You look lonely." Her voice was edged with a drip of seduction, piquing his interest even further.

He gestured to the open space beside him, ignoring his racing heart after blatantly perusing her ethereal physique. "You going to fix that?"

As she sat next to him, Miles draped an arm around the back of the sofa, casual and nonchalant, but made sure not to touch her, keeping a certain distance between them. It was a privilege to have captured Indy's attention when she'd avoided other men all night long.

"Bored?" Her red lips tipped into a mocking smile, and he narrowed his gaze on her.

"Being my antisocial self."

She laughed softly and took a small sip of her drink. "Odd choice to make in a nightclub, but you do you. I can go if I'm interrupting your peace."

He usually pushed people away, but her presence had always been addictive. "You're staying. I can make an exception for you."

"Don't flatter me."

"Wouldn't dare feed that ego of yours too much."

As she scanned the room, he took the opportunity to capture a photograph of her rosy cheeks and sparkling eyes to embed in the back of his mind. "I'll be honest. I'm surprised to see you alone. Look at all these women wanting your attention."

He didn't so much as look away from Indy. Once again, he traced the contours of her mouth with his gaze. "Not interested."

Only a soft sigh escaped as she turned back to him, a slight shake of her head perceptible. "I can't believe you did that."

Great. Keeping his distance wouldn't work. He had barely heard her voice. And he couldn't just keep on staring at her plump lips like a creep, trying to decipher her words. He shifted closer—just slightly. "Did what?"

Indy's smile was his undoing. "Win the championship."

His brows lifted in tantalising stupefaction. "Out of all people, I thought you'd be the one to have the most faith in me."

She stirred the straw around her large glass. "I did make a bet, though."

"Why am I not surprised?"

"And I won."

"I feel proud," he said, allowing a shadow of a smile to ghost over his lips.

Miles wasn't sure if he had imagined the tinge of crimson appearing on her cheekbones because of the dim light, but he tried to convince himself she was simply overwhelmed by the heat of the room.

Miles had known Indigo since he was a child as he and Malakai met when they were merely five years old when they started karting. She'd always been more than *just* Kai's little sister, and that was exactly why watching from afar was better.

"How are you feeling?" she asked, scooting closer. Her perfume whiffed in the air; something sweet, intoxicating, feminine—just like her.

It was painfully clear that the drinks she had consumed were seeping through her system, but her concern and interest seemed genuine. It was at that moment Miles wished she were sober.

Dropping his stare to her legs when she placed a thigh atop the other, he tried not to make it obvious that her presence was rendering him utterly powerless. Dressed in a little black dress, she looked regal and on the verge of pulling him towards temptation. He'd resist, especially because he knew Malakai was observing them from afar. And because she was off-limits.

The people around were probably wondering what was so special about Indigo since he hadn't allowed a single woman approach his VIP lounge, except for her. The list of things making this woman so unique was too long to even think about.

"Good," he finally answered, meeting her gaze. A satisfied gleam swirled around her pupils, as if she had followed the route of his scrutiny and saw it linger on her toned, bare legs.

She shifted just enough to fully face him, her knee digging into the side of his thigh. Miles' fingers twitched, like his body was urging him to touch her. "Just good?"

"What do you want me to say?"

"Come on, Huxley." *Huxley.* She'd always been the only person to ever call him by his last name. He loved the fact that she could own him by simply doing that. "You can find something better to describe what you're feeling. Like... Amazing. Cheerful. Happy. Ecstatic."

He nearly chuckled. "Cheerful? Do I look like a cheerful person to you?"

She lifted her glass. "I highly recommend being happy. It's good for the soul."

Miles hummed, nodding. "I can always count on you for good advice."

Indy winked playfully. "I'm your girl."

If only.

Everyone knew Indigo as the outgoing, brave, fearless woman with a sparkling personality. If she were to be a colour, she'd be yellow—the vibrant kind he could find in a field of sunflowers, the specific shade of gold he'd catch in a ray of sunlight filtering through windows in the morning. She was far too good for him—for anyone, really. But somewhere in the back of his mind, he liked to think that, one day, he could be what she needed.

"I just don't think I can find the right words to describe what I'm feeling," he said then. It was true, no word could explain that incomparable sensation. He was still high on adrenaline, trying to grasp this new reality. He could still remember the back of his throat burning after he'd crossed the finish line, listening to his race engineer and the people in the background scream with joy. Could still remember the tears blinding his vision as he entered the pit lane to park below the podium.

She eyed him in silence before chugging the remnants of her drink. "We'll circle back. You better have found the right word by then."

The smirk tugging at the corner of his mouth was out of his control. "I'm holding you onto that."

As she leaned towards the small table to deposit her empty glass, her other hand came to find support on his thigh. At the contact, Miles felt his heart starting to race. He couldn't help but observe the smoothness of her bare back, feel the press of her knee and her fingers into his leg. His breath caught when her palm slipped upwards, and he forced his hands into fists to prevent himself from touching her skin. When she straightened herself, her gaze slipped to the top of his head where a paper crown lay. She retreated her hand, her touch lingering like an invisible tattoo.

Malakai Bailey needed to plead guilty for his stupidity. He was the one who'd judged it as *fun* to put a crown on the World Champion's head.

She laughed, that beautiful, sexy melody booming louder than the music. Then, her fingers came to adjust the crown, but Miles felt paralysed. He observed her features, trying to remember when she'd become so—

Time stopped when their gazes clashed, his hammering heartbeat more deafening than all the noises around.

"You're a king," she mumbled. "Look at you."

Miles wasn't sure what had caused the blush to burn his face and the back of his neck—her words? Her seductive gaze? Their sheer proximity?

"Enough about me." He cleared his throat and jutted his chin towards her. "What's up with you?"

A mere shrug of her shoulders was her response, but her vocal answer came quickly as if her mouth had acted before her brain could. "Nothing interesting."

"Come on," he scoffed. "Everything about you is interesting."

She leaned her shoulder against the back of the sofa, colliding into his arm. It was a Herculean effort not to let his fingertips draw shapes on her arm. "I'm doing my master's in sports journalism, my internship with Thunderbolt Sports starts in February, and I'll be taking a course in motorsports analytics. The goal is to become an F1 presenter at the end of my internship. Or maybe a sports broadcaster. I'd love to work in the NHL too, but F1 is the dream. I want to change the world."

One thing he knew about Indy was that she was a dreamer, but she'd climb mountains to reach her goals. Would persist, and resist, and fight until she got what she wanted.

He smiled, although briefly, at the thought of her being an F1 presenter. She already hosted a motorsports podcast that had reached hundreds of thousands of people.

"Atta girl," he praised with a smirk. Pride danced across his chest. "It fits you well."

The memories of their childhood were as clear as day: Indy interviewing him with a spatula as a microphone when he'd stay over to eat with the Baileys after go-kart races. It was as if she'd known her destiny from an early age, and Miles simply admired the fact that she'd always been sure of what she liked and wanted.

"Thank you."

"There's a but, right?"

She sighed, looking away. "But... I'm Zachary Bailey's daughter."

His eyebrows rose. "So? You think you can't make it because you're an F1 legend's daughter?"

The question made her look back at him. "I think people will say it's too easy. I don't want Dad's help to get there. I don't want to be known just because I'm his daughter."

Miles took the risk to speak his truth. Because she was drunk. Because his words weren't meaningful to her. "You're Indy Bailey. You can do it on your own. You don't need anyone's help to prove them wrong. You want to change the world? Do it. I know you, and I know that when an idea runs through your mind you won't rest easy until you tell yourself *'I've made it.'* Besides, I think you'd do great as a presenter."

"Are you saying that just because that means you'll see me more often around the paddock?"

It felt like she had only remembered his last line, which made him laugh. "Whatever makes you happy, sweetheart."

THERE WERE two reasons that made Miles' heart somersault the next morning. The first one was the sight of Malakai sprawled over the sofa in the en-suite living room, snoring loudly. The second one was seeing Malakai's sister sitting on the counter of the kitchenette, a glass of water in hand as she rubbed her left temple.

Miles had forgotten he had brought the Bailey siblings back to his hotel room. Kai, too smashed to even find his own damn head, had insisted on staying at the club and partying until he'd fall into oblivion.

So, Miles had forced him to come back to the hotel, but Kai wouldn't leave without his sister. Trying to keep the Bailey siblings straight on their feet was chaotic to say the least. Indy had booked a room in another hotel across town, so the initial plan was to drop her off first. But when she had declared everything was spinning, Miles had decided it'd be better and easier if she crashed in his room, too.

Kai had barely made it to the sofa when he'd fallen asleep, shoes and all still on. Miles had tossed one of his t-shirts to Indy when she said she'd sleep on the other sofa.

It was when he looked at her now that he realised he should have been a gentleman. Should have given her his bed while he slept next to a nearly-unconscious Malakai.

The guilt would certainly give him a headache.

Miles didn't notice he'd been staring at her until she lifted her eyes to look at him. His cheeks heated up as he tried not to glance again at her bare legs and her body hidden beneath his t-shirt.

"Hi," she whispered as he strode towards her, rubbing the back of his neck.

"Hey. Rough morning?" He kept his voice low as well, but he knew that Malakai wouldn't wake up any time soon. He was used to taking care of his best friend after a night out.

"Your sense of observation is truly wonderful."

He gave her an amused glance. Indy liked to use sarcasm as a coping mechanism, but Indy being grumpy *and* sarcastic? Talk about his type of woman.

"You might be the only person who can make a hangover look so good." Sure, her mascara had left stains beneath her eyes, but her blonde hair still looked silken as it cascaded down her back. That faint tinge of rosy colouring the apples of her cheeks was put in evidence by the sunlight filtering through the window.

Miles felt his heartbeat speed up when her gaze sauntered over his bare chest, taking in every muscled pane of his torso and halting at the waistband of his joggers. He took another step forward, pretending to aim for the coffee machine when all he wanted was to be close to her.

"Are you flirting with me, Huxley?"

Like a natural instinct, her legs parted ever so slightly when he came to stand between them. He listened to her breath catch, his gaze settling on her parted lips. "I don't know, Indy. Am I?"

He held her gaze, losing himself in ocean eyes slightly darkened with desire. He could recognise lust in a woman's gaze, but there was something far stronger in Indy's scrutiny. Something he couldn't name nor try to understand.

He inched closer, the distance between them slowly disappearing as her legs naturally opened further for him—welcoming him.

What the fuck was happening?

Why was he losing control like this?

His hand slipped behind her, the tips of his fingers grazing her hip, as he went to retrieve an empty glass. If she was affected by the proximity, she didn't show it. But he wanted her to yield first. He'd seen the way she looked at him last night. And he knew he'd mirrored her desire.

He wouldn't have taken advantage of her when she had consumed alcohol. Regardless of her drunken state, he had spent a memorable night by her side. They'd laughed and talked until Kai came to disturb their peace. Still, there hadn't been a moment where Miles couldn't think of what could've happened if she were sober.

As if she'd read his thoughts, she gulped down the remnant of water, luring his gaze towards her gleaming lips. She was sober now, and she was trying to show him.

"Indy," he whispered—maybe like a warning.

She tipped her face upwards, letting the tip of her nose touch his.

He reached for her chin, and the mere contact set his skin ablaze. Her breath hitched and she murmured his name—like a plea. His thumb ghosted over her lower lip, as though the movement could erase the risqué invitation dripping from her sinful mouth.

The sound of Kai's loud snore startled them—a reminder that they shouldn't cross that line. Still, his body was in flames, needing *more*.

Forgetting about his glass, he took a step back. A triumphant smirk spread across his lips when he heard her hop off the counter and follow him into the bedroom. The lock clicked softly, and he pivoted in time to watch her lean against the door, fingers playing with the hem of the too-short shirt.

"Come on, Huxley," she nearly purred. "Tell me to go if you don't want this."

His chest rose and fell. His clammy palms brushed through his messy hair. His heart was racing, and Kai was on the other side of the door. Utterly passed out, but still.

"Want what?" he rasped.

A dangerous smile touched her lips. "If I'm not mistaken, you were about to kiss me out there."

He licked his lips, taking a step towards her. The woman who'd always been off-limits but who, in this very instant, didn't keep her barriers up. Who was waiting for him to break.

"Say no and I'm out of here," she continued quietly.

In perfect synchronisation, their chest heaved, and he felt like his heart was battering its way out of his body. His tongue came to wet his lips, and when her eyes settled on his mouth, he murmured, "Fuck it."

Just once, and his attraction for his best friend's sister would fade away, right?

Just once, to let all that pent-up envy explode.

Just once, and it would never happen again.

Just once.

He placed a palm on the door above her head, their breaths mingling. He was so close to finally getting what he wanted. "How quiet can you be?"

Hooking a finger beneath his chin, she stood on her tip-toes. "There's only one way to find out."

The moment their lips touched, the promise of keeping the secret hidden behind this very door was forged into an invisible tether binding them together.

CHAPTER TWO

ALPINE VALLEY, SWITZERLAND

Three years later

"So, what do you think?"

The question kept resonating in his head, tapping against every corner like a ricochet, and Miles scoffed at the sight of Malakai's smirk.

"I think it's quite possibly the worst idea you've had," he impassively said, folding his arms across his chest.

Though sunglasses were shielding Kai's eyes, Miles was certain they were narrowed behind the opaque surface. "I'm being smart," Kai corrected, a slight bite to his tone.

"You're being stupid and irrational. Nuance," Miles fired back, dragging his sunglasses to place them atop his hair.

With the sun beating down on him, his jacket unfastened,

and the sounds of delight surrounding him, Miles didn't feel like he was at Alpine Valley—save for the snow covering the mountains that was proof he was indeed here. He usually liked the weather better if it was cold, gloomy, and snowy.

"It's just a favour." Kai smiled sheepishly. "Please."

Observing Romeo Quinn and Ezra Hayes deposit their snowboards just below the terrace they were lounging on, Miles sighed heavily. "We've been here for less than twenty-four hours, Kai. You could've waited until the end of the trip."

Now his week was ruined. How was he supposed to move on from what Kai had just asked?

"You need to get your head out of your ass," Kai grumbled. "I didn't ask you to fetch me the fucking moon. Why are you getting so worked up?"

Romeo and Ezra reached the table, arguing about who was the fastest on skis.

Once a year, during the Formula 1 off-season, Miles came to Alpine Valley to reconnect with his childhood friends and unwind from racing. While some drivers liked to spend the winter break sunbathing and relaxing, Miles liked to spend his energy on a pair of skis or a snowboard.

Kai was a professional snowboarder—two-time World Champion, Olympian, and twelve-time X Games medalist—and had recently bought a home here. Romeo and Ezra, NHL players for the New York Nightingales, couldn't always free themselves during Miles' time off, so the four of them being reunited was a rare occasion that deserved the best celebration.

"Why does Miles look like he's about to kill you?" Romeo asked, his signature shit-eating grin spreading across his lips.

"Because he's a grumpy ass who won't help his best friend who's in desperate need," Kai muttered, not so much as detaching his gaze from Miles'.

Miles scoffed just as the waitress came to pour white wine in three glasses, except for his. An iced tea would suffice. "Bollocks. You asked me for the most absurd favour."

"I've known you for almost three decades, Miles—"

"Save your tears for someone else."

Ezra whistled as he sat to Miles' right. "I need some popcorn."

"What are you two even arguing about?" Romeo inquired, passing his fingers through his dark hair after taking his beanie off.

Kai huffed before reaching over to grab his wine glass. "You know how I've officially moved out of Miles' flat in Monaco?"

"Yes," the two hockey players flatly answered in unison.

"You know how my sister is debuting as an F1 presenter next month and needs a place to live in Monaco since the main office is over there?"

His sister. *Indy.*

Indy.

Indy.

Just the mere, fleeting mention of her made his heart clench.

How many times had he whispered her name against her lips when he was on the cusp of unravelling?

How many times had he wished to be good enough and deserving of tattooing those four letters on his desperate, unloved heart?

How many times had her name crossed his mind when he'd been all but trying to forget it?

It was messy. Bound to be chaotic. Indy and Miles were shooting stars, threading through each other's galaxies, dancing around one another without ever colliding and making one supernova. Perhaps he'd allow himself to make one with her—in another life. But in this lifetime, he was destined to watch her shine on her own despite constantly yearning to cradle her into the centre of his orbit.

She was Kai's sister, but she was also Miles' dirty little secret. Had been for the past three years.

"Yes." The sound of Romeo and Ezra's voices echoing again in perfect harmony distracted him from his thoughts.

"Well, I asked our charming man here, Miles Frederick Huxley, to help her out for a few weeks until she finds a place of her own."

"My middle name's not Frederick."

Kai disregarded the remark with a goddamn sneer.

Romeo hummed behind the rim of his glass. "Prices *are* insane in Monaco."

"What would you even do with that extra space?" Ezra asked Miles. "I think it's a good idea."

He wasn't surprised by these two siding with Malakai. "Are you two encouraging this shit show?"

"A bit of a woman's company would be good for you," Romeo prompted. "You know, a bit of delicacy and softness? Knowing Indy, she'll buy flowers at the farmers market and cook you breakfast. Like, I'd sign up so fast for that. You need someone to soften your rock-hard heart."

"So long as you stay away from her," Kai warned.

Miles sighed. "What's that supposed to mean?"

"Means I don't want you two to fall in love because you'll just end up hurting her."

If he knew what had happened over the past three years... Feelings weren't involved, that was a rule they had both settled on, but still, Kai didn't need to know his sister was the only woman Miles had been sleeping with.

"Stop it with your overprotective big brother speech," Miles bit out, frustrated. "And no need to worry about that because I'm not interested in her." Lies. "Besides, *you're* the one who's asking *me* to give her the spare bedroom yet you tell me to stay away. Logic ain't your thing, man."

"Grumpy," Ezra mumbled, though an amused smile danced on the corner of his mouth.

"Tell him something he doesn't know," Kai scoffed before taking a long sip of his beverage. "Seriously, Miles, do it for Indy. You two get along, right?"

That wasn't the problem. The problem was that Miles had

sworn not to get too close, but living with her? It would destroy all the walls he'd built to keep himself safe. Not only would it be dangerous for him to be in her vicinity, but he didn't want to hurt Indy either. He could never give her what she needed or wanted.

"Sure," he answered grimly.

"Why do you suddenly hate Indy?" Romeo asked, reaching to the centre of the table to snatch an olive from the amuse-bouche platter.

"I don't *hate* her. She's great, really, but... It's just—never mind." No one could know about his history with Indy. It would just complicate everything.

"You loved to annoy the shit out of her when we were younger," Kai said. "And I'd feel better knowing she lives with you rather than with some random, rich-ass stranger we never heard of and who wouldn't even talk to her."

And deep down, part of himself knew that Indy was safer with him than with anyone.

"Help her out," Kai begged. "It's just for a few weeks. A couple of months, tops. Until she gets all the paperwork settled and finds a flat. Besides, she won't bother you. The season is starting again soon, and you'll both be travelling, so you'll barely be in Monaco."

Miles' jaw hurt so badly. He had to stop tightening it, but he needed to hold a semblance of control over his emotions.

Glancing around, he expelled a heavy breath. "What's in it for me?"

"Jesus, I don't know. If you want to bargain, do it with her. But you can do us this favour, can't you?"

Miles threw his head back and shut his eyes. What was the worst that could happen? Well, she would distract him. Would make him lose all sense of focus when he'd worked hard these past few years to push away everyone who dared to come too close.

But Kai was his best friend. His brother. Miles would run

through flames to save Kai, and getting burnt for returning a favour was just the beginning of his ruination.

"Fine," he ended up saying. "Just for a few weeks. I'm doing this for you."

CHAPTER THREE

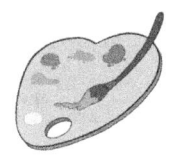

LONDON, ENGLAND

"Are you sure this is a good idea?"

Putting yet another pair of high heels in the luggage she had dedicated for shoes, Indy looked up to connect her gaze to her best friend's perplexed one. Kamari was leaning against the wall, hands in the pockets of her trousers, ankles crossed. Perched on stilettos, dressed in regal black, and an eyebrow arched, Kamari was the perfect portrait of disdain—yet absolutely beautiful.

"It's just for a few weeks," Indy said—as if she hadn't repeated those words over four times. "Until I can afford my own flat."

Indy was broke to say the least. All the money she had spent to simply *move* to Monaco was appalling, but she was ready to make the change. Deep to her core, she could feel that this new journey was made for her. That it was going to open doors to once-in-a-lifetime opportunities.

Indy could see the wheels turning in her friend's mind, the questions ready to be voiced, the uncertainty etched on her face.

"There's a spare room in Thiago's penthouse," Kamari suggested. "It's yours if you want it."

"And listen to you and Tito go at it every night? No thank you. I'm horny and single enough as it is."

Amusement sparkled in Kamari's eyes.

Indy blew out a breath. "Why do you think it's a terrible idea for me to live with *him*?"

"Because things are kind of weird between you two."

Indy winced. She couldn't even deny it. Things had been quite awkward for a while now, and she wasn't entirely sure why. Maybe because they'd been toeing a forbidden line for years. Maybe because her attraction for him had bloomed into something unfathomable, and she still had no clue about the way he felt.

Obviously, Indy was grateful for her brother who had suggested she took the bedroom he'd once used. She was also grateful that Miles had accepted this last-minute scheme, but she wasn't sure if it would work out. The last time they had spoken was at an after-party where they had ended up sneaking out to be tangled in bed sheets.

"*Please, don't fall for Miles,*" Kai had asked the day he'd called to announce that Miles was okay with her taking the spare bedroom.

"*Why?*"

"*I love him, he's a great guy, truly. But he doesn't know how to commit. Doesn't think he can settle down, and well, I know casual isn't your thing. So don't fall for him, 'kay? Just trying to look out for you. Also, don't take it personally if he struggles to open up. He has a hard time trusting people.*"

Her thoughts were interrupted when a tall figure appeared in the doorway. Thiago, Kamari's boyfriend and another Formula 1 driver who raced alongside Miles, pulled the hem of his white t-shirt to wipe his brow.

"Seriously, Indy," he started, letting out a heavy sigh. "Do you need all that shit to go with you to Monaco?"

Kamari had arrived just now due to obligations at work, but her boyfriend had kindly offered to help Indy pack and move out. Indy had always known that Thiago Valencia bore a soft heart behind the facade he'd come to show as the F1 driver—ruthless and heartless on the track. He had spent the entire day loading the moving truck, helping her pack boxes, and scoffing at her outrageous belongings.

"Yes. Thanks for your help, Tito, but you should go and enjoy the rest of the afternoon with Kam. I'll manage just fine."

"You're family, Ind. I'm not letting you move out on your own. You don't need to bring your bowls and mugs, though."

"They're handmade." She waved her fingers. "By these magic hands."

"Wow," Thiago droned, his brows lifting in mockery. "Pardon me, then. That's impressive. Bet the coffee tastes better if you drink from these."

Kamari glanced at her boyfriend. "Maybe Huxley can dedicate a shelf amongst his trophies to display her mugs. They're valuable."

"You two are so funny," Indy drawled, grabbing a pair of Louboutins to add to her stack of shoes. "Made for each other."

"Tell me something I don't know." Thiago grinned. "But Miles surely has those, right? A plate and a mug are, like, basics when you move into a place."

Indy scoffed amusedly. "Should I remind you two that Huxley used to cohabitate with my *brother?* Have you met Miles? Have you met Malakai? They are boys—"

"Whatever you're about to say is not a generality," Thiago mused.

"—and they slept on their mattresses for months before buying a bed frame. *Months.* I had to help them decorate and furnish the penthouse because, my gosh, was it pathetic."

Kamari's soft chuckle echoed. "I'm sure he's delighted to have you move in."

Indy threw a dirty glare to her friend whose response was a shrug of her shoulders.

Thiago entered the messy bedroom and plopped into the armchair by the window. "What are you two even gossiping about?"

With the back of her throat burning, Indy said, "I was just telling Kam how awkward it's going to be. Living with Huxley, I mean."

"Why do you say that?" Thiago grabbed the romance novel that was lying beside him, feigning interest so he wouldn't gape at all her lingerie scattered across the bed.

Indy wasn't embarrassed. Clothes were clothes. A body was a body. And she knew that Thiago only had eyes for his girlfriend.

"Well, to make it brief, let's just say we sleep together. He's phenomenal—"

"Spare me the details."

She grinned at Thiago's disgusted face. "It's always been quick and rough, but seriously, he's the best sex I've ever had."

"So, you guys are friends with benefits?"

Indy shrugged. "Yes."

"Exclusively?"

Shaking her head, she put a pair of knee-high boots inside her overflowing suitcase. "No. I saw other guys, and I'm pretty sure he's been with other people too. I mean, have you seen him? It was supposed to be a one-time thing, but then it happened a lot. Like, every time we saw each other. We agreed on keeping it casual, which I'm fine with, but I feel like moving in with him is going to mess everything up. Either we're going to fuck like bunnies—"

"Classy as fuck, Ind."

"—or we're going to stop everything just so it isn't weird."

"Yeah, I see why you're dreading it. Are you okay with both options?" Thiago asked as Kamari took a seat on the bed.

"I guess so. But he's been sort of distant. He didn't want me to come live with him when Kai asked him, and I just feel like I'm ruining everything by imposing."

But Indy knew he'd become this way—guarded, controlled, sometimes cold—with not just his friends, but with the entire world. As if becoming a three-time Formula 1 World Champion had changed him. Indy hated that. For the past few years, she had observed the way he kept putting on a mask whenever he was in the paddock, surrounded by cameras and reporters. Had seen the way he pushed everyone away to protect himself.

"You two could be *just* friends and see how it progresses," was Kamari's soft comment. "You'll notice he's just putting up an act to maintain his reputation. And maybe he said no to Kai in the first place so that your rule wouldn't be broken. Living with your hook-up is definitely not the same thing as seeking her out after a party."

"I *can't* be friends with a man I'm attracted to."

"Why not?" Thiago inquired, glancing up from the book.

"Because I don't think I'll be strong enough to handle the rejection when he puts me in the friend zone. How do you expect me to sit there and look at him whilst all I'll think about is the way his tongue—"

"Fucking hell, Ind."

She chuckled, avoiding the pair of socks Thiago chucked her way. "Sorry. I just think it's going to be weird, but I'm grateful he's giving me the spare room."

"When was the last time you two hooked up?"

"Like two months ago."

He tilted his head. "Why did it end?"

Another shrug. "Who knows? I was in London, he was in Monaco. We texted for a bit, but couldn't find a proper time to see each other. And that was fine with me."

"Well, I'm sure you two will figure it out," Kamari assured.

Indy knew that it was important to Kai that she and Miles got along. For her brother, she'd ruin herself, even if that meant not crossing any lines with Miles. Even if that meant pretending like nothing had ever happened between them.

"Right. Well, I'm moving to Monaco for the job of my dreams. I'm not going to let him distract me or ruin the perfect plans I've crafted for myself."

Who was she trying to convince? She had no clue.

"Good for you," Kamari said quietly yet fiercely, something like pride shining in her eyes.

Indy didn't miss the tenderness morphing onto Thiago's expression as he gazed at his lover. The flicker of envy crashing through Indy's veins nearly made her combust. Nearly made her beg the stars to give her someone to love.

She clapped her hands, moving past the detrimental emotions invading her senses. "Do you guys realise that we're going to be neighbours?"

Thiago grinned at that, and she knew he was already planning all the get-togethers either at his penthouse or at Miles'. "Why don't you try and convince Kam to move in with me too?"

Kamari travelled back and forth between London and Monaco. Though she and Thiago had moved into his townhouse in England, he was evidently still intent on having her move in with him in his Monegasque penthouse. What mattered most was that Kamari was unequivocally happy with this sunshine man, and Indy loved that for her best friend.

"The cafés," was all Kamari said. She owned two popular coffee shops in town—the second one being a sports bar which was cramped with happy patrons every single evening.

Thiago's features hardened. Indy wondered if it was a recurrent subject that led to arguing—Kamari was a hardworking woman, with a head full of ambitions and goals she wanted to achieve.

Deciding this wasn't the time nor the place to let those two argue about their future, Indy lifted two frilly nightgowns. "Do I take these negligees with me?"

Kamari chuckled. "What happened to staying away from Miles?"

"Who said it's for him? I like feeling sexy. Especially when I sleep."

Thiago threw his head back and rubbed at his temples. "Pete help me."

📍 MONTE CARLO, MONACO

WELL, maybe this was the worst idea in the entire world.

Standing in the lift and surrounded by two humongous pieces of luggage, Indy took a deep breath in. She was seconds away from arriving at his penthouse, and she didn't even know why she was so nervous.

It was just Miles Huxley.

Her brother's best friend.

The guy she'd had a crush on since she was fifteen.

And the man she'd been hooking up with for the last three years.

No big deal.

The soft ding echoed, bringing her to reality. She fixed her hair, then looked at the doors opening, revealing Miles standing across from her with his hands tucked in the pockets of his trousers. He stood there, crafted like a statue of a Greek God she could spend hours looking at, analysing and drawing.

She beamed. "Hi, roomie!"

He dipped his chin in a greeting gesture, his green gaze tracking her bags and belongings when a heavy exhale fled past his nose. "Are you moving in, or what?"

"Isn't that what the whole deal is about?"

"I wish it wasn't," he grumbled loud enough for her to hear.

A scoff was about to erupt, but she only took a step into the foyer. "God, you can be such a bellend sometimes."

He assessed her every move with an arched eyebrow. "Already told you, you can just call me Huxley."

He was infuriating! And so good-looking. All Indy wanted was to leap into his arms and straddle his lap.

Was she supposed to hug him? Shake his hand? Smack a kiss on his cheek?

As if her body had moved of its own volition, her arms wrapped around his broad shoulders. Miles was stiff, but after a beat, he relaxed into her touch, letting his palm connect with her back.

"Don't look so thrilled to see me," she huffed, taking a step back.

"Damn it. I thought the joy was so clear on my face," he deadpanned.

"Don't worry." She brushed his bicep, causing a muscle in his tight jaw to jump. The annoyance was so clear on his features that she hated herself for being the cause of his irritation. "I won't overstay my welcome."

The nerves were out of her control, and she despised this unrestrained feeling.

Indy watched a Doberman strut towards her, its tail wagging. Of course, Indy had seen Miles bring his dog to the paddock last season. This pair was the embodiment of confidence, of power.

"This is Rosie," he announced, tenderness lacing his voice as he scratched his puppy's head. "You're not allergic or scared of dogs, are you?"

She smiled, and his expression softened. "I love them."

Indy followed Miles into the penthouse, keeping her gaze on his muscled back as he pulled one of the baggages he'd taken a hold of. She couldn't help but stare at the power exuding from his body honed by countless hours of training. The sheer dominance from his demeanour.

Seeing Miles had settled an uncanny feeling inside her chest, just because it looked like it physically pained him to welcome

SPEEDING INTO OVERDRIVE

her into his home. The way he acted was unnerving, but maybe he had a reason for being so distant. Indy had decided she would keep being herself around him, and maybe he would eventually warm up to her. He'd always made an exception for her, so what was stopping him now that they lived under the same roof?

His spacious flat was exactly how she remembered it, although it felt more alive—with more pieces of furniture and decorations which were mostly all of his trophies and helmets aligned on a big shelf. Had it not been for the soft music in the background, Indy would have been able to hear the gears turning inside his head, or the grumbles he kept muttering beneath his breath.

Indy smacked her lips together. "Thank you again for doing this."

"Sure."

"I thought you'd be happier to have me as your roommate, though."

She saw his body stiffen, yet he kept walking. How was she supposed to diffuse the tension? By being an absolute walking embarrassment? Even that didn't seem to do the trick.

"You're not big on words today, are you?" Instant regret crashed over her as soon as the words escaped. Huffing at the ceiling, she winced inwardly.

"Or maybe it hasn't occurred to you that I'm not in the mood to make small talk," he snapped.

Asshole. Really, really, handsome asshole.

"That was barely small talk. But okay, sunshine. You sure do know how to make a girl feel welcome," she muttered, refraining the urge to roll her eyes.

"My pleasure. So, how was the drive down?" When he turned around and saw that she was gaping at him, bewildered, he shrugged. "What? You don't like my small talk?"

Indy wanted to laugh. Throw a shoe at him. Pour a bucket of cold water over his oversized head. "You're unbelievable. Just take me to my room, Huxley."

"I like how straightforward you are. Skipping a date and immediately heading to the bedroom," he blandly said, his rough voice making her cheeks tingle. "You know where everything is. Just make yourself at home."

Indy nodded. "Did you end up doing something with all the spare rooms?"

With a jut of his chin, he motioned to the closed door on their left. "Sim room." They passed another closed door. "There's junk in this one." And another door. "The gym."

"Of course, you have a gym."

"Feel free to use it whenever you'd like. This is your room," he indicated by opening a door and scraping a hand over the scruff on his jaw. "Everything is all set for you, so... Yeah."

Indy had already been inside this very room which had been occupied by her brother for a couple of years. All the decoration had been taken down save for the photo frame on one of the nightstands—a photo of the Bailey family. On the bed was a little basket with a blanket, a book from her favourite author, and her favourite candies. Her heart swelled, knowing that Kai was behind this sweet gesture.

Miles set her luggage by the door and turned towards her, hands finding shelter in the pockets of his loose jeans. Indy couldn't read beyond his hardened expression, his scowl, his frown.

Still, she smiled, not wanting to hold any animosity against him despite his coldness. She'd have to get used to it, anyway. "Thank you. I really appreciate it."

His response was a stiff nod before he took a step forward. "I'm going to get all your stuff up. Is Tito still downstairs unloading the car?"

"Yes."

For what felt like an eternity, his stare was on her. Like he wanted to ingrain her portrait in the back of his mind.

"Alright." He cleared his throat. "Just settle in. I'll handle the rest of it with him."

Indy knew exactly what was coming, causing a painful sensation to twist around her already aching heart.

As he brushed past her, she felt the sudden urge to catch his elbow, just to feel his skin—touch him. But she refrained from doing so by folding her arms beneath her breasts. "Huxley? I'm sorry for intruding."

The muscle in his jaw ticced as he towered over her. Next to him, she felt so small, so powerless. The scent of his cologne was too familiar, too intoxicating, and it was at that exact moment that Indy wondered how she would survive his constant presence. She didn't want her heart to be obliterated. "No worries. Happy to help Kai."

Of course, he was doing this for Kai.

"Maybe we could sit down around dinner tonight and talk about rent and the rules you expect me to follow in your home." She smiled up at him again. "I'm happy to cook."

The indifference in his eyes would have sent any person running, but Indy wasn't impressed by this cold mask. He wouldn't make her yield, so she kept her chin high.

"The only rule we're going to go by, Indigo," he started lowly, "is that we're roommates now. Nothing more, nothing less. Whatever you're expecting from me or hoping to happen between us, you can forget it."

"I—"

"I hope you understand that we have to stop what we've been doing. It can't happen again, okay?"

He turned on his heel without glimpsing at her reaction.

Well, this was going to be harder than she thought.

CHAPTER FOUR

MONTE CARLO, MONACO

His chest heaved as he tried to recuperate his breath. Pushing his locks away from his forehead, Miles peered down at his phone when it vibrated before mounting the few steps leading to the entrance of the building he lived in.

"'Sup," he said to Kai after accepting the video call.

His friend's face popped into the frame, a mocking grin spreading across his lips. "Good morning. Don't you look dashing today."

The doorman opened the door and Miles stepped inside the lobby. "I just went for a run."

Miles had found himself needing to blow off some steam more often than usual this week, and running seemed to do the trick. During the F1 season, he would train with Enzo—his physiotherapist and trainer—but when it was the off-season,

Miles liked to work out alone even though Enzo lived down the block.

Romeo's face appeared a second later. "Look at that sweat. Women are certainly falling at your feet when they see you running around the streets of Monaco. Bummer for them that it's still winter and you're not showing off your godly, tanned, sculpted body."

What a bunch of fucking morons. But truth was, Miles missed being around them.

From afar, Miles heard Ezra's snort. "They most likely will fall because of the atrocious smell of his sweat."

"Says the hockey player," Miles jested. "Everything about you stinks."

"Still doesn't stop me from bringing a girl to my condo after every home game."

A muscle in Miles' cheek twitched, but all he did was gesture to Kai to wait a second as he took an earbud out. "Hello, Teddy."

The doorman dipped his chin in a polite nod, his smile hidden by his white moustache. "Mister Huxley. Good run?"

"Pretty good. The weather's nice for a February afternoon. You? Good start to the day?"

"Very. Your new roommate is a sweetheart. Quite the opposite from her brother. But tell Mister Bailey he's missed around here."

Kai's chuckle resonated in his ear, but Miles ignored it, arching a brow sceptically. "Is she?"

"She went to the farmers market and brought back a couple of pastries for us"—he gestured to Danny, the receptionist—"which was very thoughtful."

See? To her core, she was just a good person. A caretaker.

"Sounds just like her," Kai chimed in.

If there was a certainty about Indy, it was that she was a ray of sunshine in everyone's life. But Miles was forcing himself to be a thick, impenetrable cloud who couldn't let her in, just because the man on the other side of the line was trying to protect her. Because she deserved so much more than what he could offer.

"I called to check in," Kai informed, a drip of suspicion lingering in his words.

"Why?" Miles saluted the two men standing in the lobby and walked towards the lifts.

"I haven't heard from either of you, so I thought something happened."

"Like what? Killing each other?"

"That would have been surprising. But I don't know. Indy's so fucking unpredictable. You never know what her next move is going to be."

"Happy to announce she's alive and well."

Kai chuckled. "Good to know."

It had been a week since Miles had a new roommate. As much as he tried his hardest to avoid her, it felt like torture. He knew he could only blame himself for not wanting to cross paths with her.

Miles merely didn't want any distraction. The season was starting in a couple of weeks, and he was already determined to become a four-time World Champion. Ever since his first title, his focus had shifted to racing, and racing only. No more parties (well, just a bit less than before); no more girls (even though the only woman he'd touched in years was Indy); no more anything that would make his determination waver.

But unfortunately for him, Indy was a total distraction. Always had been.

Always talking with that husky, euphonious voice. Always laughing with whomever was calling her. So far, he hadn't seen much of her around the penthouse because he'd been hiding in his sim or gaming rooms. But he dreaded the moment he would allow himself to see more of her because she would certainly walk around in taunting clothes, reminding him that their deal was off. Truth be told, knowing that he was no longer allowed to touch her hurt. For years, she'd been his, and now she was just a memory.

"Is she settling in okay?"

He cleared his throat. "I think so. She's been busy unpacking and all, but I've been busy too, so we haven't really had the chance to talk." What he didn't say though, was that he was blatantly avoiding her.

"Yeah, yeah, I know you're staying away on purpose. Don't treat her like shit," Kai warned.

"I'm a fucking gentleman," Miles bit out, annoyed by the fact his best friend knew him so well.

"Gentleman my ass. Have you checked on her? Made sure she was comfortable in the flat? Cooked her dinner? Even though you can't make a decent meal for shit."

No, no, and no.

The reason he hadn't checked on her was because he was afraid of losing control. But he knew how important it was for Kai that he got along with Indy, so he would make an effort.

"Although, I received an interesting text the other day," Kai continued. "Indy was thanking me for the little basket I left on the bed, but I didn't do anything. I bet she doesn't know it's from you. Neither does she know about the feminine products you bought for her bathroom, or her favourite brand of cereal you stocked in the pantry."

"No, she doesn't know anything, and I'd like for it to stay this way."

"What did you put in the basket?" Romeo asked, standing behind Kai with a packet of Oreos in hand. Wasn't it early morning where they were? Miles could bet everything that Romeo would complain soon enough about messing up his diet.

"A love letter," Miles deadpanned.

Romeo snickered whilst Kai frowned deeply.

"Seriously, Miles. She's my sister."

"Really? I wasn't aware. One day you're like 'stay the fuck

away from her', and the next you're all 'you should give her a cuddle and pat her hair.' There's only so much a man can do."

"Stop being weird. I just don't want you to knock her up, or something."

Miles froze. Did Kai know about— "What?"

"I'm way too young and cool to become an uncle."

"What's wrong with being cool?" Romeo asked, bemused.

Miles emitted a frustrated grunt. "You're an absolute shithead, Bailey. I don't even know how you and Indy are related."

The Bailey siblings were total opposites but complemented each other well. Aside from their identical crystal blue eyes, they didn't resemble each other much. Indy was blonde whereas Kai had dark hair. She had porcelain skin, and his was tanned. She was lean, graceful, sophisticated, and he was muscular, unruly, and loved to give Miles shit.

"Relax." Kai chuckled. "All I'm asking is for you to be her friend. Indy loves wearing that tough girl mask, but she's going through some rough times with the new job and all. She just needs some company, okay? She can't stand being alone."

He sighed. "Fine."

"She puts a lot of pressure on herself," Kai added. "She's going to want to achieve all her goals with absolute perfection, and she won't stop until she gets what she wants. I need you to look out for her, yeah? Make sure she doesn't overwork and tire herself."

Until now, Miles didn't know that Indy was an overachiever. It was a quality, and in that matter, they resembled each other a lot. "Did you ask her to look out for me too?"

"Obviously."

He refrained the urge from protesting. Miles didn't need anyone, but he'd do just about anything for his best friend. "I've got you."

"Thank you," Kai said earnestly.

The lifts stopped at the penthouse and he walked in, facing a huge bouquet of flowers set on the coffee table. He groaned, narrowing his gaze on the laptop and notebook she had left on the kitchen counter. Next to it lay a boulangerie's bag which, he supposed, contained a couple of pastries.

He toed off his sneakers and went into the kitchen to pour himself a glass of water. After taking a few sips, he unplugged his earphones, tore off his shirt, and walked towards the hallway. So far, no sign of Indy.

"Goddamn!" Romeo shouted. "Here are the abs. That's one way to flirt. Kai, sorry man, but he's trying to get Indy in his bed."

Kai flipped Romeo off. "Shut the fuck up."

Miles ruffled his hair, eyeing the mess lined up against the wall—boxes she'd left in front of the junk-room. "She's got those boxes full of pottery and paint stuff. Why did she even pack these?"

A beat passed. "Did you know she has bad anxiety?"

Miles couldn't help but frown. "Really?"

"Indy's all pretty smiles, high heels, and tough shit, but she can get really insecure about everything, so it gives her anxiety. She found comfort and peace in pottery and painting. They're the only things that help when she's in a crisis."

If Miles had known…

Something like regret pushed at his chest. He shouldn't have been so cold with her.

"I had no clue." Brushing a palm across his jaw, he sighed. "What am I supposed to do if she has a panic attack?"

"She doesn't allow anyone to see her like that, so I doubt you'll ever witness an actual attack."

Indy was, undoubtedly, out of bounds and out of his league. The times they met in the past were the strongest secret tying them together. And even though Miles had known Indy for years, he realised he didn't truly know her. Except from the softness of her skin, the sounds of her—

The door to the gym opened as he passed by it, and he said to Kai, "I'll catch up with you later."

"Wait—" The line went dead.

Indy startled when she nearly bumped into him, a hand on her chest before pulling her headphones down to rest them around the back of her neck. "Huxley! I nearly had a heart attack."

"You should look where you're going."

"Oh, wow," she scoffed. Her eyes rapidly roamed over his naked, damp chest, her gaze feeling like sparks. She needed to stop looking at him like that. "Thank you *so much* for the advice. Maybe you shouldn't stand there like a creep then."

"I was walking by," he fired back. "God forbid I walk around in my own home."

"Shirtless? I didn't know clothes were optional." Once again, she blatantly traced the curves of his torso with her eyes.

"You don't like what you're seeing?" A smirk threatened to break free when she did a double take at his v-muscle.

"What I'm seeing is that you're conceited. Are you ill?"

"Not that I know of," he muttered, frowning. "Why?"

"Because you just said more than two words to me."

He shrugged, taking in her irresistible allure. Her blonde hair was tied in a high ponytail, her tall and pristine physique hugged by a matching pink sports set. The faintest sheen of sweat was glistening on her skin, the rise and fall of her chest even as she observed him with equal interest.

His lips parted at the sight of her nose ring, the rosy tint on the apple of her freckled cheeks so enticing that he had to blink to make sure she was real.

Indigo Bailey was a walking wet dream, and he wasn't sure how long he would be able to fight the temptation.

"What are you listening to?" he asked, leaning against the doorframe. He had decided, thirty seconds ago, that he'd stop being a dick.

A dry chuckle fled past Indy's lips, and he raised his brows. She stepped forward until she stood before him, slightly twisting so her front skimmed his arm as she left the room. "Now you're talking to me?"

Throwing his head back, Miles groaned before dragging his hands through his hair. "Sorry."

"Try and sound more sincere when you apologise, Golden Boy."

Golden Boy. Only she called him that. *Her* nickname for him since they were kids.

Miles watched her form retreat, unable to glance away from her lean legs, small waist and goddamn perfect round ass. "Do you want me to get on my knees and beg?"

She peered over from her shoulder, smiling mischievously. "I'd love that."

He huffed before following her into the kitchen, frustration streaming through every nerve and vessel.

Her back was to him as she opened a cabinet to retrieve, what he supposed was, a glass. "Since you're talking, why don't you tell me why you're avoiding me?"

His next move was absolutely unnecessary and not thought through at all, but he came to stand behind her and fetched the glass before she could. She stilled. Waited. He observed the way she slowly yet barely craned her neck to peek at him. The sliver of distance between them was so minimal that, if he exhaled, they would touch. "I'm not avoiding you, Indy."

"And I don't need your help," she gritted out.

"Yeah?" he murmured, watching the hairs on her nape rise. "Is that why you're living with me while you look for your own place?"

Indy pivoted, and he couldn't breathe as he stood so closely to her. She snatched the glass from his hand, seeming unaffected by their proximity. "Whatever. You need to work on your poker face when you lie."

"You're welcome for grabbing the glass."

"I was getting there," she fired back. "*Thank you.*"

Her stare dropped to his mouth when he poked his tongue against the interior of his cheek, his breath catching when her eyes connected again with his. Miles found himself being paralysed as those cerulean irises flicked between his, unable to decide what exact colour they were. Sometimes cobalt in dim lighting—like in a club—sometimes a sapphire, crystal blue in daylight. And god fucking damn him for getting lost in that kaleidoscope of azure.

"Look," she started, slipping to the side to find the sink. "I'm sorry for being an inconvenience. I know it's bothering you to have me around, but maybe we could be civilised towards each other? Especially you. No need to glare at me. No need to be rude. I'm not asking you to hang out every damn minute of the day or cook dinner or watch my *Gossip Girl* reruns with me. I'm going to be out of here before you even know it."

God, she'd always been feisty. Straightforward. Matter-of-fact, no-bullshit kind of woman.

Miles rubbed the back of his neck before tousling his hair. "It's not—I don't mind having you around."

"Again, that lie was effortless."

There was a bite to her tone, a certain coldness he wasn't used to hearing, but maybe he deserved it.

"I don't want to make you uncomfortable, Huxley," she continued softly. "If you want me out of here, just tell me, but I'd appreciate it if you could give me at least a week to sort things out. Look for an affordable place, and all."

"You don't make me uncomfortable at all. The room is yours for as long as you need it." Miles raised his hands in surrender. "I'm sorry I made you feel like I'm annoyed to have you around, because I'm not. Let me take you up on that offer you made earlier this week. Let's chat around a good meal. Let's order in. Or cook. Or let me buy you dinner in the fanciest restaurant."

"Did Kai ask you to do that?" Incredulity shone in her eyes.

"No."

"Because it seems to me like you do everything he tells you to."

"Does he tell me to fuck you like I did the last time I took you in that bathroom at the club?"

Crimson creeped up her high cheekbones and heat flared inside her pupils. Depositing her glass atop the central island, she leaned her palms across the marble, her head slightly tilting sideways as her gaze glided across his face, then his chest, then what she could glimpse at below his waist—studying. Remembering.

"Want to make up for your douchey attitude?" He nodded.

"Try harder," she quipped.

And with that, she walked back towards her room, leaving Miles jaw-slacked and utterly irritated by her attitude.

If he was expecting her to be compliant, to be the Indy who always fell to his feet, then he was obviously wrong. She was going to play hard to get, and he loved nothing more than a good challenge—even if that meant losing focus for a heartbeat.

CHAPTER FIVE

📍 *MONTE CARLO, MONACO*

There was something so soothing and innately beautiful about Indy's aura. About the golden energy she emanated.

When Miles crossed the threshold to his flat, the smell of cinnamon filled his nostrils and opened his appetite. Music was playing from the stereo, but not loud enough to conceal Indy's soft voice as she sang to the lyrics while sitting at the central island, her attention zeroed in on her laptop.

Seeing her at first made his heart jump a beat because he still wasn't used to her presence.

She had cleaned the penthouse, including washing the dishes he had left in the sink last night with the intention of doing them in the morning. Procrastination had overpowered his senses, and Miles had decided to go on a run instead of cleaning his mess. Indy didn't need to clean up after him, but he wasn't even surprised by her kindness—even after the way he'd treated her.

With her chin in the palm of her hand, she glanced at Miles as he took off his shoes before he strode towards her.

"Morning, stud," she chirped.

Stud? Even though Indy had accepted the fact they wouldn't sleep together anymore, she wasn't afraid to show how much she was attracted to him. And listening to her flirtatious tone, seeing the salacious glint in her eyes, always made his control rattle.

"Hey." He jerked his chin towards the kitchen. "Are you baking cinnamon rolls?"

"Yes, chef."

Had she remembered they were his favourite baked goods? After an intense, rough, intimate moment in his hotel room a few months ago, he'd mentioned craving a cinnamon roll. She'd told him hers were excellent, and Miles had made her promise to make some for him one day. The only way to convince her had been to give her another orgasm. The girl knew how to bargain.

A hint of a smirk ghosted over his lips. "Are they for me?"

The scoff she emitted made him narrow his gaze. "They are, first and foremost, for my own pleasure but I guess I can share them with my rude roommate."

Offended, he parted his mouth to argue. "I'm not rude."

"I beg to differ," she huffed, diverting her attention to her laptop before sighing and locking her gaze back to his. He didn't like the way her features hardened into annoyance, into vexation. "You know what? You don't get to do this. You don't get to treat me like shit just because Kai told you to stay away, or whatever bullshit he put inside your head. Just because we aren't fucking anymore doesn't give you the right to be like this."

"Indy—"

"I'm not done," she snapped. He widened his eyes and nodded frantically. "You like to be cold and arrogant and untouchable when you're racing. But you've never acted this way with me before, and I don't understand why it's changed. Why do you suddenly hate me?"

She had a point, and he felt terrible for the pain he'd caused.

He was used to distancing himself from people, but his thoughts had kept him awake last night. Indy had always been nothing but good to him, so he needed to start giving her equal goodness. But what if he got too attached? She was bound to leave—sooner or later. "I don't hate you," he murmured. "I could never, Indy. I'm sorry. I truly am. You know I'll make it up to you."

After holding his gaze for a few beats, she looked away. "I'm holding you to that, Huxley."

He simply didn't know how to act around her. They'd gone from secretly meeting after races to hook up, to living in the same penthouse. All he knew was that he was constantly a blushing mess around her, and that he needed to get a grip if he was supposed to see her every single day.

"I think I just need a bit of time to adjust to this new lifestyle. Going from Kai to you as a housemate is different." Kai was loud, she wasn't. He was organised in a way, and she was a beautiful tornado crushing everything in her path.

A small smile pulled at the corner of her lips. "I promise my company is fun."

"I don't doubt it." He scratched the stubble across his jaw. "Can we call it a truce? Start over?"

Her eyes shone. Hope. Relief. "I'd like that."

Extending his hand, he couldn't deny the sparks jolting through his veins when her palm connected with his. "Friends?"

"Friends."

"Cool." He cleared his throat, fighting a smile. "Cool."

After downing a glass of water and not-so-discreetly observing Indy type on her keyboard, he went to the balcony. He enjoyed stretching over there just to revel in the view of the ocean, listen to the peacefulness on the coast, and watch people walk on the shore.

But it was Indy's hypnotising voice that lured him back in. Made his world spiral as she softly hummed to the tune echoing through the entire penthouse. She was the embodiment of sunshine—a light slipping through the cracks of brokenness and loneliness, rendering a once dark world entirely colourful.

Shit.

He needed to erase those thoughts from his mind. Needed to focus.

"What kind of music do you listen to?"

He pivoted, brows raised caused by her genuine intrigue, then slowly made his way towards her before taking a seat on a stool. It was an effort not to let his thigh touch hers. Not to leave lingering caresses dancing across her skin the way he used to love doing after making her reach the pinnacle of pleasure.

"Huxley." She snapped her fingers, the insolence in her demeanour making his irritation spark. "Are you going to keep staring at me or answer my question?"

"I'm still deciding," he answered tersely. "You're not too bad to look at."

"Is this how you flirt? Because it was terrible," she scoffed. "You can call me beautiful. Gorgeous. Sexy, even. No need to be shy with me."

Certainly, she was all three. Indigo was breathtaking beyond measure—the entire world was aware of that—but she'd ruin him to ashes.

"Friends don't flirt, Indy."

She had the nerve to roll her eyes. "Right. My apologies."

"Apology accepted. Here." He offered the earbud he had taken out before entering the flat, holding her gaze when she plucked it into her ear.

"Classical music?" Brows lifting, sheer surprise drew onto her expression.

"It's my favourite after a run."

"That's funny. I wouldn't have pegged you for a classical music kind of guy."

He shrugged as he went through his numerous playlists, selecting the one with more upbeat rhythms. "I listen to everything. Even audiobooks."

Her eyes snapped to him, curiosity dancing around the edges of her pupils. "What kind of audiobooks?"

"You know, about mental health and such."

She snorted softly. "Sounds like you."

It was no secret that Miles was an advocate for mental health. He spoke freely about it, wasn't afraid to show that high-performance athletes needed to take care of their health—both mental and physical.

He nodded, noticing the glass filled with a green beverage and ice cubes. Grabbing it, he asked, "What's this?"

"Iced matcha latte. Try it."

He obliged, but the regret was so instant that he grunted. Indy's laugh was akin to flowers blooming in the spring, to a ray of golden sunlight after spending an entire day in the pouring rain. The grimace he made must have been funny enough to laugh so heartily. He pushed the glass towards her before shaking his head.

"This is disgusting."

Taking a sip after him, Miles couldn't help but watch her full lips wrap around the straw, the tip of her tongue making a brief appearance to collect a stray drop. "The first time's usually hard, but you get used to it. It's really good for your health."

"No thank you. I'll stick to protein shakes." His gaze slid towards her laptop. Next to it lay a notebook on which she had scribbled information about the Saudi Arabian track—where the first Grand Prix of the season would take place next month. "What are you working on?"

"I have my first day of work on Monday. Just checking my schedule, going over what I'll have to do before we travel for the pre-season testings, doing some research. All that stuff, you know."

Miles knew she would have done it. Secretly, he'd smiled and felt a flare of pride warm his chest when he had learned she was going to be one of the lead presenters this upcoming season.

She'd worked hard—harder than anyone he knew—and it was evident her efforts had paid off.

His lips broke into a minuscule smile before he asked, "Are you nervous?"

"About my new job?"

He nodded. Making conversation with her had always been effortless. There was just something about her that encouraged him to be himself. It had been a while since he'd felt this way, but he refused to linger on the thought.

"Yeah, I am."

The waver in her voice and the slight tremble in her fingers didn't go unnoticed. He frowned, taking out his earbud and repeating the motion with hers. He remembered Kai telling him about Indy's anxiety caused by certain insecurities. That statement had piqued Miles' curiosity—what was she hiding beneath the golden girl surface?

"You're going to do great. So many people are rooting for you and are excited to see you on the screen and in the paddock. This is huge for you."

Her smile was drop-dead gorgeous. He was thankful for sitting down already, otherwise he would have fallen to the ground—plummeted into an abyss of foolishness. "I've always dreamed of this."

"I know." He winked. "I'm truly happy for you."

"Thanks." The tint of pink staining her cheekbones deepened. "I'm going out tonight by the way. A friend's in town."

"Yeah? Do I know her?"

"*His* name is Alex. And you do know him. He's Tito's best friend. The photographer."

How was he supposed to conceal his irritation? "You're going out with Alex Myers?"

Miles didn't share any animosity towards Alex. He genuinely seemed like a great guy, always smiling and creating beautiful content for Thiago. He shared some kind of similar vibes to Indy's—bright, fun, positive. Maybe that sudden wave of protectiveness crashed over him because he'd promised Kai he would look after her. Or maybe because imagining another man's hands on her made—

If she was concerned by his sudden frustration, she didn't let on. "Got a problem with that?"

Those cerulean irises dropped to his jaw that had just twitched. "Nope. I'm going to be busy the entire day, anyway."

"Are you going somewhere?"

"My sim room. Need to train." Irritation streamed through his veins as he shut down. The thought of being abandoned because Indy was going out tonight only brought his walls up.

Her gaze softened. "You never stop." It wasn't a question, just a simple statement without any hint of judgement.

"I can't stop if I want to keep on being the best." She scoffed amusedly at his remark, but he continued, "And my father's also in town so I'm going to invite him over for pizza, or something."

Her brows shot upwards. "Oh, Henry's in town? Good thing I'm going to be out then. I wouldn't want to be a burden to you two. But Diana would have *loved* to be here."

"First off, Dad would love to see you. And don't call yourself a burden because you're not and never will be. Second of all, why are we mentioning your grumpy friend?"

Diana was a friend of Indy's whom he had met a couple of times. She was pretty but had an attitude as fiery as her copper hair.

"She's got a crush on Henry," Indy casually explained.

A grunt vibrated in the back of his throat as he frowned deeply. "Why?"

"He's a DILF."

She'd said it with such nonchalance that he reared back. "Don't—seriously?"

"He's tall, handsome, in seriously good shape, and he looks like Henry Cavill. See? They even have the same name."

He shook his head. "That's disturbing."

Indy nudged his thigh with her knee before hopping off the

stool as the oven's timer went off. "If it's any consolation, you do look like your father."

"I feel so much better," he deadpanned, forcing himself not to stare at her bare legs and her tiny shorts.

She smiled brightly. "Good."

Debating if this conversation was now over as she was too focused on her freshly baked cinnamon rolls, Miles went to seek some quiet time on the balcony. But something was twisting inside his chest—something he couldn't name or describe but made him voice his thoughts without so much as thinking.

"Are you planning on coming home with Alex?" He rubbed the back of his neck, feeling an unsolicited heat.

"No." She pivoted to face him, arching an eyebrow before scanning his entire body. "Unless you *want* me to bring him back? You know I struggle to be quiet. I wouldn't want to disturb your sleep."

Anger flared through him, but he scoffed. She was toeing a dangerous line—again—by hinting what he was missing out by cutting off their deal. "I'd rather you brought no man up here."

"What about a woman?"

She's good.

Fuck.

"Don't test my patience."

The fucking audacity she had to smile innocently up at him. "As long as you don't bring your special friends up here either, we'll be fine."

"I don't bring anyone up here."

"Ever?" The fact that she sounded surprised was baffling. Indy was well aware that Miles didn't hook up with anyone else. They'd had that conversation once before he took her rough and hard in a hotel room after a party.

"Ever. You're the only woman I've invited to my home."

Though the mischief shimmering in her eyes was noticeable, he didn't miss the flicker of relief and tenderness. "I'm honoured."

"Yeah, you should be." He turned on his heel and went outside, not realising he'd been holding his breath until now.

※

The sound of heels tapping on the floorboards followed the ding of the lift.

Miles observed Indy stroll inside the penthouse, pushing her coat off her slender shoulders, revealing a satin top with a plunging décolleté.

God fucking spare him. She was so effortlessly stunning that, sometimes, it hurt to look at her.

"Oh, you're sweet," she crooned as she spotted him lounging on the sofa with Rosie at his feet. "You didn't have to wait for me."

"I wasn't." He grabbed the remote and shut off the television. "You really think the world revolves around you."

"It does," she scoffed. "Have you looked at me?"

He had, and she was absolutely gorgeous. Devastating. No wonder why so many men were at her feet everywhere she went. A beautiful woman? That was tempting. But a beautiful woman who loved cars and worked in motorsports? There was nothing sexier to him.

When he didn't react to her smug remark, she laughed. "Is Daddy Huxley still here?"

Miles rubbed his face and stood up. "Don't call him that again. And no, he left a couple of minutes ago."

He was on the cusp of telling her that Henry had loved her cinnamon rolls and helped himself to seconds, but this would only inflate her ego. She embodied arrogance and insolence, yet in a very graceful manner that tended to make his irritation prickle.

She had left a note atop the dish before leaving: *For the Huxley men. Bon appétit xx.* Of course, they were delicious. Indy was a godsend, and he'd realised he didn't regret having her around.

Her red-painted lips twisted into a pout. "I'm gutted that I missed him. Is he coming by any time soon?"

"He's going back to London in the morning. But you'll see him around the paddock. He's attending every race, or so."

The glow of tenderness in her eyes made his heart race. "He's such a great father. I love how supportive he is."

Miles smiled. He had a soft spot for very few people, and his father was at the top of the list. "He's the best. Zach is an amazing one, too."

"My dad is great, yes, but you're just saying that because he used to be your favourite F1 driver back in the days."

He admired Zachary Bailey a lot. Had so much respect for him that most times he couldn't grasp the fact that he was his best friend's dad. Zach had taught him a lot about racing, and even to this day, he was his mentor and a trustworthy man he could rely on.

"Doesn't change the fact that I still think he's good to you and Kai." When she only shrugged, he asked, "Did you have a good date?"

"It wasn't a date." She hung her coat in the closet by the entrance. "Thiago was there, then Cal"—Thiago's physio—"joined us, too."

"Ah."

Burying his hands in the pockets of his joggers, he almost chuckled when she found support on his shoulder to unstrap her stiletto. The heat of her small hand burned through the fabric of his t-shirt, her intoxicating smell rendering his knees weaker than they'd ever been. But it was the sheer proximity that almost obliterated him.

He should have stepped back, should have pried her hand off of him, but all he did was smirk as she shifted to the other foot to take off the shoe.

"Did he kiss you good night?"

The heat of her fingers lingered on his skin. "Again, it wasn't a date. Even if it was, do you kiss on the first date, Golden Boy?"

His gaze flicked from her enticing mouth to her bright sapphire eyes. The moment his right hand left the warmth of his pocket, he pulled Indy in by the waist, her body taut against his. Her eyes were wide with surprise as they flickered back and forth between his, her hand slipping to his chest. Whispering, his stare dropped to her lips. "I don't date, Daisy."

If she was affected by the nickname he'd given her—the one he liked to call her by since the day they met when she wore a daisy crown atop her head—she didn't show it. If she was affected by his previous action, she sure as hell didn't show it either.

Travelling her fingertips down his torso, she studied his expression like she was trying to solve an enigma. But all he could think about was how wild his pulse was until she stepped back. "Right." Pivoting, she went for her bedroom, making sure to sway her hips and give him a full view of those legs and that perfect backside. With one hand holding her shoes, she used the other one to bid him farewell. "Sweet dreams."

His heart was still hammering—the cause of his recklessness—but Miles watched as she halted before the spare room to which he had left the door open. She peered inside, frowning before looking over at him.

"Huxley…"

"Indigo," he deadpanned. "What?"

"You set up all my pottery and painting equipment in here?" He had to blink to make sure she wasn't teary-eyed. Had to take a step closer to hear her frail voice. "Are you serious?"

With his father, they had spent the entire evening moving out the junk boxes into the garage downstairs before setting up the room for Indy. Earlier when he'd seen how stressed she seemed to be for her new job, he simply knew that painting would help her relax and soothe her nerves. Miles hadn't been entirely sure how to set everything up, but they had unpacked it all and moved the desk so it would be facing the window. If she wanted, she could use the space to set up her laptop and microphone to host her podcast. They had also installed a reading chair and a couple of blankets in case she wanted to take all her romance novels in here. Miles had made a mental note to order a shelf if she was planning on having her entire book collection shipped to Monaco.

"You're welcome," he said gruffly.

"You didn't have to do that."

Indigo was all bravado, confidence, and sarcasm, but she was also someone who cared about the people surrounding her and took care of them. Miles thought she wasn't used to receiving freely, to be taken care of, so perhaps that was why gratitude was shining in her eyes at that moment.

He smiled, feeling like his heart was about to lodge inside his throat. "It's my apology gift to you. Part of it."

All glimmers of tenderness faded away. "There's more?"

"I'm full of surprises."

CHAPTER SIX

📍 *MONTE CARLO, MONACO*

THE FRIGID, COLD air made her skin pebble as she stepped outside, wrapping her robe around herself. She hummed to the melody still dancing across her mind as she walked to the other side of the rooftop, her breath catching at the sight of Miles lounging in the steaming hot tub, arms draped across the basin's edge as he watched the dark, starry sky. Tanned skin illuminated by the lamps. Sharp, handsome features hidden in the shadows. Long fingers passing through his hair before a lazy strand toppled over his brow.

Shit.

As if she'd voiced the curse out loud, his eyes snapped in her direction, brows rising with surprise.

"Sorry. I didn't know you were already here," she whispered, gesturing behind herself with her thumb. "I'm going to go."

There was something predatory in his gaze as his perusal trailed from her face down her body. Something quite dangerous, yet luring Indy towards him, like he was a flashing warning sign and she only ignored it.

"I don't bite." That coarse baritone made another shiver roll down her spine.

"Oh, but you should know *I* do, stud."

His lips twitched upwards into a small smirk. "I'd like to see you try."

"Don't tempt me." When his shoulders shook with a soft chuckle, she let the victory warm her vessels. "Can I join, then?"

There was a single nod as confirmation. "Step into my office, Miss Bailey."

She flashed him a grin, because she knew that it was all it took for him to let his guard down. A heartbeat later, his broad frame relaxed, and she stepped forward.

"Thank you." Reaching the tub, she deposited her wine glass on the edge before untying her robe. Under the intense scrutiny of his green eyes, Indy felt utterly naked and exposed. Hoping he wouldn't notice the blush rising on her cheekbones, she dropped the piece of clothing on the chair to her right and stepped into the water.

Not once did Miles look away from her legs and the black one-piece hugging her physique. Not once did he try to hide his blatant attraction, perusing from her thighs to her chest to her face, before blinking and making that fleeting desire darkening his eyes vanish.

Yes, this man had been invading her daydreams for years, and yes, he was attractive. But she needed to get a grip. Needed to understand that she was here for work, to forge her place in a competitive world, and to focus on herself.

No man would make her bow. Certainly not her new roommate.

Indy swallowed her moan at the feeling of the warm water lapping around her body. She sank down until her shoulders were under water, her feet accidentally brushing against Miles'.

She wasn't surprised that he retreated them quickly, his expression indecipherable.

She reached for her wineglass and took a sip, roaming her gaze over the stellar sky. It was beautiful, dotted with bright constellations. It had been a cloudy day, so seeing the heavens so clear at night was surprising.

Miles was already watching her when she looked back at him. "I interrupted your peace and quiet, didn't I?"

"Ever since you became my roommate, but whatever."

"Charming."

When he passed a hand through his hair, she couldn't help but watch his bicep flex. "No, it's fine. Your company's tolerable."

"Here I am, feeling so delighted because of all your genuine compliments." He scoffed in disbelief at her tone, then glanced at her fingers wrapped around the stem of the glass. "I don't— Does it make you uncomfortable that I'm drinking?"

Indy was aware that Miles didn't drink at all, though she wasn't exactly sure why. Asking would mean trying to peel off one of his thick layers. He wasn't one to share much about himself, and regardless of her promise to herself to focus on her career, she still wanted to have him open up. But now, as she sat here, at midnight in the tub with him, she couldn't exactly ignore that weird feeling that had settled inside her stomach.

"Of course not," he murmured. "But thank you for your concern."

She nodded, taking another sip before setting the glass down.

The crease between his brows was too deep for her own liking. "Why are you drinking anyway? Got something stressing you out?"

"Work," she said, somehow surprised by the ease of the conversation he'd started. Miles Huxley was either black or white —no in between. She was honoured to have caught his interest. "First day tomorrow."

"You'll be fine," Miles assured gently.

"I won't," she whined before blowing a strand of hair away from her eye. "Have you seen the other journalists?"

Miles shrugged, as if her argument was irrelevant. "I talk to them. I don't *look* at them."

"Hopefully you'll be more of a gentleman with me."

"No need to worry about that." When he fluttered his fingers atop the bubbly surface, Indy found herself enthralled by the size of his hands, the veins and tendons adorning them. Yeah, she was a shameless slut for men's hands. Especially Miles'.

Indy had met her new coworkers a couple of times. She was the newbie on the team, the girl straight out of her master's degree with nothing but a podcast as baggage to prove that she was worthy of being an F1 presenter. Two of her male colleagues were retired racing car drivers, and the rest of her teammates had experience in the motorsports industry. Obviously, she was Zachary Bailey's daughter, but she did not want this to be the reason why she'd gotten the job—it wasn't, anyway.

"Just a heads up," he added wryly, "I hate interviews."

"Aw. Don't worry, I'll be kind and gentle. I promise I'll make it enjoyable for you."

He gave her a bored look. "Thanks for the reassurance."

Make him smile and be comfortable during interviews? Challenge accepted.

"Anyway." She circled back to his initial question. "My room's a mess—"

"Always is."

She arched her brow. "Did you look inside my bedroom? Snooped around? Did you open the drawer on my nightstand?"

He narrowed his gaze. "What's in there?"

"Wouldn't you like to know?"

Curiosity danced along the edges of his irises, but to her disappointment, he didn't voice his answer. "Why did you make a mess?"

"I couldn't find the perfect outfit. Narrowed it down to three and had Kam help me pick."

"You invited her over?"

"No, I showed her through the window."

Miles threw his head back and laughed. His smile was a thing of savage beauty, with a dimple popping in his left cheek. But his laugh... Such a unique, rare melody only a few people had the honour of hearing once in a while.

He quickly glanced at the building across from theirs, noticing that the blinds at Thiago's penthouse were closed.

Warmth danced inside Indy's chest as she observed stars shining in his eyes when he looked back at her. She wished the butterflies in her stomach wouldn't flutter. Wished she was immune to his dazzling looks. Slowly, he shook his head. "I never know what's going to come out of your mouth."

"That's exactly why you like me."

He lifted his hands in semi-surrender. "I wouldn't go that far."

"You tolerate me?"

"Sure. You're my roomie. And my best friend's sister."

"How could I forget?" It was a constant reminder so that she wouldn't cross the line. "So what do roommates do? Watch movies together? Play board games?"

A hum rumbled in his chest. "Don't threaten me with a good time."

"I'm sure you'd be captivated by the chick-flicks I watch."

"Undoubtedly," he said with a soft chuckle.

A peaceful silence fell. She didn't enjoy the quiet that much because she would start getting lost in her own head. But as she sat there with Miles, she thought about how she didn't mind his company, even if no words were being exchanged. Even if they simply stared at each other as though they had forgotten what the other looked like. She'd sought his attention and companionship for so long, but he was obviously off-limits for numerous reasons.

He interrupted the silence after clearing his throat. "I heard you talking to Lisa on the phone earlier."

Indy rolled her eyes. "My mother is thrilled that I'm living under your roof. You're definitely her favourite."

"She makes the best lasagna."

"And you keep kissing her ass for it, which is exactly why she loves you."

When he and Kai became friends during their karting days, Miles instantly became family. Whilst Miles pursued his career in motorsports, it was snowboarding that had lured Kai in, a ski trip on his fifth birthday determining his future.

His beautiful smile made her heart thump faster. His sheer adoration for her family was precious. "True. How's she doing?"

Indy shrugged. "She's fine."

"Just fine?"

Indy wanted to tell Miles about the words her mum had told her. Lisa was a good parent, one of the best, but she'd always been hard on Indy. Always wanted her to be the best, to keep her chin high and never allow other people to glimpse at her vulnerability. She knew that her parents were this way with her and Malakai to help their confidence be steady and powerful, to remind them they were good and talented and worthy of their careers. But sometimes, a scrap of affection was all she craved and needed.

"She's busy with work," was all she said. "Getting everything ready for the Milan Fashion Week." Lisa Bailey was a popular designer, specialised in bridal couture. "So she didn't have much time to chat."

See the picture? Growing up with a Formula 1 driver and a talented fashion designer was not only resourceful, but there was no place for failure. A Bailey didn't fail—a Bailey kept climbing the mountain to reach its peak, no matter how long and hard it'd be to pass the obstacles. And a Bailey did not disappoint their parents—ever.

"Right, right."

Indy tied her hair into a bun on top of her head, observing Miles' eyes follow the slope of her shoulders and linger on her collarbones. "So... Is the hot tub the equivalent of pottery and painting to you?"

She was fully aware that Kai had told Miles about her anxiety and that only making art could soothe her nerves. She wasn't particularly mad at Kai for revealing her secret, but she wished she could have been the one to tell Miles. Although speaking about it terrified her. She hated speaking about her anxiety because people saw it as a weakness.

A small smile ghosted over his lips. "I guess so. That, and music."

"Music?" Craning her neck to look inside the penthouse, she pointed to the piano. "You play?"

"No, it's just part of the décor."

She rolled her eyes at his sardonic tone.

"Yes, I play. I've been playing since I was four, I think. Music is a big part of my life. It helps me centre myself, it grounds me. I listen to music every chance I get, but playing is another thing. I don't get much time when it's not the off-season, but I try to bring my guitar with me on the road."

She couldn't help but guffaw. "You play the guitar too?"

Miles hummed, looking amused by her flabbergasted expression. "And drums. A bit of saxophone. The bass too. Piano will always be my favourite, though."

"Wow," she breathed out. "Women must be piling at your feet. F1 driver and musician? That's incredibly sexy."

Miles ran a hand across his jaw, trying to hide his grin. "They can pile over there all they want, but I'm not interested."

"Really?" She pinned him with a look. "You seriously don't date?"

"You know I don't."

"What about hook-ups?"

"There's only been you." He cleared his throat as she tried not to let her pulse quicken. The admission, however a simple reminder she had forgotten about, set her skin ablaze. "I'm really not interested in women."

Indy reached to the side to grab her glass, her torso sliding out of the water. Miles dropped his gaze to her chest, his jaw becoming taut at the sight of her breasts nearly spilling out of the swimming suit and the nipple piercings straining against the fabric.

Indy smiled behind the rim of the wine glass.

"Men, then?"

His heady gaze locked to hers. "No," he said again, more gruffly this time.

"Why, though? You don't have to tell me if you don't want to speak about it. It's just hard to believe someone like you is single."

"Someone as good-looking and talented as me? Maybe it's because I can't have the person I want."

His eyes didn't flicker away from hers. Didn't drop her gaze. Indy's chest rose and fell, her breathing nearly becoming laboured because of the shift in his stare.

"Or maybe because you're conceited."

He scoffed. "You know, when you're someone like me who's got a couple of championships under his belt, who is not even thirty and a multi-millionaire, the people who want your attention don't want you for *you*. They want the money, the free vacations, the cars, jewellery or watches or expensive clothes. They want fame, the camera flashes and news headlines. Can you blame me for not trusting anyone? Whether these people want to become my friends or more? I've had my fair share of shitty dates. Shitty friendships. I'm happy sticking to the core four"—him, Kai, Romeo, and Ezra—"and I'm not looking for anything. Just trying to focus on F1."

At least he was clear and honest, and maybe, deep down, she was grateful that they were on the same wavelength—success and career before love.

There was something painful prodding at her chest. "I'm

sorry about your past relationships. No one deserves to be taken for granted. To be used like you're just a walking wallet. You're so much more than that."

Miles swallowed, his throat bobbing, before nodding.

"I appreciate it." He nudged his chin towards the flat. "Let's get going. It's late, and we have busy days ahead of ourselves."

"Sure." She stood up, water splashing around her body, despite being thoroughly disappointed they had to cut this moment short.

His perusal followed the route of her legs, lingering at the apex of her thighs, travelling to her torso and the slopes of her shoulders. Repeating. Photographing. Admiring. The intensity of his scrutiny felt like sparks upon her body. Indy blinked when he rose to his feet, intrigued by the tattoo on his thigh. Had he gotten it recently? It wasn't there the last time she'd been with him, and that was merely two months ago.

She was already attracted to him enough as it was, and he was just making everything worse.

She missed him. His hands. His lips. The way he knew how to make her pant, how to pleasure her until she saw stars. And even if he was at arm's length, she couldn't touch him.

"You're staring," he commented, chest glistening, muscles contracting.

"Can you blame me?" she retorted unapologetically.

"I guess not."

Miles got out first, extending his hand to help Indy out before draping her robe around her shoulders.

"These are nice," he commented huskily, referring to her nipple piercings. She'd caught him staring at them a couple of times now. "Weren't there the last time I saw you."

"I got them recently."

"Nice." He glanced down at her chest once more, a blush rising on his neck.

She contained her amusement. "You already said that."

"Right."

She wrapped the robe around herself, tipping her chin up. "If you want to see or touch them, all you have to do is ask."

"I'm not going to be home this week," he said, ignoring her remark as something flared inside his pupils. "Going back to London for a seat fit at the factory and to get ready for pre-season testing. Will you be alright on your own?"

"Do I look like I can't take care of myself?"

He gave her an unimpressed look. "Literally not what I said, Indy."

She sighed. "I will be fine."

His eyes tracked her movements as she tied the robe, his palm rubbing the back of his neck. "I'm kind of leaving on your first day at work."

Her shoulders dropped as a smile touched her lips. Miles Huxley could pretend all he wanted, but he bore a tender heart. "That's sweet of you, but again, I'll be okay."

Miles nodded, exhaling.

"Are you taking Rosie with you?"

"That was the plan. Unless you want to take care of her?"

"I'd like that. I'll feel less lonely." She despised solitude. Being alone and caged in with her own thoughts. "I can invite Kam over before she has to leave for London too."

"Of course."

She tugged at the elastic band enveloping her hair, letting the blonde locks cascade down her back. "We'll have a girls' night. Baking. Movies. Maybe a pillow fight. With just our underwear on."

"Goddamn it, Indigo." Miles threw his head back and passed wet fingers through his hair. He took one step forward, the distance between their bodies minimal. "What do you think you're doing? You're my best friend's sister. I promised not to touch you, so for the love of God, fucking help me. Don't make this harder than it already is."

Ever since she'd stepped inside his home, she thought he was indifferent to her presence. Thought he was no longer interested in seeking her out. This revelation made her heart jump until annoyance overpowered her senses because she hated that he'd made a promise to Kai. Hated that he was depriving himself from having fun because he respected Kai a little too much.

She gestured around. "Do you see Kai anywhere?"

"That's not the point."

"It's never stopped you before."

A scoff rose from his throat. "We can't let that happen, okay?"

"*You* can't or won't?" Looking at his heaving chest, she shook her head. "Be selfish for once."

For way too many heartbeats, he simply stared at her, but she couldn't help but think there was something like grief in his eyes, like he was saying goodbye. It punctured a hole inside her chest, but still, she admired his self-control and the utmost respect he had for Kai's wishes.

Indy looked at his lips. Watched the heat darken those forest green eyes. Watched as he struggled to fight the obvious temptation. The tip of her nose brushed against his, making his breath hitch, her voice becoming that sultry murmur that had once brought him to his knees. "I fucking dare you, Huxley."

The pulsing in his jaw's muscle was perceptible as it tightened. "I'm not playing this game with you."

Only his cologne whiffed in the air when he spun around, walking away from Indy—creating an immense, obliterating distance.

CHAPTER SEVEN

📍 *MONTE CARLO, MONACO*

INDY TRIED TO focus on five things surrounding her to ground herself and not let her thoughts destroy her. The feeling of the cold breeze brushing against her temple. The specific, salty scent of the ocean. The sound of waves gently colliding with each other. The—

"You're a dog-sitter, too, now?"

Startled by the deep voice, she opened her eyes and scowled at Thiago as he strode towards her, brown hair blown away from his forehead, a thick jumper hugging his torso and a smile growing on his lips. The sudden urge to claw at her tight throat vanished, and she inwardly thanked the universe for sending her friend to her rescue.

Was he...moving in slow motion? Under the setting sun of Monaco? This was utterly ridiculous.

"You scared the crap out of me," she huffed, leaning back in her seat, her hands buried in the pockets of her coat.

He stared amusedly down at her. "What were you even doing?"

"Breathing."

Thiago snorted before taking a seat next to her. "Thank fuck for that. Didn't want to give you CPR, or something."

"You're such a good friend, Tito," Indy deadpanned, eyeing him up and down. He had the audacity to mock her with a loud snicker.

"Thiago," a voice scolded from behind. "Stop bothering her."

Indy turned just in time as Kamari reached the bench they were sitting on, a thick scarf wrapped around her neck.

"Thankfully, your girlfriend is always here to defend me," Indy teased.

"She's so sexy when her claws come out." Thiago grinned as Kamari took the seat on Indy's other side.

Kamari glared at her boyfriend. "Now's not the time to hit on me, pretty boy."

He sighed, his smile widening. "God, I'm so in love with you, it's unbelievable."

"Ugh," Indy groaned, pushing Thiago away when he reached across the bench to caress Kamari's flaming cheekbone. "You two make me sick."

Truth was, Indy was undeniably enamoured by the innate love they had for each other. He was warmth whilst she was coldness, yet they were a perfect fit.

"Oh, come on. You already know you'll be our maid of honour if we ever get married."

"I better be," Indy chastised. "You would have never met without me."

"True," Kamari chimed. "And we're always so grateful for you. Now, are you going to tell us why you're wallowing alone on the beach?"

"Can't a pretty blonde enjoy the sunset with her dog and take a few moments to do her breathing exercises?"

"Isn't it Huxley's dog?" Kamari asked, looking where Rosie was playing near the water, tail wagging happily.

"Same thing." Indy whistled, and Rosie jogged towards the trio. She cutely barked at the sight of Indy's friends before sniffing them, then went to sit at Indy's feet, making herself comfortable as she watched the ocean reflecting the orange sky's colours. "She loves me. Might as well become my pup."

"How's living with Miles going, by the way?"

"Definitely better than the first couple of days. He avoided me for an entire week before coming out of his shell. I feel like he's still trying to warm up to my presence, but I'm scared he's going to close himself off again when he comes back from London."

"Maybe he's just trying to get used to the fact you're living under the same roof," Kamari said as though it was the most evident fact. "Or maybe he wants you and doesn't know how to act around you."

Miles had, in fact, told her last week that he was still trying to adjust to her presence. Indy had realised during these lonely days that she had wormed herself into his quiet and peace, and she needed to give him credit for his efforts.

"Don't give me hope, Kam. When he acts all broody and mysterious, not to mention when he walks around shirtless, I just want to bang his brains out."

"Jesus Christ," Thiago mumbled. "This situation is not too uncomfortable for you, right?"

Indy shrugged. "Not really. He's taking me in and doing it all for Kai, but I want him to do it without thinking of his best friend. Without feeling like he's forced to talk to me."

"Is your brother protective of you?"

Indy's chest warmed at the thought of Kai. The love she had for her brother was incomparable. He'd take a bullet for her, and she'd tear herself apart to see him happy. As teenagers, they only had each other. Their parents were set on letting them learn the value and life, never allowing them to use their privilege of being "rich kids" to succeed. Kai was undoubtedly her favourite person in the universe.

"Yes," Indy answered. "But in a deep brotherly love kind of way. I'm not sure how he'd react if he knew I was into Huxley, though, but at the end of the day, he simply wants me to be happy."

Miles had always been her brother's best friend. And he'd always seen her as Kai's annoying little sister. Until that one night where everything changed; the night he won the Driver's Championship and finally made a move after years of secret glances and limited interactions.

Though Indy was only three years younger than Miles and Malakai, Malakai had always made sure to include Indy if they were to hang out all together. Younger Miles used to be quite awkward around her, but he'd always been very nice. She'd watched him grow into this confident, courageous, handsome man he was today.

What hurt the most, though, was to embed inside her head that she would never feel his touch again. That he was adamant on staying friends. There was nothing wrong with that, but sometimes she wished they could have been mature enough to find closure for their previous relationship.

"Anyway," Indy continued. "My main focus has to be my career. I'm not going to let that man ruin this for me. He wants to strut out there wearing nothing but boxer briefs with 'friends' written all over his abs and 'Kai's best mate' on his ass?"—Thiago laughed at that—"Well, be my guest, Miles Huxley. Not going to complain. But it's not like there's deep feelings involved. Just mutual attraction." Though her tone stayed steady, she wondered if one day she'd find a man who would look at her as though she was his entire world. "But I get on my knees for no man, and I cry for no man. He'll open up to me if he trusts me enough. Maybe he can just fuck me into oblivion until I meet my future husband. That's a good deal to me."

Her friends chuckled at her comment, but that weight

weaving through her chest didn't go unnoticed. Indy had to repeat to herself that Miles wasn't the ultimate goal. That she hadn't moved into his home to bed him or build a romantic relationship. The thought certainly obliterated a folded corner of her heart, though she wouldn't let the foolish pain be too overpowering.

"No, seriously," said Thiago, pushing the travel mug he'd been holding into her hands. Just like that, her thoughts drifted to this moment she was sharing with her friends. "Take this, and tell me why you interrupted us. I was about to take Kam against the window when she spotted you and said you were more important than a fucking orgasm. Still made her come before we ran downstairs, though, because what the fuck was she thinking?"

"Not my fault if your girlfriend chooses me over your small dick."

Thiago snickered. "It's anything but small, Indy. Kam can confirm."

She shoved him away. "Please, shut up. I'm sorry for being an inconvenience but knowing Kam, she'll make it up to you. Just close your curtains."

Kamari huffed. "I genuinely hate you two."

"You love us," Indy and Thiago jested.

Glancing down at the steaming beverage she was holding, she smiled at the sight of hot chocolate. By the scent itself, she knew it was Kamari's recipe, and it was her all-time favourite comfort drink.

"I took the time to brew you some hot cocoa," her friend murmured softly. "You looked like you needed one."

"Thank you." Indy sighed deeply. As the sound filled with dismay echoed, Rosie lifted her head, cocking it in concern. All Indy did was scratch the spot between her ears before taking a small sip of the delicious drink. "I'm terrified, guys."

"Ah, shit," Thiago whispered, exchanging a glance with his girlfriend. "Indigo Bailey isn't afraid of anything or anyone."

"Well, breaking news, she is."

Kamari's voice caressed the shell of her ear, as soothing as the sound of the water crawling to the shore. "What happened to the fearless Indy who made me run through these very streets to hop on a boat and sneak into a party? What happened to the Indy who doesn't care what the media says about her when she leaves an event early to go clubbing?"

"She vanished."

"Shit," Thiago repeated. "This is serious."

Kamari twisted, a deep furrow of her brows perceptible. "Who do you need me to talk to? Is it the people at work? Is it those who critiqued your most recent podcast?"

She blew a raspberry, focusing on the heat seeping from the mug to her palms. "What if I mess up during my first interview? What if I suddenly stutter, or something? Maybe they'll fire me because I'm not good enough for this job—"

"Hey," Kamari coaxed gently. "I know this is scary, and I know you're working with people who've been in the job for several years, but that doesn't mean they're better than you. That doesn't mean they can't learn from you. Absolutely does not mean you're less professional or smart or capable than any of them. You were born for this, Ind. Motorsports is your thing. You live for the cameras and being under the spotlight. You've worked so hard to get the job."

"But—"

"You will do great," Thiago continued with the same delicate tone. "You can't let those fears control you now. You have to step in the paddock and prove to everyone this job was meant for you, and that no one can do it the way Indigo Bailey does."

"Fuck," she whispered, her eyes burning. "You're right. I have something in my eye."

"A grain of sand?" Thiago snorted.

Indy sniffed, and took a sip of her hot cocoa. "Yes."

"It's okay if you cry. You have a big heart, and we know you care so much about making a good impression. Trust me, we can't wait to have you interview us in the paddock."

The pride rushing through her veins made her feel alive. Reminded her why she'd gone through so much to attain her goals. "And I'm beautiful."

"Gorgeous," Kamari emphasised.

"Kind."

"The absolute kindest."

"And I deserve this."

"More than anyone."

Thiago gently squeezed her shoulder. "Indigo Bailey bows for no one."

"Damn right, she doesn't."

※

IT WAS the featherlight knock on the door that brought her back to reality.

Peering up from the canvas splayed out before her, Indy felt her heart skip a beat as Miles leaned against the doorframe, looking so ethereal that she wondered if she'd lost herself in a daydream.

She had heard him enter the penthouse as quietly as possible, but hadn't expected him to stop by her painting room, let alone check up on her.

"Holy shitballs," she whispered, dropping the paintbrush she'd just dipped into paint. "Shoot."

There was now a random stain of red in the middle of the green canopy she had painted.

Miles Huxley had no right looking this handsome this late at night. That messy chestnut hair. Those thick-framed glasses. Those biceps contracting when he folded his arms across his equally toned chest.

"Didn't mean to cuss," she whispered, blinking.

"No worries." His next move was to turn around, but then

he pivoted again to face her, a crimson flush apparent atop his cheekbones. He rubbed the back of his neck, glancing around the room. "So... I'm here. I'm home."

Amusement threatened to skitter across her body, but Indy held composure over herself, and nodded. "I can see that."

"And you're awake." He cleared his throat, scrubbing a hand over his jaw.

Tilting her head, Indy frowned at his fidgety demeanour. "I didn't know we were pointing out the obvious. Is it my turn?"

With a disinterested look, he shook his head. "Save your breath."

It was fascinating how Miles had gone from the cocky, confident man relaxing in the tub a couple of days ago, to this nervous, stuttering yet still handsome man.

"Well... Good night. Just wanted to check on you."

Chuckling softly, she grabbed her paintbrush, the tingles on her cheekbones and the warmth flooding her chest unmistakably powerful. "Good night, Clark Kent."

The frown taking over his features was downright adorable. "Oh. The glasses? I knew you were going to say that."

She made sure not to meet his gaze as she dipped the brush into paint. "You did it on purpose to seduce me, didn't you?"

"You wish," he grumbled, causing her to laugh. "Was staying on your own okay? You didn't break anything, did you?"

Oh, Indy was about to rile him up. Seeing him frustrated was one of her favourite forms of amusement.

Straightening herself, she smiled coyly. "I accidentally threw a pillow at your trophy shelf and two of them fell and broke."

His eyes widened with bewilderment, his jaw tightening. "Indigo... How the fuck did it happen?"

"Pillow fight with Kam," she stated in a matter-of-fact tone. "Then I snooped in your closet and God, man, your watch collection is insane! I touched them all with my greasy fingers after eating a pizza. One of them slipped from my grasp, the Audemars Piguet, and—"

"Please stop." Dragging his palms over his face, he sighed heavily.

The pain etched on his features was the reason a laugh bubbled out of her mouth. "Relax," she said. "I'm kidding. I didn't break anything and didn't even go in your closet. I bet you have a cool watch collection, though."

"I do. And it wasn't funny. I nearly had a hard attack."

"I'm sorry," she said softly, looking into his eyes. "You know I like messing with you."

He shook his head, a smile threatening to split on his face. "You're a brat. But I'm really going to bed now. You're going to give me grey hairs soon enough. Good night."

※

ANOTHER KNOCK RESONATED NOT EVEN ten minutes later, and Indy hid her smile when Miles peeked his head inside the room. Still wearing his glasses, he had changed into a pair of grey joggers and a large t-shirt.

She wished she could've taken a photo of him standing there to send it to Kamari, and say, *See? I'm just hopeless and defenceless. You can't blame me if I suddenly drop to my knees in front of him.*

"Yes?"

For a moment, Miles stared down at her, his expression unreadable. But when the slightest shift on his brows was noticeable, she thought she was seeing concern glimmering in his eyes.

"You okay?"

The mere question made her heart skip a beat.

She nodded. "Yes. You? Can't fall asleep?"

"I haven't given it a try yet, but I wouldn't have been able to fall asleep knowing you weren't okay."

Indy swallowed, using her free hand to tuck a loose strand of hair that had fallen out of her bun behind her ear. "I'm fine."

Miles emitted a soft scoff, running fingers through the hair at his nape. "Indigo, there might only be one woman in my life"—his older sister, Maya, who had moved to South Africa after meeting the love of her life—"but I know damn well that when a woman says she's fine, that she's not fine at all."

She couldn't tear her gaze from him as he entered the room before taking a seat across from her on the floor and grabbing a blank canvas along with a paintbrush.

"What's up with you?" he asked with a delicacy that she adored.

She looked down at her painting, uncertain of why tears were about to well in her eyes. Miles wasn't one to express his feelings with grand gestures, but when it came to caring about Indy, it was the smallest things that mattered. His genuine concern. His willingness to spend more time with her and make art, when it was obvious that he was tired from his day.

Watching him dip the paintbrush in black acrylic, she just sighed. "Do you ever get nervous?"

He drew a vertical line. "I'm not a robot."

"Some people would think otherwise."

Seeing all the comments about Miles' attitude truly broke her heart. He'd built an impenetrable brick wall around himself and refused to let anyone in. Sometimes, he was downright rude to some reporters. Sometimes, he would purposefully ignore a question regarding his private life because he simply liked his mask. Well, at least that was what Indy supposed.

He glared at her. "Of course I get nervous. All the time."

"Even before a race?"

"Especially then. A race is the moment I have to prove myself to millions of people."

"How do you deal with hate?"

Miles looked up at her. For a beat, she saw something that gripped her heart tightly before letting go as that sentiment vanished—tenderness or worry. His expression hardened then, and he looked exactly like the man ready to get into his race car, ready to show the world he was the best. "Who's hating on you?"

With a shake of her head, she said, "No one. I'm just bracing myself for the criticism I'm going to face after my first appearance on live TV."

Indy looked away, loathing the way she allowed her thoughts to tear her down.

"I'm sorry," she said when the silence stretched out for too long. "We don't have to talk about me—"

"Hey, look at me," he demanded with such a chilling softness that she couldn't help but follow the command. His green eyes flicked between hers. "Life doesn't end because someone didn't like something you said or did. If anything, you should rise above the hatred and use all the constructive criticism to become the person they envy."

"I'm so terrified of messing up."

"And that's okay," he said in a whisper. "Your feelings are valid. But I know you, and you will work so hard not to mess up. You're going to go out there and smash it, Indy. You're going to show everyone that the key to success is perseverance, the way you do it so seamlessly. You're going to stand in front of those cameras and smile, and everyone's going to worship you. But when you're with me, or whoever you want to talk to, you can always share the way you feel because I'm never going to invalidate your feelings or thoughts. I'm never going to judge you."

And that was exactly why it was always so easy to talk to him. Why her heart had been beating so fast for him, and solely him.

She gave him a wobbly smile. And just like that, her confidence sparked again. All she'd needed was encouraging words. "Thank you."

"Of course. You're capable, alright?" She nodded. "Say it."

"I'm capable," she repeated with confidence.

He studied her for a beat, then the ghost of a smile appeared. "Good girl."

Were her cheeks red? Certainly. "Don't say things like that, Huxley."

His lips twitched. "Couldn't help myself."

Silence fell again as they both went back to completing their paintings. As she caught a glimpse of his careful hold around the paintbrush—like she imagined the way he'd touch a sheet of music—she thought about getting used to this—pouring her worries and hopes into swirls of colours in Miles' company. The high crashed down as soon as it bloomed, the constant reminder that she was only temporarily staying here ringing like a bell.

"You'd tell me if someone bothers you, right?"

With her hand freezing above her canvas, she took a small breath in. "I can defend myself just fine."

"Right. But what's so bad about having someone to take care of you?"

A lump thickened in her throat at the idea of Miles caring for her. Not a lot of people had come to her defence because she'd always felt strong enough to stand up for herself, but it felt nice to know he'd have her back in case she became powerless.

"Don't be like this," she said quietly, keeping her attention on the colour palette. "You're making things hard for me too."

The silence, however brief, made her peer up into his eyes. "Would being an asshole help then?"

She chuckled. "I'm not sure because it appears that I'm into sarcastic jackasses."

"Noted." A grin spread across his lips as he teased her with a wink.

Making art and sharing it with someone else wasn't something she was always comfortable with, but there was something about him that procured her solace. The glimpses he kept stealing weren't judgemental. They were simply made of admiration, and that only eased her more and more as her paintbrush caressed the canvas.

"You're so fucking talented," Miles whispered in awe.

When she slid her gaze towards him, he was focusing on his artwork, but she didn't miss the heat crawling up his cheeks.

"So many compliments in such a short amount of time."

He scowled. "I see you still don't know how to accept kindness. Just say thanks."

"Thank you," she said earnestly. "What are you drawing?"

When he turned the canvas towards her, she barked out a laugh. He'd drawn a stick figure standing next to a Formula 1 car. "Autoportrait," he said, grinning.

And as they laughed together, unrestrained and carefree, Indy knew that everything would be alright.

Maybe she could do this—just be friends with Miles. Maybe she was okay with it after all. Because focusing on her career was way more important than giving out her heart to a man who could shatter it too easily.

CHAPTER EIGHT

📍 *SAKHIR, BAHRAIN*

"Wow, Miss Bailey. Look at all those men queuing just to be interviewed by you."

Giggling at the cameraman beside her, Indy adjusted the lanyard strapped around her neck before glancing at him. Scott Cassidy was part of the filming crew at Thunderbolt Sports and the only coworker she had clicked with —mostly because they'd been assigned to work together for the entire season.

Last week had been her first week at work, which had consisted of preparing for the beginning of the season. She'd been right to dread it, because she had sensed that her coworkers weren't particularly excited for her to join the team, whereas she had walked in with pride rushing through her bloodstream and greeted everyone with a big smile, delighted to start this journey. Indy loved the lead presenter who was also her boss, Carmen Stenfield, an ex-race car driver, who saw her as a true force and had expressed her gratitude for joining the team.

Still, there was nothing worse than feeling unwelcome and as though she didn't fit in at work.

But this was, and had always been, Indy's dream job, and she wouldn't let anything or anyone ruin this experience for her.

Indy was now standing in the media pen, waiting to interview the drivers about their first run of the pre-season testing. During three days, all twenty drivers were able to test out their cars before the actual first race, allowing the teams to gain valuable information about the cars' performances as they'd be put through their paces on track. Testings also allowed drivers to put their skills to use.

She cleared her throat and lifted her chin, trying to ease the ball of anxiety rolling inside the pit of her stomach. She'd been assigned to conduct post-practice and race interviews for this weekend and the next one.

"You should capture this, Scotty," she said, smiling at the grey-haired man. "It's not everyday that I have this many drivers begging for my attention."

Scott crossed his arms over his chest, his camera set up by his side. "I bet everyone envies you right now."

Before her stood Rowan Emerson, driver for Primavera Racing, as he chatted quietly with his press officer, a guy named Joey. Right behind them was Miles and his publicist, Ava, both of them talking with Thiago, Rowan's teammate.

Indy chuckled when Rowan winked at Ava, his girlfriend, making the latter blush furiously. Miles grumbled something from her side before throwing his hands in the air.

Jealousy was a vicious thing, something Indy shouldn't be feeling. But she wanted this friendship with Miles, the one he and Ava had since they were children. But she also wanted what Ava and Rowan had, that kind of unwavering love where they'd find each other in every universe and lifetime.

"I call dibs!" Charlie Beaumont stepped before Indy, raking

his fingers through his dark hair and pushing them back. He then scratched his beard, grinning handsomely. "Hello."

His broad grin instantly eased her nerves, and she mirrored his smile. "Hey, Charlie."

"Yo, it was my turn," Rowan said, stepping behind Charlie.

Charlie smirked. "Shoulda been faster, mate."

Chuckling, Indy turned to Scott. "Let's get the camera rolling."

"Good luck," whispered Scott. "You're doing great, Miss Bailey."

Indy offered a grateful smile to the cameraman before turning to Charlie.

She'd known Charlie since she was a child because her relatives who lived in Montana were close to Charlie's family. In a way, she liked to think of him as a distant cousin. He was ruggedly handsome, with those dark eyes and brown locks slightly longer than any other drivers' on the grid.

A lady working for F1 entered the media pen, waving her hands in the air. "Why are you all waiting in line? There's at least ten other reporters you all have to go to. Move. All of you. Now!"

"So goddamn bossy," Rowan muttered.

"Rowan," Ava hissed, but Indy could still perceive the amusement glinting in her eyes.

He raised a tattooed hand. "Ah-ah. You're not my press officer anymore. You cannot scold me, sunflower."

Ava narrowed her gaze before pulling Miles by his elbow towards a journalist on the opposite end of the pen.

Indy slipped her gaze towards Charlie who was toying with his earring, chuckling. "So, Charlie. You were the second fastest today despite the minor issue with the gearbox at the beginning of the session. How does it feel to be back in the car?"

SPEEDING INTO OVERDRIVE

WHEN IT WAS Huxley's turn, her heart went into overdrive, exploded, and turned into fragments in the pit of her stomach.

She hated the way her body would react to his presence, even if her demeanour didn't give way to her weakness. There was no denying that Miles Huxley was extremely hot in his racing suit, cheeks slightly flushed and traces of his balaclava still marking his cheeks.

"Indigo," Miles greeted with a dip of his chin, holding her gaze.

The late afternoon sun shone softly upon his features, outlining the evidence of his regal cheekbones, and brightening the unique, mesmerising colour of his irises. For a moment, she almost got lost in him.

"Huxley." She smiled brightly, watching the way he gripped the railing between them. "How does it feel to be back in the car after a three-month break?"

"Amazing and refreshing."

"It looked like you struggled a bit today, though. I noticed you couldn't manage to control the car as easily as usual."

He rubbed the back of his neck. "Yeah, I kept losing the rear. Too much oversteer. It's frustrating because the car worked well on this track last season, so we have some improvements to make. But we still have two more days of testing, and that gives us enough time to do what we have to do to perfect the car for next weekend."

A couple of questions and answers flew between them, their gazes never disconnecting as though no one, nothing surrounded them. His posture was casual, yet stoic—the same way he'd acted with other reporters. But his eyes... Indy saw the tenderness in them, and she wondered if she was the only one able to see how he'd brought his walls down around her, albeit faintly and slowly.

"Thank you for your time," she said softly after he finished answering the last question.

And then, he smiled. Subtle, but there. The entire world felt like coming to a full stop, this moment feeling like exploding fireworks—the highlight of her day. "Thank *you*."

⁂

WHEN SHE WRAPPED up the interviews, she turned to Scott and squealed before slanting her palm over her lips. "Sorry. Sorry. I got too excited for a moment."

Scott chuckled as he turned the camera off before raising his hand, inviting Indy to high-five him. "Awesome?"

She sighed in relief, elated. "So awesome!"

There was no comparison to that blissful sensation skittering down her spine as she grinned, not yet grasping the fact that she'd just conducted her very first round of interviews of the season without having any slip-ups.

"You're perfect for this job. Dynamic and enthusiastic, but still very professional. It shows that you paid attention to each driver during their laps and wrote down everything you needed to ask. Good job."

She swore the back of her throat was tightening. "Thanks, Scotty. I can call you Scotty, right?"

He chuckled again. "You call me whatever you want, Miss Bailey. I'm going to put in a good word for you to Carmen. She'll be happy to know you nailed your first interview session."

Fuck yes!

She sauntered away, happy. She wanted to dance and jump around and tell her friends about it all, but she simply walked the paddock with her chin held high, her slightly trembling fingers still holding onto the microphone.

"Indigo! Indigo! An autograph, pleaaaase."

Turning around, she watched Alex jog towards her, his dear camera strapped around his neck. She chuckled, lightly smacking his chest when he fell into step beside her.

"You're going to be a famous journalist," he said, "and I

want to sell your autograph. It could cost hundreds of thousands of bucks."

"I'll sign the prettiest shot you have of me."

"Is that a yes?"

She rolled her eyes in amusement.

The adrenaline crashed down way too quickly for her liking, letting place to unsettling nerves and self-doubt. "How did I do?"

Alex mussed his blonde hair with a hand. "From what I saw and heard, you did great. You were made for this."

She nudged her shoulder to her friend's, still beaming despite her inner battle. Convincing herself she'd aced it would be a struggle even with all the praise. "Thanks, Alex."

"Plus, you did the impossible."

She looked over to him, arching a brow incredulously. "Which is?"

"You made Huxley smile. This is a first, and we're all shocked to our core right now."

She blinked, casting that sensation of flutters inside her stomach aside. "That's overly dramatic."

"No, I promise. The guy doesn't smile at anyone. Doesn't talk to anyone except his press officer and trainer. He smiled at you, Ind. You know what it means, right?"

"No?"

"That the World Champion is going to let you in."

CHAPTER NINE

SAKHIR, BAHRAIN

"So, what I'm thinking right now is that we go for a run this afternoon. Tomorrow we'll do some reflex exercises before focusing on your neck, and..."

As much as Miles loved Enzo and his strict plan to keep Miles in shape and moving on his day off, he couldn't help but tune out the sound of his voice when a silhouette caught his eye.

So much for not wanting to be distracted by anyone.

Indigo Bailey just knew how to steal his breath away by simply walking into a room. Today, she was wearing a sundress that accentuated the tan of her skin and the curves of her pristine physique.

She was so effortlessly, breathtakingly beautiful.

And Miles must have allowed his jaw to go slack, or his breath to hitch audibly, because Enzo elbowed him.

"You were saying?" Miles asked after blinking and looking away from Indy sauntering towards the buffet. Settling his gaze on his empty cup of coffee, he ignored the amused glare his trainer gave him.

"Never mind," Enzo said. "I see you're distracted."

"Yeah, I had a rough night," Miles confessed, leaning back in his chair. Again, he looked over to where Indy was, busy choosing her breakfast amongst a large selection of delicious food.

"Rough night," Enzo repeated, followed by a chuckle. "Is that the excuse we now make when we see a pretty chick enter the room?"

"Fuck off," Miles muttered.

Usually, during race week, Imperium Racing shared a hotel with another team. In addition to seeing members of Primavera Racing walk around in their red uniform, people working in the media were staying in this very hotel, too. Hence why he'd been seeing Indy grab breakfast at the same time as him for the past couple of days.

"Want to talk about it?"

Miles stood up and clapped his friend's shoulder. "I appreciate it, but I think I just need to eat something. I'll be back."

Enzo simply hummed, a little smirk dancing at the corner of his mouth, as he looked down at his phone.

Walking over to Indy, snatching a plate along the way and pretending to look at all the food scattered before him, he murmured, "Hey, Daisy."

She pivoted to face him, her perfume dancing in the air with the movement. Jasmine, amber, maybe cedar—a sexy, rich, gourmand floral scent that instantly weakened his knees.

At the sight of him standing so close, she smiled. Prominent freckles dotted the bridge of her nose—the result of the time she'd been spending under the sun. "Hey, stranger."

He hadn't spoken to her since last Friday in the media pen after she'd asked him about the third and last day of pre-season testing. Miles wasn't one to seek companionship outside of his inner circle, but there was something so soothing yet thrilling about being in Indy's company. Scratching the back of his head, he studied the way she carefully scooped some scrambled eggs and added them to her plate. Everything she did was so graceful and alluring. "How were your first few days of work?"

She glanced to their right, and he followed the route of her perusal to watch four women sitting around a table, recognising them as Indy's colleagues. Two of them were journalists, the other two were assistants, or something.

"They were great," she earnestly answered, looking back at him.

"Are you sure about that?"

Indy nodded, but Miles didn't miss the way her unoccupied fingers were toying with the rings before her pointer finger came to scratch the skin between her thumb and palm.

He frowned, noticing the slight flare in her pupils as subtle panic danced in them.

What wasn't she telling him? Was she anxious? Did she not know people had been praising her, watching her like she was some kind of goddess marching upon still water?

"What about you?" she asked as they walked back towards the open space where tables were scattered around. They halted in the middle of the room, uncaring of the whispers floating in the air and the glances thrown their way.

"The car is great," he said. "I can't wait for the race this Sunday."

Amusement danced in her gaze as it trailed from his face to his chest. There was nothing risqué or sensual about the scrutiny, but it still made his skin burn. "You pretended to struggle last week, didn't you? Your car is perfectly fine and you're going to be the fastest this weekend."

How did she know?

He shrugged. "Don't you think I'm a good man for letting all the other drivers have hope? Imagine beating The Lion. And I'm not going to lie, I've enjoyed seeing them excited during the interviews when some of them noticed they had run a faster lap than mine. Especially Valencia and Emerson. I swear those two share a soul, or something."

She shook her head. "You can be such an ass sometimes."

"Does it look like I care?"

"Perhaps you should care about what the media says about your behaviour when they realise you've been tricking the entire grid."

He leaned forward, their breaths nearly entwining. The moment his lips broke into a smile, he couldn't control the soft chuckle escaping either. "It's our secret, okay?"

Indy turned on her heel. "Amongst many other secrets, right? Don't worry, you know you're safe with me."

"Good. Also, prepare yourself because you're doing hot laps with me on Sunday morning." Whilst Indy would sit in the passenger seat of a Ferrari, Miles would drive around the circuit as fast as he could all the while trying to answer questions. This activity's purpose was to entertain the public—those sitting in the grandstands waiting for the Grand Prix to start, and those who would watch the video—but as Miles got forced by Ava to do this, he'd asked for Indy to be his guest instead of some random beauty influencer who knew nothing about motorsports or F1 itself.

"Am I now?"

"Yeah, and I'm not going to go easy on you," he whispered, smirking.

"That's fine because you know I hate it when you're too vanilla," she whispered back, a brow raised. "And you're aware you'll have to answer questions, right?"

"Like Twenty Questions on a first date?"

"How many times have you had to play that game on first dates?"

"Zero. You'll be my first."

Obviously, she was pleasantly surprised with his comebacks, and it made delight dance around his chest. "I promise I'll make it fun."

He grinned. "And I promise I'll make you scream. My name, preferably."

Crimson tinted her cheeks as laughter bubbled out of her mouth. "Good luck with that. See you around, Golden Boy."

You're safe with me. Those words still lingered in his head as she walked to the other side of the room whilst he settled down across from Enzo. When Indy reached her coworkers' table, one of them shook her head, saying the last seat was reserved.

For whom? Miles scoffed. He'd seen them sit at this very table for the past few days, and not once had the last chair been occupied.

"Where's your breakfast?" Enzo asked amusedly.

"Just fuck off."

It was obvious that Indy was disappointed, but she simply smiled and walked over to where Ava was sitting with Rowan and Thiago. They welcomed her with open arms, telling her something that made her laugh.

Good. These were good people who would treat Indy the way she deserved to be treated.

And as Miles watched Indy shrug off the rudeness of her coworkers, ignore all the curious stares sent her way, and keep her chin high, he knew exactly why she was the most attractive woman he'd ever settled eyes on.

Still, all he could do was look at her from afar, and repeat like a constant reminder that she was a distraction and, first and foremost, off-limits.

Was the sauna the equivalent to a hot tub? Probably not, but it would still satisfy Miles' need to relax.

"Thanks, Shelby," he said to the hotel receptionist for giving him the key to access the closed sauna room. "I owe you."

She shook her head, darting her attention to her computer.

"Every damn year, Huxley. Everything's ready, by the way. Just sit and relax, and stay out of trouble."

"I always behave."

The look Shelby gave him was enough to let him know she didn't believe him.

Entering the room, he flicked the lights on, a slow smile spreading across his lips as he saw the farthest sauna ready for him to use.

Just as he was about to close the door, a woman's voice filtered the room. "Wait, wait, wait."

And not just any voice. Indy's.

Of course.

When she stumbled before him, clutching a white towel around her chest, he suddenly felt paralysed.

"What are you doing?" Miles hissed.

Indy looked up at him, slightly rearing back before the shock disappeared from her expression. Her stare dropped to the sliver of skin shown on his chest where his robe couldn't hide his nakedness beneath. "What are *you* doing?"

Leaning against the doorframe, he smirked down at the devastating, beautiful, infuriating woman. "Isn't it obvious? About to play golf."

"What a coincidence," Indy chastised with dramatised enthusiasm. "I was about to do the same."

She took a step forward, but with a swift movement, he put his hand against the door jamb, causing her nose to almost come in contact with his bicep. He tutted, "Who said you could come in here when it's obviously closed?"

"Well, if it's closed, why are you trespassing?"

"Who," he repeated lowly, "said you could use the room, Indy?"

She raised her nose, the insolence he knew so well shining in her eyes. "Shelby."

"Shelby? No way."

Lifting herself on her tiptoes, Miles couldn't help but gaze into those ocean eyes brimmed with mischief. "Nobody says no to this pretty face."

Fucking hell. That was true.

A resigned grunt vibrated in his throat as he let his arm fall. She pushed past him, purposely grazing her bare skin against his, sending every single one of his blood vessels to an untameable inferno.

"Thank you," she chirped sweetly, marching over to the only heated space—the one he had reserved for himself.

Closing the door and locking it to ensure no one would disturb his—well, now, *their*—peace, Miles tousled his hair before following Indy.

She halted, slowly looking over her shoulder. "I'm bothering you, aren't I? You wanted to be alone."

The fact that she could read him even when he hadn't said a thing made his heart race. "It's fine."

"Well, no. I need to stop invading—"

He walked over to where she stood still, towering over her. "When have I ever said no to you, Indy? You'll always be the only exception to me. So get in there before I do it myself."

Her cheeks flushed. "So bossy."

"You know I like to be in control."

Heat flared in her pupils before she acted like his remark hadn't affected her. But he knew, by the salacious gleam, that his words from their secret moments were echoing in her head.

Spread your legs.

Eyes on me, Indy. Be quiet.

Don't come until I allow you to, got it?

The small cubicle was already fuming, causing his body to warm in a heartbeat. He didn't miss her not-so-discreet glance when he shrugged his robe off, hanging it outside the small shed and leaving him in his swimming trunks.

They sat opposite from one another, and as he spread his legs and watched her blatantly, he smirked as she looked everywhere but into his eyes. If he shifted his foot slightly to the right, he would be touching her. The way she was acting so timidly was unnerving. Indy was bold, fearless, and ballsy—not fucking shy.

He studied the slope of her lean shoulders and toned arms as she tied her wild locks into a bun, rebellious locks framing her otherworldly, beautiful face.

"What are you staring at, Golden Boy?"

"Can't blame me for looking at the only person sitting in this tiny sauna with me, can you?"

Their gazes finally clashed, and the way she unashamedly traced the route of his naked, sculpted torso made his breath catch. A thin sheen of sweat had started coating her golden skin, and he found himself desperate to see what kind of swimwear she was wearing beneath that white towel.

Full lips curved upwards into a tantalising smile, then came a suggestion: "Truth or dare?"

Baffled by the question, Miles scoffed and shook his head. "Are we seriously doing that? Playing games?"

"You like to play games with me."

He squinted at her. "I'm not sure what that's supposed to mean." If anything, she was the one who found pleasure in initiating and playing games.

"Well?" She raised a brow. "Are you going to answer? Or just stare at me until you decide to make a move?"

"You're so goddamn infuriating," he bit out. "Fine. Truth."

If she was disappointed, she didn't let on.

"What brings you here?" she asked, tilting her head in concern.

As wary as he was regarding people's kindness, there was no doubt in the back of his mind that Indy's curiosity was genuine. That she didn't have bad intentions or needed something from him. "I like to relax before quali day. I usually like going to the pool, then hitting the hot tub, but Ava and Rowan were already there. Didn't want to disturb their alone time."

"They're so cute together." Indy sighed dreamily. "They both sacrificed a lot to be happy."

The thought of his press officer—first and foremost childhood friend—finding happiness made him smile. Sure, Rowan was one of his most ferocious and competitive rivals on the track, but outside of racing, he believed him to be a fun, outgoing, and dynamic person.

"So to the sauna you came," she said, not even giving him a beat to reply.

"Good conclusion. What are *you* doing here?"

"Hang on, you didn't ask me if I wanted to pick truth or dare."

He gave her a blank stare, and she sighed.

"Needed to relax, too," was her response.

He straightened himself. "You okay?"

He cared about her more than he'd care to admit. More than he could ever voice. Playing games with Indy was always thrilling, but her wellbeing was more important than anything else. The worry consuming his senses was impossible to fathom.

A faux smile touched her mouth. "Always."

He could see through the terse smile. The effortless lie. The image of the golden girl. "Don't give me that bullshit. Not with me."

The same motion she always did when anxious caught his attention—the gentle yet firm rub of her forefinger on the skin between her thumb and palm. "I forgot my sketch pad and all at home—your place, I mean. It's stupid, and I shouldn't depend on that, but—"

"It's not stupid, Indy. If it's the only thing that makes you feel at peace after a chaotic day, then you shouldn't belittle the comfort it provides you. I admire the fact you're trying to ease your mind by painting, or drawing, or doing something crafty."

A frown touched her brows. "You really think so?"

"Yeah."

Miles was utterly flabbergasted by her uncertainty. She was a confident woman, empowering and optimistic, but behind the image of the Princess of the Paddock lay a vulnerability so beautiful to him. Somehow, he could relate to her feelings—to the want of needing something totally different from real life to lose himself in another world.

To him, music was the equivalent of art for Indy.

"Thank you." She blew out a breath. "I didn't realise I needed to hear those words until now."

When he pushed his hair away from his forehead, she glanced at his bicep. "Don't let anyone make you feel like you aren't allowed to feel negative emotions, okay? Don't let people make you think that being creative is stupid or whatever they tell you."

"I don't like feeling negative," she countered.

And he knew that. Kai was quite similar to her. Their parents didn't truly allow them to linger in negative feelings, always urging them to lift themselves up after a breakdown. Miles, on the other hand, grew up with a father who gave him the space to feel as much as he wanted, but had the consciousness to come to him when he wasn't angered or saddened any longer.

"I know," he said softly. "But allowing yourself to feel whatever you're feeling doesn't make you less of an amazing person."

"You think I'm amazing?"

"I think you like to deflect."

She exhaled, a quiet laugh rumbling. "You're right. Thank you."

He didn't quite know when they had entered a staring contest, but he found himself feeling triumphant when she looked away first, dropping her glance to his torso where beads of sweat were making their way down the valley of his pectorals.

"Truth or dare?" she murmured, finding his gaze.

Too many things were procuring him an exhilarating sensation as chilling as racing: sitting almost bare before Indy in this confined space, playing this game, and holding together every sliver of self-control he could find so he wouldn't leap towards her, rip the towel off her body, and bend her over the bench.

"Huxley," she whispered. "Don't look at me like that."

Knowing exactly what gleamed in his eyes—want, desperation—he clenched his jaw, darting his gaze away. "Truth."

Silence fell for a few beats as she contemplated her words. "Why are you single?"

A smirk touched the corner of his mouth. "We've already been through that. The question is, why are *you*?"

He didn't know he'd been holding his breath until she admitted, "I've also had my fair share of shitty dates, so…"

"Have you been with anyone since the last time we…"

"Fucked? Yes, this one guy," she said. "Lasted a total of three days. He was whatever, anyway. He was a finance bro."

A snort erupted. "Ah, so you're into men who wear fancy shirts and dress pants?"

He felt like combusting under her scrutiny when she held his gaze, a sultry gleam in her eyes. "I'm more into athletes. High-performance athletes to be more specific. Racers."

With a slow nod of his head, Miles tried not to show how her comment was affecting him—pulse hammering, fingers trembling with the need to touch her. Claim her. "I see. And why did it end? He talked too much about work?"

"Oh, no. He admitted he wanted to date me to get close to my dad."

"God fucking damn it, Indy."

She shrugged like it didn't matter. Like she was used to facing hypocrites. "Nothing I'm not used to."

"People trying to befriend you and Kai just because you're Zach and Lisa's kids drive me nuts."

But Indy was a tough kid. She could handle people's shit without letting anything break her. She wasn't one to linger in the past and dwell on actions that had hurt, and he truly admired that.

She smiled softly. "It's okay. Those people are not worth our time and energy."

See? Inspiring and strong were two words to describe her.

Amongst a humongous list of qualities that he kept secured in the back of his mind.

He sighed, rubbing a hand across his damp jaw. "You're right."

Her chin was high, some kind of challenge glinting around her pupils. "Ask me."

And instead of stopping this foolish game, he walked right into the fire. "Truth or dare, Indigo?"

He already knew that she was going to reply, "Dare."

And two could play at this game. "Take off that towel."

Slowly, so deliberately, she untied the cloth and let it pool behind her on the bench. With one thigh placed over the other, her torso slightly leaned forward as she braced her hands on the bench, fingers gripping the edge, she tilted her head and innocently smiled.

And God. Fucking. Damn him.

She was perfection.

A goddess intent on ruining him by luring him towards a precipice where there was no safety net to catch him after a dangerous fall.

She was wearing a black one-piece, its neckline plunging to give him a full view of the slope of her cleavage. Her smooth skin, now shining with perspiration, was visible around her collarbones, and the fabric covering her most intimate parts did absolutely nothing to hide them.

His gulp was audible as he ran his fingers through his hair, taking in her physique. When he'd dared her to take the towel off, he'd been intent on keeping his eyes on her face, but he was always helpless when it came to her.

Yeah. He was utterly, royally fucked.

God, this perfect body.

Those perfect, full breasts.

He'd never seen Indy naked. This was the closest to being bare she'd been before his eyes. All the times they were intimate in the past were quick, rough, fuelled by the thrill of getting caught, neither of them fully unclothed. That had never stopped hands from wandering, though, and he could still feel how her breasts had felt in his palms—round, heavy. Could still hear her soft moans as his fingers grazed her peaked nipples, played and tugged at them.

He wondered how it would feel to play with the metal barbells across her nipples. How loud she'd moan if he swirled his tongue—

"Quit staring at my tits," she snapped. "Or do something about it. I can't stand that look in your eyes."

She was trying to provoke him. Get a reaction out of him. She was trying to break him, and fuck, he could not give in to the destructive power of temptation.

"And I can't stand the fact that you think I'm just going to unleash myself on you."

Her gaze dropped to his lap, where his desire was growing and obvious. "Look at you, Huxley. You want to."

He stood up the moment she did, their bodies nearly touching. All he needed to do was lean down, and his world would rattle.

"What game are you playing, Indy?"

Defiance burned in her gaze as she studied his reaction. Waited for him to, perhaps, put an end to whatever this was. "The first one to break loses."

He smirked. Her flames should have kept him away, but perhaps he was a desperate moth, undeniably drawn, helpless and ready to get burned. "You're cute if you think I'm going to let you win. I do not lose, and you know that."

She stepped forward again, the featherlight graze of her breasts against his chest making his breath hitch. She stood on her tiptoes, her sinful, full mouth brushing against his. The next second, she was turning around and her bare ass splayed before him was almost the reason he unravelled.

Fuck, he needed to get laid.

She grabbed her discarded towel, her hand ready to open the

door. She found him watching her firm, round bottom from over her shoulder and said, "Challenge accepted."

Leaving him standing there, Miles wondered how they had ended up in this situation, and how long he would last in the shower later when he'd jerk off to the image of Indigo Bailey wearing that swimsuit and talking sultrily at him—a seductress waiting for his downfall.

CHAPTER TEN

📍 *SAKHIR, BAHRAIN*

"I THINK I'M about to vomit."

"Real sexy, Ind," Alex deadpanned after lowering the camera and showing her the shot he had just taken of her standing in front of Primavera Racing's garage, smiling.

"I'm so nervous," she whispered after approving of the photo.

She was wearing white suit-pants, high heels, and her hair was flowing down her back in gentle waves. The people around the paddock were looking at her in awe, begging to be photographed with her by their side, and having all that attention on her didn't help with unsettled nerves.

She followed Alex towards the pit lane when he said, "Come on, it's not your first time speaking on camera."

"It'll be my first time being on live TV!"

She took a deep breath in, trying to think of anything but the ball of stress stirring inside her stomach. Delicious, gooey cookies. A fresh iced coffee. A cheesy pizza. A new pair of Louboutins. Maybe some lingerie.

"Hey," Alex crooned, elbowing her. "I need to go, but you've got this, okay?"

With a nod, she accepted the side hug and watched her friend saunter off to Thiago, who was busy chatting with his race engineer.

Today was the first Grand Prix of the season.

And this would be Indy's very first live TV appearance as a Formula 1 presenter. She was getting ready to walk through the pit lane with Carmen, and they would debrief about the weekend so far (free practices and qualifying session) and give their predictions for the race.

"We're going live in five," announced Scott.

Indy walked over to where Carmen was standing, a stylist fixing her long, brown hair. She smiled at Indy when she approached, but Indy glanced towards Imperium Racing's garage, observing a group of car mechanics round Miles' car.

A gentle, amicable pat fell upon her back, and Indy grinned at Charlie who was rushing towards his own garage—the one right in between Thiago's and Miles'. "Good luck!"

A warm sensation danced across her chest. "To you, too."

He winked, then disappeared inside his garage.

"Hey, Indy." It was Henry Huxley, leaning against the wall, hands in the pockets of his trousers. *Diana would have enjoyed the sight.* She walked up to the man, waving. "Amazing job. You've been dreaming of this for quite some time, haven't you? I talked to your dad just earlier, and he and your mum are so proud of you."

The back of Indy's nose burned. She'd received so many messages from friends and family congratulating her on her TV debut, but seeing pride shine in her parents' eyes felt akin to being held tightly. Even Kai was here for the first race. In fact, he was standing at the back of Huxley's garage, phone in hand, trying to film Indy.

"Thanks, Henry."

He smiled, then drifted his attention towards David Rogers, Imperium Racing's team principal. That was Indy's cue to leave, but a hand caught her elbow, obliging her to pivot.

How many photographers had been able to capture this moment—the rapid motion of Miles holding onto Indy so she wouldn't slip away?

Her heart thundered when her gaze fell upon a broad chest clad with a black fireproof shirt. Slowly, she found breathtaking green eyes, watching her with so much tenderness that she almost felt her heart shatter to pieces.

"Hi, Daisy."

His hand had left her elbow a while ago, but its warmth still lingered on her skin.

"Hi, Golden Boy." An easy smile spread across her lips, drawing his attention towards her mouth. "Ready to beat everyone else?"

"I didn't know this was an interview," he taunted, and she huffed out an amused laugh. "Look, I don't like talking too fast or being too cocky, but I'm starting from pole, so it should be easy."

Of course, he'd had an amazing weekend and results, topping every driver on the grid every time he was in the car. Indy had seen many comments on the internet regarding Miles' behaviour during pre-season testing, speculating he'd pretended to struggle just to spite his rivals. If he was affected by the rudeness of those people, he didn't show it.

"How are you feeling?"

"A bit nervous," she admitted. This morning's activity—sitting in the passenger seat whilst Miles rushed down the track—had made adrenaline crash through her veins, making her forget about the real world. She'd shouted his name when he went full throttle through the track, and he had laughed heartily. But now, she couldn't exactly ignore her trembling hands and churning stomach.

"That's normal. But you're going to be amazing. You know what you're doing." His magnifying eyes tracked down her outfit. "And you look very pretty."

Indy didn't miss the scarlet blush staining his cheekbones. Was this man really the World Champion the world had categorised as too distant and uncaring?

"Are you hitting on me?" she whispered, chuckling. Behind him, Kai was walking over to them.

"That wouldn't be very professional of me," he said breezily.

She wondered what would have happened two nights ago if they hadn't started playing this foolish, meaningless game. Would he have brought her to his room? Torn off her swimsuit—

"Miss Bailey?" Scott called. "Two minutes."

"Okay, I need to go." Just as she started pivoting, she halted and looked at him again, finding his expression now unreadable. He must have remembered where he was. "Thank you for the sketch pad and pencils. Ava didn't say they were from you, but I'm not dumb."

"I knew you'd put two and two together easily," Miles said softly. "I know it's not acrylic paint or watercolour and a canvas, but I hope they were helpful."

It had been a small act, but its meaning and the intention behind getting her those supplies as quickly as possible had almost swept her off her feet.

She gave his fingers a small squeeze, tingles dancing on her palm. "You have no idea. Good luck, Huxley."

The most subtle smile ghosted over his lips. "You too."

She sauntered over to the filming crew, waving over her shoulder when she heard Kai cheer for her.

Grabbing the microphone Carmen extended her way, she smiled. "Let's do this."

She placed herself on Carmen's left, allowing the stylist to quickly rearrange her hair before facing the camera, chin high and burning determination seeping through her veins.

"Thirty seconds," Scott announced.

All it took was a glance behind the cameraman to make Indy's heart somersault. Between Primavera Racing and Imperium Racing garages stood Miles, watching her with his arms folded across his chest, a glimmer of pride shining in his eyes. And next to him stood Kai, his phone in hand. Was that a tear streaming down his face? Ava was on Miles' other side, beaming brightly, tucked under Rowan's arm who gave her a thumbs-up. Kamari was next to the Australian driver, leaning close to Thiago, who kissed her temple, before nodding enthusiastically at Indy. Even Alex, Cal, and Tate were standing there, cheering her on for this memorable moment.

All her friends were there. Her family. All ready to witness her first, big step.

She swallowed the emotions and looked at the camera.

When the signal was given, they began recording.

"Good afternoon, ladies and gentlemen," Carmen started. "F1 is back! Today, I'm in the wonderful company of Indigo Bailey, our newest presenter at Thunderbolt Sports. Indy, welcome. What's your first impression of the weekend so far?"

She brought the microphone to her mouth, her smile so big that her cheeks hurt. "Hi, Carmen. Thank you. Well, the atmosphere is sizzling and hectic in the best way possible. I can feel a great energy emanating from everyone as they're getting ready for the race. Qualifying was absolutely thrilling. Can you believe there were only nine thousandths of a second separating Huxley and Valencia from pole position?"

They started taking a few steps forward. "I was on the edge of my seat the entire time. Here, let's grab Thiago and ask how he's feeling to start the race on the front row."

As Thiago fell into step between them, Indy cast a glance at her friends, and the sheer pride and admiration etched on each of their faces sent a wave of comfort through her.

She'd made it. And she'd make it to the mountain's peak, too.

CHAPTER ELEVEN

♟ SAKHIR, BAHRAIN

"Do you want to share a wings platter with me?" Charlie asked, rubbing his stomach like the dramatic man he was. "I've been craving those for days. Weeks, even."

"No."

"Fine, so no wings. Nachos? I'm in the mood for something greasy."

A heavy sigh. "No."

"Jeez, you're moody tonight."

"I'll share with you," Kai said from the other side of the table. "Mister Grump is brooding, so just let him be."

Though his focus was zeroed in on the menu leaflet between his hands, Miles could feel Charlie's amused gaze burning on his profile. "And *why* exactly are you like this? I can't believe this guy. He won a fucking Grand Prix, *again*—"

"It was the first one of the season," Miles interjected, his words echoing like a grumble. As he realised it, he cleared his throat, but didn't relax his frown.

"Yeah, but you won the five last of the last season, so your streak is still going strong. So please, enlighten me and tell me why you're acting so ungrateful."

Miles threw a dirty glare over to Charlie. His teammate bristled exaggeratedly. To the world, Miles always appeared rude and cold, but to his inner circle, his impertinence was always taken as a joke.

"He's in a bad mood because his face is all over the internet," Kai clarified, snickering.

"And why is it a bad thing?" Charlie lifted his hands. "I'm trying to understand here because I'd love to be the centre of attention for once."

"You can take the spotlight from me," Miles said. "I fucking hate the media and all the shit they make up."

"Which is?"

The joy and thorough amusement illuminating Kai's features made Miles glower with annoyance. "He was spotted talking *and* smiling to a woman more than once, so now the media is saying that he finally found a heart inside himself."

Gathering all the pieces together, Charlie nodded. "Oooh," he mused. "Because you were making lovey eyes at Indigo."

"We were just talking," Miles snapped coldly.

Charlie frowned. "You've never been affected by what the media says about you, so why are you letting it get to your head now?"

Scrubbing a hand over his jaw, he let his gaze drift around the restaurant where all the tables were occupied, mostly by people working in F1 and celebrating the weekend. "It's not about me," he muttered loud enough for his two friends to hear. "It's about Indy and all the weird stuff they say about her. I seriously want to kick all those machos who think she's not good enough for her job, or the so-called fans saying she's only here because of her dad.

That she's trying to date me to get a free pass or something."

"A free pass?" Charlie echoed, confusion laced into his tone. "That makes no sense at all."

"It's seriously pissing me off. They can say whatever they want about me because to be honest, I don't give a shit. But I don't like the way they speak about Indy."

Miles had yet to realise his hands had curled into fists, his blood boiling and his pulse thumping against his temple.

"Shit," Kai whispered, eyes wide. "Do you, like, have the hots for my sister?"

Miles scoffed. "Nobody says that, Malakai. And no, I'm just protective of her because she's your sister, and you asked me to look after her."

Kai and Charlie exchanged a weighted glance, and what bemused Miles more than their silent conversation was the perspiration starting to clam up his hands.

Miles had one goal in mind, though, and it was to be the best Formula 1 driver to ever compete, to secure another championship under his belt, and nothing would distract him. Especially not Indigo and her little games. He needed to put some distance between them, needed to let her know he wasn't so much as tempted to fall into her trap.

"Ah, fuck me," Charlie whispered, drawing Miles' attention towards his face, stricken with a mixture of panic and admiration, before following the route of his regard towards the entrance of the restaurant.

So much for not allowing himself to be distracted by Indigo. Her mere presence stole his breath away, and as she entered the room, Miles felt a thorough skip in his heartbeat before it started battering erratically.

"What's got you all fidgety?" he asked Charlie who was frustratingly raking a hand through his hair.

"Aïda," was his response.

Behind Indy, who was talking to a waiter, was Aïda, Simon

Romano's daughter. Simon was the team principal of Primavera Racing—Imperium Racing's biggest rival on track. She'd just been announced as a reserve driver for the rival team, but had yet to make her debut in F1. Truth was, Miles was excited to see her behind the wheel. Not that he wished for Thiago or Rowan to not be able to drive during the season, but it was about damn time to see a woman on the grid.

Charlie was tracking each one of her movements, something like devastation and longing shining in his dark eyes. Miles watched Aïda exchange a word with Kamari and Ava who had entered the restaurant, her dark curls cascading down her back, her eyes as cold as ice sliding across the room to find Charlie.

"Fucking hell," Charlie said, hiding his face behind the menu. "If one look could kill, I'd be buried six feet under already."

"What did you do to her?" Miles asked, glancing at the group of girls slowly making their way to them. Thiago and Rowan were ahead of them, already sliding into the booth next to Kai.

His face was crimson with what looked like embarrassment and regret. "I fucked up with her, that's what I did."

"Oh," Miles said. "I kind of forgot you were related."

Charlie reared back. "Woah, woah, man. I'm not related to the Romano's, like at all. I mean, yeah, Kai and Indy are more like distant cousins, but my family just owns a ranch next to the Romanos in Montana."

"So you're childhood friends with Aïda?"

"Something like that."

Miles looked at Kai. "And are you related to the Romanos?"

"Not at all."

"Okay. Just wanted to make sure you're not doing some weird shit or anything."

"Do you miss country life?" Thiago asked, his interest genuine as he joined the conversation whilst Rowan waved for the girls to join.

"Sure do, man." Charlie sighed wistfully.

"I don't," Kai said. "Me and Ind are more city people. Heard Stevie and Wyatt are getting married next summer, yeah?"

Miles had no clue who they were talking about, but he watched Charlie roll his eyes. "Guess who's the best man?"

"You?" all the men around the table suggested.

"Bingo. Guess who's maid of honour?"

Rowan emitted a dramatic gasp. "Aïda?"

"Yes!" Charlie threw his hands in the air. "This is going to be a disaster, mates."

Kai tried to hide his snicker by coughing. "If it's any reassurance, Indy and I will be attending. It's been years since we've visited."

"Thank God. At least you'll be there to defend me if she tries to murder me."

"What in the bleeding hell did you do to this girl?" Thiago asked.

Before Charlie could even respond, a group of four women appeared beside the table. Ava slid into the booth to sit next to Rowan, Aïda stumbling in next. Indy's presence sent Miles' mind into a frenzy when she sat across from him, pretending not to notice the intensity of his stare upon her as she waved for Alex to join. He sat next to her, draping his arm around the back of her seat, causing Miles to scoff behind the rim of the glass he had brought to his lips.

Kamari sat next to Miles. "What's that look on your face?" she asked quietly.

"What look?"

"Honestly," Charlie joined in a hushed voice as conversation started to stir around the table, "if you keep on frowning like that, you might just get a permanent line between your brows."

"Just bug off," he sighed.

When he looked up, Indy was already looking at him, concern etched on her features.

"Are you okay?" she asked, bringing the entire table's attention to him. "You look distraught."

Great. Just fucking great.

His gaze dropped to the small distance separating her shoulder from Alex's side, and he couldn't fathom why his insides twisted all of a sudden. He despised that sensation.

"He's just being his grumpy self," Kai remarked while scanning the menu and tapping on the name of a dish that had caught his interest. "He'll be okay once he eats something."

Once the attention wasn't no longer on him, Miles took the chance to look at Indy again, and when their eyes clashed, he didn't miss the way her cheeks turned into a darker shade of rose. Something like relief washed over him as he realised that Alex Myers couldn't make her blush this way, but then something like annoyance overpowered his senses as he noticed how much of an idiot he was.

Indy's attention was brought to her phone that had just chimed, and when a deep line appeared between her brows, the sudden urge to make everyone go away so that he could comfort her became overwhelming. Alex peered at the screen and he, too, frowned before saying something Miles couldn't make out.

"What are you two whispering about?"

Indy's blue eyes found his, and she shook her head. "Nothing important. Just read a comment on my latest post."

She slid her phone towards him, and he felt Kamari hovering over his shoulder as she also read the most sexist comment he'd ever seen under the photo she had posted—a shot of her standing in the pit lane, high heels on and the most beautiful smile brightening her features.

Go back in the kitchen. Bet you don't even know how to parallel park, so watcha doin' commenting about F1?

"Well," Miles said, jaw clenching. "Tell @jon1234primavera to go fuck himself."

"I already did. I know where I belong," she said, beaming, like she wasn't any longer affected. That made his irritation spark, the anger simmering in the pit of his stomach becoming uncomfortable. Indy was everything he wasn't: strong, down to earth, and optimistic. The way she could shrug off the negativity was praiseworthy, but he hoped that it wouldn't destroy her if she thought too much into it.

"Good. Don't listen to those pricks." He gave her phone back, lingering his gaze on her smile when it didn't waver.

"Something you want to tell me?" Kamari whispered when Indy was back to chatting with Alex.

"About what?"

Discreetly, she motioned with her eyes towards Indy.

He shook his head, taking a large gulp of his water. "There's nothing to say."

And maybe one day Miles would find the courage to stop lying—to himself. But for now, hiding behind his walls was the safest option.

CHAPTER TWELVE

📍 *JEDDAH, SAUDI ARABIA*

INDY HELD HER breath as she watched Thiago and Charlie battle for P2. As she stood in the media pen next to Scott, arms folded beneath her breasts and attention entirely focused on the two cars almost driving wheel to wheel inside a narrow corner, she couldn't help but nibble her lower lip.

A bead of sweat made its way down her neck, not only because of the heat, but mostly because of the nerves rattling her body.

At heart, she was a die-hard fan of Primavera Racing because her father had raced for them in his early F1 days, and she also thought the team was at its peak with their two talented drivers.

On the other hand, she genuinely admired Imperium Racing —their rapid cars, their two drivers who were unbeatable and stronger than anyone else on the grid.

But she was now a journalist, so she needed to stay neutral and objective. She couldn't act as though she was in Kamari's living room, squealing with excitement when Thiago managed to overtake Charlie. Couldn't hold her breath when Huxley took a turn too wide and nearly let his car come in contact with a wall, and exhale in relief when nothing happened to him. Couldn't curse when other drivers at the end of the grid were acting reckless and colliding into each other.

So all she did was keep her thoughts inside her head, her expression blank, save for the tiny winces every time an incident was on the cusp of happening.

She was also taking notes to ask each driver during the postrace interview she'd be conducting in a few minutes. Only ten laps were left before the chequered flag would be brandished.

"What a race," Scott muttered, mostly to himself, but still made Indy nod in agreement.

The transcription of the radio exchange between Miles and his race engineer appeared on the bottom of the screen, causing Indy to frown. "I think I'm losing power. Can you check?"

"Checking now."

On the left side of the screen were the twenty drivers' positions, Miles being at the top as he'd been leading the race since the beginning. Thiago, who was right behind, was over five seconds away, but the gap between them seemed to be decreasing.

"Put mode eighteen on," AJ commanded. "Should be good to go."

"I swear to god, AJ, if you fuck this up..."

"You're allowed to go flat-out on the last couple of laps." Even if it would degrade his tyres, Miles could allow himself to do it because he was so far ahead of the rest of the drivers.

Lap after lap, Miles continued to lead the race, roaring off the track with unbridled speed.

When he passed the chequered flag, Indy kept her smile from growing, pride flooding inside her chest.

The public could say whatever they wanted about Miles— some of them hated his arrogance and dominance during most races, while others admired his ferocity—but it had never stopped Indy from applauding his sheer talent.

Someone came to stand beside her, and Indy didn't even have to turn to know who it was. Tara's perfume was overwhelming and strong, and not in a positive way. Indy didn't like holding any animosity against anyone, especially against her colleagues, but Tara was toeing a dangerous line. Only few knew how venomous Indy could be if someone ever struck the wrong nerve.

"Heard a rumour," Tara said.

Indy forced a smile, turning to face her colleague. "Nice."

"Do you not want to know?"

"Burying my nose where it doesn't belong isn't my thing."

Tara scoffed. "Even when it concerns you?"

"Do tell, then," she answered with a sigh, her annoyance ready to bubble to the surface.

"Heard you're roomies with Huxley."

She arched a brow. "Who did you hear this from?"

"Are you confirming it?"

"No," Indy said with a chilling calmness. "I'm just wondering why you're so interested in something that clearly doesn't concern you."

Tara's brows were lifted in slight puzzlement. "What, exactly, are you doing, Indy? Your daddy paid enough money to get you this job, and now you're dating Huxley? Just to hold on to your spot? It doesn't work that way. Besides, you don't even know what you're talking about when you're on live TV."

Those accusations were absolutely insane.

"Sorry," Indy said, "but who's conducting the interviews and doing the pit lane walk with Carmen every race day? Apparently, it's not you."

"Yet."

She was fuming on the inside, her stomach churning with frustration. "Listen, Tara, I wish you all the success and happiness, and I hope that one day you can get promoted to be a

SPEEDING INTO OVERDRIVE

presenter. But you don't know anything about *my* situation, so I'd suggest you walk away."

Utter disdain was etched on Tara's face. "Huxley would never date you."

Indy blinked, listening to the sounds surrounding her instead of letting her anger take over. She took a small breath. "Ooh, I get it. Is this why you're working in F1? Not to prove we, women, belong here too, but to score a driver? Come on, Tara, we're better than this."

When Tara simply scoffed, Indy decided to walk away. She could feel the tension straining her shoulders, the slow, burning anger seeping through her veins.

How dare she say those things? How dare she assume she'd arrived here without breaking a sweat when all she did was struggle to forge her place into this universe? How dare she?

Walking furiously through the crowded paddock, Indy texted Scott to let him know she'd be back in a minute. He responded with a thumbs-up emoji, having certainly heard every word of the conversation she'd had with Tara since he was standing right beside them.

Don't let her get to you. Don't let her win.

By storming off like a mad woman, she was probably making a mistake, and she'd probably be scolded by her boss for it. But she needed to breathe to calm herself. She couldn't conduct the interviews while being angry.

"Indy!"

Now was not the time.

"Why are you walking like you're pissed off?"

Okay, maybe it was fine that Miles had fallen into step beside her, Ava on her other side.

"I'm fine," she muttered.

"Doesn't work with me, Daisy." When his fingers delicately looped around her wrist, she halted. "What's going on?"

Gently, Miles pulled her behind the wall of Imperium

Racing's motorhome. "We have exactly three minutes before you need to start with your interviews, so talk to me."

"I'm going to wait for you...there," Ava announced, pointing to a table in front of the motorhome.

Indy folded her arms across her chest. She felt her torso rise and fall with every breath she took and released, a knot building in her throat. "She said I got this job because my dad paid Thunderbolt Sports to have me as a lead presenter."

Slowly, bewilderment drew itself upon Miles' face. "Who?"

"Tara."

"Who's that?"

Indy was a better woman than that, but fuck, she couldn't control the little smirk of victory ghosting over her lips. "My coworker. She's an assistant. Provides all the texts I need to read on live TV and such."

He nodded. "Got it."

"She also said I was dating you to keep my job. Like, that doesn't make sense? God, I'm so angry right now!"

"Hey," Miles coaxed softly. "You know she's just trying to piss you off—"

"Well, congrats to her because she succeeded."

He chuckled, as if amused by her frustration. "Don't let her get to you. You're letting her win by acting this way. Everyone knows you didn't need or want Zach's help to get this job. Everyone who's listened to your podcast knows how hard you've worked to get here."

Exhaling, she felt her shoulders drop, the tension slowly fading away. That was when she realised he had run after her to make sure she was okay.

Miles Huxley would always break his rules for her, and she couldn't exactly fathom why.

Wearing a cap atop his damp hair, his face flushed and sweaty, his racing suit unzipped and hanging at his hips, Miles was utterly enthralling after winning a race. For a beat, Indy forgot about her anger and distress, mesmerised by the tall man.

Regardless of her strong attraction for Miles, she refused to let people think she'd gotten the job to be with him. Refused to let them say she had it easy when it was anything but.

He took a sip of water, his attention still focused on her as he blatantly ignored the people gawking at them.

"You're right," she said, exhaling heavily. "I'm sorry."

"Don't apologise. Your feelings are always valid when you're with me, remember? Just don't let anyone break you. You're not worth their childish behaviour."

"Right. I'm too pretty for that drama."

He chuckled. "There she is."

Ava peered around the corner. "I hate to interrupt, but you need to head back to the media pen, Ind."

"Crap," she said, turning on her heel. "See you in a minute."

"You better run," Miles suggested amusedly. "Wouldn't want you to get in trouble."

"Watch me."

Trotting in her high heels, she waved at Alex photographing her. Then, she looked over her shoulder to smile at Miles who stood there, hiding his grin beside Ava who was laughing heartily.

"Thank you, Huxley!"

And what he did next almost sent her toppling over a bench. His voice was loud and clear, sincerity woven into his tone: "I've got you!"

CHAPTER THIRTEEN

ᴑ *MONTE CARLO, MONACO*

THE SOUND OF Indy's laughter fed his soul. Melodious, feathery, and joyous—it felt akin to a ray of sunshine.

It was the first thing he heard when he stepped into the flat. It was always the first thing that would procure him solace whenever he was in her presence—even if he heard her laugh through the closed door of her room when he passed by.

Sitting at the kitchen's island with her laptop opened and her phone in hand, Indy didn't seem to acknowledge his presence just yet. But it was when he started whistling, toeing his shoes off, that she dragged her attention towards him.

With the grocery bags in hand, he walked into the kitchen. "Thought you were going out with Ava and Kam?"

He'd once been startled by her being there, but now the contentment he felt any time he would see her roaming around couldn't be ignored. The relief to know he wasn't enveloped by solitude. The ease and serenity her company provided.

"Change of plans."

"Oh." He was aware of how much she cherished her time with her friends. "Hope you're not too disappointed to spend the evening here."

Her shoulders popped. "I love slow nights, too. I might just run myself a bath and read a good, smutty romance."

Miles couldn't help but lift his brows, slightly curious about the type of books that were scattered around her room.

She interrupted his thoughts by saying, "*You* look disappointed to see me here, though."

A scowl took over his features. "Come on, Indigo. We've been through this. I don't mind your company. In fact, I think I'm happy to know that we're both home tonight. Doesn't mean I'm agreeing to putting a chick-flick on."

"Damn it. We were getting somewhere."

"With that being said, I'm not opposed to watching a horror movie."

"You're just saying that in hopes that I'll end up curling in your chest and stay in your arms."

He hummed, the corner of his mouth tipping upwards. "Maybe."

"You wish. I'm a tough kid."

"That's not what I remember from the times we had movie night over at your place and you'd end up hiding under the blankets."

She scoffed. "Honestly, Huxley, you simply missed your chance to comfort me. That was when I was young. Now I'm brave."

He barked out a laugh, seeing right through her shit. "It's never too late to give it a try."

She put her phone down, eyeing him suspiciously. "You must be ill."

"Pardon me?"

"You seem to be in a good mood."

"I am." His grin widened.

She blinked. "That's unusual."

Shrugging, he took the groceries out of the bag. "I had a good day off. Ran twelve kilometres this morning, then trained on the sim all afternoon."

"*That's* your definition of a good day off? You and I are so not alike."

He chuckled. "What's that saying again? Opposites attract?"

Dragging her reading glasses atop her head, she said, "Did you just admit that you're attracted to me?"

Miles turned around to wash his hands, but mostly to hide his face where a burning blush had bloomed. He couldn't voice the confirmation for numerous reasons, but he didn't deny it either. Physically, she was everything. But it was her soul and heart that he was desperately trying not to adore. "Don't put words in my mouth, Indy."

She hummed, and when he peered over his shoulder, she was looking at the groceries he had splayed out atop the counter. "What are you making?"

"Bolognese, but I wasn't sure if you liked it."

Sparks ignited in her eyes. "Are you kidding? I love it. Let me finish writing this email, and I'll help."

"You don't have to."

Her soft smile sent his mind into overdrive. "I want to."

While he took a cutting board and knife out, he couldn't help but observe the way Indy was thoroughly focused on the screen of her laptop. He rolled the sleeves of his shirt to his elbows, not missing her fleeting glance when he did so. "What are you working on?"

For a heartbeat, their eyes locked, and her brows tugged together like she couldn't believe his interest was genuine. Like she was wondering if his kindness was real. But the walls surrounding him always came down when he talked to her. "I just sent over my report from last weekend, and now I'm just reading over my text for the video I'm shooting on Thursday."

Even as he tried to busy himself by sorting everything out to

SPEEDING INTO OVERDRIVE

make the dish, he couldn't help but be concerned by the soft sigh escaping her nose. "Is something bothering you?"

"No?"

"Is that a question or your answer?" His frown deepened when his gaze dropped to her right hand, where she was busy rubbing the spot between her thumb and forefinger. "Indy. What's going on?"

Loosening a heavy breath, she closed her laptop. "Don't make fun of me."

"Don't ask too much of me," he teased. It made her lips pull upwards, though the twisting feeling in his chest was a sensation he despised.

A beat passed before she confessed, "I'm dyslexic."

Miles blinked, crossing his arms over his chest. Relief flooded his senses—he'd been expecting something terrible. "And? You thought I was going to laugh at you or judge you for that?"

Her shoulders dropped. "Well, I'm used to it, so—"

"People have made fun of you for being dyslexic?"

She nodded, her expression solemn.

Miles ran a hand through his hair in frustration. "Shit, Indy. That's not okay."

"It's not a big deal. A lot of people suffer from it."

"Yeah, exactly, but it doesn't make it okay for people to belittle you because you struggle to read or write at a normal pace. Do your colleagues know?"

"They do. I just need more time to read, but I do get how it can be inconvenient for the team. Also, what kind of reporter is dyslexic?" She emitted a nervous laugh, rolling her eyes.

But Miles didn't find it funny in the slightest. He cocked his head in curiosity. "Can I help in any way?"

She shook her head. "No, but thank you. That's why I wake up extra early and go to bed later than I should during a race weekend because I take the time I need to read over my texts and memorise them perfectly. I try avoiding checking my cards because they can confuse me."

Miles nodded. He wished he'd known. Wished she could see how strong and brave she was.

She went to wash her hands as Miles took out the flour from the pantry. "It can take me two weeks to read a book," she admitted.

A smile nearly made its appearance on his lips at the sight of her slippers. His gaze trailed up her legs to settle on the shorts hidden below the oversized jumper she was wearing. "So? Life's not a competition."

"Says the guy who competes in a racing car for a living."

"It's different, and you know it. I know you love reading, and you do it for your own pleasure. Ava can read three books in a week while you take two weeks to read one, so what? It's your journey, your life. You go at your own pace."

Leaning her hip against the counter, she grabbed a hair tie to gather her locks in a messy knot at the nape of her neck. "Do you know how hard it is not to compare yourself to others? I feel like everything's a competition. Even reading. It's just so overwhelming."

"Comparing yourself to others is inevitable, but don't let others ruin this for you. You're smart, and if the people around you make you second-guess yourself, then they are not your friends or worthy of your time."

Her blue eyes shone with emotions he couldn't exactly name, but made his breath catch. The twitch in his fingers forced him to curl his hand by his side, otherwise he would let his control slip away and tuck a rogue strand of blonde hair behind her ear.

"Thank you," she whispered. "You always know how to reassure me."

"Always," he murmured, smiling down at her. "A woman with a burning confidence like yours shouldn't let worthless people step over her flame."

She laughed. "So poetic. Careful, I might start thinking you're flirting."

Time seemed to freeze the exact moment Indy smiled, bright and unrestrained, and he took a mental picture to which he would hold on for eternity.

Miles had always found Indigo beautiful. But when she was herself, not fancied up or not trying to impress her entourage with rouge lips and high heels; when she was laughing heartily with her hair unbound and that paint-stained jumper, that was when he found her most beautiful.

Her smile dropped ever so slightly, her eyes flickering between his, her cheekbones tinted with a smattering of rose as she looked at his lips.

He cleared his throat. "Okay, let's cook."

Her mesmerising eyes sparkled. "I'm listening, chef. What do you want me to do?"

Hearing Indy call him *chef* made his blood heat up. But to conceal the obvious effect of her words, he just said as nonchalantly as he could: "You can cut up the carrots and celery while I make the pasta?"

She beamed. "That works for me."

Not that the calmness between them was ever disturbing or uncomfortable, but Miles liked having music in the background, and he knew that Indy loved it just as much. He glanced over at her, only to see her thoroughly focused on the carrot she was busy peeling as he clicked on the playlist he'd created on the plane a few days ago.

Songs for Daisy.

Would he ever share it with her? Probably not. But this playlist was filled with over a hundred songs that reminded him of her.

"Oh!" she squealed as Noah Kahan's *Orange Juice* weaved through the room. "I love this song."

And how did he know that? He had heard her play it on repeat during one of her pottery sessions.

As he kneaded the dough, he could feel her whole attention

on his moving hands. Catching the reverence in her gaze, he smirked. "Want a photo?"

"Thanks for the offer, but I'll pass." He smirked again at the way she peered at his hands before focusing back on her task.

Indy interrupted her soft singing to ask, "When did you learn how to cook?"

The pasta was ready to be cooked, so he helped her cut the remaining vegetables. "I think I was around nine or ten."

"Wow," she whispered. "Really?"

He nodded. Usually, he'd shut himself down or would change subjects when people wanted to pry into his past, but this was different. This was Indy. And everything felt easy and natural with her. "My dad, he's always worked hard. When he would leave the office late he'd either bring us some take-out food or ask if we were okay making ourselves something quick. Maya and I would eat grilled cheese or pasta. Sometimes, Zoya and Andrew would come knocking on the door and have us over to eat with them."

Indy was now standing next to him, leaned against the counter as he waited for the saucepan to heat. "Ava's parents, right?"

"Yeah." He smiled at the thought of the girl who he had considered a sister his whole life, who was now his press officer. Smiled at the thought of the two people who had taken him and Maya under their wing when they were on their own. "Such good people. Anyway, I just wanted to help Dad. I could see how tired he was, working two jobs at a time, driving me left and right for my karting competitions, taking care of Maya and I. So I learned to cook on my own, with books and TV shows."

"That's very admirable. Would you be a chef if you weren't an F1 driver?"

"Probably. What about you?"

"This isn't about me."

"So? I want to learn about you every second of the day." That was a foolish thing to say—a paradox to the rules he'd set.

She smiled softly. "Actually, I don't know. I've never thought about it because I've always had one goal in mind. I remember hearing Mum and Dad talking one night, saying how badly they wanted to help your family. I guess I never realised how much you struggled to survive whilst I grew up with a maid and personal chef."

A lump started to build inside his throat, but he swallowed it before the dismay could be heard through his words. "It's okay. Dad sacrificed so much for me, but I also needed to take care of my sister. She cooked at first, just to fulfil her duty as a big sister, but then she stopped. She was so angry at our Dad for working so much, for not being home, but she couldn't understand at the time that without him, we'd be nowhere today. I started taking care of them, of the little flat we lived in, just to allow Dad to breathe when he got home."

"Oh, Huxley..."

For a moment, only the sounds of onions sizzling in the pan filled the silence. The smell of it swivelling in the air. The empathic regard in Indy's eyes.

"What about your mother?"

A phone ringing prevented him from answering, and instead of sighing with relief, he found himself wanting to reveal his deepest secrets to Indy. Secrets he'd kept to himself, ones he hadn't told anyone. Secrets that had obliterated him, but simmered deep within him, asking to be freed.

"It's Daddy Huxley," Indy said, lifting his phone that he had left on the counter.

He jutted his chin all the while stirring the mix of vegetables in the pan. "Go ahead, answer it."

She shrugged, bringing the phone to her ear. "Hello! Hi, Henry. Yes, it's Indy...Well, he's cooking, but...Oh, he's making bolognese. Oh? It's the best I'll ever have?" She raised her eyebrows, and Miles chuckled. "Well, I can't wait to have a taste. I'm doing good, thank you for asking...Yeah, jet lag is a bitch. I don't know how you do it...Yes, hang on, let me ask him."

Miles closed his agape mouth, rubbing his chest where he felt like a cord had pulled and released his vital organ. Seeing Indy and his dad bonding so easily did something unexplainable to him.

"Your dad asks: navy blue or grey?"

He frowned, ready to ask for more context, but then he understood. "Blue."

She repeated, "He says blue, Henry." She gave Miles a thumbs-up to which he returned a solemn nod. He listened to their conversation whilst continuing to cook, a small smile dancing on the corner of his lips. "Flowers? Yes, flowers are always a good idea! First date? That's so exciting! What's her name? Oh, pretty. Well, have fun. Be careful. Yes? Of course." Her voice had just cracked, causing Miles to look at her with a frown. Indy nodded, her gaze on the floor as she rubbed her nose. "Bye."

Gently, she deposited the phone atop the counter and found his gaze. "Your dad is going on a date."

Miles chuckled. "I figured. He was asking me about the suit he should wear."

"He's adorable."

He grabbed two plates as Indy retrieved glasses and the cutlery. "I hope it goes well. He hasn't been on a date in a while."

"How come?"

It was when their plates were full and they were sitting across from each other at the table that he continued, "The women he dated were awful."

When Indy complimented him on the food after taking the first bite, he smiled and thanked her. "But Henry is such a wonderful man."

"He is," Miles agreed. "The best man I know. But the women he tried dating in the past only wanted him for one thing: money."

Indy groaned frustratingly. "That's not fair. Why can't good people find happiness?"

He twirled his pasta around his fork. "I'd love to see my dad happy. Not with the watches and cars I buy him, but with a woman who will love him for his true self, you know?"

Indy nodded. "He's... Your mother... Actually, you don't have to answer me. I remember Kai telling me to never ask about her."

He took a sip of water. "You know, I'm really grateful for Kai. We met when we were just kids but he's been there during my worst moments. That guy pulled me up every time I kept falling."

Emotions swamped her eyes. "Kai is an amazing guy."

"He is." He cleared his throat, deciding to give more pieces of himself. "I don't know if you already knew that, but...my mother left when I was ten."

"Did you completely lose touch with her?" Sadness was woven to her tone, questions dancing in that crystal gaze. "I just know she's out of the picture."

"Yeah. We don't talk about her."

"I'm sorry," Indy whispered. "Let's move on. But if you ever feel the want to talk about her, or about anything, you know where to find me."

"Thank you," he said earnestly. The glow of the fading sun shone softly upon her face, and he was absolutely enthralled by her effortless beauty. Her beautiful aura. He could get lost in those ocean eyes, so he needed to hold control over himself lest he fell and drowned. "I really appreciate it."

"Of course." She smiled. "I have one thing to ask."

"You get one free pass. I already told you so much about me tonight."

She shrugged. "If you want to make it fair, I usually spill a lot about myself on dates."

He barked out a laugh. "Keeping that in mind. Ask away then."

When her expression softened, the warmth dancing inside

his chest enveloped him in a cosmos of comfort. "Do you have a dream?"

Miles should've been alarmed by the rapidity of his answer coming to mind, but then he realised that it was okay to be hopeful. "I want to be happy. You know, happiness that doesn't involve racing and winning."

He also wanted to tell her that he wanted to be enough, worth it, and good. But no matter how much he would voice it or wish upon the stars for it to happen, he simply knew that he wasn't worthy of that.

Indy's fingers twitched around her fork, but her eyes stayed locked to his. She gave him a devastating, beautiful smile. "You'll get there. I know you will."

Miles was grateful to Indy for changing subjects and telling him about a canvas she'd seen in Thiago's flat, but he felt the urge to ask her something in return.

"Can I ask a question?"

She nodded. "Hit me."

"What did my dad say to you? You seemed a bit emotional over there."

She set her cutlery down, the tenderness etched on her face stealing the air straight out of his lungs. "He thanked me for looking after you because you've always been the one to take care of others. I hope your father knows that he raised an incredible man. Whoever you marry will be one lucky woman, Huxley."

Heartbeat speeding up and threatening to go in overdrive, he gaped at her in awe. It was at that moment that Miles felt everything shift.

CHAPTER FOURTEEN

📍 *MONTE CARLO, MONACO*

Kai blinked repeatedly, his expression morphing into utter shock as he gaped at Miles. "Pardon me?"

Staring at the screen of his phone, Miles huffed, slouching further into the sofa. "You heard me."

"You're asking me about the things my sister likes, like it's the most normal thing to ask. Are you planning on taking her out on a date, or something?"

Miles drifted his gaze to the window, where he could see the sun setting in the sky, casting a hue of pink and tangerine on the calm ocean. "No. I just want to do nice things for her. Does she like watches? I could take her out and choose a Cartier. Or maybe a Van Cleef & Arpels bracelet?"

Kai emitted a small snort. "Dude, you're so used to talking to girls who want you for your money that you don't know how to be romantic anymore."

"I'm not trying to be romantic," he corrected grimly, though the heat creeping up the back of his neck threatened to betray him. "Just friendly."

"Bull-fucking-shit!" a voice shouted from somewhere before Romeo's face appeared on the screen next to Kai. "You can admit that you have a crush on—"

Kai pushed Romeo away. "Don't finish that sentence."

Romeo grinned. "Did she bring sunshine into your life yet?"

Miles kept his expression blank, but truth was Indigo was the embodiment of a summery sun ray. She was a coalescence of bright colours, bringing warmth wherever she went.

It was not only her presence that illuminated his otherwise quiet and dull life, but the little things she did in order to fuel her love for life: baking cookies and bringing one to him whilst he raced on the simulator; going to the farmers market and getting flowers; painting outside no matter the weather; taking Rosie on walks and sending him photos of the sunset.

"Can you just answer my question?" he addressed Malakai.

"Indy doesn't give a shit about watches or jewellery. She's got everything she wants. My sister likes small things. Small gestures. Honestly, take her to watch the sunset on the beach and she'll be the happiest girl ever. She doesn't ask for much."

He truly admired the fact that she was able to find peace in the smallest things.

"Watching the sunset with her sounds like a date."

"Cook her a nice meal," Kai suggested, ignoring the previous statement. "She loves food. I've never seen a chick love food as much as Indy does."

"What's her favourite dish?"

At that, Kai blinked.

Fucking idiot.

"Lisa's lasagna!" Romeo shouted from wherever he was.

Well, Lisa Bailey's lasagna was probably everyone's favourite dish. God, didn't he miss those days where he'd spend evenings at the Bailey's mansion and stuff his belly with the incredible lasagna.

"Miles, whatever you're doing with my sister, please don't fucking play with her feelings."

Annoyance flared through his bloodstream. "Again, Kai, I'm just trying to be friendly."

"Yeah, you better not cross any fucking line."

The sound of heels tapping on the floorboards resonated, and Miles shifted on the sofa to see Indy walk into the living room, her gaze on her phone. Wearing a regal black jumpsuit with its neckline so low, she looked yet again like the seductress intent on ruining him.

"Hey, Huxley," she said. "I'm going—oh, are you calling my brother?"

"Yeah." He cleared his throat. "Come say hi."

"Hello, dear brother." She leaned over the back of the sofa, her cheek almost nestled against his as she waved at the phone. "How's training going?"

"Pretty great. Just nailed a Triple Cork 1440 this morning."

Miles whistled. "Impressive."

"Good job," Indy praised. "Where are you?"

Miles swallowed, the sheer proximity of Indy's body setting his skin ablaze. She smelled intoxicatingly sweet, and as he watched their reflection in the small rectangle in the corner of the screen, he couldn't help but think she looked devastatingly gorgeous.

"Romeo's hotel room."

Speaking of the devil, Romeo appeared in the frame again, smiling broadly at the sight of Indy. "Yo, blondie! Thought I heard your voice. Don't you look beautiful?"

She chuckled, its melodious sound feeding his soul again. "Thank you. Your game kept me on the edge of my seat last night. Great assists."

Romeo sat down next to Kai. "Fucking exhausting game, is what it was. Ezra spent four minutes in the penalty box."

"He's done worse," Kai jested.

When Miles had awoken in the middle of the night, thirsty,

he'd walked into the living room to find Indy sleeping on the sofa, the hockey game's highlights playing on the TV. After turning it off and draping a blanket over her, he'd brushed her hair out of her face, sighing softly.

Guilt had pushed at his chest the remainder of the night as he tossed and turned in his bed. He should have picked her up and brought her to her own bed. Should have stayed up to watch Romeo and Ezra's game to support them like he normally would.

"When are you inviting me to one of your games?"

Miles just loved how deep and genuine her interest in sports was. How supportive she was of her friends.

"Well, you guys are travelling to America for the Miami Grand Prix in May, right?" Indy and Miles nodded in sync. "If we make it to the playoffs, I can get you two tickets if it works with your schedule, and all."

"We can make this work."

Romeo grinned. "Cool. So, are you still single?"

Indy giggled, and Miles felt the back of his throat tighten. His jaw clenched, and he couldn't help but look elsewhere. He was certain their relationship was platonic, and that Romeo was doing this to rile him up, so why was he feeling so furious?

"Are you?"

Miles narrowed his gaze on Indy's reflection. Was she flirting back?

"Fuck, no, please," Kai whined. "He's been pining after the same girl for years."

Indy came to sit next to Miles, her shoulder pressed against his. Shifting, he draped his arm over the back of the sofa, allowing Indy to come closer. He took a tremulous breath in, an uncanny sensation floating around his stomach.

"Oh, tell me more."

"Isla," was all Kai managed to say before receiving a punch in the shoulder. "Ow, fuck."

"Isla St James?" she asked. "The ski instructor?"

"Yes," Kai answered for Romeo whose face was as red as Indy's nail polish.

"Says the guy who's still in love with the girl who broke his heart almost ten years ago," Romeo countered.

"Amara?" Miles whispered to Indy. She nodded in confirmation.

"Shut the fuck up," Kai groaned. "You don't know shit."

Romeo scoffed. "Oh, because you do?"

"Okay," Miles said slowly, brows lifting. "Gotta go. Bye, guys. Kai, thanks for your help."

"Wait!" Romeo called, grabbing the phone. "Miles, if you don't date Indy, I will. See ya at the playoffs, baby."

"Why the fuck would you say that?" Kai bellowed. "I'm going to—"

The call ended, and Indy laughed. Pushing herself forward to sit on the edge of the sofa, Miles took in her bare back. He wanted to trace the route of her spine, caress her smooth skin and pepper light kisses—

"Well, that was interesting."

He cleared his throat, rubbing at his flushed face. "Yeah."

She peered over at him, amusement dancing around the edges of her irises. "I'm going out. Join me?"

Glancing down at himself, he let that primal part of him take over. If she were to go out like this and steal everyone's attention, then he'd be the one to claim her—one way or another.

"Give me a minute to change."

<hr />

INDIGO WAS LIVELY, spirited, and absolutely mesmerising to the point he'd forgotten all about his surroundings and where he was supposed to be.

He probably looked like a fool, staring at her from across the room, dumbfounded and speechless. She was near the bar, dancing with Ava and Rowan with a drink in hand as she sang along to the music reverberating off the walls.

Miles felt a kick against his shin. "You good?"

Slipping his attention to the couple sitting across from him, he nodded curtly. "All grand."

Kamari, who was tucked under Thiago's arm, narrowed her gaze on him. "You seem distracted."

Thiago smirked. "By a wild blonde over there?"

"No clue who you're talking about," he said nonchalantly. "I was just thinking of tomorrow's plan."

"Which is?" Kamari asked, seeming genuinely curious.

"Doing Indy." Thiago snickered.

He threw a glare at his friend and decided to ignore his comment. "I think I want to go on a fifteen-kilometre run, then train, and—"

"Woah," Thiago interrupted, eyes wide. "You need to relax. I know it's difficult to stay put when we're not racing, but why are you training so hard?"

He shrugged, though he knew he was too hard on himself at times. "Helps me stay focused."

"And not be distracted by the wild blonde living with you?"

Miles sent another dirty glare to his friend.

"When are you going to make a move on her?" There was no rudeness or animosity in Kamari's tone.

Was the longing on his face that obvious?

What did Kamari know about his and Indy's history? Certainly everything.

"Not that I owe you an explanation, but it's actually more complicated than that."

"You're right, you don't owe me anything," she said gently. "But if you won't do anything about the way you look at her, you should just stay clear. She's not going to sit around and wait for you. Don't give her mixed signals, Miles."

Miles knew that Kamari was protective of Indy, and he liked that. In fact, Kamari was protective of every single person in their group of friends—it was in her nature to be a caretaker and a shield all at once. She looked out for everyone and made sure no one got hurt.

"Look at her."

He'd never looked over to where Indy was this fast. The feeling of his stomach dropping was one of the worst sensations he'd experienced. The sight of Indy smiling broadly at her interlocutor made his blood boil with unsolicited annoyance.

Alex, who had just taken a step closer to her as they leaned against the bar, was harmless. Miles knew that because Indy had never taken, let alone mentioned an interest in him. Sure, they were friendly and always laughing together, but they were just friends. Platonic. No feelings involved. Right? *Right?*

The only confirmation he needed was witnessing a brunette demanding Alex's attention by tapping on his shoulder.

It was the other man stealing her attention when Alex left that pushed Miles to his feet. At first, the guy offered his hand to shake, but then he kissed the back of Indy's hand. They exchanged a few words, but Miles didn't like the way he was crowding Indy's personal space. Without Indy's permission, the man put a hand on her hip. Without Indy's permission, he leaned into her ear. And without her goddamn consent, he tried pulling her into his chest, his lips a millimetre away from her neck.

Gently, Indy pushed him away. According to Miles, she could've been more aggressive and firm, but that wasn't like Indy. She was always gentle.

It was just a matter of seconds before Miles would reach them and knock some sense and respect into this man.

"I'm not interested," Indy said slowly and firmly, taking a step back.

The man said something that made her smile tightly, uneasiness perceptible on her taut shoulders. Then, he grabbed her wrist again and Indy emitted a nervous, dry chuckle.

"Don't touch me," she gritted out.

"You heard her," Miles bit out, impressed by the calmness of his tone. "Get your hand off her."

When Miles came to stand behind Indy, he brushed his fingers to her hip, letting her know through the delicacy of the caress that it was him. She startled, turning to look at him, before smiling in relief. And when his arm came to loop around her collarbones, crushing her back into his chest, he felt his own breath hitch.

The man let go of her, gulping as he looked up at Miles.

"Hey," he murmured against her temple, finding the other man's gaze in the corner of his eye. "You good?"

Indy relaxed against him, one hand finding his forearm. "I'm okay."

"Shouldn't you be apologising?" Miles drawled out to the stranger who was still standing there.

"Didn't know she was taken."

"Taken or not, you don't touch a woman without her permission. Fucking apologise."

It was only after Miles threw him the coldest glare that he scrambled away, mumbling a weak apology.

Miles' heart was still thundering furiously as he tightened his hold over Indy. "Tell me you're okay, Daisy."

He could feel the slight shudder of her body beneath his palm. Could feel the even rise and fall of her chest as she caught her breath.

Gingerly, he made her spin around. Delicately, he lifted her chin with the help of his forefinger, sapphire eyes brimmed with uncertainty locking to his. "You want to get out of here?"

She nodded, stepping back. He felt cold in an instant before she came to entwine her fingers with his. Miles let himself be pulled away, pushing past dancing bodies, to stumble into a dimly lit corridor, then into a quiet room.

Indy let go of his hand, and he instantly missed the warmth of her skin, the softness of her touch. She went to lean against the billiard table at the centre of the room, sighing.

"I'm sorry," Miles said, running a hand in utter frustration through his hair. "I know you can defend yourself, and I shouldn't have stepped in and acted this way, and I'm so sorry for—"

"Thank you," she cut in softly.

He paused, holding his breath. "Fuck, are you okay?"

Caring for Indigo had always been the one weakness he allowed to consume him. He wasn't usually a jealous person, but seeing another man touch her made him feral. He wanted to dot her porcelain skin with his kisses, with his caresses, to let any other man know that she was off-limits. Part of himself tried to convince his head that he'd stepped in because it was his duty as Kai's best friend to protect her. But the other part simply knew that it was a lie. So, intervening in the earlier situation had not only been because he cared about her, but because he was so fucking jealous and furious too—and yes, he had no right to feel this way.

She nodded. "I'm totally fine. It all just happened so fast."

Taking slow steps towards her, he searched her eyes. Brushing her hair away from her cheek to tuck it behind her ear, he asked, "Promise?"

There was something like anguish, sadness, in her gaze as she held his stare. He swore he could feel her jaw tremble beneath his fingers. Swore he could feel his heartbeat go into overdrive when her eyes fell upon his mouth.

"I promise." The flutter of her lashes when his thumb grazed her cheekbone made him swallow. She turned her face away, gripping his hand. "Don't do this, Huxley. Don't be like this."

He let his hand fall, though the urge to touch her again almost became unbearable.

"Why did you do it? Why did you come and save me?"

His gaze flicked to hers, a lump building inside his throat. "Don't make me say it."

Hurt flashed across her eyes. "Is it going to kill you if you admit that you care?"

He didn't answer because he was already breaking his rules. Was already allowing himself to be distracted when it was the one thing he had sworn not to do. Indy deserved everything that was beautiful and good in the world, and he wasn't quite sure he could meet her expectations. Could be this kind of person for her. Even Kai had asked him to stay away for good measure—because he didn't know how to put his heart to good use. If he was going to hurt someone, it was going to be himself.

"Just tell me what you want," Indy whispered, anguish blending into her words.

Finding her fingers, he waited for her to retreat, but she didn't so much as move. She looked at their connected palms, fitting like magnets, a small crease between her brows. "I'm not above breaking my rules for you, but if I'm willing to lose, I need to do this the right way. We're both focused on our careers right now. We're both at the peak of our lives, and we can't just let ourselves be distracted."

"A distraction," she repeated, her grip loosening. "It's all I'll ever be, right?"

"No," he replied, almost panicking that she wanted to put some distance between them. He caged her in against the table, hands settling on either side of her hips. She'd been holding onto that invisible cord tying his heart to hers for years, and if he gave in to the temptation, it meant that he was willing to let her ruin him. "What's the rush, Indy?"

Back and forth, she looked between his eyes and his lips, like she didn't know where to settle her gaze. Like she didn't know what to say, because she didn't know the answer.

"If you were expecting me to drag you into the nearest bathroom and take you against the wall like all the times we hooked up in the past, then sorry to disappoint, but it's not going to happen."

She nodded slowly. "Because it's different now?"

"Because everything's changed since you came to live under my roof, and you know it. I'm trying my hardest to respect

Kai's wishes and stay friends with you. I don't want to fuck it up, and I need you to understand that I'm not the guy you used to fuck and walk away from. I don't want to be like that anymore."

"I don't want that, either."

"What do *you* want? You want to date?" No answer. Deep down, neither of them were ready for that step, and he was relieved to know she felt the same way. "You want to fuck? If so, just say the word, but I can't do casual like before."

"Why? Cause you think I'm the one who's going to get attached if we start fucking on a regular basis again? That I'm going to have feelings for you?"

"All I think is that you're my best—"

"Use Kai as a fucking excuse one more time. I dare you. This is not about him, and you know it." She exhaled. "Forgive me for being confused about the mixed signals you're giving me. You look at me like you want to rip my clothes off, but you don't want anything to do with me."

"I'm sorry. I'm sorry, Indy." He dropped his head, feeling her warm breath fan across his forehead. "I never meant to make you feel like this, but you've got to understand that I'd love to give you everything I have." How long had he wished for this? How many times had he dreamed of being hers? "But not now, okay? I'm just not ready."

Miles needed the time, the courage, to be worthy of her. To understand she wasn't someone who would walk away. Having been abandoned too many times meant that he was still healing from the shattered pieces, and he wasn't ready for Indy to go because her absence would obliterate him more than any loss he'd experienced.

She'd always been the only woman on his mind, consuming his thoughts albeit against his will. He'd always thought she was special, and quite frankly, he'd always been attracted to her. But admitting his feelings could be deeper, all-consuming, was terrifying.

Though Indy had a reason to leave, he would do everything in his power to make her stay.

The side of his forefinger held her chin in place. The turmoil and affliction were clear in those cerulean irises, causing his heart to clench. "I'm just confused about the way you make me feel," he whispered.

When his hand slipped to her cheek, she leaned into his touch, her brows creasing. "Then let me help you understand those feelings. Please."

※

"Do you even know how to play?"

"No," she said. "You'll teach me."

"Okay." He rubbed the back of his neck. Teaching Indy how to play eight-ball should be easy, right? "Cool. Cool."

She hadn't wanted to go back to their friends, and Miles was more than fine with that. Spending some alone time with Indy meant learning to trust her. Be close to her. Escape in a world alone where nothing else mattered. He wasn't sure of how she would manage to help him understand his feelings, but knowing he wasn't alone made relief crash through him.

As he took hold of a cue, he explained the basics to her. She listened thoroughly, nodding to each piece of information he gave, and watched as he demonstrated how to hold the cue before assembling the balls inside the triangular rack.

"Here." He handed Indy a cue after chalking its end, then proceeded to take off his jacket. "Ladies first."

"So chivalrous," she teased, placing herself at the end of the table.

When she leaned forward over the table, Miles rubbed his face. She was a goddamn temptation, and he needed to hold a semblance of control over himself.

"Okay, so..." She held the end of the cue a few centimetres away from the white ball placed behind the service line. "I need to break the triangle, and whichever ball I pot is the kind I have to pocket throughout the game?"

"Yes."

"Should be easy."

Instead of focusing on what she was doing, he was looking at the slope of her shoulders, the smoothness of her delicate skin, the beautiful shape of her physique—

"Is my arm's position okay?"

He blinked, finding her looking over at him from her shoulder, a suggestive glint in her eyes. He cleared his throat, getting the hint. "Your elbow's too high."

"Oh."

He placed the cue he'd been holding against the table, and stepped behind Indy, his senses already heightening. "Can I touch you?"

"Yes," she whispered.

This was so fucking cliché, and Miles snickered as he realised it had been her intention all along. Brushing his palm from her shoulder down her arm, he lowered her elbow, tingles dancing on his fingertips at the contact of their skin. His chest nearly brushed her bare back, her body caged in below his. She truly fitted him as though she was the missing puzzle piece he'd been looking for.

An electric frisson jolted from her skin to his when his murmur caressed the shell of her ear. "Now, you want to be gentle but firm. No need to be aggressive with your movement. Steady, focused, and"—he helped her break the triangle, potting two solids—"you've got the solids."

"Okay." Turning her neck to look at him, she smiled softly. "Thank you. I think I've got it."

All it would take for everything to change was a kiss. A tangle of their breaths. An entwine of their souls. Only mere centimetres stood in between them. The impulse was there, thrumming and burning. Especially when her soft, sultry laugh echoed, sending chills down his spine.

In the vicinity of Indigo Bailey, Miles was a simple man, powerless and at her complete mercy. But he wouldn't succumb. Not yet.

Finding the sliver of strength he possessed to pull himself back to reality, he winked and took a step back. "Let's see that."

He folded his arms across his chest and watched the sheer concentration on her face as she took her aim. And then, the most baffling thing happened. He tipped his head back as a dry laugh broke free.

"You fucking, sneaky brat," he spat, shaking his head in disbelief. Her shot had been perfectly aimed, smooth and controlled, its motion so precise that she had potted two balls at once. "You know how to fucking play eight-ball."

She had the nerve to smile, shrugging. "I do. Just wanted to play pretend and have you touch me."

"Unbelievable."

⁂

THREE ROUNDS OF EIGHT-BALL, non-alcoholic drinks, and numerous flying insults later, Miles scoffed as he studied his next shot.

It was near impossible.

He'd lose.

Again.

Fuck, she was too good at this. And she was having too much fun winning.

"Hey, Huxley?"

"Mmh?" From where he was hunched over the table, gaze narrowed on his target at the end of the cue, he waited for her response. When it didn't come, he made the mistake of peering at her. With her small hands placed on the edge of the table, her head tilted sideways as she calculated his movements, her breasts were pushed together, their shape and fullness so distracting that he grumbled.

"Stop trying to distract me," he told her, lowering his gaze.

"Sorry." Her apology was everything but sincere. "Not my fault if you can't stop staring at my tits."

He shot her a cold glare, finding that light sliver of control he still possessed to stop himself from ogling at her cleavage.

Giggles echoed in the corridor, the volume of the music from the pub still loud. For a moment, Miles had forgotten there was a world out there. Ava popped her head inside the room, Rowan coming behind her to wrap his arms around her shoulders.

The sight of them together, but especially the stars dancing in Ava's eyes and her blatant happiness, made Miles' heart swell. He smiled at Ava, and she smiled back, leaning further into her boyfriend's chest.

"Are you two hiding?" Rowan asked, grinning.

"Let them be," Ava said. "We're obviously interrupting their date."

"Not a date," Miles muttered in harmony with Indy.

"Rooting for you two," Rowan commented with a wink.

They left then, laughing together.

"Bet they're going to shag?" Indy asked.

"Obviously."

"At least they're getting some."

After not being able to pot his ball, he watched Indy take her turn.

"Hey, Huxley," she mumbled. "Truth or dare?"

He couldn't hide his smile as he took a sip of his soda. "Truth."

Indy rounded the table, and as she stood beside him, she pushed him away with her hip. "What was your first impression of me?"

His heart stalled before going back to thumping erratically. That day, when he'd met Indy for the first time, he'd known she was special.

Thankfully, she was too focused on the game to see the blush on his cheeks. "Well, I think I was completely mesmerised by you. How old were we? I think I was six and you were three? And you wanted to get into the go-kart and compete with Kai and I. You looked like the princess of my dreams."

He didn't miss the scarlet tinge on the apple of her cheeks even if she didn't meet his gaze. "Hey, I thought we agreed on not flirting. Friends don't flirt."

"Can't help myself when I'm with you," he jested with a grin. "I'd never met a girl who liked cars. My mother never came to my karting races, and Maya was into ballet. She'd pretend to gag at every mention of cars. She'd made me believe girls were *allergic* to cars. Imagine how I felt when my new best friend told me he had a sister who loved racing just as much."

She pocketed her ball smoothly. "It's kind of inevitable when you grow up with a father who was at the peak of his F1 career."

"True. That never stopped you from doing typical girl stuff, though." He remembered laughing when she'd show up to karting races wearing a tiara, or a tutu because she had ballet afterwards—he'd never meant it in a mocking way, but more in admiration.

"Oh, absolutely. I loved dance class, art, and fashion all the same."

"You're so brilliant," he murmured truthfully, which brought a devastating smile to her lips. "Your turn: truth or dare?"

"Dare."

Brushing his fingertips against her hip, he came to stand beside her and leaned his forearms on the edge of the table, looking at her profile. She was undoubtedly the most beautiful woman he'd ever had the privilege of setting his eyes on. This close, the freckles splattered across the bridge of her nose and dusting faintly on her cheekbones were visible like constellations.

"I dare you to let me win this round."

She laughed coldly. "No can do, Golden Boy."

"Fine. I dare you to say on live TV that you love me, and that I'm the best, hottest, most glorious driver—"

"So basically you want me to lose my job?" She missed her next shot, taking a step back to give him more space to play. "You suck at this game."

"You're so annoying," he said.

"Trying to be smart," she countered breezily.

"Fine. I dare you to set the world on fire by showing all your followers that you're here with me tonight."

All the rumours circulating around and speculating that Miles was in a relationship with Indy had made him laugh. Seriously, weren't there more important things going on in the world than a driver's personal life?

He was aware of the many comments about the way he talked to her—softly, openly, as if his guard lowered any time she was around—and the way he walked by her side in the paddock. He was aware of everything the media said about him, he just didn't give one single flying fuck—never had.

But if he could create chaos just for one minute...

She sighed. "You're trouble."

"As if you didn't already know."

"Done." The phone she shoved into his face displayed a photo of his back as he held the cue, his forearms and expensive watch perceptible. Enough to raise suspicions, enough to give hints. "Easy, baby."

Miles smirked. This woman was fearless.

As he continued on potting another ball, he said, "Ask me."

"Truth or dare?"

"Truth."

"Were you jealous?"

At that, Miles straightened himself, immediately finding Indy's electric gaze. He could feel the push and pull between them—two magnets fighting to cross that tempting field. "Yes."

"No need to be," she assured softly, though the small smile tilting her mouth upwards was indication of her triumph.

"See, it's only with you that I have all those weird feelings bubbling inside me. I see Alex Myers chatting and having a giggle with another girl? I don't give a shit. But I see him touching your back? I'm fuming, and I realise my self-control shatters for you. I see a stranger take advantage of you, and there's this voice in my head saying that it should be *me* touching you."

"Then act on it," she whispered fiercely.

"I already told you; I'm not going to ruin this situation for any of us."

Hurt flared across her gaze—comprehension, too.

"Okay." She cleared her throat, holding his gaze. "Truth or dare?"

"I didn't get to ask you."

"Answer me."

This feisty woman.... "Dare."

With her chin tipped up, her determined gaze locked to his, and her nose almost touching his, Miles thought his weak knees would suddenly give up. If he wasn't already a fool, he was absolutely reckless for accepting her challenge. "If and when you realise that you want me, I dare you to show me how much. Words will never matter to me. Actions do. So if you want me, I dare you to grow some balls."

CHAPTER FIFTEEN

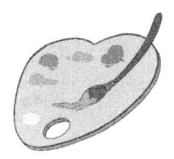

📍 *MELBOURNE, AUSTRALIA*

THE TORRENTIAL RAIN splattered onto the concrete, the softer rumble of thunder nearly drowned out by the noise of the deluge.

Indy glanced skywards, grimacing at the sight of the dark, calamitous heavens. It was only early morning, and the race was set to start at three p.m. She hoped the rain would stop so that the Grand Prix wouldn't be delayed. Still, a wet race was always exhilarating to watch, and she had no doubt that today was about to be chaotic.

In the shelter of the building, she braced herself for the gust of cold wind that would brush into her face the moment she'd open the door. She needed to cross the paddock to enter another building to attend a press conference.

What a stupid idea to wear a skirt when rain had been predicted all weekend long. At least she was wearing knee-high boots, but fashion before anything, right? That's what her mother had always taught her. *Dress like it's your last day on Earth.*

Despite the apocalyptic weather, the paddock was quite busy: car mechanics roaming around, drivers arriving at the circuit, journalists and photographers rushing towards shelter, and VIP members being guided into a team's motorhome.

Checking the time again, Indy sighed and decided to leave the building. She stepped outside, and came face to face with Miles.

"Wrong building, Golden Boy," she said, still standing below that tiny roof.

"Such a nice way of greeting." He was holding a large umbrella with a to-go cup of coffee in his other hand, the tops of his cheekbones slightly rosy because of the weather. He took her in with a once-over—rapid and fleeting yet powerful enough to make her forget about the chilly wind. "Just the person I was looking for."

"Me?" Her brows knitted together in slight confusion. If there was one thing she hated, it was her heart always skipping a beat at the mere attention he brought upon her.

"No," he deadpanned. "Your coworker who's staring at us."

Tara.

Indy didn't have to turn around to know she was the one watching them. She'd been hanging out in the lobby for a while, chattering quietly with other people, though always observing Indy from the corner of her eye. Indy couldn't recall the amount of times she wanted to shift with uneasiness, wondering why she was being so blatantly judged.

"I'm sure she'd love to receive the tiniest bit of your attention."

Miles' expression didn't break—like an unmovable mask he had slipped on that wouldn't budge no matter what. "Do I look like I want to talk to her?"

"And you want to with me?"

Something in his gaze softened. "I always want to talk to

you, Indy." He held out the umbrella, urging her to step beneath it. "Come on, I'll walk you."

"What a gentleman," she teased as they started walking.

"Only with you."

She paused, the rain beating down on the umbrella they stood under, and shivered, not expecting it to be so cold.

Well, maybe that frisson jolting throughout her bones was caused by their proximity, by his presence. The memories from their late night at the club in Monaco were still vivid. They'd played pool for hours, laughing and getting to know each other without being interrupted. Then, they had joined their friends in the main area and had danced until fatigue took over (well, Miles sat with the boys whilst Indy had dragged the girls to the dance floor, but still, he looked like he was having a good time).

It had felt nice to spend an evening out of the flat with him. She'd found herself lying in bed later that night, wishing for more alone time with Miles.

"This weather is so shitty," she muttered to diffuse the butterflies stirring inside her stomach. "You'd think we're in Spa, or something, with heavy rain like this."

"True." Miles chuckled. "But I love wet races. Okay, so, hold the umbrella and the coffee for a sec."

She did, rolling her eyes in pleasantry. "Remember what I just said about you being a gentleman? Forget it."

"Just give me a moment, woman."

The specific notes of ginger and nutmeg mixed with pepper danced in the air as he shrugged his jacket off, leaving him in a thick, black Imperium Racing jumper. He draped the warm piece of clothing around Indy's shoulders, offering her a secret, soft smile as he did so, untucking her hair from under the collar.

"Wouldn't want you to catch a cold," he murmured, letting his perusal travel from the slope of her nose to her lips. "Who else is going to interview me after I win today?"

"First of all, there are tons of other reporters in the media pen. Secondly, who says you're the winner of today's GP?"

The glint in his eyes was pure arrogance and burning mischief. "I like to start my day being confident."

"You're such an inspiring person." She grinned, and he huffed at the sarcasm woven into her tone. "Teach me your ways."

As he grabbed the umbrella, their fingers brushed. She tried to give him the coffee, only for him to push it back towards her.

"Coffee's for you."

She guffawed. "Do you know my coffee order? It's quite specific."

"Double espresso with a splash of oat milk and brown sugar," he said without missing a beat.

"How?" Her word was a simple whisper, blended in with all the noises booming around.

"Texted Kam," he answered casually. So nonchalantly.

Indy could feel her heart expand, on the brink of bursting at the seams.

No one had ever taken interest in her favourite hot drink, let alone memorise its specific composition.

"Thank you," she whispered, rapidly squeezing his hand. His thumb ran along the side of her wrist before letting the coaxing caress vanish.

Crimson tinged his cheeks. "You're welcome." When thunder cracked overhead, he flinched. Although it was barely noticeable, Indy saw everything in him and frowned with concern.

"What's wrong?"

Finding the small of her back with his free hand, he urged her forward. "Nothing. Let's get inside."

As they stopped in front of the building she was supposed to go in, she smiled at him. "You really didn't have to give me your jacket, or get me a coffee, or walk me here."

"I wanted to."

Ugh. Why did he have to be so...perfect? Even though they were finally getting comfortable with one another, Indy still felt

SPEEDING INTO OVERDRIVE

like she was overstaying her welcome and bothering him with her constant presence. She'd been thinking of moving out as soon as possible, and she needed to give him a heads-up. Now was maybe not the time, but she decided to speak up.

"Well, thanks." Tucking a strand of hair behind her ear, she inhaled. "I'm looking for an extra job for when we're not travelling and back in Monaco."

His expression was blank. "Why?"

"To save more money to find a place of my own. I don't want to be a burden and invade your—"

"Indigo," he interjected. "Where is this coming from? You'll never be a burden, and I refuse to let you take on an extra job to get out of my place. Unless it's what you really want, but I like having you around, and I'm not kicking you out."

She didn't reply, because of course she didn't want to leave. His place was a dream. And even though she was a hardworking person, she didn't want to exhaust herself on days off.

"Let me pay my share of the rent." It wasn't a question. Until now, he had avoided every conversation revolving around rent and money.

"No. It's my penthouse."

"But—"

His jaw ticced. "Here's a rule we can settle on. How about you just let yourself be taken care of without worrying about me?"

She was certain her cheeks had heated up. "Well, forgive me for being an independent woman who hates taking advantage of people."

"Apology accepted. Your independence is so sexy, but stop trying to bargain because it won't work. And for your information, you're not taking advantage of me if I'm finding pleasure in helping you out."

Indy huffed. "Will you watch chick-flicks with me?"

"Depends. What's the first one we're putting on?"

"*How to Lose a Guy in 10 Days*." Probably her favourite one.

The corner of his mouth quirked. "Deal."

If she could just stand there, under the pouring rain, admiring the specific shade of green of his eyes blended with hues of gold and red, she would. If she could just stop time and take a photo of him staring at her like there wasn't a world around them, she would. But reality struck when another thunder vibrated. "Good luck for today."

As she handed his jacket back and entered the lobby, she blushed at his wink, trying her hardest to calm her racing heart. This was bad news. Trouble.

She was fucked. So much for wanting to focus on the new job and pretend like her crush on her roommate and brother's best friend had faded.

"Fascinating," a soft voice came from behind.

"What is?" Indy asked Carmen as the latter deposited a wet umbrella by the door.

"Miles Huxley. I've never seen him act this way with anyone before. Are you two..."

She frowned, understanding the question that lingered behind the thought.

"Oh, no. Friends." The simple action of voicing this word pinched her chest.

Carmen nodded, studying Indy's expression. "Well, I do think it'd be a good thing for him to be seen with you. It'd be good PR, and maybe the public would start liking him more when he's off the track too. You're showing them that he's a good man."

And he was. He was becoming the best man she'd ever met. She'd do anything to show how big of a heart Miles Huxley bore. He wasn't heartless, or rude, or uncaring. Quite the contrary. He was golden, but that was something the world had yet to discover under the thick layers of his mask.

CHAPTER SIXTEEN

⚑ *MELBOURNE, AUSTRALIA*

THE VISOR OF his helmet was dotted with droplets of rain, the road ahead barely visible because of the thin drizzle falling onto the track. Good thing that he knew the trajectory of the circuit like he'd been born on it.

His breathing was staggered, the zipping roar of his engine a melody to his ears. Gripping the steering wheel tightly between his gloved fingers, he embraced all those frissons skittering down his spine as he took a high-speed chicane. This particular circuit was one of his favourites because 1) it was bumpy and slippery until it rubbered in after a few progressing sessions, rendering the competition quite challenging for most drivers; 2) this was where he'd had his maiden win five years ago.

As his foot pressed on the throttle, AJ's voice boomed in his earplugs the very moment he passed a yellow flag being waved in the air. "Yellow flag in sector two. The safety car is arriving. Keep delta positive."

Slowing down, he cast a quick glance in his rear-view mirror to see if the chaos had unravelled behind him. Charlie was following him closely, now zig-zagging to keep his tyres warm, as overtaking was forbidden until the green flag was brandished and the safety car was out of the track.

"What happened? Is everyone okay?" he demanded. The sun was now peeking through clouds, although slowly, the rain falling down in thin, irregular rivulets.

"There's a McMillan in the gravel. Locked up and almost collided with the wall. Hugo's okay, but he's retiring because there's an issue with his gearbox."

The safety car came to lead the queue of fast cars in front of Miles. "Sucks for the team."

"Yeah. Box on the next lap."

As he kept dragging his vehicle on the asphalt, switching between slowing down and accelerating, he almost chuckled at the sight of Charlie attempting to drift in the rain.

In the pit lane, he stopped where his pit crew waited for him in front of his garage, ready to replace the tyres.

"Inters?" Miles asked, bemused. "Don't mess up."

Less than three seconds later, his car had a fresh set of compounds on, and he was driving out of the pit lane, falling back into fifth place. He'd seen other drivers opt for the same strategy: pitting during the safety car.

"Track's drying out. Trust me," AJ said.

Miles sighed, ignoring the spray misting from the car in front. "You're going to give me grey hairs, AJ."

His race engineer huffed. "You'll thank me when you win another title."

It took six laps for the track to be cleared and the green flag to be brandished. Accelerating easily, Miles overtook two cars in the long, fast turn.

"Great job," AJ praised as Miles fell into third place. "Seventeen laps to go."

Three laps later, the track dried out, but not enough to put soft compounds on, though not wet enough to keep wet tyres on. The two Primavera Racing drivers that had been leading the race went into the pit lane, leaving Miles to be the leader of the race.

"Good call," he finally told AJ.

"Please, do you know who you're talking to?"

All Miles did was grunt before pushing on the throttle, leaving a big gap between him and Charlie.

※

MILES WON THE GRAND PRIX.

As he stood on the podium, hands behind his back, and gaze settled on the now blue sky, he listened to the British Anthem.

This—this sensational and incomparable feeling—was what fuelled him.

This was what made him happy.

This was what he was made for.

Glancing down, he dipped his chin in a curt nod when he locked his stare with his team principal, David, before looking at the car mechanics cheering him on, and all the fans chanting his name.

Despite the pride flaring inside his chest, despite the awareness that he'd fought his whole life to stand here today, he couldn't help but feel as though he was doing something wrong. As though he would get more hate for winning again, for being a ferocious and unbeatable driver.

He wasn't enough despite his greatest efforts. And he didn't know what to do anymore.

As he grabbed the bottle of champagne, rammed it against the step to let the bubbles fizzle out and throw the liquid on Charlie and Rowan, he wondered what he needed to achieve in order to show the world he wasn't *that* inaccessible. That agonising feeling of being unloved was starting to become overwhelming, and he just needed it to stop.

Perhaps the breathtaking blonde chatting with a cameraman,

whose gaze found his in a heartbeat when he stepped inside the media pen, would help him salvage himself.

And if salvation meant breaking each one of his rules, then he'd ruin himself to win.

❧

"Can I run an idea by you? You might hate it, though."

"Consider me intrigued," he drawled lazily to Ava as he glanced to where she was sitting, tablet opened before her as she typed hastily.

She stopped whatever she'd been doing for the past half-hour, walked up to the door, closed it, then sat beside him on the sofa. Miles had been relaxing after his interviews, soaking it all in before he needed to head out to grab a post-race dinner with his friends.

"I'm telling you this as your press officer," she began. "Not your friend."

"Shit, I hate it when you use that tone." He raised his hands. "I promise I've been trying to be good during interviews."

"You have," Ava assured sweetly and took a breath in. "You're allowed to say no, okay?"

"Get straight to the point, Ave."

"Right, right. What do you think of PR relationships?"

He blinked. "Pardon me?"

"With Indy," she added, her expression indecipherable.

Frowning, he leaned forward to place his elbows atop his thighs and ran a hand across his jaw. At the simple mention of the beautiful blonde, his pulse started picking up its pace. "I don't like this idea. Where are you going with it?"

"I've noticed a sudden interest in whatever's going on between you and Indy from your followers. Lots of encouragement. Lots of questions. The whole fake dating thing would not only help you polish your image, but it could be beneficial for her, too, in many ways."

Miles stared at the wall ahead, shaking his head. "Does she know about this?"

"Not yet. I wanted to run the idea by you first. And to be honest, it was Carmen who came up to me. She thinks it would be good PR, especially for you, and since you and Indy hang out a lot..."

Redemption could be his, but was this the sole solution? Miles had one shot at making everything right with Indy, but playing pretence would destroy everything.

"What's your opinion as my friend?" he asked.

"I want your thoughts first," she said firmly.

He straightened himself. "The idea has potential, but I won't go with it. Things are going great between Indy and I, and this could ruin everything. I don't want to fake anything with her."

Ava expelled a breath full of relief after a moment of silence. "I hoped you'd say that. Indy's liked you for a while—"

"She has?"

"God, you're so blind. Yes, you imbecile. But I don't think she'd like the idea of having you under the guise of pretending. With that being said, though, she'd do anything for you, so if dating for PR is something that you'd want, I'll talk to her."

His pulse was pounding against his temple, his blood roaring to life. He'd always thought Indy's attraction for him was simply physical, but knowing it was deeper made him feel like an ass for the way he'd treated her.

Applying a much-needed pressure against his temple, he sighed. "I'm not cleaning my image by fake dating Indy."

"But would you date her for real?"

Rubbing the back of his neck, he contemplated the question for a few beats. "I'm just letting time do its own thing."

"You didn't deny it," Ava countered with a smile.

"Wipe that cheeky smile off your face." He shrugged. "There's no other girl like her, and I'm aware of that. I constantly think about her. But I'm not ready to be in a relationship." Ava was probably the only person who knew about the way he felt. "I don't think I can give her what she needs or be remotely close to being enough for her."

"I know, and that's okay. But don't belittle yourself this way. You're a good man, and I'm certain she sees it. I think you've been so used to people saying you're kind of cold and that's why you don't see yourself as a caring person, but trust me, you're kind and absolutely worthy of happiness." The reassurance in her voice made him feel at peace. It would take him months, if not years, to believe that he was good. "Say you could date someone else for PR, though. A model, a celebrity? Is that something you'd—?"

"No. Just drop the idea."

She nodded. "Okay. Just wanted to make sure. I'm glad you don't want to destroy yours and Indy's friendship."

"Yeah," he said. "I don't want to lose her."

Admitting everything he'd just said should have scared him. Instead, peace simply threaded through his bloodstream—an indication that facing his sentiments wasn't a cause for self-destruction.

Ava patted his shoulder and stood up. "Your secret's safe with me, Miles."

And damn him for opening up to his friend. Damn him for allowing himself to break, even for the sliver of truth he'd given. He would need to build his walls up again, because protecting his friendship with Indy was way more important than acting on his growing feelings for her.

CHAPTER SEVENTEEN

📍 *MONTE CARLO, MONACO*

THE HAZE OF fatigue was still fogging her mind as she deposited her empty glass by the sink. Yawning, Indy padded back towards her room, the coldness of the floorboards making chills prickle the back of her neck.

She'd caught a glimpse of the time before entering the dark hallway: two in the morning.

Indy hadn't been able to sleep well since she'd entered her bedroom after watching a romantic comedy with Miles (yes, he had caved in). She'd woken up every hour, an unsettling sensation stirring deep inside her gut, and she still didn't know why. Like every night before switching the lights off, she had done her breathing exercises which should have helped her sleep peacefully.

Just as she stepped inside her room, a scream echoed from the other end of the corridor, making her heart leap out of her chest.

"*NO!*" Huxley shouted, a crack in his voice.

With a hand placed above her chest, she could feel the uneven and wild beat of her organ. She hurried to his room without a second thought. Uncaring of the consequences.

Miles wasn't trashing or turning in his bed like she'd expected to find him, but he was lying immobile, his skin damp with sweat, his fists curled into tight balls atop the sheets.

He whimpered, the sound filled with agony, his head turning to face Indy. The deep crease between his eyebrows was illuminated by the faint glow of the moonlight streaming through the gap in the curtains, his hair sticking to his forehead.

"No, please," he whispered, followed by a gut-wrenching sob. Whatever he was dreaming about was destroying him, and Indy could feel her heart drop inside her stomach at the sight.

Indy had never seen him like this. She could feel tears gather at the corners of her eyes, but she took a breath and braced herself as she walked further into the room.

"Huxley?" she attempted softly.

She wasn't sure of how to handle the situation. She didn't want to startle him but also didn't want to leave him so distressed any longer.

She kneeled on the carpet, her bare knees digging into the soft fabric just as she shook his shoulder. "Huxley."

A tear streamed down his cheek, causing the ache in her chest to grow—like vines wrapping around her heart, squeezing, compressing, and squashing in order to break it.

"Huxley!" She shook his shoulder more firmly and he finally jolted upright into a sitting position. His bare torso shone with perspiration, the blanket pooling at his waist. The dismay and concern etched on his handsome face truly broke her.

His chest heaved, his bated breaths reverberating off the walls as his empty gaze searched her face. The sheer fear marring his features, the confusion in his gaze... She simply hated whatever affliction he was going through.

"Hey," she whispered, coming to sit on the edge of the mattress. "It's me."

His gaze softened, a sigh filled with relief escaping his mouth. "Indy?" God, she'd never seen him so out of control, so lost, so tormented.

She nodded, offering him a reassuring smile. "Are you okay?" What a daft question. Of course, he wasn't.

His swallow was audible as he pushed his hair away from his forehead, his fingers shaking.

"Can I touch you?" Indy's voice was above a mere whisper.

Miles gave her a nod, and even if she'd have wanted to hear a verbal response, she didn't want to leave him with his internal battle any longer. Delicately, she ran her hands from his wrists to his shoulders. He shivered beneath her palms, his wide eyes pleading for her to lift him out of this nightmare. "Come here."

The moment she pulled him into her chest, he wrapped his arms around her waist, tightly so. Like he was tethering himself to her. Like he didn't want to let go.

His entire body trembled beneath her hands, her caresses floating between his shoulder blades where the muscles were taut with fear. Discomfort. Anguish.

She felt something wet cascade down her shoulder and that was when she felt a knot twisting inside her throat. He shook when her fingers wove into the hair at his nape, his embrace tightening.

She could feel his heart beating fast, wild, as if it had gone into racing mode. Could feel the utter pain in his demeanour as he clung to her as though she was his lifeline.

"It's okay," she soothed, passing gentle fingers through his hair. "You're safe."

"You're here," he said, so quietly that it had almost been inaudible.

She swallowed. "I'm not going anywhere."

Miles pulled her onto his lap, and Indy didn't care about his naked chest. Didn't care about the thin silky camisole hugging her torso being the only piece of clothing between them. She simply cared about the fact he was being held, that she did not want to loosen her hold.

They stayed attached to one another for minutes—like two perfectly fitted puzzle pieces—without saying a word, without moving.

"You're okay. Everything's all right."

Repeatedly, she whispered that he was safe with her. That nothing could hurt him.

Eventually, his body stopped trembling and his breathing calmed down to even puffs of air.

Her mind was flooded with questions, but she didn't dare voice any of them.

Without warning, he flipped them over until Indy was lying down, facing him. He pulled her in by the hip, engulfing her between strong arms as she placed her head on his chest.

Soon enough, their legs were tangled, her arms looped around his waist.

She felt so safe, so at peace between his arms, listening to the steady yet loud patter of his heartbeat. Like this, she almost felt complete.

She wondered if he also felt this way. Or if he was holding onto her because she'd been there at the right time. Slightly shifting to make herself more comfortable, she felt his grip tightening.

"Don't go just yet," he demanded, his raspy voice feeling akin to a cool breeze slipping through the crack of an open window.

It hurt—to be this close to Miles and wanting to be even closer, but knowing there was a line between them. But being here and not knowing the cause of his utter distress hurt just as much.

She drew soft circles along his ribs, feeling goosebumps arise in the wake of her touch. "Huxley?"

He hummed, as if to respond *yes*, the vibration rumbling inside his chest.

"Do you want to talk about it?"

The lengthy silence made her move just enough to look at him. His eyes were shut, the crease that had once formed a line between his brows now gone. "Not today," he answered in a whisper.

"Okay."

His features relaxed, but his arms stayed firmly around her shoulders. She sighed, observing his handsome face—those regal cheekbones, that little scar atop his right brow, his full lips, the shadow of a moustache growing and the stubble smattered across his jawline.

"Can you stay? Just for a bit."

Indy exhaled, sinking further into him. "Anything you need."

"Thank you, Daisy."

When his breaths became even, soft, she understood he'd fallen asleep.

Perhaps having Indy here had helped him find a sliver of strength to forget about his demons and fall asleep peacefully.

Delicately, Indy brushed a dark strand of hair away from his brow. He didn't so much as stir, his lips parting to let a breath escape.

Even asleep he looked distraught and tortured. Indy hated seeing him like this.

What was she supposed to do? Stay here and fall asleep in the comfort of his arms, his sheets? Go and give him some space until he was ready to open up?

The former option was the one she wanted to lean on, the one she'd been waiting for. But the latter seemed like the smartest decision—because she knew Miles, and she did not want him to panic in the morning if he found her sleeping in his bed. Especially not after a moment like the one she had witnessed, which he certainly hadn't wanted her to see.

She waited a moment—minutes, an hour—to ensure that he

was sound asleep, that he wasn't about to wake up again screaming and drenched in sweat.

It was when her eyelids felt heavy that she forced herself to move. Slowly escaping his embrace, she tried to ignore the tight feeling inside her chest and slipped out of his room.

☙

SEVERAL HOURS later when Indy walked into the kitchen, she found herself being surprised at the sight of Miles standing at the counter, focused on his task.

His head jerked up when she approached, a ghost of a smile touching his lips. "Morning."

She yawned, wrapping her robe around herself. "Hey, stud."

"You good?"

Indy blinked. His hair was tousled as if he'd run his fingers through it multiple times, his eyes slightly glossy from the lack of sleep, even hidden behind his glasses. Worry consumed her senses as she wondered why he wasn't getting the rest he desperately needed.

"Yes," she lied. She hadn't been able to sleep at all until five in the morning. It was now seven. "You?"

"Doing pretty great." Did he also just blatantly lie in her face? "I'm trying to make you a matcha latte."

That was when she noticed the mess on the counter, the strawberries in a bowl, the bottle of oat milk. "You are?"

Miles cleared his throat, dropping his gaze to the little bowl set before him. "I woke up again and couldn't fall asleep. Watched videos on how to make your favourite drink."

She couldn't control the furious blush heating her cheeks. "You didn't have to."

"Shouldn't you be thanking me?"

"I was getting there, Golden Boy." She gave him a smile that made a tinge of rose appear on his face. "Thank you, but you didn't have to."

"Everything I do for you is because I genuinely want to. Not because you think I feel obligated."

Sure, Indy had friends—a lot of them—but he was one of the rare ones who enjoyed doing something for her without wanting anything in exchange.

Indy had left the door to her room ajar just in case he'd wake up again. Guilt gripped at her nerves because she shouldn't have left—especially since he had asked for her to stay.

"This is really sweet of you." She let her mouth tip upwards into a beam.

When his gaze dropped to her lips, everything stopped. "Anything to see your beautiful smile."

"Stop flirting."

"Can't resist the temptation. I made a strawberry purée," he said then. "Thought I'd make an iced strawberry matcha latte, but then I realised that I don't know if you like strawberries or—"

"I love them," she cut in, smiling.

"I never asked if you have any allergies."

"Just to assholes," she muttered, patting Rosie's head who was sleeping on a fluffy mat by the floor-to-ceiling window.

Miles snorted. That felt like a victory to Indy. She collected his smiles and laughs like rare gemstones. "So basically you've been allergic to me for the past couple of years?"

"Basically, yeah. Seems like the allergy is getting better, though."

"Glad to hear that." His palm rubbed the back of his neck. "I'm just not sure how to whisk the powder properly."

She watched as he attempted to mix the green powder with the water, obliging her to step in. "Hold on." She came to stand by his side, the lingering memories of his arms around her making the warmth inside her chest expand. "Here." She placed her hand atop his, guiding his movement, the zip of electricity from his skin directly seeping into her veins. "You want to make an M and Z motion with the whisk. You can be thorough. We don't want clumps of matcha at the bottom of our glass."

She helped Miles finish the mixture and took a slight step away. She was in awe of how meticulous he was when it came to cooking. After being done with her drink, he handed it to her.

Indy brought the straw to her lips, and the first sip sent her straight to heaven. She moaned, going in for another sip. "This is delicious."

It wasn't the scarlet blush on his cheekbones that had caught her attention, but his broad smile. "I'm glad."

He caught her wrist, bringing the drink towards him. If he heard the way her breath had hitched, he didn't show it. He hummed in approval after taking a sip. "I like this one better than the one you made me drink when you first moved in."

She scoffed. "You make it sound like I forced you to drink it."

He chuckled, then grabbed her free hand. His thumb drew circles on her palm before he laced their fingers together. For a few seconds, he didn't look into her eyes, but when he did, there was a gloom that had misted over his bright green irises.

"I'm sorry," he whispered. "For last night."

She squeezed his hand. "Don't apologise."

"I woke you up, and I bet you were worried. And I'm sorry for pushing you away when you asked if I wanted to talk about it. I'm just so, so sorry."

Putting down the glass, she cupped the side of his broad neck. "I appreciate the apology, but I promise that it's not necessary. I was just scared and worried. And I just want you to know that I'm here if you want to talk about it. Whenever you're ready."

The subtle clench in his jaw didn't go unnoticed, but when he wrapped his arms around her and pulled her in, all worries seemed to fade away. She held Miles just as tightly, balling his t-shirt between her fists. One of his hands cupped the back of her head, his fingers tangling with her locks.

"Thank you," he whispered against the crown of her head. "For coming. For staying. Just—thank you."

"Of course. You call, I come running."

When Miles kissed her temple softly, she felt her heart burst —fireworks on a summer night.

And when he didn't pull away, slowly swaying to Mazzy Star's *Fade Into You*, he asked, "Is it okay if I hold you a little bit longer?" Indy nodded because this may be the only glimpse she could take at his vulnerability. May be the only time he would hold her close.

This was better than receiving nothing at all, and perhaps Indy was a fool for thinking she could live with the tiny pieces of himself that he was handing her.

"More than okay." She inhaled his addictive scent, keeping her eyes closed to linger in the moment. "It feels nice to be hugged."

"Especially when it feels right," he murmured.

Indy nodded in agreement, feeling the back of her throat tighten. "Did you know my parents hugged Kai and I on rare occasions?"

"I'm sorry," Miles said. "I know how that feels, and it sucks. Your parents might not have given you that kind of affection, but that doesn't mean they don't love you, and it doesn't mean that you don't deserve to be held. I'll hold you, Indy, and I won't let go."

At that exact moment, she felt a shard go through her organ, letting all those broken pieces that had been hanging by a thin thread fracture into dust. She was all too familiar with what heartbreak felt like—but the worst of it all was that she wanted *him* to mend the fragmented pieces.

Indy simply wanted him—dark facets, scars, fears and insecurities, and even bits of brokenness. She wanted all of him, and she didn't know how to tell him. How to let him know without scaring him away. Because if there was one thing she was sure of, it was that Miles tended to shield himself when something good came his way.

※

MALAKAI ANSWERED on the third ring, sounds of laughter booming on his side of the line.

"What's up, Ind?" The smile in his tone was evident, and the thought of seeing her brother happy and enjoying life so thoroughly enveloped her in a bubble of pure delight.

"Are you busy?"

"Nah," he said. "Just eating out with Rome and Ez."

Indy had texted Kai to call her as soon as he was free, and her phone rang not even two seconds later. At the time, she was still in the flat, so she had declined the call and waited until she was outside to call her brother back.

"Tell them I said hi."

Kai echoed her demand, and she chuckled when his two best friends greeted her so joyfully that she couldn't help but smile, too.

"Where are you?" Kai asked. "You sound out of breath."

"I'm crossing the road. Taking Rosie on a walk." The dog peered up at the sound of her name.

Indy had suggested taking Rosie out and coming back with some take away food. Miles had grinned, broad and beautiful, settling for Thai before asking which rom-com to watch tonight.

She was starting to love this ordeal of spending more time together.

"Holy shit, you're so out of shape," Kai mocked.

"Tell me about it. Listen, it's about Huxley."

"Hang on." A few heartbeats later, the sound of chatter sounded more distant. "What about him?"

Indy halted on the sidewalk, blowing out a breath. "Do you know about his nightmares?"

The lengthy silence made her check her phone to ensure the call hadn't been disconnected.

"Do you—"

"Don't tell me what causes them, don't tell me anything. I just wanted to know if you knew of them."

She imagined Kai passing his fingers through his dark hair. "It's not my place to tell, anyway. But yeah, he doesn't get them often, but when he does, they're really bad."

"Last night was terrifying," she admitted, a lump growing in her throat. "I was so scared, and he looked so pained, and I wanted to cry too, and—"

"What did you do?" Sympathy was woven into his tone.

"Just held him."

Kai paused again. "Do you like him?"

"Of course, we've known each other—"

"No, like, do you have feelings for Miles?"

She couldn't. She wasn't allowed to. Miles was Kai's best friend. She couldn't do this to her brother. Couldn't steal him. Therefore, Indy really needed to find the courage to step back.

"No," she answered quietly, her stomach churning with the lie escaping her mouth. "Don't worry. He's super attractive, though."

"Facts," he chuckled. "Thanks, Ind. Thank you for being there for him."

"He's not alone. I hope he knows that."

"He might be an F1 World Champion, has tons of people looking up at him and friends on the other side of the world, but I think he's a bit lonely at times. I think you're making this a bit better for him."

"How do you know that?"

"He talks a lot about you. He won't ever say it, but he loves having you around. Not because you remind him of me, but because he likes you."

She paused. "As a friend?"

"Yeah. Miles doesn't do feelings. Don't get your hopes up."

A knot was growing inside her throat, the urge to claw at her skin becoming overwhelming. "Are you sure about that?"

"Positive. I know he's been seeing this girl for the past couple of years, although they're keeping it casual. He never mentioned her name, but I just know he's only been with her, and I'm just baffled by the fact he still hasn't fallen for her."

"Lucky girl." The way her heart was nearly on the brink of shattering was not a good sign. The idea of being the only woman for Miles but still feeling as though she wasn't good enough for him was putting her in an endless spiral of affliction. "He made me a matcha latte this morning, though. Be prepared to receive an invitation to our wedding soon."

"For fuck's sake," Kai grumbled.

She sniffled, then waved at Thiago who came out of his building. "You're not mad that I care about him, are you?"

Kai chuckled. "Of course not. Makes me happy to see my two best friends care about each other."

She smiled. "Thanks, Kai."

"Yup. I'm always a call away if you need anything." There was a small beat of silence. "Oh, and Ind? In case I don't say it enough, I'm really, really fucking proud of you. Love you."

Kai didn't give her the chance to respond and hung up.

Thiago grinned as he reached Indy, hands in the pockets of his baggy jeans. "What's up, blondie?"

She rolled her eyes at the given nickname. "I'm walking to grab some Thai food. Want to join me?"

"Sure." They fell into step on the sidewalk, the cool breeze brushing her hair away from her face. "Where's Huxley?"

"He was in his sim room when I left, but he's probably chilling now."

"Does he ever stop?" There was simple curiosity in Thiago's question.

Indy shook her head, her grip around Rosie's leash tightening. "No. He's a hardworking man."

Thiago hummed. "He reminds me of Kam in a way."

She side-glanced at her friend, noticing the blush on his face. "How is she doing by the way? I feel like I barely see her nowadays."

"You know how she is. Working day and night to make sure everything's perfect. Now that the second café is open, she's running left and right, but I truly admire her courage. She's phenomenal and doing amazing."

"She's so brave," Indy whispered. "Her hard work has paid off."

"Sure has. She's doing big things."

Indy blew a raspberry. "I love Kam. She's the coolest."

There were three women that Indy looked up to: her mother who'd taught her so much; Kamari, her inspiring best friend who was the embodiment of bravery; and Carmen, her boss, who was the living proof that women belonged in a male-dominated world, and that nothing and no one could tear them apart.

"Hey," Thiago teased, elbowing her. "She's *my* girl."

Chuckling, she dropped her gaze to her shoes. "Tito, can I ask you something?"

"Anything."

"How did you manage to have Kam open up when she tried to shut herself off?"

She could feel Thiago's gaze on her. "Be patient. Show Huxley that you care about him. Give him pieces of yourself—parts no one knows about you—and he'll open up. I'm sure he's terrified of something that doesn't have to do with you, and all you can do during those moments is hold his hand and prove to him that you're not going anywhere."

"And if he keeps pushing me away?"

The gentle squeeze he applied on her shoulder was coaxing. "You know your worth, Ind. You don't bow for anyone, so if fighting for him destroys you more than it gives you hope to, one day, be with him, please protect your heart. You deserve more than a man who makes you second-guess yourself. You deserve more than a man who makes you wait."

Fuck. He was right.

"I know what I want, though. And I'm going to do everything I can for it to be mine."

"I like your determination, but I thought your main focus was work?"

"It is. It will always be. But Tito, at the end of the day, I'm just a girl who lives under the same roof as her childhood crush."

But Indy was too full of life, full of love, to be someone's maybe—*his* maybe. She longed to be his certainty, the object of his daydreams, his future but also his anchor to the present moment—his everything. Clinging to the hope would destroy her, but it was no secret that she was a fool for Miles Huxley. And if there was one thing aside from racing he was excellent at, it was shattering her heart.

CHAPTER EIGHTEEN

MONTE CARLO, MONACO

O<small>N</small> S<small>ATURDAY MORNING</small>, Miles was waiting for Indy in the living room, holding a to-go cup filled with iced matcha latte. He'd tried to perfect it this morning, and if he could make her one every single morning, he would.

A few weeks ago Indy had dared him to show how much he wanted her, and this was him getting into action, though he wasn't certain if he was doing things the right way.

He wanted to be someone worthy of Indigo Bailey.

She was the only person he could be his true self with, and he'd do whatever she asked of him. He would fall to his knees. Would crawl if he needed to. He couldn't let go of Indy—not after what she'd seen, not after showing him that she didn't care about his demons.

She stepped out of her room, her attention zeroed in on her phone before coming to a halt, their stares locking, the world ceasing to exist. Even dressed in simple jeans and a cardigan, she managed to look breathtaking. In her vicinity, his heartbeat sped up, almost going into a frenzy—a terrifying sensation only she could provoke.

"Do you look at everyone like that?" She raised a brow. "Careful, because I'm not sure where to draw the line."

A smirk danced across his lips. She was a shameless flirt, and her boldness was quite enticing. "I just look at *you* like that."

"Good to know," she breathed out, tilting her head to look at him from head to toe. Sunglasses were folded at the neckline of his t-shirt, a jumper draped over his shoulders, a cap atop his hair, and a tote bag hanging from an arm. "Going somewhere?"

"To the farmers market with you."

The raw joy those simple words had created made Miles believe, firmly so, that he could make Indy happy if he let himself fall. If he let himself believe that he was good enough for her—a woman so incredibly passionate, with a beautiful soul, who constantly fought her way through the labyrinth leading to his heart.

"Are you asking me out on a date?"

"I know I can't articulate well when I speak fast, but I'm pretty sure I didn't say that."

Indy laughed heartily, shaking her head. "Can't wait for you to grow some balls and ask me out."

His control was hanging by a thin, loose thread, and he was trying his best not to snap it. "Keep dreaming."

"Chivalry is clearly dead," she muttered.

Taking a step towards her, he handed her the drink. "Is it?"

Their fingers brushed when she took hold of the cup, a wave of chills racing down his spine. "That's sweet of you. Thanks."

He flicked her cheek, amused by the scepticism gleaming in her perusal. "Why do you look so doubtful?"

After humming whilst sipping her beverage, she planted the back of her hand on his forehead, causing him to bat it away.

"What are you doing?"

"What are *you* doing? Are you sick? Do you need something from me?"

He huffed then walked towards the door. "I want to spend some time with you and suddenly I have a fever? God forbid I'm nice to you."

Her soft laughter floated across the penthouse, across his mind, slowly imprinting itself like an unforgettable melody. She rushed towards him, planting an equally soft kiss on his cheek.

"Sorry," Indy said, the blush on the apple of her cheeks as burning as the one creeping up the back of his neck. She brushed past him, but he didn't miss the way she glowered and rolled her eyes, like she was inwardly scolding herself. "You're just so cute."

"I'm not cute," he grumbled.

"What are you then?"

Letting his hand trail across her stomach, he reached around her to call the lift. "I don't know. Sexy? Handsome? Talented and extremely funny?"

"Yeah, right. I'm not stroking your humongous ego."

"Please?"

She turned around, a gleam of mischief around her pupils. "That sounded nice. Do that again, but this time, get on your knees."

"You'd like that, wouldn't you?"

"Yes."

Miles barked out a laugh and pinched her side. "You're insufferable. Rosie, let's go!"

When the dog trotted towards them, her leash in her mouth, Miles groaned. "Indy. You did not put a pink bow on her collar."

She pressed a kiss to Rosie's head before attaching the leash. "I did. She looks adorable, doesn't she?"

Rosie was his baby, and seeing Indy give her unrestrained love did unexplainable things to him. He almost rubbed the spot on his chest where warmth had expanded. He needed to have a talk with Rosie and tell her that this was temporary, that she couldn't get too attached to Indy. Because Indy was bound to leave, right? Just like every good thing that came his way tended to go away.

"She's a goddamn Doberman, Daisy. She's supposed to be ferocious and intimidating. Not cute."

Indy gave him a dirty look before exiting the penthouse. "Should've named her Zelda or something then."

Fine, maybe the bow looked rather cute on Rosie.

He led Indy out of the penthouse, and when she walked towards the exit of the building, he tugged her by the wrist towards the garage. "I know you like to go to Menton, but I thought we could go to Cannes, and we can take one of my cars. The market over there is very pretty and lively, and I think you'd love their flower selection."

She beamed at him. "I'd love that."

In the car (they had settled for the BMW M4 to not attract too much attention—to be fair, it was the most simple car he owned amongst Ferraris, McLaren's, and Porsches), he put on the playlist he'd made for her. She immediately hummed to the lyrics, gaze settled on the moving landscape.

"How'd you sleep?" No matter the amount of times he had excused himself for waking her up, and no matter how many times she had told him it was no trouble, he still felt guilty for dragging her into his chaotic world.

Apparently, she didn't mind, and he didn't know what to do with that. Didn't know how to process the fact that she always welcomed him into her open arms—scars, darkness, secrets, and all.

"Good," she answered cheerily. "You?"

He drummed his fingers on the steering wheel. "Better."

He hadn't had any nightmares last night, but he'd awoken in cold sweats around three in the morning. He'd found himself stopping short in front of Indy's door, a sudden urge to crawl into her bed and seek comfort crashing over him.

Even now, Miles still couldn't fathom how easily she had been able to sooth his nerves, to coax his anguish. He had never felt at peace with anyone before. Had never been able to fall asleep after a nightmare—albeit for a few hours.

He could still remember how perfectly she fitted in his arms, how he'd wanted to cage her in for eternity. How he had held her so closely, but she was embracing him just as tightly. And the way she had looked at him—no judgement, no fear. Just like she saw him.

It was like she'd wanted to keep him safe. Wanted to put a safety net below him.

But telling her what caused his nightmares would mean peeling another layer off him. Not that he wasn't ready for that, but he simply wanted Indy to be ready to hear his full story. He wanted her to know everything about him because she was the first woman to ever make him feel like this—like he was safe.

"I'm glad," she said softly, looking over at him and making his heart drum a little faster, a little bit more hers.

"How much money do you want?"

Miles lowered his glass onto the table and frowned at Charlie who was sitting across from him. "What for?"

Charlie jerked his chin somewhere behind Miles' shoulder. "For giving your number or buying a drink to that girl who won't stop looking at you. But don't look now— Dude, I said not to look now."

Miles looked away from the woman, but his three friends were still glancing in her direction.

"Isn't she one of Indy's coworkers?" Thiago asked before taking the last bite of his taco.

"Tara," Miles informed, indifferent.

"Oh, yeah," Rowan said. "Heard she got a warning from Thunderbolt Sports about her behaviour in the paddock."

"She looks like a mean girl," Thiago remarked. "I don't like using the b-word, but she's definitely one."

"She's pretty, though." Charlie's brows pumped suggestively, and Miles gave him a disinterested look.

"*You* buy her a drink, then."

"Nah. She's looking at you, not me, or Rowan, or Tito."

Miles shrugged. "Not interested. She's not my type."

Rowan snickered behind his beer.

"What?"

"Nothing. Just wondering when you're going to settle down. Haven't seen you with a woman in ages."

"I'm not interested in anyone."

"Who's not Indigo Bailey," Charlie prompted with a grin.

Feeling the back of his neck heat up, Miles ruffled his hair and shook his head. "It's not like that. We're just friends."

"Keep lying to yourself, bro."

"He's blushing," Rowan whispered to the boys. "Miles, mate, you don't have to pretend you're immune to Indy's charms."

"Can we talk about *your* love lives?" he grumbled, leaning back in his seat. "Mine's as interesting as watching clouds drift in a blue sky."

"I'm single and as miserable as you," Charlie protested, lifting his hand to call a waiter.

Rowan grinned. "I'm in love and really happy. Avery is amazing. And yo, Miles, don't glare at me like that. That overprotective big brother shit isn't working."

"Kam is incredible." Thiago sighed wistfully, his eyes shining with utter adoration. "I can't believe I have the chance to be with her. Like, I mean, she's just so... Extraordinary."

"I'm really happy for you guys," Miles commented earnestly.

He had faith that he would feel like this one day, too. Maybe not in this lifetime, but maybe he'd allow himself to find love in the next one.

His attention was brought to his vibrating phone, and a smile tugged at his lips when Indy's name flashed on the screen.

SPEEDING INTO OVERDRIVE

DAISY

Heading to bed soon. Hope you're having a great time with the boys!

I am. How was your evening?

Pretty great. Taking a bath right now and reading smut. Couldn't ask for better.

Send pics.

Remember, you asked for it.

Attachment: 1 photo

Miles felt his jaw go slack as an image of Indy relaxing in the bathtub filled his screen. Bubbles floated around her body, but the swell of her breasts caught his attention, a soft smile on her lips as she held a wineglass in the air. He glanced around the table, but his friends were busy laughing amongst themselves, so he allowed himself to stare at the blonde beauty for a few seconds longer.

Fuck, you're gorgeous.

And you're trouble.

Sorry, not sorry.

Shaking his head, Miles pocketed his phone, the photo still ingrained in the back of his mind. Was there any harm to their friendship by exchanging those kinds of provocative—sensual—photos?

When the waiter came back to deposit another round of beers for Charlie, Thiago, and Rowan, he placed one in front of Miles along with a note. "From the lady over there."

Tara lifted her cocktail when his gaze clashed with hers.

A chorus of *oooooh's* danced around the table, and Miles sighed. He didn't even open the note, and left the beer untouched before pushing his chair back.

"I'll be back."

"Do you want a condom?" Charlie asked, grinning. "I'll even let you go to my place because it's the closest. I'll crash at yours and spend time with Indy. It's a win-win situation."

"No. Fuck you. I'm a gentleman, so I'm just going to thank her for the drink."

"And then tell her to fuck off?"

"You got that right."

Rowan cackled. "There he is."

He gave a kind smile to Tara when he stopped before her and her friend, who pretended to be interested in the barman's activities. "Thanks for the beer, Tara."

Surprise flashed in her eyes as she straightened herself, taking a sip from her drink. "You know who I am?"

He nodded, tucking his hands in the pockets of his jeans. Her wandering gaze made his skin prickle in an uncomfortable way. "You work with Indy."

He tried not to narrow his gaze when annoyance drew upon her face. "Yes."

"Well, thanks again." He cleared his throat. "Enjoy your night."

When he turned on his heel, a cold hand grabbed his wrist. "Would you like to spend the rest of the night with me? I'll buy you more beers. We can head to my place afterwards. Small bed, but it does the trick. Or maybe we can go to your place? I'm sure Indy won't mind hearing us."

Gently, he shrugged Tara's hand off, taking a step back and trying to control his temper that was on the verge of sparkling into an unwelcome inferno. That was when he realised that Indy's touch was his favourite—the one that calmed him. "Look, I'm flattered, but I'm not interested."

She frowned. "I thought you were single?"

"Yes, and?"

"Okay, so we can still—"

"It's a no. You must be naïve to think I'd sleep with you after the way you've been treating Indy. I have a great thing going on, alright? Have a *really* good feeling about it." He winked, then smiled at Tara's friend whose mouth was twisted in a pout. "Cheers, girls. See you around."

CHAPTER NINETEEN

♀ *SUZUKA, JAPAN*

His goal was to cross the paddock as quickly as possible, to ignore all photographers and fans begging for his attention, and lock himself in his room before starting his pre-race ritual. But of course, the fiery, wild, energetic blonde perched on high heels managed to distract him.

Damn it.

He decided he'd talk to her later, but there was this invisible force obliging him to go and find her. As if Indigo was the centre of gravity in his orbit, and he was innately drawn to her.

He changed his trajectory and jogged towards her.

Indy was pacing back and forth between two motorhomes, notes between her fingers. The closer he got to her, the more he could see the panic in her demeanour. To the entire world, it simply looked like she was revising her speech, but Miles knew better.

"Hey, Daisy. Need a hand?" He pulled his earphones out, aware that a horde of photographers was still surrounding him. "Can y'all give me two damn seconds?" Even though they all scattered around, the cameras were still pointed at him, causing irritation to flare through his bloodstream.

Mesmerising cerulean eyes locked to his gaze, weakening him in the knees. She huffed, lifting the sheet of paper. "Unless you can inject the new speech inside my brain in less than thirty minutes, then no."

"New?"

She studied his physique clad in his racing suit. "Yes, last minute changes happen quite often, but I just cannot read this font, and I can't memorise the last bit of it, and it's stressing me out. I'm sorry."

"Don't be sorry. Can you relax for me?" he demanded softly. "Take deep breaths?"

"I don't know." She sounded so panicked, so out of control, and he hated seeing her in this state.

He stepped closer, and her shoulders sagged. "Look at me," he murmured, fingers twitching like his body yearned to touch her delicate face. "Breathe, Indy."

She inhaled deeply through her nose, expelling through her mouth. He nodded, encouraging her to repeat the motion over and over again, until her panic-stricken face relaxed.

"Give me your notes."

Without asking questions, she handed him the paper. He snapped a photo and sent it to Ava, followed by a text of what she needed to do—quickly.

She frowned. "What did you do?"

"You'll see in a few minutes." Extending an earplug, he eliminated the distance between them by taking yet another step closer. Her fingers brushed against his, the lingering touch setting his flesh ablaze, before grabbing the earphone. "Listen to this."

She folded her arms beneath her breasts, the anxiety coiling through her bones still evident by the way she was shielding herself. At the first note of piano filling their ears, she looked at him in relief, then closed her eyes for a beat. The cord was the only thing binding them together—enveloping them in an invisible bubble where the outside world was nonexistent.

"I understand why classical music helps you relax."

"It's the best," he confirmed.

"Will you share this playlist with me? It might come in handy when I get anxious."

A smile touched his lips. "I'll make you one. Anything you need." What she didn't know, though, was that he had already created a couple of playlists for her. "I usually switch between piano and songs that hype me up, but sometimes an audiobook is what I need when my nerves aren't all over the place."

She tilted her head. "About mental health, right?"

"What if I told you I started the one you're currently listening to?"

Her lips parted, and he snickered at the shock painted over her face. "You mean—not the—"

He leaned closer. "Indy, you naughty, filthy woman. I got to the cabin part, and I had to pause it to catch my breath several times."

"Huxley!" she hissed in a whisper before gently smacking his chest with the back of her hand. "I listen to smutty audiobooks."

"Yeah, I figured. Quite instructive, if you ask me."

She raised her brows. "Are you going to show me what you learned?"

All flicker of amusement vanished from his veins as he paused. "Are you challenging me?"

Fire blazed in her eyes. "I dare you."

The boldness this woman possessed was both unnerving and sexy. He couldn't help but glance at her mouth, pulled into a taunting smile.

Ava was his saving grace—she always was—as she came up to

them, smiling brightly. "Here." She gave Indy a folded sheet of paper.

"What is it?"

When it unfolded, Miles almost laughed at the flabbergasted gasp escaping her mouth. She glanced from the notes to him, to Ava, and back down.

"Huxley," she murmured.

"Indy," he deadpanned.

"Ava!"

"Indy," Ava mimicked. "It was all him." She then squeezed his forearm. "Warmup starts in five," she told him before heading towards Imperium's motorhome.

"You—" Indy's voice was already thick with emotion.

"Are extraordinarily amazing? Yes."

A wobbly smile touched her lips. "Asked Ava to type out my speech—"

"And told her to put it in a font and size that is easier for you to read? Absolutely. And I'll do it again."

He didn't know why he'd expected her to throw herself at him and hug him. Didn't know why he was thoroughly disappointed when her fingers tangled with his. He realised it was because too many prying eyes were settled on them, and he despised that they had no privacy.

Blue eyes were shining with gratitude. "You have no idea how much this means to me. Thank you for having my back."

He applied pressure around her fingers, his heartbeat speeding up at the sight of her devastating smile. "Always."

When she wished him good luck for the race, he told her to smash it on live TV before they parted ways.

Miles rolled his eyes when he passed by his father who was sitting across from Ava in front of the motorhome. "Not a word, Dad."

Henry's teasing smile was a thing of pure mischief as he lifted his hands in surrender. "Didn't say a thing."

It was official, Miles was doomed.

He was starting P11 because of the grid-penalty he had faced after changing his car's power unit yesterday morning. Obviously, he had made the fastest lap during qualifying and was supposed to start the race from pole. Starting further down the grid wasn't an actual problem, though—if anything, Miles liked the challenge.

Proving to the world he was the best wasn't always by winning race after race, but showing that he could claim the trophy by facing obstacles.

After repositioning himself on the starting grid following the formation lap, he watched the other cars line up behind him. He cast a quick glance to the front row where Charlie was starting P2, right behind Valencia. The goal for today was to secure a double podium for Imperium Racing, but if Charlie could manage to have his maiden win here, then Miles would do anything to defend his teammate.

Suzuka's circuit was an exhilarating one. It was a high-speed track filled with challenges, and undoubtedly one of Miles' favourites.

The sound of engines revving around him was his all-time favourite. As he gripped his steering wheel, he sank into his seat, letting the car's vibrations jolt through his body.

Stare zeroed in on the horizontal lights placed above the starting line, he waited for them to light up.

The first one flashed to red, and the engines started buzzing. The second one lit up. Until all five were red.

Four seconds later, they went out, and Miles pushed on the throttle.

Slotting in between two cars, he managed to overtake them, claiming P9 in a matter of seconds. Going at full speed down the straight line and braking late before taking the first turn on the inside, he overtook two other cars. The succession of *S* curves was his favourite part of the track, and as he raced through it, he was fairly certain that he could fall into fifth position by the end of the lap.

His fingers worked the forward gear clutches, his feet working in tandem to either push on the throttle or decelerate near a corner.

"Yellow flag," AJ announced during the second lap. Miles was P6, on the verge of overtaking the driver in front of him. "Safety car is coming."

Miles wanted to huff out in frustration, but he only decreased his pace, zig-zagging and keeping the warm temperatures on his tyres. "Already? What happened?"

"Collision between three cars at the end of the grid in turn one."

"Shit," he muttered. "Is everyone okay?"

"I think so."

Checking his rear-view mirror, he noticed that Rowan had been overtaken by Hugo Bauer, a rookie racing for McMillan Motorsports.

He frowned. "Did Bauer just overtake Emerson under the safety car?"

"Yep," AJ breathed out.

Miles winced. That meant Hugo would be getting a penalty because overtaking under the yellow flag and safety car was forbidden.

As Miles kept his distance from the car in front, he suddenly felt his stomach flip as a force went into him. The next moment, he felt the rear of his car lifting before being entirely pushed out of the track.

"What the fuck!"

"You okay?" AJ asked.

"He just went into me!"

"I saw that, mate. But are you okay?"

He groaned. "Yeah."

"Good. I need you to get out of the car. There's damage."

Stopping in the gravel, he turned off his engine before

unplugging the steering wheel. After pulling himself out of the cockpit, he unbuckled his helmet and rounded the car to observe the damage, blood pounding in his ear.

Miles could feel his heart racing furiously, his gloved hands curling into fists as he pivoted. Bauer was still sitting in his car, its front wing totally wrung out.

"Fucking idiot," Miles said under his breath.

For good measure, and because he needed to evacuate the fury seeping through his veins, he kicked one of his car's tyres before rushing towards the closest exit.

⁂

THE LUMP RISING in his throat was becoming uncomfortable, but so were the poisonous vines growing inside the pit of his stomach, tangling into a ball of anger he couldn't get rid of no matter how hard he tried.

He took a sip of water, stopping at where Indy was in the media pen, watching him with so much tenderness that his frustration almost vanished. *Almost.*

"Hey, Huxley," she said, glancing at Ava who was now standing by his side, portable recorder in hand.

He gripped the railing between them, offering Indy a curt nod, his jaw tightening.

"So, I just got done interviewing Hugo," she announced coyly.

"I hope he's doing great," he coldly spit out.

"Well, he said the incident was caused by you because you braked."

His scoff was rightfully outraged as he took a step back, his tongue poking at the interior of his cheek. He shielded his mouth with a fist, drifting his gaze towards Ava who shook her head in warning.

He aimed a finger at his chest. "He said it was *my* fault?"

Indy nodded.

Unbelievable.

Because of Bauer's reckless mistake, Miles had been forced to DNF the race. On a positive note, Charlie had finished P3, and had scored points for the team. Miles was still leading the championship, though, but if he lost his title because of someone else's bullshit, he would lose it.

Miles knew better than to act on his anger, but he was trembling with utter vexation. He scoffed again, shaking his head in disbelief and running his hand across his mouth. "Okay, I just listened to his radio, and he had the fu—audacity to say I was in his way. The guy literally overtook Emerson under the safety car then went into me, and *I* was in his way? I had just started to calm down, but now knowing that he still blames *me* for his own stupidity is just... I won't say it, but this is truly pissing me off."

"Have you—"

"Do you think I'm the one to blame?"

"I can't answer this, Huxley, but—"

"You know what? I'm just fucking tired and this is bullshit. Hugo Bauer is a spoiled brat who got into F1 because he's got money. He's not man enough to take responsibility for his actions, so can you do me a favour? Tell him this sport is for tough kids. Get your shit together, people."

He simply walked away, irritation boiling through his veins.

"Sorry," he heard Ava whisper to Indy before rushing after him. "Miles, you're in trouble. You said some things—"

"I really don't give a shit right now, Ava. I just need to be alone and punch something."

CHAPTER TWENTY

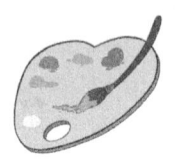

📍 *SUZUKA, JAPAN*

It was past ten at night when Indy's phone lit up with a text from Miles.

GOLDEN BOY
You up?

Is this is a booty call?

Come to my room. 609

Take me out on a date first.

He replied with an emoji rolling its eyes, which made her chuckle. Pulling a jumper over her top, she walked out of her room towards the lifts.

Miles opened his door the moment she stopped knocking, like he'd been waiting for her arrival.

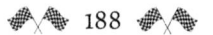

She felt her heart jump against her ribcage. He looked annoyingly good with his dishevelled hair, the stubble on his jaw, and his casual attire. Had he called her upstairs to hook up? God, she hoped not. She didn't look attractive at all right now, but maybe he was still turned on by the photo she had sent earlier—a risqué shot displaying the top of her frilly negligee, to which he'd responded with a simple "*Fuck, you're sexy.*"

"Sorry for texting you so late."

"It's okay," she assured sweetly. "You call, I come running. Remember?"

He paused, frowning. "I'm—I've never had someone put me first."

"Well, might as well get used to it, stud."

He'd been texting her since the end of the Grand Prix. At first, it had been to ask how her day went, then to apologise for his behaviour in the media pen, then started the music recommendations as well as exchanges of cat memes.

Indy had understood his reaction earlier. Deep down, she'd felt furious for him, too, but she'd managed to keep those feelings to herself. Now that she had stepped out of her journalist's shoes for the day, she could express her sentiments.

"Are *you* okay?" She stepped closer, cataloguing his features stricken with something that made her chest ache. He was upset —she hated seeing him like this.

"I'm grand." When he took a seat on the edge of the bed, he passed his fingers through his hair frustratingly.

Though she was craving to touch him, she folded her arms across her chest. "You're not hurt, are you?"

"Careful," he droned, elbows atop his thighs. "I might start thinking you care about me."

Indy held his gaze. "What are you going to do if I admit that I, in fact, care about you, Huxley? You're going to walk away? Act like it doesn't mean anything?"

"You shouldn't care about me."

"Well, that's too bad. Because I do and I always have, so just accept it."

He was silent—and she could almost hear the thoughts ricocheting against his mind. Scrubbing a hand over his jaw, he scoffed a cold laugh before standing up. "I feel like a dick, Indy. I shouldn't have talked to you that way in the media pen. I shouldn't have walked away like that in the middle of the interview, but I was pissed off. Now I'm fine, but I'm so sorry for disrespecting you."

A sigh fled past her lips, her shoulders falling. "You were totally entitled to react this way, and it's okay. I'm not angry at you."

"But I'm angry at myself. I've been working so fucking hard to be the man you know outside of racing in front of cameras, too. I'm trying my best to prove that I'm not some heartless man, and they saw the way I was with you, and I messed it up today by—by—"

"Huxley," she coaxed softly, coming to grip his shoulders. The tension pulling taut at his body went away, relief morphing onto his expression, into tenderness when her hands glided to his neck. "It's okay."

"How can you be so calm after seeing all the bullshit the media has said?"

She let her brows pinch together. "I'm not following."

"They say you're too sweet for me. That I'm an asshole who doesn't deserve your attention. Who doesn't respect your time or work in the paddock. They say I'll never change. Never be worthy of you, of anything good in the world if I keep being a dick."

Indy could feel a squeeze around her heart, hurting and destroying everything in its path. She blinked the burning feeling in her eyes away because to her, Miles was everything that was good and beautiful in this messy, imperfect world.

Keeping her gaze on his heaving chest for a moment, she started applying featherlight circles on the side of his neck. Although his body shuddered lightly, she could feel it inside her bones. "Fuck those people who criticise everything you do, everything you say. Fuck them, really. I know you, and I *see* you, both my friend and the F1 driver. I'm never going to be mad at you for expressing the way you feel after a race, and I'm certainly not going to let you treat me like I'm made of glass when we're inside or outside of the paddock."

He blinked. "What?"

"I can handle it, you know." She kept her head high, refusing to crumble to pieces. "The anger. The frustration. The silence that says more than words. I can handle it all. It's my job, and I need you to stop treating me like I can't handle your rage when we're on live TV, because I can."

A deep crease appeared between his knitted brows. "Where is this coming from? I know you can. You're the strongest person I know."

She dropped her hands from his skin. "So stop acting like I'm fragile."

The confusion brimming his irises was crystal clear. "I'm not."

He took a step forward, and Indy inhaled tremulously. She was sick and tired of the comments accusing her of being treated differently because she was Zachary Bailey's daughter. Sick and tired of thinking she wasn't tough enough to be a presenter.

The rage blended to his deep voice made her skin pebble. "Who the fuck hurt you?"

"I'm sick and tired of all those people treating me like I'm not good enough for this job. Of those saying that I don't belong here because the Princess of the Paddock is nothing more than Zach's spoiled daughter. I'm tired of the people saying I'm only working in F1 to date you."

Because she wasn't! This job had been her dream way before Miles came into her life.

It was when she furiously batted a tear away that she realised she'd started crying in the midst of her monologue.

She had felt that upsetting sensation flooding her senses all evening long—that feeling of knowing she would be crying soon enough, but refused to break down until she was alone. Of course, it had to be now that the dam went bursting, all her emotions taking over.

"I'm sorry," she whispered, looking away. She wiped at her cheeks again. "This wasn't supposed to be about me."

Gently, Miles lifted her chin with the help of his finger. "Can you look at me?"

When she found his gaze, she felt that familiar devastation crash over her. He was looking at her with so much adoration, tenderness, comprehension, yet she couldn't fall into him.

He cupped her face between both hands, forcing her to maintain his hypnotising stare. When his thumb collected a tear beneath her eye, she shivered and leaned into his touch.

"Never apologise for expressing your feelings when you're with me. You know I won't judge you, right? You know I won't undermine you. You're safe here."

She nodded, throat too tight and eyes too watery.

"What's got you so upset?"

She was tired. Lonely. Stressed out. But she said, "I'm afraid of disappointing everyone. I feel pressured. I work so hard, but it's always the little mistakes that people remember instead of my accomplishments and milestones. I'm terrified of failure. Of failing the fans, my parents, my brother, my friends."

It had never felt so good to finally set her thoughts free. Being the positive and uplifting friend had always made her believe that she wasn't allowed to feel down. To be negative.

"Indy," he murmured, "everyone is so proud of you. You're inspiring, empowering, and courageous. Girls look up to you. Boys do, too. Hell, even us drivers do."

"But my parents—"

"Are the best kind of people. Lisa and Zach are amazing, and you're so lucky to be their daughter. I know they weren't often at home when you and Kai were growing up, and I know they've always been hard on you, but that's because they want to see you succeed. But I know that the moment you make a silly mistake,

Lisa and Zach will fly across the world to cheer you up, just because you're simply a human being. You were raised by extraordinary people. You're surrounded by people who love you so fucking much, Indy."

She blinked rapidly. "You're making me cry."

His thumb ran below her eye. "I hate seeing you like this."

See this man? This was the man she wanted to keep to herself. He would go through fires to keep her safe and unscathed, to pull her out of that abyss of worry.

"Come here." He pulled her towards the bed, and they sat close to each other as he took hold of her hand, lacing their fingers together. Indy laid her head on his shoulder, and she sighed when his cheek touched the top of her head. "We live in a world where failure isn't an option. If we fail, if we make a mistake, we get laughed at and we disappoint many people. But I'm going to tell you something: I think failing is the best lesson life can teach us. You can learn from your mistakes, rise above them, and become the version no one expected you to be."

"Is that why you became like this after your first title?"

She felt him shrug. "I guess so. I wanted to put a mask on to let the public see what they were working with. Who they were watching. I've been doubted for many, many years, read countless articles enumerating reasons why I wasn't champion-worthy. I think part of me didn't want the world to see how vulnerable I could be. It's like I built a barrier between racing and my private life, you know? But sometimes I wish they could stop criticising me."

Keeping her gaze on their interlocked fingers, she observed the way his thumb caressed her skin. "I think I understand that shift. Sometimes I just want to become a bitch, become a woman people fear. I want to show my teeth, make them fear me. But it's not me, it's not in my nature."

"Don't change. For anyone. You know why you're such a great presenter? You're authentic, real. You're simply *you*, and it's so fucking beautiful and refreshing."

The lump in her throat grew again. "Thank you." Despite it all, she was having a hard time seeing the positive outcome of her work. It was exhausting because she was an overachiever, and all she craved was validation and good results.

For a moment, there was silence—peace, comfort. She squeezed his hand, and he squeezed it back—although firmly, causing her to chuckle lightly when she did it again, trying to apply more force.

"Look at me," he murmured with such delicacy that she felt the softness caress her bones. With his finger beneath her chin, he brought her gaze to him. The sight of her tear-stained cheeks and glossy eyes made him sigh, like the sight of her detriment shattered him. "Do not let your fears break you. Do not let anyone or anything break you. They don't deserve your tears. Keep your chin high. Give them your beautiful smile."

And she gave it to him, a smile broad and unrestrained. A soft exhale fled past his lips as he watched her adoringly, the pad of his thumb skimming her under-eye then her dimple.

"You're going to be so successful, Indigo. More successful than me, and I cannot wait to see you thrive and cheer you on. I just cannot wait to watch you accomplish big goals, change the world, and be the person who inspires our generation to take the leap and live their dream."

"Huxley..."

"I mean it," he whispered, leaning forward to let his forehead rest against hers. The ache in her chest stretched out, hurting, breaking her to pieces. She closed her eyes to hold a semblance of control over her emotions. "I'm going to wear merch that says *'Indy Bailey's #1 Babe'* and proudly wear it every time I walk through the paddock. Going to make everyone wear it. Even Kai when he snowboards. Even Romeo and Ez before they hit the ice."

She chuckled as streams of tears rolled down her cheeks. She didn't even know why she was still crying. Perhaps she needed to let go—all of it. The past few months were tough, and she hadn't realised how much energy she'd been pouring into her work until today. "Is that my fandom name?"

"From now on it is. We're your babes."

She covered her mouth when a giggle erupted, and Miles pulled away to bring her hand down. "Don't hide from me."

He meant her laugh, but maybe also her vulnerability. She wanted to give him everything.

"My real laugh is obnoxious."

He smiled so beautifully that she blushed. "I find it endearing. It's cute. And funny. Like, it makes me want to laugh, too. When you laugh, your entire face lights up. You have those little crinkles on the outsides of your eyes, that little dimple on your chin appearing."

"You—you noticed all that?"

He was silent for a beat. "How could I not?" he breathed out.

No one had ever noticed the tiniest details about her.

She was used to men looking at her, to grab someone's attention by simply walking into a room, but with Miles... He'd always looked at her differently—like he *saw* her.

When Miles cradled her jaw, his thumb ghosting over the spot where a dimple would pop if she laughed too hard, she felt the tremble in his fingers. Their gazes locked, and she heard the way he swallowed. His pupils expanded, his fingers moving until they cupped the back of her head, tangling into her hair.

The distance between them was minuscule as the tip of his nose grazed hers. Her breath caught, then she was fisting his shirt. She shivered when his palm landed on her waist, delicate and burning.

"Indy," he whispered. And she heard it through his gruff tone—the yearning, the longing, the craving. The way his voice was strained, like it physically pained him to be so close yet so far away. She wanted him to break his rules, to finally give in.

Their breaths entwined, and their lips were so, so close to locking. His chest rose and fell, his skin blazing when her free hand travelled up his arm. Indy shut her eyes, revelling in the moment, memorising the feel of his hands in her hair, his thumb dusting over her pulse, her name sounding like a prayer on his lips.

The taut, invisible cord between them was on the cusp of breaking, and yet...

"I should go," she said, backing away just enough to watch his reaction: utter wreckage before it shifted into understanding. She refused to be the one to cross the line first, no matter how much she wanted this.

She was waiting for it—for him to say *"don't go"*, but it never came.

Though he said, "Yeah. It's getting late," he didn't disentangle his hand from her locks, a staggered breath brushing past his parted mouth.

She didn't want any more pity fucks. Didn't want to sleep with him to release the anxiety, and stress, and chagrin. If she were to give herself to him, she needed to know that he was willing to accept all of her. No games, no chasing. She didn't want either of them to walk away after finding release. Didn't want to go back to the way it was before—casual.

She still couldn't fathom why he made her want him so bad but gave her nothing back. Pulling away was such a torturous sensation that made her chest twist and ache—a sensation she had learned to live with.

Miles ran a hand over his flushed face—in frustration she supposed—and walked her to the door.

He cleared his throat. "You okay?"

No, she was not. She'd probably cry again in her room by replaying his words, his verbal applause. Then she'd cry by remembering she had pushed him away. And she'd cry again just because she felt like sobbing.

"Yes. Thank you."

He studied her expression for a beat. Like he could see past her tough layers and knew she was lying. Like he understood her need of being alone to break. "Of course. I'll text you."

She was already out of his room when she peered over her shoulder and said, "I don't expect anything less coming from you, Golden Boy. Good night."

His whisper caressed the shell of her ear. "Night, Daisy."

And as Indy stood in the lift, observing her rosy cheeks, glinting eyes, and small smile, she wondered what would have happened if she had just leaned forward to finally kiss the man she'd loved her entire life.

CHAPTER TWENTY-ONE

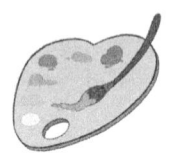

📍 *MONTE CARLO, MONACO*

When Indy emerged from the gym, Miles was stretched out on the sofa, scrolling through his phone, absently scratching Rosie's head as the dog laid beside him.

She could feel his gaze follow her movements as she marched towards the kitchen, and she smiled in triumph at the thought of it—knowing she'd been able to distract him by simply existing.

As she poured herself a glass of water, she peered over her shoulder to watch Miles sit up. She leaned against the counter and sipped her drink in silence, feeling her pulse settle into a steady rhythm.

She could get used to this routine on days off, but sometimes she forgot about the original ordeal. Forgot this was only a temporary solution and that she needed to go back to looking for a small flat she could afford. Her parents had offered numerous times to buy a place for her, but she kept refusing their kindness and generosity.

Miles' phone chimed, and he read the text message he'd received, scoffing.

"I wonder what kind of messages the talented Miles Huxley receives on a daily basis," she prompted. "How many girls try to slide into your DMs to hook up?"

"A lot," he muttered in a huff. "As much as haters messaging me to say they're bothered by the fact I win most races."

"Oh, I—"

He rapidly glanced at her. "It's fine. These messages make me laugh."

She truly admired Miles' resilience. Receiving hate freely wasn't fun, and it certainly wasn't easy to be under the spotlight and be critiqued so openly.

"But Tara just texted me," he announced, setting his phone down as he leaned back, hands locking behind his head. Slowly, a smirk spread across his lips. Like this, he was the perfect portrait of arrogance, and she committed the sight to memory to draw him later.

"Tara?" Indy repeated slowly, setting her glass down. "Like, Tara, my coworker?"

"Yes."

"Why is she texting you?" Indy tried not to let jealousy and irritation weave into her voice as she asked the question with faux sweetness.

"You'd be surprised by the amount of times this girl tries to grab my attention. I mostly ignore her texts, but the one she's just sent me is very, very interesting."

She gripped the counter behind a bit too tightly. "Humour me."

Miles' expression was blank. He didn't let on whether he was amused or bothered by this situation, but Indy was definitely fuming inside. She knew Tara wanted to rile her up. For what reason? Indy didn't know.

"She asked me if I have a date to the gala we're attending this weekend," he informed, standing up. He was tall and handsome, and the power he innately exuded made her heart race.

Indy held his gaze as he stepped towards her. "Well, what are you going to tell her?"

He blinked, then lifted his shoulders in a shrug. "Firstly, she's rude to you and thinks she's better than you. She constantly talks to me even when I told her I wasn't interested."

"Wait, what?"

"The other night when I was out with the guys, she was there and wanted to hook up. I told her no."

Indy felt the frustration flare through her veins, making her blood boil. Regardless, she refused to show how upset she truly was. "You know, I'm sure she'd be a sweetheart with you. Plus, she has great hair. Beautiful, long, brown hair. I've always wanted to be a brunette, like Mum. Do you think I could pull it off? Also, she's curvier, and really pretty. She's shorter than me, but still has got a good height, so that when you kiss her you won't hurt your neck, and—"

"She's not you, Indy."

"Oh, and she—" The entire world paused as she whispered, "What?"

Miles now stood in front of her, but the distance felt immense. The way he looked at her, glanced at her mouth, stepped into her personal space without so much as darting his gaze away... She felt like combusting under the intensity of it all. "She isn't you."

"But—"

The moment he caged her in by placing his hands on the counter, his thumb coming to brush over her knuckles, she felt her breath catch. "Do you have a date for the gala?"

"Do *you*?"

His jaw tightened. "I hate these kinds of events. I was planning on going on my own since it's mandatory for me to attend, but I'm surprised no one's asked you to accompany them."

"There's one person who hasn't asked," she retorted, holding his gaze.

Obviously, she had gotten quite a few invitations to the gala. Charlie was even willing to take her, but she had declined the sweet offer just because, deep down, she'd been wishing that Miles would grow some balls and ask her out. Sure, a work event couldn't be considered a date per se, but Indy would take every single scrap of affection she could get from him. Even if it was for a couple of hours where cameras would be pointed at them.

Was her desperation pathetic? One hundred percent.

Amusement shone in his eyes as a shadow of a smirk ghosted over his lips. "I see. Well, Daisy, you're my date to the gala."

She raised her brows. "I am? Can I at least think about it? I have tons of applications to go through."

His chuckle was music to her ears. "Sure. I already know your answer, anyway."

With a huff, she rolled her eyes in mock annoyance. "So sure of yourself."

"Don't look so surprised." His whisper caressed her lips, softly, teasingly. "If I'm going to the gala, it's you that I'm taking. No one else."

"Fine." Indy tipped her chin up, her nose grazing his. "I'm only accepting because I don't have a date yet and time's running short."

"Great." He smiled, then pecked her cheek, his lips coming to hover above the shell of her ear. "Besides, I have a type. I've always been into blondes. Tall women. Snarky. Ferocious. My best mate's sister. You, specifically."

After rummaging through her closet, throwing clothes on the bed, and calling her mother to see if she could borrow a dress, Indy found Miles leaning against the door of her bedroom, amused by the mess she had made.

Because the timing was too short for Lisa to ship a dress to Monaco and have it arrive on time for the gala, Miles suggested taking Indy shopping.

She expected him to drop her off in front of the shop whilst he would go purchase a new watch or something, but not for him to walk in with her, pick dresses, and wait as she tried them on.

Indy was currently watching her reflection, doubt pinching at her expression.

She planted her hands on her hips and tore the curtains open. Miles was sitting in a loveseat, scrolling through his phone. He looked up at Indy, blinking, then roaming his stare up and down her body.

"Nope."

"Agreed. I look dumb."

He frowned. "You don't. This dress just isn't made for you."

Huffing, she went back into the dressing room. There was one dress left on the hanger—the one Miles had chosen. She hadn't intended on wearing black at the gala, just because she'd wanted something different, but this dress looked like onyx dotted with tiny silver gemstones.

"Huxley?" she called out.

"Yeah?"

"You can go, you know." Carefully, she undressed herself, placing the navy blue dress on its hanger. "I don't want to be a burden. I could meet you later to grab some food if you'd like. I don't want to bore you to death. I mean, this could take ages. I look awful in everything!"

He chuckled dryly. "You could never bore me. I'd sit here all day and watch you try on every dress this store has."

She was thankful for the curtains shielding herself from him because the blush blooming across her chest was almost embarrassing.

"You're enjoying yourself, aren't you?"

His smile was evident through his tone. "You have no idea."

The dress clinging to her body was utterly beautiful. Strapless, the corset hugged her torso and breasts, putting their swell in perfect evidence. The black fabric was cinched at the waist before floating down her legs, a long slit perceptible along her left thigh.

Indy hummed, impressed, pushing her breasts up. She peered at her reflection from over her shoulder, enjoying the way most of her back was exposed.

Now, she needed to tug the zipper upwards.

And of course, it got stuck.

She laughed, shaking her head. "Of fucking course."

She took a deep breath in after trying again, only to fail miserably.

"Huxley?" She kept her voice steady and calm despite the furious beating of her heart.

"What's up?"

"Can you come here for a sec?" She couldn't help but laugh nervously again when he opened the curtain and took a step back. "Zipper's stuck."

Miles fell against the wall, like he'd lost his balance, his hand coming to rub the back of his neck. His brows lifted in pleasant surprise as he took his time to scrutinise her. Slowly. Taking in every detail. "Indy," he breathed out. "You look stunning."

"I'm not even wearing any makeup. Don't have my heels on."

"Still." He stepped inside the small room, tugging the curtains to shield them from the world. "You could wear PJs for all I care, and I'd still think you're breathtaking."

She blushed, turning around to hide it from him.

He stepped closer, closer, closer, until the heat emanating from his body radiated upon her bare back.

"What do you say when I compliment you?" He brushed her hair away from her back to splay it on her shoulder.

She met his gaze through the mirror. "Thank you."

Receiving compliments wasn't something she was unaccustomed to. On the contrary, she got them daily. She loved them. They helped her build her confidence. But being praised and applauded by Miles was different. It always had been.

He smiled softly, then his knuckles grazed her spine, and her breath got stuck somewhere in her body. "How cliché is this?"

With one hand, she held the bodice to her chest as she gathered her hair with the other one, exposing the length of her neck to him. If he noticed her skin pebbling, he didn't show it. "Trust me, I would have avoided this situation."

"Really?" he droned amusedly. A frown settled on his brows when he tried to tug the zipper up as gently as he could. "Damn it." He stepped even closer, and Indy could feel his breath fan across the back of her neck. "This is really stuck."

"No shit, Sherlock." She felt her breath catch for numerous reasons: his hands on her, their sheer proximity, and the awe blended with utter concentration etched on his features. "I mean, as much as I love your hands on me and seeing you so flustered, I still think this is embarrassing."

"Happens to everyone," he gruffly assured.

"How many of your dates have you had to rescue when they couldn't zip their dress?"

"None," he said. "Just you. It's always just you, Daisy."

He flicked his eyes to her, a charming smile spreading across his lips. Then, as he raked his stare over her with such intensity, she saw a flash of vehemence heat up his gaze.

"Got it," he murmured.

Indy was certain goosebumps had appeared in the wake of his touch as his knuckles caressed her skin. His delicacy felt akin to a serenade, poetry, but the blatant desire glinting around his pupils set her skin ablaze.

Miles leaned forward, planting one brief, powerful kiss on the back of her neck. The contact of his lips upon her flesh made her tremble, and she closed her eyes for a moment, losing herself in the desire burning her veins.

"Huxley..." she breathed out, unable to do anything except feel the way his breath warmed her skin.

Instead of backing away, instead of putting some distance between them, he took hold of her hips, pressing her back into his chest, his lips skimming over the side of her neck until they reached the shell of her ear.

Indy had stopped breathing, had stopped existing. She leaned into him, powerless. His big hands ran up her ribs, halting below her breasts, and that was when she felt the sheer size of him press against the small of her back.

Oh, God.

"This dress..." His voice was gruff, husky, and Indy was ready to succumb. All she had to do was spin around to crash her lips to his. "You..." He kissed her neck again, and she shivered. He smirked against her skin, like he'd noticed the noxious power he had over her. "You drive me mad."

"Do something about it." She was surprised by the steadiness of her command.

"Indy," he warned slowly.

She grabbed his left hand, trailing it down her waist, her hip, her upper thigh, until it reached the opening of the slit. His fingers were hot, and the featherlight caress on her skin felt as though he'd already stripped her naked. As though the flutter of his digits were embedding one single word he wanted to whisper: *mine.*

Tangling her fingers in the hair at his nape, she compelled him to lock his gaze with hers in the reflection. His eyes were almost black with intense desire, his fingers travelling up and down her exposed flesh as his perusal halted on her breasts. A groan vibrated when his palm disappeared beneath the dress, inching towards the inside of her thigh.

"If I dare you to take it off of me after the gala," she started, "will you do it?"

The smirk pulling at his mouth was all mischief and defiance. "You already know I don't back out from a challenge, love."

"And if I dare you to slip your hand between my thighs now, will you do it?"

A low grunt rumbled in his chest as his jaw tightened. His nostrils flared slightly, his lips parting as his stare stayed on her heaving chest.

"Ask me," he whispered.

Indy smiled—a triumphant queen. Pulling at his hair, she turned her face to let her lips find his ear. He was on the brink of panting, she presumed, by the rapid movement of his torso. Was on the cusp of finally touching her, and that made the arousal pooling inside her belly expand to the point of becoming torturous. "Huxley, I dare you to—"

A knock resonated on the wall, startling the both of them. "Everything alright in there? Need a hand?"

"It's not a goddamn hand that I need," she huffed in a whisper. "It's just your cock."

"Fucking hell, Indy."

Miles dropped his forehead on her shoulder as Indy chuckled. She linked her fingers through his, bringing his arm around her waist. "Just fine," Indy called out. "I'll be out in a minute."

Miles made her spin around, his fingers tilting her chin upwards. The heat in his gaze, the slight tremor in his fingers, the anticipation in the way his chest heaved. Indy could get down on her knees for him, but she wouldn't do it without seeing him bow first.

"Next time, I'll make sure we're not interrupted," he promised huskily.

"Good," she murmured. "I'm holding you to that, Golden Boy."

CHAPTER TWENTY-TWO

MONTE CARLO, MONACO

THERE WAS A certain possessiveness in the way he held her, showed her to the world, and kept her close as though they belonged together. There was a risqué gleam in his gaze every time their eyes collided, a salacious note in its negligence when his hand touched the small of her back and lingered there. But there was this longing, envious, adoring caress every time they moved in sync to pose for the photographers.

Being in Miles' arms felt like being held by the universe—magnetised to the centre of gravity of her world. And she just wanted to bask in his comfort for an eternity.

Indy peered up at him, sighing softly. He was magnificent, standing under the blinding flashlights, dressed in an expensive suit, his hair pushed back and his jaw tight. Their gazes collided again, and she smiled. Instantly, tenderness drew upon his features.

"You're doing great," she encouraged as they moved to the last spot of the red carpet.

"I hate this," he grumbled under his breath.

"I know," she whispered. "I'm sorry."

His thumb brushed her hip. "Don't be. I'd do anything for you."

When she had emerged from her room earlier, she found Miles standing in the foyer, fixing his tie, watching her utterly speechless. He'd blinked repeatedly, stuttering as she approached. A blush had bloomed on his face, and Indy had laughed at his expression. When she kissed his cheek, she thought he'd faint.

In the backseat of the car, she'd noticed how nervous he looked. She was aware that he didn't enjoy these kinds of events, being under the spotlight like this, so she had grabbed his hand to interlace their fingers, and he had let her.

With his hand splayed across her back, they stopped in front of Carmen—who was conducting all interviews for the gala—and Indy smiled up at her boss. She offered a smile back, dipping her chin in some sort of approval after glancing at Miles, who had let his hands find shelter in the pockets of his dress pants.

"Don't you two look dashing together," Carmen commented, beaming.

"That's all her," Miles said, nudging her elbow. "She always steals the spotlight."

"I can't handle all those compliments," Indy teased.

"Right. Your ego is going to inflate like a hot-air balloon."

Carmen chuckled. "Give me a run-down. What are you wearing?"

"He's wearing Armani," Indy said, looking at him from head to toe. He kept stealing her breath away every time she'd look in his direction. "And a nice Tudor on his wrist."

"And she's wearing full Christian Dior."

"You look beautiful, Indy," Carmen praised.

Miles' next words seared through her veins. "She really does."

"And you look great, too, Miles. It's great seeing you attending the event. Items will be auctioned to help children in need get access to education, medicine, and care all around the world. Did you donate anything?"

"Yes, the helmet I wore when I got my maiden win. It has a special design, and I think it's one of the most beautiful helmets I used to own."

"This is amazing." Carmen turned to Indy. "All the drivers have donated an item, but did you, too?"

She nodded. "I'm not certain anyone will buy it, but I did donate a painting I made a few years back. It's called *Hope*, and it's one of my favourites."

"I love this. Well, enjoy your night, guys."

"We will," Miles said. "Thanks, Carmen."

He led Indy into the venue, still touching her lower back, like he needed to feel her skin to be grounded.

"So," he started as they searched for their table. "I heard Rowan, Thiago, and a couple of other guys make a bet on how long you would stay put before leaving the gala."

Indy huffed and threw him a glare. "Please, don't tell me you bet with them."

"I did," he confessed sheepishly. "But I was the only one to bet you'd get through the entire evening without leaving."

"Wow," she drawled. "I don't know if I should thank you or tell you to go fuck yourself."

Miles chuckled, the warmth of his hand leaving her body but still lingering. "Just behave." Gently, he took hold of her chin, and the tiny grip was what kept her knees from wobbling. All eyes were on them. All cameras turned towards them, yet he didn't seem to care in the slightest. "I have faith in you."

"Please," she scoffed. "I know I used to be young and reckless, but I'm a sports broadcaster now. I can't just get up and leave. Don't worry, baby, you'll win the bet."

He grinned. "That's my girl."

"I WANT TO LEAVE," Indy huffed behind the rim of her empty flute of champagne.

Laughter bubbled out of everyone sitting around her.

"I knew you'd say that ten minutes into the event," Kamari said, feigning exasperation when amusement shone in her eyes.

"You can pay up," Alex said from her side, facing his palm upwards and curling his fingers in a *give me* motion. "Huxley owes us a shit-ton of money."

Indy narrowed her gaze. "How much?"

"A hundred bucks each."

"Oh my God." Indy threw her hands in the air. "I can't believe you all bet that money because you don't think I can stay here and have fun."

"By all means, Indy," Rowan interjected, smirking smugly, "show us how much fun you're having right now."

She rolled her eyes, then pushed herself to stand up when a host walked up the small stage. "Oh, look, I can't. It's about to start."

Laughter reverberated again, and Indy longed to hear one particular chuckle that had the tendency of bringing her joy. She looked around the crowded place, finding Miles standing by the bar with Charlie. Miles was nursing a glass of water, calmly chatting with his teammate, but when his gaze collided with hers, time stopped.

The corner of his mouth ticced, his chest falling with a sigh as he stared at her from across the room, the softness in his expression almost making her weep.

"What?" she mouthed.

With a shake of his head, he smiled, and the cry in her heart was so desperately loud that she feared it could be heard through the entire venue. "Nothing," he mouthed back.

The next heartbeat, his eyes slid to Alex, who was sitting next to her and sipping on his champagne. Miles' features hardened, his eyes flaring with something she couldn't name. As a muscle in his jaw jumped, he looked away.

Was he jealous? Of *Alex*? Oh, this was good.

"I have a question for you," she announced to her friends. They all turned to her, uncaring that someone was speaking on stage. "Is there something wrong with me? My dress? My makeup?"

"I feel like this is a trick question," Rowan said, gaze narrowed.

"Nothing's wrong with you," Thiago shared. "Except for the fact that you can't stay put. Also, you're fearless sometimes, and it scares me to death."

"Thank you?"

"You two can be such bellends sometimes," Ava bit out with such gentleness that no one could ever strike her to be a bad person. "You look beautiful, Ind. Why do you even have to ask?"

"Everyone keeps staring at me like I've grown a second head or something."

They all exchanged glances, turmoil overpowering her senses.

Ava was the one to speak again, "Have you ever wondered why the world is so fascinated by whatever is going on between you and Miles?" Indy shook her head. "There's a reason why the tabloids speak a lot about him. This man is breaking all his rules for you. He doesn't like to attend events. He will donate, he will invest in a cause, but he won't step on the red carpet. He doesn't smile. He doesn't speak to anyone in the paddock except me, Enzo, Charlie, and his dad. Sometimes Tito and Rowan, but that's about it."

"So why doesn't he tell me that he wants me?" she whispered. She didn't want to attract any more attention. Her other friends had turned their focus towards the stage, anyway.

"He's scared," Ava said quietly. "He doesn't know how to let anyone in. He doesn't know what love is. But he's slowly accepting the fact that you mean something to him. I'm sure he's told you about his childhood, and you have to understand that he doesn't know what love looks like. He never saw his parents show affection towards each other."

Indy absently nodded. She understood his fears, his inability to trust, and all she could do was hold his hand through the storm and wait for it to settle down.

"He's been abandoned in the past," Ava continued. "All he needs is time. Reassurance. Stability and trust. He adores you—"

"He just doesn't know it," Rowan interjected. "But the realisation will hit soon enough."

She'd waited long enough for him, but for how long could she hang onto that thread of hope? For how long could she listen to her desperate heart calling out his name? Indy deserved to feel something real, something strong, something all-consuming—she was worthy of love the same way her friends were.

She sighed heavily. "Do you think it's bratty of me to try and make him jealous?"

Ava chuckled. At her side, Rowan was shaking his head, yet a glint of mischief made his hazel eyes twinkle. "Oh, absolutely not. I'm sick and tired of seeing you two run around each other. We all know you're into each other, so please, make him realise that he really wants you and put us all out of our misery."

A general echo of agreement fled around the table.

Indy peered over her shoulder to look at Miles. His helmet was being auctioned, and he was nodding every time someone placed a bid. Why had he decided to sit at another table, though? The seat to her right was unoccupied, reserved for him.

"I have a suggestion," Rowan said. "Try and break him. Tease him some more."

"That's what I've been trying to do, but he seems unbreakable."

"Trust me, from the look of it, my guy is about to snap."

A little fun wouldn't ruin the strong friendship they had built, right?

Indy leaned towards Alex. "Alex, I need you to act like you're into me when we go out later."

Her friend turned to her, his lips pursed before he barked out a laugh. "What? Hell no. Look, I like you. You're stunning and really cool. But I just don't want to fall in love with you."

She reared back. "I'm offended."

"You're just the type of girl who makes everyone around you fall in love so easily. I don't want to be heartbroken."

"Is that a compliment? Alex, I'm not asking you to fall in love, get married, and have babies. I just need you to be all over me for a hot minute. I'll buy you a burger."

His beautiful, blue eyes raked across her face, trailing down to her body. He gave in with a sigh, but the amusement glinting in his gaze didn't go unnoticed. "The stupid things I do for you, Ind... You owe me a week's worth of food. Who are we making jealous?"

CHAPTER TWENTY-THREE

📍 *MONTE CARLO, MONACO*

When, exactly, had Indigo Bailey become an addiction?

It was never supposed to happen. Or perhaps it had always been bound to happen, and he needed to stop fighting the temptation.

As Miles stood in the archway leading to Thiago's rooftop, his hands in the pockets of his pants and his head leaned against the doorframe, he watched Indy be the life of the party. She danced to the beat of the music, grabbing Ava's hand to make her spin around.

Miles glanced at Rowan, who was sitting on a lounge chair, elbows atop his thighs as he smiled at Ava. Miles was genuinely happy for his publicist; she deserved that kind of fierce, unwavering love.

He remembered when they were merely eight years old that they'd agreed to marry each other if they were still single by the time they were thirty. He winced at the memory. Ava had always felt like a sister to him.

But it was Indy who grabbed his attention as she tugged Alex from where he'd been playing a drinking game with the other guys. His hand found the small of her back, hers looping around the back of his neck as they danced too close to one another, laughing.

Miles narrowed his gaze and loosened his tie, suddenly feeling like he was suffocating when Alex dipped his mouth to Indy's ear to whisper something that made her giggle.

Indy had gone back to the penthouse to change into some short, tight dress, while he'd gone to Thiago's flat.

Maybe he should've followed her.

Should've ripped the gala dress off of her.

Should've taken her against the window and shown Alex fucking Myers who owned her.

Especially when she had sent him a photo of herself sitting on the edge of her bed, leaning on a hand as a thigh was placed atop the other. The skirt had hiked up so high that he had asked if she were wearing any underwear. *Do you think I want to walk around with a panty line? Get your shit together, stud*, had been her response. Miles had to retreat to the bathroom to arrange his erection, but only after he'd sent back a mirror selfie, his arousal clearly noticeable.

And Miles had expected her to come up to him at some point during the gala, to whisper in his ear that she dared him to slip his hand between her thighs and find how ready she was.

But she never did.

That's what he got for avoiding her all night long. For sitting at another table, keeping himself busy with other athletes. Because many lines would have been crossed if he'd stayed in her vicinity.

And now, she was in another man's arms. Laughing. Dancing. Whispering in his ear.

Indy squeezed Alex's bicep as she talked, his hand drifting to the curve of her ass as his gaze locked with Miles'.

Oh, hell no.

He was done with this shit show.

"You look pathetic," Charlie said, clapping him on the chest as he went inside.

He blew out a breath, undoing the first few buttons of his shirt and rolling the sleeves up to his elbows. "Thanks."

"What's up with you, anyway? You just won, like, five hundred bucks because of that bet."

Despite complaining about being bored to her core, Indy had proved to Miles everything he already knew about her—that she was fiercely loyal, and that she never backed out from a challenge. Miles knew he'd been right to have faith in her.

Miles turned around, following Charlie into the kitchen. He didn't need to witness Alex touching his Daisy any longer. He rubbed his face, groaning. "Nothing. What's going on with *you?*"

If Indy was the female representation of pure sunshine, Charlie was her male equal. But lately, Miles had noticed a shift in his demeanour—his smiles were forced, his mind was absent, and his eyes didn't hold the joy he'd been used to seeing.

"Just going through some tough times," Charlie said, pouring himself another glass of whiskey.

"Is this about racing?"

The entire world knew how pressured Charlie felt. With his contract with Imperium Racing ending next season, rumours going around that he would be replaced soon by another driver who could win a championship, and threats by his own team principal that he needed to win soon to keep his seat; it was evident that he wasn't doing okay.

"Nah," Charlie mumbled. "It's uh, we really don't need to talk about it."

"It's your choice. I won't force you. But you know I'm here, right?"

"Yeah, I know. Actually, I think you deserve to know." There were a few beats of silence as Charlie stared at his glass, his jaw tightening. "I found my girlfriend of almost two years banging some random guy a couple of months ago..."

"Ah, man..." Miles pulled his teammate in, patting his back in comfort. Charlie dropped his forehead on his shoulder, sighing with sadness and defeat. "I'm so sorry."

"It's fine. I'm never around, so maybe it was my fault."

"No, it wasn't. It's her loss."

"Yeah, that's what I'm telling myself. I was good to her. I gave her everything she wanted." Charlie's eyes were glossy as they pulled away. "My mind just keeps replaying this moment where I found them in *my* bed. I'm so disgusted. It's been months, and I should move on. But she texted me tonight and I guess the memories just came back."

"I'm not the best when it comes to relationship advice, but the fact she messaged you after what she's done is shitty. You shouldn't blame yourself, and you're allowed to have a hard time moving on. But I thought you had a thing for Aïda Romano? I mean, don't get me wrong, but the way you looked at her a few weeks ago when we went out..."

Charlie's cheeks flushed. "Aïda and I were a thing a few years back, but I fucked up with her, and some part of myself can't let her go. You know when you feel like your heart belongs to one person, and no matter what forces you to be away from that person, you refuse to give it out to someone else? You know when you feel like you've loved one person for so long that the thought of having feelings for someone else makes you sick?"

Miles nodded absently, his gaze slipping to the balcony where Indy was still dancing. He felt his heart drum hastily, an invisible thread pulling him towards her, but he was resisting, again, and again, and again.

"I mean, don't get me wrong," Charlie continued, "I loved Daniella, but..."

His voice became distant as Miles kept his gaze on Indy shining brighter than stars.

Of course, he knew the feeling all too well. His heart craved for her so fiercely, so violently, that it was near impossible to deny how drawn he was to her. The initial attraction he shared for Indy had turned into longing and adoration, had bled into his very bones and soul, had utterly shattered him, and yet he wanted *more*.

But for how long would he be able to pretend he didn't want anything from her? That he didn't *want* her?

Fuck. He needed to put an end to his misery.

MILES WAS STARING at the bouquet adorning the centre of the island when Indy stepped inside the penthouse.

"Ah, it's you." She sighed after uttering those words as she walked towards him, those long legs taunting him.

He almost chuckled at the faux annoyance etched on her face. "You look so thrilled to see me."

When she came to stand by his side to fill her empty glass with tap water, a zip of electricity coursed through him. He didn't move, and she didn't either.

"I'm actually surprised to see that you're still here."

"What do you mean?" he asked, frowning down at her.

Indy pivoted to face him. "You've been ignoring me."

Dropping his head, he sighed. "Don't be like this, Indy. All cameras were pointed at you all night long, and everyone was looking at you. You don't need my attention. Besides, it looks like Alex is taking great care of you."

The simple thought of Alex having his hands on Indy made a lump rise in the back of his throat. The way he touched her. The way he smiled down at her. Miles thought Indy had no interest in Alex, but perhaps he'd been wrong the whole time.

Indy set her glass down, her tongue making a brief appearance to wet her lips. He looked at her full mouth, and he almost made the distance between them go away. But he refused to succumb because he didn't want to kiss her. Didn't want it to be fuelled by recklessness. He wanted the kiss to mean *everything* to her.

Indy stepped closer, the space between their chests so minimal that if he exhaled, his torso would touch hers. "Does it piss you off to see me with him?"

Miles was done with her games. His jaw tightened. "It fucking kills me, Indigo."

"Are you jealous?"

He smirked. "Is this what you're playing at? Trying to make me jealous by showing me any man can have his hands on you?"

Victory gleamed in her gaze. "Is it working?"

Swiftly, he caught her waist and pinned her to the counter. A gasp got stuck in her throat, and he wondered if she'd emit this sound if he kissed her. His hips pressed into hers as he stared into her eyes. "Why are you doing this?"

"Because I don't get you, Huxley."

"There's nothing to understand—"

"No, you don't get to do that." When her hands pushed at his chest, he didn't budge, only pressing his fingers into her clothed flesh, making her chest heave as her stare dropped to his mouth. "You were all over me in the dressing room, ready to fuck me. You couldn't stop touching me on the red carpet, like you wanted to show everyone that I'm yours. You couldn't stop looking at me, yet you stayed away during the entire event. You bought my painting for three million euros, for fuck's sake! But once we're here, with just our friends, you avoid me. You don't talk to me. You let me be in another man's arms like it doesn't bother you. Are you embarrassed? Ashamed of me? Of being attracted to someone who's so messy and imperfect? Is that—"

"I don't trust myself when I'm around you, Indy," he interrupted in a low voice. "I feel like I'm losing control whenever you're near me."

It was barely noticeable, but her shoulders dropped. "What are you so afraid of?"

Everything.

He was terrified of losing her. Losing control over himself. Ruining everything between them.

Of not being enough for her. Not being worthy of her.

Of falling in love—because Miles knew nothing of love. And Indy deserved the kind of loud, burning red love.

"What's so bad about wanting me?" Her voice cracked, tears pooling in the corners of her eyes. She was hurt, and it was all because of him. "Am I only desirable for just one night, is that it?"

He let a deep breath out, his forehead falling on hers. "Can we talk about it when you're not drunk?"

Indy shoved him away, hard. "I've sobered up. God, you make me mad. Why do you keep running away when you're about to break? Can't you understand that I'm on the same boat as you?"

"This is beyond simply wanting you," he confessed, passing his hands through his hair.

"And that's fine! Just stop fighting it."

He swallowed the tight, uncomfortable knot. "If you were willing to go to Alex's, then just—"

Indy turned around, but he didn't miss the pain in her eyes. "I can't do this. I'm going home."

Home.

He didn't know why, but hearing this word coming out of her mouth cemented something in him.

"Indy—"

She lifted a hand. "No, Huxley. Stop. Yes, I tried making you jealous. And yes I'm trying to piss you off because the only thing I want to know is whether you want me or not. It seems like you don't, so there, I have my answer." She tripped on her way out, cursing. Miles rushed to her as she took her heels off. "I'm just so tired."

The anguish and fatigue in her voice made his chest ache. He was the cause of this pain.

She was tired of waiting for him. For always making the first move, and he realised he'd been a fool all along. She'd always been there, right before his eyes, but his focus had been elsewhere. The damages he'd done almost shattered him to irreparable pieces.

He caught her elbow, then hooked an arm beneath her knees, the other under her back as he carried her towards the lift. Hopefully, Alex was watching and understood that Miles was Indy's man. That Indy was *his*.

"I'm angry at you." Still, she held on tight. Still, she placed her head on his shoulder. "This game is stupid."

"I know, baby. I'm sorry." There was a voice reminding him that she was the one who'd started it all, who wanted to see who would resist the longest, but he didn't comment on it. Obviously, this game had wrecked them more than intended, and Miles didn't want to hurt her any more.

Her ear rested against his thumping heart as he crossed the road. As he dipped his chin in a curt nod at Teddy who opened the door. As he stood in the lift, holding her tightly against him.

"For the record," he murmured, "I hate seeing you with someone else." He set her down in front of her bedroom, tucking a strand of hair behind her ear before grabbing her chin. "I hate that he got to touch you and make you laugh. I hate that you make me feel this way."

"Is that it? You're scared of just *feeling*?" The thing was, with her, he felt too much. So much. And it terrified him. When he didn't dare voice his answer, she continued. "Let me ask you something."

His heart stalled. Was she about to invite him inside her room?

She studied his expression, the emotions in his eyes, the desperation in his trembling hands. "I always thought you simply wanted to stay friends. Why admit you didn't like seeing me with Alex?"

He gripped her jaw, perusing those lovely lips. "Do friends do what we do, Indy? Do friends send each other sensual pictures? Do they tease and flirt and touch the way we do? Seeing you with Alex only made me realise that I'm sick of pretending. I'm sick of being just your friend, and trust me, I've been feeling this way long before he got to put his hands on you tonight."

"Huxley," she breathed, his name echoing like a plea. "Just say it."

He released her face, distancing himself from the devastating woman. "I dream of tasting you. Fucking you. I'd love nothing more than to make you understand that the word *friends* doesn't work with us." His chest heaved in perfect sync with hers, his pulse erratic and deafening. "But right now, I'm going to ask you to go into your room and lock the door."

She didn't ask questions. Didn't let her expression break.

With her shoes in hand, she stepped into her bedroom. Rapidly, she cast a quick glance his way, then disappeared through the darkness.

Miles waited for the lock to click, but the sound never resonated.

Maybe it was time for Miles to be selfish and take what he wanted.

CHAPTER TWENTY-FOUR

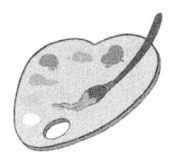

📍 *MONTE CARLO, MONACO*

"You have got to be kidding me."

Grunting with complete frustration, Indy fell back onto her pillows and tossed the once vibrating toy to the side.

How could she have forgotten to charge it?

Well, guess her fingers would be her friends tonight.

Except it seemed like her mind did not want to cooperate with her body's needs. She was desperate for release, aching for a soul-shattering orgasm that would send her to the stars, but she simply couldn't get there. Any time she'd start to writhe, nearly reaching that line, her mind would wander off elsewhere, and that high crashed down.

She tipped her head back, closing her eyes as her hand drifted down her abdomen.

Indy hadn't been able to sleep since she came back from the after-party at Thiago's.

She'd left her door unlocked, hoping that Miles would come

to his senses and seek her out. But he didn't. All she'd heard was his shower running for a long moment.

When she tried to fall asleep, all that had popped in her mind was the fantasy of Miles touching himself at the thought of her in the shower. And that had led to opening her nightstand's drawer.

This little vibrating toy was her best friend when she was travelling. Despite procuring her the satisfying release she needed after long days at the track, it had been too long since she'd truly had an orgasm that left her shaking and panting.

Indy sighed when her fingers grazed her clit—more in frustration than in pleasure—imagining them being Miles'. Imagining his touch burning her skin. Imagining his lips on her.

All she had was the vague memory of their stolen moments in the past. How he'd dragged her skirt up to her hips. How he'd parted her legs, nudging the tip of his hard cock to her entrance from behind, how he'd fucked her so hard that he'd ruined her forever.

But why wouldn't he come to her? Why was he trying to lead her on? Why—

"Okay, fuck this." This wouldn't work. She would never find release if she let her overpowering thoughts control her.

Indy pulled her silk shorts back up to her hips, then put her feet into slippers. She tied her hair in a messy bun, feeling her skin slick with unreleased tension.

She needed fresh air. A glass of water. Maybe hop into the goddamn ocean to clear her head.

She startled at the sight of Miles standing in the dim lighting of the kitchen, hands braced atop the counter as his head hung low.

Her soft gasp made him look at her.

"Shit, you scared me," she said, a hand on her chest as she approached him. Only the moon's light filtered through the windows.

"*You* nearly gave me a heart attack." His voice was hoarse, and he cleared his throat.

"That's a very negative way to say I look like shit when I'm not wearing heels and a fancy dress."

Miles looked amused as he straightened himself. That's when she realised he was simply wearing a pair of joggers, hanging low around his hips.

"You always look pristine." As he said those words, his eyes meandered across her physique, halting at her chest more than once. She didn't dare look down, but she guessed her nipples were still peaking, straining against the thin fabric of her camisole.

"I know." He chuckled at her answer, then kept his gaze on her as she went to grab a glass. "Why are you awake? Did you have—was it a nightmare?"

The heat in his eyes vanished, leaving place to sudden tenderness. "No, not at all. Just couldn't sleep."

"Have you had them lately?"

"Not since that night."

She nodded. "Will you tell me if they come back?"

"Why?" he asked, frowning.

A soft sigh escaped. "So that you don't have to do it alone." The thought that he could bask in his anguish and detriment any night made her heart ache, especially if he was alone and woke up drenched in sweat with tears running down his face, with no one to keep him safe.

His throat worked as he swallowed. "That's not necessary—"

"Please," she whispered.

"Okay," he said quietly. "I will. Thank you, I appreciate it."

That's when she noticed his damp hair, ruffled like he'd just run his fingers through it even after trying to dry it. His muscular chest, still glinting with water, like he hadn't taken the time to really dry himself off.

She frowned. Did he just take another shower?

But when the breeze hit her skin, pebbling it, she understood he'd gone into the hot tub—his solace, his getaway.

She gulped her water down, still feeling hot. Especially under the intensity of his scrutiny.

"What about you?" His gravelly voice caressed her ear, making its descent all the way to her core. "It's two in the morning."

"Couldn't sleep either."

"Got something on your mind?" His interest was genuine, but her answer would ruin everything.

So, she said, "No." But she had wanted to say, *You.*

The crease between his brows deepened. He stepped forward, and she stepped backwards, hitting the central island.

"I know when you're lying to me, Indy," he whispered, looking at her mouth.

She didn't respond, holding his gaze.

His hands fell atop the marble counter, caging her in. She sucked in a breath, the desire that had taken over her body an hour ago already sparkling back to life. "Truth or dare?" he asked.

This was a trap—he would ask the same question no matter what her response was.

Still, she said, "Dare."

Miles smirked, like he knew she'd accept the challenge without hesitating.

"I dare you to tell me why you couldn't fall asleep."

"Fine." She tipped her chin upwards, just enough for their breaths to entwine. She listened to the loud thud of her heart, to the way his breathing became shallow, like the anticipation was killing him. Like the proximity was driving him as wild as it was driving her. "I can't come."

Miles blinked. Then his face flushed, and she was positive her cheeks were as reddish as his. Raw desire caused his pupils to expand. "You—couldn't make yourself orgasm?"

"You heard me."

He inhaled, stepping closer until their chests were aligned. "You were touching yourself."

She nodded. "And failing at my task."

"And why haven't you been able to pleasure yourself?"

"I can't stop thinking," she whispered, trailing her hands up his veiny forearms, chills rattling in the wake of her touch.

"About what?"

"About you."

His gulp was audible. Then, he dipped his head down, his mouth pressing at the base of her throat. He skimmed his lips over her skin, the side of her neck, peppering kisses so light that they felt non-existent. She arched into him, and he grunted. She realised her nipples had just brushed at his bare chest. The friction set her body on fire.

"Were you imagining *me* touching you?"

"Yes," she whispered, her nails digging into his shoulders.

Miles was breathing heavily against her skin, his hands finding her waist. "You know how my fingers feel inside you. What stopped you from coming?"

"Because I want *you* to make me come."

Miles groaned again, and when his eyes found hers, they were black with unrelenting lust.

With his hips pressed to hers, she could feel his hard-on against her lower stomach, making her want more, and more, and more.

She moved, her lips brushing his, and they both inhaled at the same time. Her lashes fluttered, her body already shaking with desperation.

"Huxley." A plea. A request. A need for him to claim her.

He groaned, then muttered, "Fuck it."

And then, his mouth fell upon hers, and time stopped. They exhaled at the same time, separating just enough to breathe, before crashing into one another again, drumming heartbeats aligning and making one symphony.

He cradled her jaw, his hands trembling, a soft moan

escaping his mouth as she returned the kiss with equal passion. Indy wound her arms around his neck, afraid he might slip away if she didn't latch onto him. Had it not been for his tight hold on her, the way he swallowed her gasps would have swept her off the ground.

A groan caught in the back of his throat when her fingers tangled through his hair, just as he tugged her closer by the waist, his fingers branding her skin when they slipped beneath her shirt.

It felt as though everything had come to a halt around them, the only living element being the two of them, tethered by the sizzling energy coursing through their veins as they kissed, and kissed, and kissed, without ever wanting to stop.

Indy was panting by the time he moved to pepper her jaw with light kisses, her back arching into the palm of his hands.

She shook as the realisation rocked into her like a reckless tidal wave: Miles wanted her, just as much as she wanted him. He kissed and touched her like she was his salvation. Still, she needed to hear him say it, otherwise she would feel like she was stuck in a fever dream.

"Fuck," he murmured, releasing a shaky breath. Effortlessly, he hoisted her up onto the counter, spreading her thighs with his hips. He dotted her jaw with kisses before pulling back to look into her eyes.

Miles' gaze softened, like he saw something in her eyes. His forehead fell on hers, and he kissed her again. More softly this time, more carefully, like he was trying to understand whether this was real or not.

"You're shaking," he said against her mouth.

Indy's throat burned, and before she could realise it, tears were threatening to escape.

"What's wrong?" The pad of his thumb ran under her eye, his other hand caressing the small of her bare back.

"I thought—never mind."

"Hey, talk to me. No secrets between us, okay?"

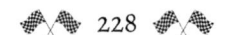

Indy dropped her gaze to his chest, watching it rise and fall as she placed her palm above his thundering heart. "I thought you really didn't want me. All this back and forth—I just thought you weren't interested or attracted to me anymore. That I'm just Kai's sister to you, and nothing more."

Miles lifted her chin, obliging her to look into his eyes. "Indy, you've *always* been so much more than my best friend's little sister. I've always been into you."

Her brows shot up in surprise. "Always?"

The timid nod Miles gave her was utterly adorable. "Yes. I can't think of a single moment where you weren't on my mind."

"So why haven't you sought me out?"

He swallowed thickly. "I just don't want to fuck it up."

She frowned. "I don't get it."

"You know this is different from the times we were together before. All of this... It's foreign to me. We spend a lot of time together, we *live* together, and I just wasn't expecting you to mark your territory into my life this way. And I'm starting to feel something really intense for you, and I don't know what to do with it. How to handle it."

Indy's head was spinning as she let the phrases echo inside her head. He was laying his heart open, giving her an insight into his sentiments. "I thought breaking your walls was impossible to do."

His thumb ran across her jawline. "There are...things about me that I will tell you one day, but I'm sorry if I'm slow at letting my guard down."

"You don't have to be—"

"But that doesn't mean that I'm not attracted to you." Pressing his hard bulge against her centre, he showed how desired she was by him. "Doesn't mean I don't want to dive my tongue in between your thighs every time you strut around in those skirts and high heels around the paddock. Doesn't mean I don't want to fuck you senseless. And doesn't mean I don't jerk off by thinking of you in the shower."

"Oh, is that why your showers run for so long?"

He smirked. "Maybe." He kissed her jaw, her throat. "Do you want an invitation to the show?"

"Tempting. Can I give you one of my own?" She brushed her lips to his, leading to him capturing hers into a fervent kiss.

"Fuck, yes. That's so hot."

She was already panting, and he hadn't even properly touched her yet. "I really thought you forgot about the times we were together."

When his palms skittered along her spine beneath her blouse, she shivered. When his hoarse voice echoed, she locked her legs around his hips. "I haven't stopped thinking about you for a single minute. I can still taste you on my tongue. I can still hear your moans. Feel your nails dig into my shoulders. Feel your greedy cunt squeeze my cock dry. But this is different now, and you know it. This is not us bumping into each other at a club and finding the closest washroom because we're both high on adrenaline and need to get it out of our system. This is me breaking my fucking rules for you, so you have to be sure of what you want. You're the only one I let in. The only one I want."

"You want me?" Indy echoed steadily, firmly.

"Yes."

"Then beg for it, Golden Boy."

Trailing his lips from her thigh to the inside of her knee and down her shin, Miles sank to the floor—slowly, deliberately—without so much as detaching his gaze from hers. A heartbeat later, he was on both knees, pleading eyes looking up at her—brimmed with desperation and unwavering desire. He continued to brand featherlight kisses to her skin and making uncontrollable shivers appear in the wake of his devastating touch. "Please, Indy. Let me have you."

She pulled him up by his hair, her heartbeat erratic inside her chest.

There was no hesitation slamming through her mind. There was no doubt clinging to her heart. Holding his gaze, she made sure the sincerity alighting her eyes was as earnest as her confession. "I want you," she said softly yet firmly. "I want you, Huxley, and I need you to get me naked right now, or else I'll lose my mind."

His lips tilted upwards. "So damn bossy."

Nevertheless, he slanted his mouth upon hers, stealing the breath straight from her lungs. His tongue was seeking dominance, brushing against hers in a salacious dance as his hands slipped to her bottom. He groaned, palming her through her shorts, then bucking his arousal into her. Indy moaned at the friction, and she felt his smug smirk against her mouth.

The next moment, he picked her up. Without so much as breaking their heady kiss, he walked them over to the sofa, laying her down on the arm of it.

His fingers trailed over her shoulders, toying with the thin straps of her shirt. He pushed them down her upper arms, then moved to the hem of her top to slip his big, warm hands to touch her skin. He groaned softly in the back of his throat, bucking his hips into hers.

"Does Alex touch you like this?" he asked.

There it was—the possessiveness she'd seen flash in his eyes when he watched her dance with Alex earlier tonight.

Indy didn't respond. She wanted to rile him up. Didn't want him to hold back.

When his thumb skimmed the underside of her breast, she sighed. Then, he fully grabbed it, like he'd done so many times in the past, except the most masculine, guttural groan rumbled in his throat as he felt the nipple piercing. "Goddamn it, Indy." He played with the barbell, causing Indy to writhe under him. "Does Alex make you moan like this?"

Miles pressed a light kiss on the swell of her breast, then found her peaked nipple over her camisole, taking it between his lips.

"Answer me," he demanded, pushing the top until it rested below her breasts.

"Don't tell me what to do," she bit out, fingers tangling through his dishevelled locks.

"Baby, if you don't do what I ask of you, I'm going to play with you. I'm going to edge you and not let you come until you prove to me that you're a good girl. I'm going to make you wait, moan, and pant. You'll be begging me to come. And I know you're already frustrated for not being able to find release on your own, so just answer me. As much as I'd love to torture you, I want my girl to be satisfied as soon as possible."

In other circumstances, she would have played games with him, would have challenged him. But as she felt her pulse fall between her legs, all she could do was listen to his command. "No, he doesn't."

He smiled up at her. "Good girl."

As he used a hand to pull the straps of her shirt off her shoulders, the other one found her aroused centre through the shorts. Miles pressed a finger to her clit, gently circling. "And does Alex make you feel like this?"

Indy dragged the other strap down. "No."

"That's what I fucking thought."

"Green doesn't suit you," she jested, arching into him. "He's just a friend. I've never wanted to fuck him. He was just helping me to make you jealous."

"Good to know. It worked." Miles pulled her camisole down to her midriff, exposing her bare, heavy breasts. His jaw went slack as he sat back on his heels, pushing his locks away from his forehead. "Holy shit," he whispered gruffly, staring at every exposed inch of her—like he was studying a sculpture. "You are beautiful."

Indy pinched her pierced nipples, chuckling. "At least look at me in the eyes when you compliment me."

He found her gaze, admiration and lust darkening his eyes. "I've never—"

He'd never seen her naked, was maybe what he meant to say before stopping short.

His hands replaced hers, and she was amazed at how Miles was so perfectly made for her. His tongue came to lap at her nipple, flickered across the piercing, and he repeated the motion on the other breast. "I can't stop thinking about your tits. Your perfect ass. Your body. You look like a goddess."

"What do you think about when you jerk off?"

Miles' lips descended down her stomach. He smirked as he noticed the shivers appearing on her skin. "You. Riding me as I suck on your pink nipples. Taking you from behind. Having my cock pushed inside your tight cunt." He pushed her shorts to the side, fingers sliding through her slickness. They moaned at the same time. "I think of going down on you. Eating your soaked cunt until you can't breathe."

"Please," Indy cried out when he inserted one finger in a slow, teasing motion.

He looked up at her through thick lashes. "Please what?"

"Please stop teasing me."

"So polite." He tugged her shorts down, and there she was, completely bare and exposed, save for the bunched camisole around her midriff. Miles expelled a breath and stood up, raking his gaze all over her body. "And so fucking perfect."

She blushed. "Thank you."

He tugged his joggers down. "Show me what you were just doing in your bed."

Indy blinked at his cock springing upwards, hard and impressive. She moaned when his hand wrapped around the base, then let her cold fingers find her clit. She circled it, looking up into his eyes.

"My vibrator died," she admitted.

"You—fuck. You're so hot. Will you let me play with you sometime?"

Indy nodded, shifting on the sofa. Still lying down, she positioned herself by his knees and let her head dangle in emptiness, baring her throat to him as he stood by her head. "Only if you come here."

Stepping forward, Miles smirked down at her. He nudged her plump lips with the tip of his cock, already leaking with pre-cum, then whimpered when her tongue swirled around the crown.

"Fuck," he groaned. "I forgot how amazing your mouth is. I can't wait to fuck you again."

Indy moaned around him as he pushed forward. With this angle, she couldn't see the look on his face, but imagining his expression made the wetness between her thighs dribble down her skin. She listened to his whimper, pictured his lips parting, brows bunched together, chest heaving.

Indy let him fuck her throat at an even pace all the while she drew fast circles around her clit, driving herself towards the precipice as she sucked on his thick, throbbing cock.

"Fuck, baby. Just like that. You're a masterpiece."

Miles grabbed her breasts, played with her nipples, then let his fingers travel from her torso to her navel. He plunged two fingers inside her drenched core, and Indy moaned again. She stopped pleasuring herself, his fingers filling her so perfectly.

"You're drenching my hand already," he rasped. "Making such a mess."

Indy responded with a moan, and his body jerked on a spasm.

"Take big breaths for me," he ordered. "Gonna fuck this perfect, bratty mouth until I come. I missed this. Missed you. I dreamed of your mouth every single night."

She could feel her head spinning, not just because of the way she was positioned, but because of the way he was working his fingers inside her.

She was a moaning mess, feeling beads of saliva trickle down her cheek. Miles used his other hand to rub her clit, and she played with her nipples, bucking into his hands and taking more of him in her mouth. Her tongue brushed his pulsing shaft, her throat welcoming him.

"Atta girl. You're taking it so well," he panted. "Won't last long."

He released a guttural groan, chanting her name, and when her core clenched around his fingers, he retreated from her mouth to let her fall apart. She arched off the sofa, her thighs closing as she cried out, tremors taking over her body whilst her vision whitened.

"I love the way you come. You're so beautiful."

Coming down from her high, she felt Miles' release hit her breasts, and she opened her eyes to see him pump his cock dry, hoarse moans escaping his mouth.

He was panting hard, but then, he was on his knees, dragging her towards the edge of the sofa and spreading her legs apart.

"Absolutely drenched."

"Are you complaining?" she scoffed.

"No. Just admiring my work." He kissed the inside of her thigh and pulled his phone out of his pocket. "Would you be okay if I recorded us?"

Indy nodded, her lips parting.

"I need to hear your voice, baby."

Pushing his locks away from his brows, she said, "Yes, you can record us."

He hit the record button, setting his phone by her side before taking hold of her heaving breasts. "I'll listen to it every time we're travelling if we're not in the same hotel room. Don't want to forget the way you sound when you moan my name. The way you pant when you're about to come."

Indy didn't have the time to think as his lips wrapped around her clit, his hands kneading her breasts. His tongue lapped fiercely at her clit with abandon, like a man starved.

"Oh, fuck, Huxley," she moaned, trembling when his tongue went flat out from her entrance to her clit. He suctioned on it, smirking when her hips bucked into his face.

"I can't get enough of you. You taste just like I remembered, if not even better." He inserted two fingers all at once, his tongue continuing to lap steadily.

Her fingers dug into his skull when she pulled him as close as she could, throwing her head back when he kitten-licked her folds. When she looked down at him, he was watching her, smiling devilishly against her clit.

"Oh, God."

He groaned against her, and she whispered his name.

Applying the perfect amount of pressure around her nipples, the stars bursting behind her eyes made her moan loudly. When she unravelled again, she held his head in place, just where she wanted him, the rapid motions of his tongue never ceasing and coaxing her through the high.

"Shit, woman," he breathed, rising until his hands caressed her hips. "You are the sexiest person I know."

Gently, Indy cradled his jaw and he was the one to lean in and kiss her tenderly. She moaned at the taste of herself on his tongue, already wanting more.

"Thank you," she whispered.

"No, thank *you*. You're incredible."

As he helped her clean up with a warm cloth, then got her into sleeping clothes, she couldn't help but notice the softness in his gaze, the blush on his face, the smile on his lips. He carried her into her bed, despite her complaints, and tucked her in.

"We'll talk in the morning," he promised, kissing her temple. "Good night, Daisy."

Indy didn't want him to go. Didn't want this to turn into the situation she'd lived too many times.

She was too tangled in him. This was beyond physical attraction, and she needed him to reciprocate those feelings. She was tired of the heartbreak, of watching him walk away. She needed him to stay, but this time, she had a feeling he wasn't going to hide. This time, she knew he was going to fight for her.

CHAPTER TWENTY-FIVE

📍 *MONTE CARLO, MONACO*

INDY WOKE UP to the soft morning light filtering through the curtains. She sighed contently, shifting on her back, only to hear rustling around her room.

Slowly, she opened her eyes, blinking a couple of times to adjust her vision to the bright light. Miles was standing next to the window, busy with something he had set on the desk.

Sitting up, Indy rubbed her face. The swishing sound of her sheets made him turn around, and a soft smile spread across his lips when their gazes locked.

She felt her heartbeat pick up its pace, warmth dancing around her chest. The power he had over her was terrifying, yet exhilarating. "Good morning, stud. What a joy to be awoken by Clark Kent himself."

Miles chuckled, adjusting his glasses atop his nose. "Morning, baby. You like the glasses, don't you?" His morning voice, raspy and low, sent flashes of what happened a few hours ago through her mind. Scarlet bloomed on his cheekbones, and perhaps he'd been thinking about the exact same thing.

"Love them. You look sexy wearing them."

"Am I not without them?"

Indy rolled her eyes. "Don't put words in my mouth."

His broad grin, beautiful and rare, was a thing of savage beauty. Slipping his hands in his pockets, he sighed softly, and she felt like free falling in an endless abyss of devastation as she stared back into his starry eyes full of adoration.

"What?" she asked when he slightly shook his head.

"Nothing. Nothing at all." The blush on his face deepened before he cleared his throat. "Here."

He brought a tray to the nightstand, then handed her a glass of water. Atop the tray sat a tall glass of iced matcha latte and a bowl of oatmeal, topped with fruit and a drizzle of peanut butter.

"Wow," she said after taking a long sip of water. "All of this to thank me for giving you head last night?"

Miles pinned her with a glare, though the corner of his lips twitched. "All of this to show I care about you, you damn *idiot*. Best head of my life, though."

Not wanting to think about the fact Miles had been with other girls before her, she leaned back against her pillows, chuckling. After taming her hair in a braid, she grabbed the iced beverage. "Thank you, Golden Boy."

The soft look on his face, the small smile etched on his lips, made her want to pull him in between her bedsheets. Then, she thought again about his fingers bringing her towards the pinnacle of pleasure, his lips claiming hers, his tongue on her.

"Don't look at me like that," he warned, jaw tightening as his eyes drifted to her chest.

"Can't help myself."

"As much as I adore having your pretty eyes on me, I just have to remind you that we're leaving for Miami today, and you need to pack."

Indy's head fell backward. "Way to ruin the mood."

Miles looked amused by her sudden frustration and walked to her closet to retrieve a large suitcase. "Don't worry about it. I'll get it started for you."

"No, it's fine, I'll just—"

"Indy," he cut in. "Just tell me what to put in there. You're taking your little vibrator?"

Choking on her drink, she gave him wide eyes, feeling heat creep up her neck. "Depends. If you plan on making me come with your tongue, fingers, or cock, then I won't be needing it."

A muscle popped in his tight jaw. "Who says you can't use everything?"

"Keep talking like that, and we will definitely miss our flight."

"Tempting." From her desk, he grabbed the sketch pad he'd gotten her at the beginning of the season. "We're taking this, right?"

She smiled at the gentleness woven into his tone. "Yes, please."

"Can I look through it?" he asked, taking a seat at the foot of the bed. At least he wasn't running away from what had happened last night. Still, they needed to talk about it.

"Go ahead. They're not especially good, but drawing helps me clear my head when we travel."

He was silent as he flipped page after page. Anxiety was clawing at her stomach as she sipped on the drink, watching his muscular back rise and fall. Showing her art was akin to sharing deep secrets. Not many people in her life had the opportunity of flipping through her sketches, but Miles made her feel safe. Something about him made her want to share the deepest parts of herself, knowing he'd see and understand her.

"Indy," he exhaled without turning around. He ruffled his hair, chuckling like he couldn't believe what he was staring at. "These are amazing. I'm so in awe of your talent, it's unbelievable."

Indy could feel the emotion burning her eyes. Of course, she'd been complimented in the past for her art. Of course, she'd sold a couple of commissions. But not once had someone told her they liked her art when it was still a draft, messy and incomplete. Not once had she been told that she was talented when the initial intention behind a drawing was simply to let her mind loose.

She felt a lump grow inside her throat. Setting the glass down, she pushed the duvet off her legs. "Huxley?"

He was still flipping through the book. "Yeah?"

"Why did you buy my painting? Why did you bid so much on it?"

Finally, he turned to her. Her heart nearly lodged into her throat, battering so furiously that she wondered why this man was having such a powerful effect over her. "Because I love your art. I love the way you pour your soul into it. Because it speaks to me."

"Three million euros, Huxley... I'm not worth this much money. I'm—I don't matter that way."

He set the book down, tugging her in by the hip until she was straddling his lap. He searched her gaze as his fingers gently tucked a strand of hair behind an ear. "You are priceless, Indigo. I will spend my money on you, no matter how much anything costs me. I will buy your work and open a gallery just to expose your art, even those silly mugs with hearts painted on them. You matter so much, and so does everything you do. I bought the painting because for one, those people who bid a couple of thousand bucks for it do not know a single thing about art. They wanted it because *the* Indigo Bailey made it, and they would have never looked at it the way I do. And two, I truly love it."

It was way too early to be shedding tears. She sniffled, a wobbly smile growing on her face. "Thank you. I'm so glad you bought it."

"So am I," he whispered.

Searching for her words carefully, she wound her arms

around his neck, his gaze darkening at their sheer proximity. As her fingers found their way through his soft hair, his hands roamed over the outsides of her thighs. His soothing touch was everything to her. "Can we talk about last night?"

"You mean this morning," he teased with a knowing smile.

"Yes, smartass," she huffed, rolling her eyes. "Can we just talk?"

"Of course."

She felt her cheeks heat up as he patiently waited for her to open up.

"I know it used to be different before I became your roommate. I didn't mind hooking up and keeping it casual—"

"But it hurt you, didn't it? *I* hurt you."

She swallowed the tight knot that had built inside her throat. "You did," she confessed. Pain flashed in his eyes, but he simply nodded, like he understood her feelings. Like he was accepting the damages he'd done. "I don't want you to use me and run away. I want you to communicate with me, tell me about your feelings, even tell me when you want space for some reason. I'd rather that than be left confused and asking myself what I did wrong for you to distance yourself like that."

His brows knitted together. "I'm so, so sorry. You know I never meant to hurt you. I was so focused on racing—I still am—and to be honest, seeing you was always a good distraction in the way that you made me feel good, both physically and emotionally. Being in your company simply reminds me that I can be myself. That there's no need to pretend. I've never wanted to use you, Indy. Now that we're always together, I know that what I've been feeling for you is not just lust. It's always been more than that, and like I said last night, I'm scared of feeling."

She loved his honesty. His sincerity as he held her gaze. Deep down, he was just a man exploring his feelings, and perhaps he was terrified of his blooming sentiments for her. If she, too, consumed his every thought the exact same way he did with hers, Indy would understand why he was confused.

"I thought you didn't do feelings."

"I didn't," he confirmed. "Past tense."

"So this is not just sex?"

He shook his head. "It's not like before."

Knowing he was on the same wavelength made her sigh in relief. "Is there something else you're scared of?"

He seemed to think for a second, his thumb drawing light circles on her thigh. "Iguanas? There's just something about them—"

"No, you idiot," she chuckled, lightly smacking his chest. "Are you scared of falling for me?"

"I think, deep down, we're all terrified of falling in love. What if I not only hurt you, but I end up hurting myself in the process? What if I fully let you in and you betray me? What if it's just temporary and you end up leaving? I've been abandoned in the past, and that isn't something I wish to live again. I'm trying my hardest to understand that I can trust you, that I'm safe with you."

She cradled his face, the roughness of his stubble scraping against her palms. "You are safe with me. You will always be. It's okay to be scared, because I am, too. But if you let yourself fall, I promise that I'll fall with you. Just don't push me away."

"I won't, I promise." He brushed a light kiss to her lips, and there was so much adoration in his act. So many promises. "You're so good to me, Indy, and I'm terrified of losing you. Of making a mistake. I've walked away from you one time too many, and it hurt me, too. I'm not leaving this time, alright?"

She'd wait for him—no matter how long it would take for him to be ready. To commit. To fall in love and accept to be loved, too.

"I'm holding you onto that," she whispered.

"Besides, if Kai ever learns that I've hurt you, he will strangle me to death."

She snorted softly. "Kai doesn't even have the guts to kill a spider. He could never harm you."

Miles gave her a look. "Are you sure about that? He loves you more than anything. I'm pretty sure no one can harm his baby sister."

"True."

"But what about you? What scares you? And don't say pigeons, because I already know you're scared shitless of them."

Indy shuddered, burying her face in the crook of his neck. His soft chuckle rumbled against her, and he gently caressed her back in soothing circles.

"I'm scared of being alone," she admitted, a weight being lifted off her shoulders. "Of rejection. Of failing and not being good enough. I'm scared of being replaced, whether it's at work or with my friends."

His forehead fell against hers. She closed her eyes, letting his murmur caress the indentations on her heart—giving him the power to mend the secretly broken pieces. "There's no one like you, Indigo Bailey. You are irreplaceable. You're unique, captivating, intelligent, and worthy of good things. You're also a human being who can make mistakes, but you'll always be enough, okay? And those mistakes don't make you less of a great woman because you're selfless with the way you always put others' happiness before your own. And you are not alone. Never."

She allowed him to wipe a stray tear from her cheek, leaning into his touch.

"Tell me you understand," he demanded in a whisper.

"I understand."

The gentle kiss he placed on her mouth made the butterflies caged inside her chest bat their wings wildly. "We've got each other."

And as long as they had each other, as long as there was a place for her in his once jet-black heart, Indy was okay. Everything she had once wished for was finally becoming hers, and there was no greater feeling than knowing the dreams she had chased were on the cusp of falling into the palm of her hand.

CHAPTER TWENTY-SIX

MIAMI, UNITED STATES OF AMERICA

"Yellow flag in sector three," AJ announced on the twentieth lap. "VSC."

Virtual safety car. Meaning all twenty drivers had to decelerate and were forbidden to overtake until the green flag was brandished again.

Miles made haste to decrease his pace, listening to his ragged breathing as he held a firm grip over his steering wheel. He kept a safe distance from Rowan who was leading the race, following the route of his zig-zags to keep his tyres warm.

Rowan was extremely good on this track.

Miles would love to see his friend win, but he'd love to stand on that first step more. Off track, Rowan had become one of his closest friends, but the moment they were behind their steering wheel, helmet and racing suit on, they were rivals, fighting for the shiniest trophy. So, he would reclaim his initial position back once the yellow flag would end, and he was confident he could easily do it.

"What happened?" he asked, checking his rear-view mirror. Charlie was right behind him.

Good, he thought. *Let's make this a double podium for Imperium Racing.*

"Two cars made contact. Nothing too bad. Just be careful with the little debris on the track."

"Got it."

※

EXITING the pit lane after a quick pit stop, Miles fell back into seventh place, right behind Hugo Bauer. He stayed aligned behind Hugo's car to seek a slipstream, but the dirty air caused slight turbulences to rattle his car. When he gained the extra speed he wanted, he slipped on the inside of a corner and overtook, easily so.

Staying close, Hugo tried to attempt a similar strategy, but Miles was faster and swifter.

When Miles was close to overtaking the car in front, Hugo had managed to catch up, causing him to be sandwiched between two cars as they went through a turn.

Being able to anticipate Hugo's moves, Miles accelerated and widened his trajectory as his rival almost touched his car with the rear wing of his.

"What the fuck is he doing?" he bellowed, drifting to the left to push Hugo out of his way. Their cars had almost come in contact, and the race could've been ruined. "He's trying to go into me. Someone teach him to fucking drive."

"Don't curse on live radio," AJ said. "And yeah, I saw."

"Tell him to stay away from me, or else I won't be gentle." With a push on the throttle, he roared off the track, sparks igniting on the asphalt as he focused on claiming back his leading position.

※

"There's something wrong with my tyres," Miles said to AJ as he started the fifty-fifth lap. Three more to go.

Until now, the race had been quite boring save for his overtake on Rowan in turn seven as DRS had been enabled. He'd driven inside the corner, then put a gap of two seconds after passing in front and taking the lead.

"Checking," AJ answered, unfazed.

Miles frowned as the back of his car lightly slipped when he drove inside a corner. "I just oversteered."

"Everything looks fine... You already know that we've reduced the downforce, but I don't think that's the issue."

"It's not! I told you, it's my tyres."

"Check the management."

He'd pitted about fifteen laps earlier. The hard compounds shouldn't have degraded so fast. "I did."

"Okay, Miles. Put mode fourteen on, and—"

AJ couldn't finish his sentence because Miles heard a hissing sound as his car trembled, then smoke came out from his front left tyre.

"Holy fuck," he said, his heart pounding. Nevertheless, he kept on driving, maintaining the big gap between him and Rowan. "What happened?"

There was a beat of silence before AJ's voice came through his earbuds. "Your tyre exploded. Like, literally."

Miles didn't know what baffled him the most: AJ's nonchalance or the fact that he was still roaring off the track with only three wheels on.

"It blew off because of the heat," AJ explained. "What's your call?"

"What do you mean, 'what's my call'? I'm finishing the race and I'm winning it, man."

"But—"

"Just fucking trust me."

There were now two laps to go, and Miles was drenched in sweat, his head was pounding, and his heart was thundering too wildly for his own liking. He kept the grip on his steering wheel firm, his focus intact, and his determination unwavering.

End the race with one blown-off tyre? Challenge accepted.

※

JUMPING OUT OF THE CAR, Miles pumped his fist in the air before sprinting towards his team that was waiting for him behind barriers. He got pulled in between arms and received pats of encouragement all over his back and helmet.

No matter how many races he'd won, his team would always cheer him on and treat him like he'd fetched the sun for them.

He slipped into his father's arms who was smiling proudly—like he always was.

"Great job," Henry murmured as he clapped the back of his helmet. "You impress me every day."

"Thanks, Dad." He squeezed his father tightly. "Love you."

Henry smiled, pride glinting in his eyes. "Love you, man."

Without his dad, Miles wouldn't have been here. Henry had sacrificed so much, had given up everything to help Miles achieve his dreams. And despite the chaos in his own life, he'd never once lost faith in Miles.

Having his dad follow him around the world and cheer him on during races was a true form of encouragement, one Miles would always be grateful for.

He spun on his heel, planting his hands on his hips as he observed the damage on the black and gold car. He sighed, then chuckled when Rowan pulled him into his chest, clapping his back.

"You're unbelievable," Rowan said. "I was so close to catching up to you. How did you manage to be faster than any of us with a blown-off tyre?"

He unstrapped his helmet. "I don't reveal my secrets to success."

"Jackass," Rowan muttered.

"When are you going to tell her?"

Finding whatever sliver of strength he could find deep within his bones, Miles looked away from Indy to find Ava's curious gaze. The chatter continued to reverberate around the large table, but one particular laugh managed to fill his ears like music. Too powerless to fight the temptation, he glanced towards the end of the table where Indy and Thiago were laughing heartily.

He shrugged to answer Ava's question.

"You like her, right?"

He sighed, unable to control the blush heating his face, and settled his attention on the plate that had just been deposited in front of him. "So much. I always have."

"Ha! I knew it." Ava nudged his elbow. "Took you long enough to admit it."

Throwing a dirty glare at his friend, he grabbed a fork. "Just taking things slow. I can't screw it up."

"I'm rooting for you." Rowan grinned from Ava's other side.

"Thanks, bro."

"Indy sort of got into an argument outside the washroom," Ava informed quietly after taking a long sip of her wine.

Miles frowned. "What? With whom?" It wasn't like Indy to pick up a fight unless she was provoked.

"Tara." The mere mention of her name made annoyance roll down his spine. "I don't know what the matter is with that girl, but she won't leave Indy alone."

"She's just a jealous brat," he bit out frustratingly. "What happened?"

"We were just leaving to come out here when Tara asked Indy if she was aware that dating you would discredit her objectivity."

Scoffing, Miles met Rowan's bewildered stare. "That's bullshit."

"Tammy needs to move on," Rowan mumbled.

"You mean Tara?" Ava chuckled.

"Whatever her name is needs to stop acting like a child. Indy is allowed to date whoever she wants."

"Did she take her claws out?" Miles asked, knowing all too well that Indy was perfectly capable of defending herself. She was excellent at staying professional, neutral, and objective when she was working. She would never let an envious coworker undermine her.

Ava smiled. "What do you think? Indy will always defend and stand up for you. She does it with so much class, too."

He met with crystal blue eyes from across the room, bringing a smile to his mouth. *That's my girl.* It would take so much more than petty remarks to let someone else step on her fire. Indy knew what she wanted, what she fought for, and there was nothing sexier to him than this empowering woman.

He winked, then turned back to Ava.

"Marry her," Rowan said.

I will, his head responded.

Indy was slowly, yet surely, turning his cold heart into something that craved for a reason to beat. Consuming his every thought. Becoming nearly as important to him as racing.

His passion, his devotion for racing had never been beaten by anything or anyone. But his heart was screaming at him to give Indy the unoccupied space to be filled with something he had been craving for: happiness.

The realisation should have terrified him, but only now was he thrilled by this unnerving yet exciting feeling, helpless by the fact he wanted to be good for her. That he simply *wanted* her.

Step by step, he would hand out his heart to Indy. But was she willing to accept his demons? His scars? His past and broken pieces? The small smile she sent him from the other side of the table was proof that, yes, she wanted him. Armour and all.

CHAPTER TWENTY-SEVEN

♟ *MIAMI, UNITED STATES OF AMERICA*

THE SOFT KNOCK on her door brought a smile to her lips. Indy looked up from the book she'd been reading to check the time—nearly eight p.m.

Later than she had anticipated.

When she opened the door, Miles was leaning against the doorway, a smug smile on his lips.

"Can I help you?" She feigned annoyance by huffing. "I was in the middle of reading."

He peered behind her shoulder. "I bet it was a steamy scene."

"Do you want me to show you?"

Mischief shimmered in his gaze as he lifted a card—the key to her room. "Actually, this is a very creative way of telling me you want to hook up. Giving your key to Ava and asking her to give it to me."

Indy shrugged. "Took you long enough to get the hint."

As he walked past her, the brush of his shoulder against hers made electricity barrel through her bones. "You could've handed it to me yourself."

"Where's the fun in that?" she teased, closing the door. "So, I was wondering what you do with the photos I send you."

Ever since they'd landed in Miami days ago, they hadn't been able to catch a moment alone, but their nights had been filled with text exchanges—photos, to be specific. Indy in the bath. Miles' naked chest reflecting in the mirror. Another photo of him a while later, drops of water glistening on his abs, his arousal straining against the white towel. A peek of Indy's thong. A selfie with her shirt unbuttoned, giving him a glimpse of her lacy bra. Later at night, a hand shielding her bare breasts as she lay naked and alone in her bed.

"Take a wild guess, Daisy."

"I have an idea."

Maybe he'd fisted himself in the shower, thinking of all the photos they had sent to each other and listening to their recording from a few nights ago. Indy had certainly used her vibrator every single night, wishing he would come and seek her out.

Her hands trembled with anticipation as she wondered what was about to happen. During the post-Grand Prix dinner, all they had done was look at each other, even from either ends of the large table. Secret, stolen glances, even when she was busy talking to someone. Secret smiles and heated looks.

He looked so handsome with his linen pants and matching shirt, his hair ruffled like he'd passed his fingers through it. Indy was ready to take her clothes off, but it was his frown that stopped her in her tracks.

"You were painting." It wasn't a question. He turned to her, his brows high.

"I was," she admitted, taking a seat on the edge of the mattress.

Miles didn't say anything. He threw her keycard onto the

bed, though, which elicited confusion to rock through her. "I'll be back."

"Wow, if you're not interested in me, just tell me," she teased—just because she loved to give him shit.

Before he could walk towards the door, he went up to her, grabbing her chin. The softness in his gaze made all the anxiety coiling in her gut taper off. "You know how I feel about you, Indy. I'm just going back to my room to grab something."

"So you're coming back?" Indy wasn't sure why she was so worried about him abandoning her.

The pad of his thumb grazed the corner of her lips. "Always for you," he whispered. "You should change, though. I'm taking you somewhere."

"Where?"

"I know places."

※

MILES CAME BACK twenty minutes later, holding a basket with a jumper tied around his shoulders.

"Ready?" he asked, grabbing a sketch pad from the desk along with a few paintbrushes and tubes of acrylic paint. Miles wandered his gaze all over her physique, like he didn't quite know where to look, his eyes brightening. "You look beautiful."

"Thank you." She smiled timidly, as if he rendered her powerless. As though she lost all senses of herself whenever he looked at her like *this*.

"Come on." He extended his hand, blushing when their fingers entwined. "We need to hurry."

They walked out of the hotel holding hands. If there was one thing Miles was a professional at, it was ignoring and not giving a damn about what people said about him. He proudly walked by her side, his chin held high, as Indy noticed everyone looking at them and snapping pictures.

"Hey, Miles?" one fan wearing an Imperium t-shirt asked as they passed the hotel's gate. "Can we take a pic?"

"Sorry," he said, "but I'm on a date right now, and I need you all to respect my privacy. I'll come back in the morning to take photos with you."

Indy tried to keep up with his hasty footfalls as they walked to the beach. He talked about everything and anything before stopping on the sand where there weren't too many people around.

Indy lifted her gaze to the sky, painted in a multitude of colour splashes—orange filaments weaving through pink clouds, waves of blue and violet dancing across the beautiful painting. She felt her breath catch at the sight, Miles' fingers letting go of hers.

Still in awe of the scenery, she looked over to where Miles stood, the sounds of waves gently crashing with each other filling her ears. She caught his tender gaze, the golden light falling over him. He was smiling softly, complete devotion etched on his expression.

When something slipped out of his grasp, he snapped back to reality. "Fuck!" He turned around and ran after the blanket being blown away by the wind.

When he came back, cheeks rosy and hair untamed, a laugh bubbled out of her. The sound of her delight caused him to chuckle, and a nanosecond later, he was shaking his head whilst grinning broadly.

At that moment, nothing around them existed. Indy managed to tune out all the sounds ringing around her, capturing this instant as he smiled down at her like she was the embodiment of sunlight.

Miles settled the blanket on the sand just as Indy stepped out of her sandals. She sat down, observing him take out the painting equipment along with snacks and bottled water he poured into two wineglasses.

"This is fancy."

She squeezed some paint onto the palette as he opened a packet of Sour Patch Kids. He threw a sweet into the air and caught it swiftly before giving her a roguish wink.

"Anything for you," he murmured. Digging further into the basket, he retrieved a vibrant, pink flower. Delicately tucking a strand of her hair behind an ear, Miles let his touch linger upon her skin. He popped the flower behind her ear, smiling. "Beautiful."

"Where'd you get that?" She grazed a petal with her finger.

"Plucked it from a bush outside of the hotel," he admitted without an ounce of guilt weaving through his tone.

"Delinquent."

"I guess being with you makes me reckless."

Then he took out a little vintage digital camera, and snapped a picture as she burst out in laughter.

"What else do you have in that basket, Mary Poppins?"

Miles mirrored her delight then set the camera down before propping himself onto an elbow. He popped another candy into his mouth, humming in pleasure.

"Man, eating shitty food after a GP is my favourite thing to do."

"I bet it is. I couldn't do what you do. Train hard all year long, follow a strict diet."

"I'm just very hard on myself for everything. Some drivers aren't as harsh with themselves as I am."

She reached for a sweet. "I think that being hard on yourself can be a good quality."

"How do you do that?" he asked softly. "How do you always see the good in every situation?"

Indy lifted her shoulders in a small shrug, smiling as a response.

He didn't press and handed her a paintbrush.

There was something so innately comforting about this— sitting under the setting sun, snacks scattered around them whilst painting, the soothing sound of waves gently crawling to the shore as background noise.

When he gave her a square canvas and set another one before him, she stared at him dumbfounded. "Where did you even get all those things?"

"Ava," he simply said. "She's got my back."

She smiled at the thought of her two friends having each other's backs no matter what. "I love that. Thank you for doing all of this."

Indy sighed in contentment. She'd dreamed of this her entire life. She was aware that Miles didn't act like this with anyone but her, so she wouldn't ruin this for him. He didn't trust easily, and being able to catch a glimpse of Miles' vulnerability, to have his trust, was akin to holding a ball made of crystal—fragile, unique, and precious. She wouldn't break it.

"Would you look at this view?" she asked quietly, her stare wandering across the breathtaking sky.

When his fingertips caressed her forearm, she shivered, but she tried convincing herself they were caused by the cool wind. "I am. It's spectacular."

But when she turned to look at him, wanting to see the raw awe on his expression, she found him watching her adoringly. The look of affection itself was enough to make her heart clench.

"You're such a flirt," she fired at him.

He laughed heartily before shifting into a seated position. "Only with you."

"I'm honoured."

"You should be," he said smugly. "So, what's going on inside that pretty head of yours?"

Indy shrugged. "Oh, you know, the usual same. Nothing for you to worry about."

She could feel how intensely he was observing her reaction as she painted. "Don't do this, don't act like it's going to bother me to talk about what's making you upset. I know you're the cheerful friend who always lifts others up, the one who comes running when someone calls for help. I know you're the optimistic, bright, incredible girl who loves to say that everything's going to be all right. Who always says that she's fine. Except you don't let yourself ask for help when you struggle. So talk to me, okay?"

"I don't want to ruin the date."

"Indy... Please, stop. I want you to trust me the way I trust you. I'm here to listen or just be a shoulder to cry on. Normally, I wouldn't push you to talk about it, but knowing that you're bottling your feelings inside is hurting me. Seeing you in pain is literally destroying me."

She swallowed down the knot inside her throat. "I broke down today."

"So?" Indy didn't respond, already feeling tears burn her eyes. Gently, he lifted her chin, obliging her to look at the concern etched on his face. "Baby, that's okay. You're allowed to cry, to let go. You're strong and brave, and crying doesn't make you weak."

With her free hand, she wiped a tear that had escaped of its free will. "I feel pressured."

"I know you do," he murmured. "It means that you take your job to heart. I'm proud of you for speaking about it."

"You're proud of me?" That was not the point, but these were words she'd rarely heard throughout her life. It was odd how a few words could spark her determination.

"So much. Always."

Indy sniffed, blinking up at the sky. She couldn't control her small smile when Miles leaned forward to peck her cheek—collecting a tear. "I'm proud of myself too. I think I'm doing a great job at broadcasting, conducting the interviews, and being a sports journalist in general. I'm making good progress, but... I don't know, I just can't help but compare myself to others. I overthink a lot, and it gives me anxiety. It's like I can't get those thoughts out of my head no matter how hard I convince myself that I'm enough."

"Comparing yourself to others is inevitable," he said softly. Indy frowned and looked at him while he busied himself painting. What? She didn't know, but the concentration on his face was utterly adorable. "It happens to you too?"

"All the time."

"But you're the best. You're the World Champion."

"So? Doesn't mean I don't crave to be different and do better. I love Thiago's driving style, especially the way he masters the late brakings. Rowan is a phenomenal driver in the rain, if not the best I've ever seen. Charlie has perfect control of his car and is excellent during a race start. I might have three championships under my belt, I might be the best in some people's regard, but it doesn't mean that I *feel* like I'm the best."

"And what do you do to stop comparing yourself to them?"

"I work harder to become better. And I'm not saying that you need to push yourself to become someone you're not happy with, because I know you feel comfortable in your own skin. *I love how fierce you are, how strong and inspiring you are.* I've already told you, and I'll say it a million times again, but you're doing an amazing job. When you step into a world like this one, it's obvious that people are going to compare your work with someone else's. It's obvious that it's not going to be easy, because life's never pink and full of butterflies. But Indy, it's your first time experiencing life, too. Don't be this hard on yourself. Don't let anyone break you. You're way too full of life to listen to someone's bullshit."

His last word made her chuckle, but it didn't conceal the tear streaming down her face. God, why did she always cry so easily?

"Life doesn't stop because someone didn't like what I said or did," she whispered, repeating the words he'd said to her a couple of months ago.

"No, it doesn't, baby. It's your life, you're living your dream, and you need to get inside your head that your happiness cannot be defined by someone's expectations. You're doing a phenomenal job at what you're doing, so you have to focus on the positive outcome. Not the negative. You're simply incredible, Indy. Fuck everyone and everything that make you feel less than that."

"Thank you, Huxley. I—I'm sorry," she said frustratingly.

"Come here." He shifted until he could pull her into his chest without knocking over the paint supplies. She exhaled, tightening her embrace. "What are you sorry for?"

After basking in his warmth for a moment, they separated and went back to focusing on their respective paintings. "For crying. For being so...sensitive?"

"There's no need to apologise for being yourself."

Swallowing, she took a deep breath. "When I was younger, I wasn't allowed to cry. It annoyed my parents to see me cry over the most stupid things, and it made me think that I was weak. I had to learn to contain my emotions and cry when I was locked inside my room." Despite it all, her parents were the best and she wouldn't trade them for anyone else.

"I'm sorry, Indy." Some sort of gloom had misted over his eyes. "You've grown into a courageous and empowering woman. I hope you know that."

She nodded. "And I'm also sorry that you're feeling this way towards your friends."

"Don't be sorry for me." He caressed her knee. "It's part of the sport."

"For the record, I think you're deserving of your three championships. You might even become a four-time World Champion, and you totally deserve it. You make driving a Formula 1 car look so easy, but it's your mindset that I admire so much."

"Your words mean a lot." He was focused on what he was doing, but he rapidly glanced her way. "We both put a mask on when we face the world, but I've always loved the fact that we don't have to do it around each other."

"Me too."

The silence falling between them was never uncomfortable or awkward. It was always peaceful. Between small smiles and secret glances, Indy noticed the slight tremor in his hands, the stars in his eyes, and the blush on the back of his neck that he kept rubbing.

Was he nervous? Indy could never fathom how this powerful, sexy man could lose control around her.

"What are you thinking of right now?" she asked as he popped a candy into his mouth.

"I'm thinking that I'm an idiot for waiting so long to ask you out. That you're one in a million. That you're the only woman I've opened up to without feeling like I'm being judged. I'm thinking that I really like you, Indy."

"I really like you, too, and I'm not going anywhere," she whispered, holding his gaze. "I know you like your solitude and that you don't need anyone but yourself. But I'm here, and you can have me if you want. I will wait for you, Huxley."

There was a flicker of pain perceptible in his irises. He grabbed her free hand, brushing his lips over her knuckles. "I don't deserve you. Thank you for seeing me."

It was her turn to kiss the centre of his palm. "Always."

He grinned, and the entire world came to a halt. No beauty in this universe could compare to the masterpiece that was Miles Huxley.

"So, I keep waiting for you to walk into the paddock wearing a shirt claiming that you love me unconditionally and that I'm your entire world."

Throwing his head back, he barked out a laugh, the sound warming her chest. "Please, I'll wear that when you least expect it, and only if you invite me to your podcast."

Surprise rattled through her. The man who didn't like interviews, who always answered coldly to reporters, wanted to be a guest on her podcast. "Really?"

"Yeah. I think it's obvious that the people like seeing me with you. You're kind and funny, and you'll know how to put me at ease. If I want them to see that I'm not an asshole outside of racing, I want *you* to show them."

"Well, I'm honoured."

She'd always wanted to invite Miles onto her podcast, so hearing the enthusiasm laced in his tone made delight crash over her. She was certain that everyone would fall in love with him if they knew how good of a man he truly was.

Just as she finished her painting, she shivered. The colours in the sky had faded into more sombre shades, indicating that soon enough, the moon would claim its place, and the stars would shine.

Miles grabbed the jumper he'd taken with him and pulled it over her head, untucking her hair from the collar. "There." He pecked her nose, making her cheeks heat up.

Indy thanked him, controlling herself from taking a whiff of the piece of clothing. The scent of Miles' cologne was intoxicating.

And every time he acted like this—tender, loving—and talked to her like she was genuinely amazing and worthy of good things, it made Indy's world rattle. As if he couldn't stand having her on the borders of his universe, needing to nestle her into its centre and keeping her there.

But did Miles know that he'd already become her centre of gravity a long time ago? That no matter what she did to build a fortress around her, she still gravitated towards him?

He suggested going back to the hotel, and she agreed. He snapped a photo of the mess scattered atop the blanket, complimenting her painting. She'd drawn the sky, splashes of pink tangled with orange and red—as if the heavens had screamed of burning love.

"What did you paint?" she asked, leaning over his shoulder to watch his own masterpiece.

He tucked a strand of hair behind her ear. "A sunrise."

"Why?"

"It makes me think of you," he confessed before brushing a kiss to her temple. "These colours remind me of you, just like a sunrise because they're bright. Because a sunrise is exactly the way you make me feel: happy and alive. A sunrise is a promise to a good day, a good life, with brightness around us even when I surrounded myself with darkness for a while. Sunrise means hope to me."

Wrapping her arms around his shoulders, she sighed happily when he returned the embrace. She could feel the wild beating of his heart against her own. "You can't just say that and not kiss me."

He chuckled against the crook of her neck. "Trust me, I want to kiss you so badly, but I stand by my rule; I don't kiss on the first date."

"You better ask me out again, then."

He gripped her chin, forcing her to look into his mesmerising eyes. "I will. In fact, you're coming to Romeo and Ez's game tomorrow night as my date."

"Wow," she teased. "So eager to be my man."

His smile was broad and unrestrained. Just for her. "You have no idea. I like to consider myself lucky."

CHAPTER TWENTY-EIGHT

NEW YORK CITY, NEW YORK

Well, Miles was absolutely, utterly, undoubtedly fucked.

Surrounded by the entire Bailey family, he was supposed to act like he didn't feel a damn thing for Indigo. How was he supposed to do it? Especially as she walked up the stairs to the VIP box, wearing Romeo Quinn's jersey paired with a short skirt and knee-high boots.

She was talking to one of the New York Nightingales' marketing managers, her signature, beautiful smile plastered to her lips.

Miles forgot about the drink he had brought to his lips when their gazes collided. Her eyes were full of mirth and mischief, yet he had to keep his poker face on. Had to pretend like he didn't want to pull her into his arms and whisper in her ear that she belonged right there.

The woman Indy was talking to left, and Indy walked up to her parents who were chatting with Henry.

Miles felt content to be in the company of these people, cheering on his best friends who were warming up. Perhaps one day he could bring Charlie, Thiago, and Rowan along with their girlfriends to a game and let his two worlds collide.

"Is there something you're not telling me, Miles?"

Realising his perusal had lingered on Indy's beaming smile, he tightened his jaw and glared at Kai, whose gaze was settled on the ice rink below.

Romeo's face appeared on the jumbotron as he was passing the puck to one of his teammates, eliciting roars from the crowd. Miles smiled at the sight of his friend—the captain of the New York Nightingales and one of the best forwards in the league— who had worked so hard to earn this position.

"So you're not going to answer?" Kai asked then. "Deny or confirm anything?"

"I don't even know what you're talking about, Malakai."

Kai snorted. "*Ouch*. Full name and all? You must be extra grouchy today. Anyway, how's it going with my sister?"

"What?"

"How's the whole roommate thing going?"

For a second, he thought Kai knew about their date, the late nights, the secret touches, but how? Photos had been circulating all over the internet for months—rumours, but still. It was a mystery why Kai hadn't confronted him yet.

"I like her," he confessed, slipping his free hand in the pocket of his jeans. "Living with her, I mean. She's less messy than you, even though she's pure chaos walking on sunshine. We have dinner together when we're not travelling. I cook for her, and she makes the most delicious desserts. I bought her painting at the auction a couple of weeks ago—yeah, you already know that—and we hung it up in the living room above the sofa. She loves taking Rosie on walks. She brings Teddy breakfast every time she goes to the farmer's market."

Indy truly belonged there. With him. And that was all that mattered to him.

In a short amount of time, she had made his penthouse a home, her own heart a safe place for him, allowing him to carve his name in the organ and giving him the power to shatter or protect it. Still, he needed to convince himself that she wasn't leaving. He needed to give her a reason to stay.

"Say it."

"Say what?" That he was utterly obsessed with Indy? No fucking way. He didn't want to tell Kai just yet.

"Admit that I was right. Living and being friends with Indy has brought nothing but positivity into your life."

"Go fuck yourself. I'd rather have a puck thrown in my face than ever admit I was wrong."

Aside from the amusement sparkling in Kai's gaze, there was a softer emotion gleaming there. He nodded, clearing his throat. "Glad it all worked out, though."

"She's giving me grey hair," Miles continued, chuckling. "Shoes all around the foyer. Clothes scattered here and there. But I know that she's dyslexic, and it appears that it can cause her to be disorganised. That's what I read when I did my research."

And truth was, Miles liked her messy side. He liked every version of her—he wouldn't have her any other way.

Kai paused. "She told you about her dyslexia?"

"Yes. I've been helping her out with her work. Bought her a couple of audiobooks I sent to her phone, too."

Raw surprise was drawn onto his best friend's face. Kai blinked, then blew out a breath, slowly nodding to himself. "Wow. Okay. Cool. Cool. Cool."

"You're being weird."

"No, I'm totally fine. I'll be back. Need a refill."

Miles glanced down. "Your glass is full."

Kai downed his beer. "Is it?"

Sometimes Miles genuinely wondered why he was best friends with Malakai Bailey.

※

"How are you doing, my love?"

Miles instantly smiled at Lisa when she took a seat by his side. She offered him some popcorn which he gratefully grabbed a handful of.

The second period was about to end, and the Nightingales had scored two goals, both assists from their captain, Romeo. Ezra was currently in the penalty box, his busted lip being tended to.

"I'm good," he answered. "How about you?"

"I'm doing amazing! I have so many projects which I'm excited about. Thank you for inviting us to the Grand Prix, by the way. I love seeing you behind that steering wheel and captivating the entire track with your skills and speed."

"Don't make me cry, Lisa," he grumbled through the lump of emotion that had formed in his throat.

"I'm just telling the truth. Seeing you go through all that shit, and watching you grow into this inspiring man... You're breaking records, and I'm so happy to be able to see you succeed."

Miles may not have a mother, but Lisa Bailey had always been a motherly figure to him. And Zach, who'd become Henry's best friend through the years, was akin to an uncle for Miles.

As Miles was about to voice his gratitude to Lisa, voices boomed from the other side of the room. He turned towards the source of disturbance, chuckling under his breath at the sight of Indy and Kai standing and throwing their arms in the air.

"Ref!" Indy shouted. "That's bullshit!"

"Yeah!" Kai bellowed. "That's a penalty shot, bro!"

They started screaming profanities, and Miles shook his head whilst laughing.

Lisa nudged his side, and he realised he had been staring at the stunning blonde for a few beats too long. "Indy is not making your life a misery, is she?"

"Never. She's truly incredible. Fun. Makes life exciting in a way I didn't know could be possible." The words had escaped of their free will, but he didn't regret confessing to Lisa.

There was a knowing gleam in the woman's eyes. "You like her, don't you?"

He took a breath in, looking back over to where Indy stood with her hands on her hips, an aggravated expression on her face. He'd continue to lie to Kai, but the truth could never be hidden from Lisa. "She makes me want to be better. I haven't felt this way in forever, and there's just something about her that makes me want to stay, grow, be alive. So to answer your question, yeah, I really do. There's this consistency about her that keeps me grounded. I love that she always lifts others up, and I admire her so much for that. She pours her heart into everything she does, and it's mind-blowing how gentle her soul is. She's a fighter—she doesn't look down or turn around, she just does everything with her head held high and, honestly, Lisa, she just renders me speechless."

"Miles... For someone who can't find the words to say, you know exactly how to describe what you feel for my daughter." Lisa smiled, then stood up. She kissed the crown of Miles' head, whispering, "Thank you for taking care of my baby. She needs someone like you in her life. You keep this wild girl grounded."

But did Lisa know that Indy was his anchor, too?

"STOP STARING at my ass and answer my question."

Miles blinked, darting his gaze upwards to find Indy's. He shrugged sheepishly as he followed her into the crowded pub, unable to control himself from looking again at her backside hugged by this tiny thing she called a skirt. What he hated most, though, was Romeo's name displayed on her back like she belonged to him, or something.

"But you're so beautiful to look at."

She scoffed. "You're lucky I like you. So? Do you want something to drink?"

He waved her off. "Just whatever you're getting for yourself is fine with me."

Indy didn't drink alcohol in his presence anymore, but still, she taunted him by saying, "I'm getting the girliest drink, then."

He made sure his annoyed groan could be heard through the loud bass of the music. "What have I done to deserve this? I hate you."

Halting and pivoting, she faced him, and his chest nearly came in contact with hers. She lifted a brow in defiance. God, didn't the devilish glint shimmering in her gaze and that smirk dancing on the corner of her lips turn him on.

She fisted his shirt and pulled him towards her. "Hate sex? Yes, please."

"Indy," he warned, looking behind her shoulder to where Kai had sat down.

"I dare you."

Then, she left, squeezing between dancing patrons to access the bar.

§

RUBBING HIS TENSE JAW, Miles observed the steady sway of her hips as she walked towards the booth he was sitting in, Romeo in tow with drinks in both hands.

Miles hadn't listened to a single word Kai said. Instead, he'd watched Indy and Romeo talk as they waited for their beverages to be served, standing close to one another due to the lack of space around them. At one point, Indy had engulfed Romeo in a tight hug, and even after separating, he'd kept his arm looped around her shoulders. What the fuck had he said to make her laugh so loudly? And why the hell was his pulse thrumming any time he would glance at the jersey clinging to her chest?

Then, Miles had watched a woman come up to Indy and ask for a photo. She looked so emotional that he felt his chest tighten with pride.

Now, as she slid into the booth and was forced to sit in his lap—thanks to half of the hockey team hogging the space—Miles looped an arm around her waist, placing his chin atop her shoulder.

There was just something about touching her that he loved so thoroughly.

She was his anchor. His steadiness in an ocean rattled by reckless waves.

She was his favourite place. His getaway.

"Hi, stud."

He smiled, then glanced at Kai who was busy showing something on his phone to Ezra. Neither of them were paying attention to their surroundings, but it was only a matter of time until Kai would notice where Indy was sitting.

"Hey," he murmured. "What was that about?"

She leaned forward to snatch a mozzarella stick from the table. Miles suppressed a grunt as she rubbed herself on him. It was already an effort not to let the blood rush south, but he was fairly certain that she was provoking him. "Please be more specific, darling."

Kai looked up, frowning. "Jesus fuck. Get a room. Wait. No, don't do that, but why are you sitting on Miles, Ind?"

"Do you want me to sit on Ezra?" she retorted, causing Miles to pinch her hip.

"I'm not opposed to that." Ezra bristled dramatically when he met Miles' cold glare.

"Nah," Kai said, looking back down at his phone. "You're a player. I'm not letting my sister near you."

"Well, damn. For the record, I don't sleep around that much anymore."

"Since you met your new neighbour, right?" Indy asked, smiling teasingly.

"What? Who?" Miles asked in unison with Kai.

Ezra blushed furiously. "Doesn't matter. She's got a boyfriend."

Okay, Miles really needed to catch up with his friends.

"Well, shit."

When Kai and Ezra were back to minding their business, Miles leaned closer to whisper in her ear. "You want me to ask about Romeo, don't you? You want me to tell you how much it's pissing me off to see another man's hands on you? How I'm fuming inside at the thought of someone else touching you?"

She tensed at the sound of his low voice, and Miles took the opportunity to drag her backwards into his chest.

His hand slid up her bare thigh, her breath hitching at the contact. "You want me to tell you how much I hate seeing you wear his jersey?"

"Huxley." Her voice was strangled. "Come on, have some self-respect."

He huffed out a dry laugh, applying pressure on her leg. "You're such a brat."

"I'm loving the compliment." She turned to him, smiling. "What are you going to do about it?"

She could probably feel him growing, right?

Oh, she could. Because she started moving, pretending to make herself more comfortable before leaning forward to grab her glass.

Holding her hips, he forced her to stay sill. "Damn it, Indy. Don't move."

"Why?" She blinked, feigning innocence.

"You know why," he gritted out. "I've been trying my hardest to be a gentleman all night long, and I'm not going to drag you into the washroom. So please, just stay still until we have to leave."

"Are you still going to be a gentleman when we get back to the hotel?"

His temper sparked, and his jaw tightened. "Only good girls get rewarded."

She nodded, her pulse racing beneath his fingers when he pushed her hair away from her neck. "Okay."

"Do you want to get out of—"

"Okay, I can't do this anymore," Kai snapped, frowning at them. The confusion and frustration in his eyes made Miles' stomach bottom out, guilt consuming his senses for still not saying the truth to his best friend. "What's going on between you two?"

"Are you aware they've been flirting right under your nose?" Ezra commented around a mouthful of nachos.

"What the fuck?!"

⁂

"Kai's face was epic."

Unable to contain his laughter, Miles tucked her into his side as they walked towards the hotel's entrance, his arm secured around her shoulders. "We need to stop fucking with him."

"But he really believed that you were in love with me," she countered, still smiling widely.

Why, do you think, would Kai believe that? Perhaps because of the way Miles had clung to her the entire evening. That he only talked to her.

He tensed, knots forming inside his throat. As he opened the door, he whispered, "Would that be a bad thing?"

She glanced over at him, shrugging. "Kai's a good guy. He would just want me to be happy."

"So would I." He found her hand, interlacing their fingers

together. They'd walked from the pub to the hotel, laughing and holding hands as if the world didn't matter.

"Are you going to tell him? The truth about us?"

His heartbeat sped up. "I will one day. Just let me have you for myself for a while longer, okay?"

She squeezed his hand. "Okay."

"I had your bags moved into my room," he announced as they stepped inside the lift.

"Why?" She turned around slowly, lifting a perplexed eyebrow.

"You know exactly why," he murmured huskily, looking at her full lips. "We wouldn't have made it to your room. You would have begged to spend the night tangled in my bed sheets."

The salacious gleam in her eyes made his breath hitch. He backed her up until she was against the wall, her hands fisting the front of his shirt. God, he couldn't wait to rip that fucking jersey off of her and replace it with one of his own—well, at least with team merch that had his name on it. "Doubtful."

"Can I change your mind in"—he glanced at the numbers going up. They were already on the fourth floor, and their room was on the fifteenth—"less than thirty seconds?"

Challenge flashed in her eyes, and she gave him that seductive smile that made him more aroused than ever. "I dare you."

CHAPTER TWENTY-NINE

♀ *NEW YORK CITY, NEW YORK*

Indy's mind went into a frenzy the instant he crashed his mouth to hers, swallowing her gasp like he owned every sound she emitted.

He pushed her further into the wall, pressing his chest to hers like he couldn't bear any sliver of distance that stood between them. His fingers cupped the back of her head, tangling with her hair as he kissed her fervently.

Miles kissed her like she was the air he breathed. Like this was the last time he'd touch her. Like he just couldn't get enough.

"You drive me insane," he mumbled against her swollen lips before attacking them again like a starved man. Indy moaned, melting into him as she clung to his shirt.

The moment he pushed her legs apart by moving his thigh in between them, Indy felt like combusting. She started tugging at his hair, eliciting a grunt to rise from his throat. His rock-hard length pressed into her hip, and she writhed at the feel of him.

All this push and pull, years of longing and pining and daydreams burst into fireworks as that invisible string between them finally snapped, allowing their crying hearts to be aligned and frantically drum in symphony. No one had ever made her feel this way. No one had ever held a power so devastating yet exciting over her. There was no way she could fight the alchemy, and it looked like he was succumbing too.

His hand bared her throat, lips skimming her jawline. "Indy—"

But then, the lift stopped.

Miles pulled back, the smug smirk spreading across his lips only making her want to jump and wrap her legs around his waist.

Someone cleared their throat, and Miles turned around. "Good evening," he said to the couple staring amusedly at them, his voice a gravelly rasp that made her spine tingle, then pulled her out of the lift.

She beamed, following his hasty footfalls. "Have a lovely night!"

The very instant they stepped into his dark room, he pushed her against the door, his hand slipping to her throat as he claimed her mouth.

"Huxley," she breathed out as he pecked the side of her neck, letting her fingers entwine with his soft hair. The mere contact of his lips upon her blazing skin was already making her pant.

"What, baby?" he rasped, sliding his large hands under her jersey. "Tell me what you want."

"You."

His lips brushed the spot below her ear. "What was that? Didn't quite hear you."

"I want you." She didn't care if she sounded desperate. She just needed to feel him everywhere. His hands. Fingers. Mouth. Tongue. Everything.

"Yeah?" He cupped her breasts and kneaded them through her bra. A groan rumbled in his throat as he pinched a pebbled nipple before dragging his thumb across the piercing. "You want me to fuck you? You want me to make you understand that I'm the only one who can make you come so hard that you see stars? That I find you to be the prettiest when you whimper, and beg, and then come with my name on your lips?"

Trying her hardest to hold her whimper in, she failed. The sound of her desperation made him smirk—a triumphant king. "Yes."

Stepping back, he tore his shirt off by the back of the collar. Indy's mouth had never felt drier at the sight of his tanned, muscled chest, honed by hours of intense physical training, highlighted by the city's glow filtering through the window.

"On your knees, Indigo."

She couldn't do anything but follow his command, sinking down onto the carpeted floor. His smirk was a reflection to the way he felt—victorious. Miles had always been a man in control, but Indy needed him to snap. Break. Shatter. He thought he was having the upper hand right now, but he didn't know that Indy would challenge him all the same.

The pad of his thumb ran across her lower lip. "God, you're beautiful. I've seen you wear expensive dresses, smile and talk in front of cameras, pose under flashing lights. But right now, you on your knees for me, ready to take my cock? You're goddamn breathtaking."

She gave him a smile that made his jaw go slack. "Thank you, stud."

Then, she unbuttoned and unzipped his jeans, her knuckles grazing over his erection. His breath caught as she held eye contact before pulling the trousers down his thighs.

"You've been such a teasing brat today." He gathered her hair into a make-shift ponytail, his jaw clenching when she rubbed the heel of her palm against the length of him. "Strutting around in that tiny thing you call a skirt. Wearing Romeo's name like you're his or something. Giving me the most painful hard-on in a crowded pub as you rub your perfect ass over me."

SPEEDING INTO OVERDRIVE

She tilted her head, giving him a taunting smile. "Oh, I'm sorry. That sounds terrible."

He scoffed. She loved the disbelief in his tone. The arrogance in his demeanour. The ember of annoyance blazing around his pupils. "Are you? Come on then, show me how you beg for forgiveness."

Closing her thighs in search of friction, she pulled down his briefs and let his hard cock spring free. Its head was already leaking pre-cum, and knowing he was so turned on only amplified her confidence. Indy wrapped her hand around the thick base, giving it a slow pump as she watched the way he licked his lips leisurely.

Miles breathed heavily, his gaze dropping to where they were connected. She pumped her fist, slightly twisting it as she reached the crown before swiping her thumb over the bead of moisture to spread it around. He was big, throbbing with need, and it made more arousal dampen her underwear.

Keeping her gaze locked to his, Indy wrapped her lips around the head as she dragged her fist down to the base. Miles whimpered as her tongue swept across the slit, his walls shattering instantly.

His grip around her hair tightened as he bucked his hips into her mouth. Indy sank down, taking as much as she could whilst using her hand to pump what she couldn't fit into her mouth.

"Fuck," he groaned, causing her to huff out a quiet laugh. "You take my cock so goddamn well."

Her tongue swirled across the crown, and she tugged firmly on the base, which caused Miles to unleash himself. His hips snapped into her mouth, his movements frantic as he moaned loudly when she sucked harder.

She took him until he hit the back of her throat, her small hands braced on his thighs, just as his fingers dug into her skull. She breathed through her nose and looked up, adoring his expression full of lust and desire. His brows bunched together as he tipped his head back, guiding her movements with his hands.

She watched his abdomen clench, his lips part, and his thighs tremble. He pried her away, breathing heavily.

"That's enough."

Miles pulled her onto her feet, wiping the dribble of saliva off her chin.

She blinked innocently. "Have you forgiven me yet?"

He tsked. "Not so fast." She knew he wasn't mad at her, per se. Jealous and possessive, perhaps, but not angry. He just loved having this control over her, and quite frankly, she enjoyed it as well. "Get on the bed."

She obliged after taking her boots off as he switched the light on. She observed him take his jeans and briefs off, tossing them somewhere in the room before rushing towards her, his eyes an onyx pool of desire.

He grabbed her by the throat, sealing their lips in a kiss that left her breathless. Her knees sank into the mattress, her hands trailing across his hard torso. She wrapped her hand around his slick shaft, eliciting a moan from the back of his throat.

As though his self-control snapped whenever it came to her.

As though she, too, held some kind of power over him that could make him shatter to pieces.

She broke away from the kiss and took his cock back into her mouth.

"Shit," he whimpered as she massaged his balls with her left hand. "Those lips look perfect around me. Thought of this moment all week long."

Indy moaned in response.

The noises of utter pleasure echoing inside the room were music to her ears. "Just like that, baby. You feel so good. You're so good at sucking my cock."

She felt his hands roam all over her back until he leaned forward, tugging her skirt up to her waist.

"Are you trying to kill me?" His rough palm rubbed at her bottom and gave it a harsh slap. She moaned around his cock, feeling it twitch when her nails grazed its underside. "Dark purple?"

She pulled away to catch her breath. "Just like you asked."

He smirked. "You knew I would seek you out tonight, didn't you?"

"I'm a woman with confidence."

"And I fucking love that."

Indy wrapped her lips around the reddish head, swirling her tongue around the crown as she pumped him in tandem with the help of both hands. Miles' whimper sent a jolt of electricity down her spine, then she felt his cock twitch again.

"You need to stop now, or else I'll come," he warned.

She looked up at him through her lashes, shaking her head. The tip of his cock hit the back of her throat as he fucked her mouth relentlessly. "Fuck, Indy. This feels so good. I can't last any longer."

His guttural groan reverberated off the walls as he came hard, trembling and chanting her name like a prayer.

He was panting by the time she rose to her knees, his thumbs caressing her cheekbones.

"Swallow." She loved the flush on his cheeks, the stars in his gaze—all caused by her.

She obliged, holding his gaze.

"Open."

Sticking her tongue out, she smirked when he grabbed her jaw, grunting. Then, he spit into her mouth, and Indy moaned again. This side of him? The man who disrespected her in the sheets and treated her like a queen out of it? It was her favourite. He didn't treat her like she was made of glass, like she'd break.

"Good girl," he rasped as she swallowed again. "Filthy, good fucking girl."

Miles got onto the bed, made her pivot, and placed himself behind her when they faced the full-length mirror set between two armchairs.

She stared at the reflection—at how good they looked together. Her hair mussed out because of his fingers. Her cheeks as equally flushed as his. His hands holding her hips, pressing his fingers into her porcelain skin like he wanted to embed his mark on her.

There was always a reverence in the way he touched her. The way he looked at her. It emboldened her in ways she couldn't describe.

"Always challenging me," he said, a bite to his tone. "Fighting me."

"You love it."

"And damn me if I don't." Pushing her hair away from her shoulder, he dotted a few kisses over the side of her neck, smiling against it. His right hand trailed down her stomach, straight to her clit. He circled it through the deep purple lace with three fingers, making Indy gasp with pleasure. "And as beautiful as you look right now, I can't stand this fucking jersey. Take it off."

Indy loved that downright jealous guy act. He didn't hide the fact that he hated seeing her with another man. Indy pulled the shirt off her body, baring herself to him.

Miles' jaw went slack as he raked his gaze over her physique from the mirror's reflection. "Look at you. You're absolutely perfect."

Slipping his hand beneath the flimsy panties, he groaned at the feeling of her aroused centre. "You're soaked. Taking my cock into your mouth makes you wet, doesn't it?"

She gasped. "Yes."

His fingers gathered the wetness and spread it across her clit before applying pressure over it. Indy tipped her head back against his shoulder, emitting a moan when he found the perfect rhythm that made her hips roll against his palm. With his other hand, he came to cup her breast through the bra.

Her hips jerked when he pinched her nipple.

"Your nipples get hard so fast," he said, palming the full

flesh. "And they're so sensitive. Bet I can make you come by playing with these alone. Those piercings are so hot."

"You've thought of them whilst jerking off?"

"Obviously," he said, like it was an evidence. "These incredible tits. That ass. *You.*"

"Huxley," she cried out. She could already feel the orgasm building like flames in the pit of her stomach.

"But today you're coming on my fingers."

He tugged the cups of her bra down and rolled her taut nipple between his fingers, then gave equal attention to the other.

Indy was a writhing and moaning mess, and when he inserted two fingers in, she blinked the stars away.

She grabbed his hand, having it exactly where she needed it as she ground over his palm, his fingers curling to hit the exact spot that made her thighs clench.

"Look in the mirror."

This exact image was enthralling and so hot. His fingers inside her, hidden by the lace underwear. His big hand palming her heavy breasts. His dark gaze locked to hers.

"Watch how I make you come. How pretty you look."

The moment his lips came in contact with her pulse point, she fell apart. Shaking. Crying out his name. Stilling as the orgasm crashed over her like a reckless wave.

"Beautiful when you come, baby."

She had barely caught her breath that he flipped her over on all fours, pushing her chest into the mattress as he forced her trembling legs apart.

"What—"

"Now you're going to come on my tongue." He tugged her underwear to the side, his tongue instantly lapping at her drenched core. "My girl comes at least twice a night. Got it?"

She fisted the sheets, bucking her ass into his face. "Yes."

He smirked against her, then went to leave a languid stroke

from her clit to her entrance, his hands spread out on her bottom.

He devoured her with abandon, feasting on her like she was his last meal. His tongue lapped against her clit, repeatedly so, and she felt her body ready to give into another climax.

He moaned against her, the vibrations sending chills down her spine.

With a final lap against her clit, Indy came undone, whispering his name into the sheets like a sinful secret.

He knew exactly what she needed, what she liked, as he continued to suck and lick until she rode out her orgasm. Gently, he trailed kisses over her spine before hovering over her, his lips millimetres away from her ear.

She could feel his erection rubbing against her skin, and honestly, she was ready for more. But Miles wasn't, and she was more than alright with it because when she reached behind to feel him, he gently stopped her.

"Not tonight, baby," he murmured, kissing the corner of her mouth. "We've got time. We don't have to rush, okay?"

She blushed, because no man had ever been this gentle and patient with her. "Okay."

Miles raced fast cars for a living, yet he was everything calm and peaceful, soothing her in a way she didn't know existed until him. He was an entire paradox, yet he simply made sense to her.

She was having him bit by bit, and it was all that mattered. But Indy's body was burning like an inferno. She wanted to be pinned between him and the mattress—like words printed on a page—and get lost in endless, infinite circles. Wanted to whisper his name over and over, like it was the only word she'd ever known, like it was the only melody she'd ever listened to.

"You amaze me," he whispered after turning her around and pulling her on his lap. Delicately, he brushed her hair away from her face. "Stay with me tonight."

Indy's heart swelled. She wanted forever with him, but for now, one night was enough. "For tonight."

His eyes held a raw sincerity she came to love, a vulnerability she came to adore. But then, his words made her world rattle as she understood that he was finally on the same page as her. "I don't want you for just one night anymore, Indy. You know it's beyond that. So please, don't go."

CHAPTER THIRTY

NEW YORK CITY, NEW YORK

Was it a dream? To wake up beside Indy with the soft morning light lurking upon the walls, falling atop her angelic face like a heaven's glow. To feel her limbs tangled with his as her soft, steady breaths fanned across his bare chest. To realise he'd had the best night of sleep in a while.

Miles didn't want to move. Basking in the moment, smiling at the thought that they'd spent the night talking and laughing before falling asleep, he kept his eyes closed, fearing that if he opened them Indy would simply leave.

But eventually, he looked down at her and smiled again. Softly, he placed a kiss on the crown of her head. She stirred, then rolled over to her side. Her steady breathing filled the room, seeming like she was still sound asleep.

She was real.

She was *here*.

After all these years of pining, secrets, longing, she was here, and she was a treasure he would keep safely tucked inside his heart.

His pulse drummed hastily when he kept his gaze on her peaceful face, and he thought he had never seen anything quite as amazing as this exact instant. Indigo Bailey was a magnificent canvas so rare, so beautiful, that nothing in this universe could so much as equal her beauty. It was the way her bright soul and unwavering string of light collided that set his whole heart on fire. Miles couldn't fathom how he had once managed to fight the relentless sparks, because now that they had burst like fireworks, he refused to go back in time.

He liked it—that feeling whenever he was around Indy. Because he had never met a woman with an aura like hers before. Had never met someone who made him feel so deeply. Had never been more infatuated and enamoured than he was right now.

When Indy woke up a few minutes later to the melody of his guitar strings creating soft notes, she smiled brightly. She stretched out, her hair an adorable mess of tangled locks, that sleepy haze still lingering in her eyes.

"Good morning, Golden Boy."

He smiled. "Hi, Daisy."

She pushed herself into a sitting position against massive pillows. "Being serenaded first thing in the morning has always been a dream of mine."

Miles dropped his gaze to her chest clad in one of his t-shirts. "I'm glad I can contribute to making your dreams come true in any kind of way."

"So next time, you can wake me up by going down on me."

He choked on air then barked out a laugh. "God, you're unhinged."

"You love it."

He sighed softly. "I do."

She reached to the nightstand to grab an elastic band and pulled her hair into a bun. "How'd you sleep?"

"Like a baby." Certainly, she was the reason for the peacefulness buzzing around his mind. "You?"

God, her smile. It was beautiful. Unrestrained. Probably his favourite feature of hers because she had the one she offered to the world, and then she had *the* smile only reserved for him. "Pretty damn well. Did you know that you kick in your sleep, though?"

"I do?" His eyes widened. "I didn't hurt you, did I?"

She chuckled, and the melody fed his soul. "No, don't worry."

Rubbing the back of his neck, he gently deposited the guitar at her feet. He was about to confess that he wasn't used to sleeping with someone, but loved having her in his arms, when a knock on the door resonated.

"Perfect timing."

He rushed to the door, accepted the tray the kind lady gave him, and thanked her before going up to Indy.

"Oh my God," she mumbled at the sight of the full breakfast tray. "Is this Princess treatment?"

Safely putting the large plate down in the middle of the bed, he nodded. "*Queen* treatment," he corrected.

"Aren't I lucky?"

With his hands placed on either side of her hips, he leaned down to leave a lingering kiss on her lips. She sighed, smiling against his mouth as her small hand cradled his stubbled jaw.

Kissing Indy made him want to anchor himself to the moment. Made him want to tether his soul to hers in every way possible. Miles never thought that love was meant for him. Never even *believed* it was possible to be so deeply consumed by a person.

Not until *her*. Not until she made him lose all semblance of control and became an addiction.

"Anything for you," he whispered when they parted ways.

He grabbed a grape from the fruit bowl, tossed it into the air, and caught it smoothly in his mouth, chuckling when she brazenly traced the lines of his abdomen with her ocean gaze.

When he sat across from her and draped the guitar over his lap, she asked, "When did you start playing?"

"The guitar? I think I was eight."

For a moment, there was only the tune of *Californication* resonating around the room. Miles was intently watching Indy —the awe on her expression, the longing in her gaze, the steady rise and fall of her chest.

"Did you start playing for a specific reason?"

A couple of months ago, he was set on keeping his secrets safe, cornered into his soul. But now, as he realised he trusted Indy with everything, he knew that she needed to know about that part of him—that darkness he bore. Hated.

Indy handed him a cup of coffee, letting his fingers brush hers as he grabbed it. He took a sip and deposited the mug on the nightstand.

"Music and karting were my only escape as a kid. The only things I truly loved. At that point, I'd been playing the piano for a few years already, but I wanted to learn to play another instrument."

"That's so cool. I love that you knew from an early age what you liked and made you happy."

A knot got stuck inside his throat as he strummed absently. "My mother... She never understood what communication was. When she was angry at me, she'd just tell me to go to my room. She would never apologise, talk about the issue, or hug me. The next day, she would just move on and act like she hadn't hurt me. My only way of clearing my mind was to play music. But she'd yell at me because the volume of the piano was too loud. Or because I wasn't playing well enough."

Her brows bunched together. "But you were just a kid."

"I know." He exhaled heavily. "Anyway, I started learning the guitar because I supposed it was a bit quieter."

She brought her knees to her chest, leaning her chin atop one of them before sipping her coffee. "And your dad?"

"Worked his ass off for everything. Came to kiss me goodnight every day, asked me to play on the piano for him, brought my mother flowers, and exhausted himself to make sure we were all happy."

A light veil of sadness misted over her eyes. "Were you? Happy?"

Miles shrugged. "I was. I had everything I wanted."

"But?"

"But I always wondered what I did wrong to make my mum so mad. Why she never hugged me or told me she loved me, whereas it was evident that I was my dad's world."

Her expression fell, a sigh escaping her mouth. She reached forward, placing her hand on his wrist. "Huxley, I'm so sorry. No one should be neglected by a parent."

He thought he was numb to the feeling, that he was indifferent regarding the situation, but talking so openly about it with Indy made his chest tighten.

"My dad kept telling me she was just tired. That it wasn't my fault that she snapped like this. And then"—his voice cracked, his gaze darting to the window—"she left him. She left us."

Indy's lower lip quivered, but she didn't say anything. Didn't rush him. Merely gave him the time to go at his own pace.

"What I'm going to say might sound so wrong," he continued quietly, "but deep down, I've always thought we were better off without her. It took me years to realise it, though. Of course, I was confused at first. I didn't understand why she left without a word, why my dad was so devastated but still kept being the best man ever. Then I learned a couple of years later that he was the one to kick her out."

"Do you know why? You don't have to tell me if you're not comfortable or ready, though. I'll understand."

"I appreciate you. But talking about it feels really good.

You're important to me, and I just want you to know everything about me."

She smiled softly, grabbing his hand. Her thumb caressed his skin—coaxing and reassuring. "Good. I feel the same way about you."

After kissing the centre of her palm, he took a deep breath in. "Apparently, my mother had wanted to divorce my dad for a while, but he'd always fought for her. Always did everything to prove to her they were good together. Did you know they met when she was seventeen and him fifteen?" Indy shook her head. "They had Maya when Mum was twenty, and then me when she was twenty-three. They were young. Didn't expect to be pregnant twice. That's never stopped Dad from giving us the world, you know?"

A shaky exhale escaped his mouth, and Indy applied a gentle pressure around his fingers. She had scooted closer, her eyes never leaving his—beautiful sapphires full of attention, full of love.

"Anyway, my father caught my mother stealing money from the trust fund they had set up for me—the money I won from karting races."

"Oh, shit. Why did she do that?"

"For drugs."

Indy's brows shot up. "What?"

He nodded, sighing. "Yeah. My mother was an addict. An emotional and physical abuser. She was shitty."

"Physical—what did she do? Did she lay a fucking finger on you?" There was not only anger blended into her tone, but anguish and perhaps disgust, too.

"She—" He licked his lips, scoffing dryly. The back of his throat tightened further. "When she hit me, it was the last straw. That was when my dad kicked her out. Told her to never come back. He got full custody. She never even tried to come back, apologise, or go to rehab. I don't even know where she is today.

If she's alive. We moved out of that small flat when I got into secondary school, and yeah."

Her voice was brittle as she asked, "She hit you?"

Miles tightened his jaw. Aside from his father and sister, there were only two people who were aware of the physical *and* emotional abuse he'd been through: Kai and Ava. Kai because he was his best friend. Ava because he would go and find shelter in her flat when he needed to get out of his own house.

Indy was a smart woman—one of the most intelligent, wise, and loving people he'd ever met. Her gaze fell to his forearm, where a thick scar slashed from his elbow to his wrist.

"She got really mad at me one day," he explained. "It was just us two at home because Dad was at Maya's dance recital. I—fuck, this is such a crazy story. I wanted to have dinner with her because, despite the negligence, she was still my *mother* and I missed her. I remember seeing her pouring the last drop of wine into her glass. She'd consumed the whole bottle by herself, and she didn't want to eat with me. Said she wasn't hungry. Then said I was bothering her, that I was too needy. Everything's a blur from the moment she started saying atrocities to me such as I ruined her life, until the moment she started throwing stuff around. She'd gone mad. At one point she just grabbed one of those plastic chairs we used to sit in as children, you know? She threw it at me. I protected my face with my arms, and yeah..."

"How—I don't—" Indy's voice was shaky as one single tear rolled down her face. Carefully, she grabbed the guitar to lay it aside. She swallowed. Breathed in. "Is it okay if I touch you?"

An invisible yet powerful force closed around his heart, squeezing and crushing. He nodded, realising he *needed* her. Yearned for her. "Yes."

As she settled in his lap, wrapping her arms around his neck, he didn't miss a beat to loop his own around her waist, holding her as though she was his safety net. He inhaled her scent, her perfume from last night still lingering.

Her soft caresses upon his back were delicate. "I'm so sorry," she whispered. "I'm sorry you had to go through that. You are brave. You are so strong. I can't even imagine how much this situation hurt you. I can't even fathom what you went through. I'm—are you okay?"

He pushed her away just enough to stare into her eyes. Another tear trickled down her skin, which he wiped away with the pad of his thumb. "I'm okay, baby. Thank you for your words."

"Are you *really* okay?" She sniffed, searching his gaze for something.

"Yes. I promise. I went to see a therapist for multiple years to help me overcome the trauma. My dad's okay, so is Maya. We all went to get help to get better. And I'm so lucky to be surrounded by friends who helped me when I needed it. Do you know how many times your mum came over to cook for us? To help us with groceries when Dad was out late? Your dad once sent Maya and I a bit of money to go treat ourselves for our birthdays."

"I had no idea," she choked out.

Miles brushed her hair away from her cheek, tucking it behind an ear. "I'm so grateful for them. For Kai. And you."

"My parents have always spoken so highly of you, and I always noticed that Mum was extra protective of you. I now understand why." She cradled his broad neck, and he wondered if she could feel his erratic pulse. "We all love you, Huxley."

He knew that. But Indy's love was different—stronger. He just still couldn't believe that she could love him like *that*. He wasn't worthy of it. Of her.

He shook the thought aside for a moment. "But you do understand why I push a lot of people away?"

She nodded, though the hurt flashing in her gaze didn't go unnoticed. "I do. The walls you built, the no-drinking rule... They're caused by your mother?"

"Mostly, yeah."

He slipped his hands beneath her shirt, needing to feel her

skin. Needing to be closer. Through the waves in a tempestuous sea, she was his anchor. Through a storm, she was the aftermath—a golden ray of sunshine peeking through the granite sky. And through chaos, she was his calm.

Indy was *everything* to him.

She was just staring at his arm, feather-lightly tracing the healed wound as though she was scared of hurting him. The raw compassion in her expression made his chest warm. It was evident that she was deeply affected by his story. She understood him in ways no other person had ever done. She provided for him in any capacity he needed. He felt safe, and loved, and seen.

"What are you thinking, baby?" he whispered, cupping her chin to lift her gaze towards him.

"That I want to hurt everyone who's caused you pain. That I just can't understand how someone as good as you was treated this way. That I just—I just—"

"It's okay," he murmured, pulling her into his chest. He held the back of her head, kissing away the tear streaming down her cheek. "I'm okay."

Indy lifted his forearm just enough to pepper soft, gentle, delicate kisses atop his scar. He shivered, then felt a burning sensation in his eyes. He blinked, melting into her touch. Just like that, she was pulling on his heart strings, one by one, making him understand that she was quickly becoming the owner of the pounding organ.

And then, she hugged him. Tightly. Without saying a word. Only letting their hearts beat against one another, syncing like two metronomes.

"Can I tell you a secret?"

Indy nodded, pulling away. She smiled softly, her eyes still glassy as she sifted her fingers through his dishevelled hair.

He dropped his gaze to her chest. "The way my mother left us without batting an eyelash, without putting up a fight, and the way the world thinks of me as such a distant man... It just strikes me as unlovable, right? I keep thinking that I'm not deserving of good things. That beautiful things are just ephemeral and will always go away. That's why I'm scared to hurt you, because I know that losing you will destroy me, too. So, with every piece of me that I gave you today, you can decide if you want to leave. And if you do, please just do it now because I already completely fucking adore you, and—"

"Huxley." His name on her lips was a soft whisper. Her small, trembling hands touched his jaw, lifting his face. "You are the most loveable man I know. I love everything about you— your secrets, your darker side, and your big heart in which you made sure to leave a space for everyone you love. The way you care about Kai, Romeo, and Ezra, and even Ava, Tito, Rowan, Charlie, Kam... Me... You care about us so fiercely. I love how protective you are of your dad, how you'd give the world to my parents after what they did for you. You are good. The people who can't see you for who you truly are, who have walked away from you, are a waste of your time. There's so many people out there who love you unconditionally, including your fans. Everyone has so much respect for you—not because you're a three-time F1 World Champion, but because you are an amazing man, on and off the track."

When he let out a shaky exhale, he realised he'd freed a single tear. Indy wiped it off his face, kissing the tip of his nose. "But I don't deserve you. I'm not good enough—"

"That is not something you can decide for me," she said with a chilling softness. "I know what I want, what's good for me, and it's you. You make me happy. You make me feel beautiful, and wanted, and appreciated. I can be myself around you. I just want you to understand that I am yours, and that I'm not going anywhere. I've been patient, and I will be patient until you're ready to walk out there with my hand in yours."

And just like that, he felt cords tangling around his heart, securing it solely for Indigo Bailey. He was already ready to give it to her, but he just needed time to give its fullest to the woman of his dreams.

Perhaps it was time for Miles to allow himself to be happy.

Perhaps the only thing he needed to understand that he was genuinely a good person, was to believe what his entourage said.

Starting with this woman who always pulled him out of the darkness surrounding him. Who always saw the good in him—in everyone. Who just loved him without any limits, and made his heart speed into overdrive.

Miles kissed her softly. Gave her his utter devotion. "Thank you."

※

MILES RUSHED to his dad who was sitting in the hotel lobby, chuckling at something he was reading from the magazine opened on his lap.

"Hey, man," Henry said, smiling up at him. "Look, there's an article about Romeo."

"I don't care."

"Oh?" A frown touched Henry's brows. "Did something happen?"

"No. I mean, I do care. I'm proud of him, and I'll read the article right after. But come here first, Dad."

There was amusement but also concern shining in Henry's gaze. Regardless, he stood up and fell into Miles' open arms.

Miles tightened his embrace around his father, exhaling in relief. "I love you, Dad. I know I don't say it enough, but I love you."

CHAPTER THIRTY-ONE

📍 *MONTE CARLO, MONACO*

"We meet again." Indy's smoky voice filled the air, her silhouette catching his attention as she stepped onto the rooftop.

Miles looked away from the colourful sky to stare at Indy as she walked towards where he was lounging in the hot tub, all unwavering confidence and jaw-dropping demeanour, smiling like a queen. She was wearing that black swimsuit she'd once worn in the sauna at the beginning of the season, and he felt his mouth go dry.

Not only was she sexy, but her burning confidence was one of his favourite things about her. The way she salaciously looked at him. The way she knew she could have him on his knees if she asked.

"You should take a pic," she pointed out. "It'll last longer."

"I have plenty in my secret folder, but I'm not opposed to adding some more."

"That's what I thought."

Passing wet fingers through his hair, he chuckled. If there was something that he really liked about his relationship—or whatever it was—with Indy, it was how much she loved giving him shit.

"What's up, Golden Boy?" She got into the tub across from him, her toes poking at his shin. "Nervous about the weekend?"

Well, it was only Wednesday, but the race weekend always started on Thursday. The Monaco Grand Prix was one of his favourites because of the tricky track, the sinuous and tight corners, and how challenging the seventy-eight laps were. "A bit, yeah. How are you feeling about it?"

Her smile widened. "I'm excited. I get to attend the press conferences this time, and it's great to be doing something different even though I enjoy conducting the interviews in the media pen, too."

He loved her excitement. Her blatant love for her job and the sport. "When is it that you're interviewing me after I win a race?" There was always a journalist who interviewed the top three drivers after each Grand Prix before the podium, and secretly, Miles was waiting for Indy to be that person because she deserved it.

"Perhaps the day you *don't* win."

Miles barked out a laugh at her mocking tone. "Don't challenge me."

"You don't know me well enough. I *love* challenging you."

He draped his arms along the edge of the hot tub. "Oh, baby, I know. But I would really love to see you out there."

She nodded with determination. "It would be another dream come true. One day I'll stand there. When I've earned it."

Miles couldn't help but smile at her. Indy had already come so far, had progressed well, and had proved to everyone that she was meant for this job.

"You're powerful. You'll earn this quicker than you think."

"Powerful?" Indy repeated in a whisper, blinking. "No one's ever said that to me."

"Well, I mean it."

She threw her head back. "*Ugh*. I hate it when you say things like that to me."

"Why?" He laughed just because she was so full of shit.

"Makes me want to jump on you."

He jerked his chin at her. "Do it."

The fading sunlight softly shone upon her skin, casting the outline of a golden halo atop her head. Full lips tilted upwards into a knowing smirk. Sapphire eyes gleaming with longing.

"What are you thinking of?" she asked.

"That your lips would look really good wrapped around my cock right now."

"Wow," she droned, her brows flicking upwards. "You can go from sweet to dirty in ten seconds. Impressive."

"I can also make you come in less than a minute."

Heat flared in her gaze, and Miles could already feel himself hardening inside his swimming shorts.

"Doubtful." What a liar.

He pushed himself off the edge, inching towards her. "I know I can."

She met him in the middle, her fingers tracing his pectorals. "Well, then. Show me what you can do."

He didn't waste a beat. Pulling her in by her waist, he slanted his mouth onto hers, his tongue sliding into her mouth as she moaned softly. He swallowed her gasp, her breath, like they all belonged to him. Her fingers tangled through the wet hair on his nape, pulling and tugging, causing him to groan.

Miles' hands descended to the ass he loved so much, kneading at the flesh as he pressed his hips into hers, letting her know how turned on he already was. Indy pulled herself up, wrapping her legs around his hips, and their kiss turned more fervent. Needy. Hurried.

Miles sat her down on the edge of the tub, keeping her legs

locked around his waist. His hands found her breasts, and he smirked at the feeling of her hardened nipples scraping against his palms.

"Someone's greedy," he mocked between kisses when she started whimpering.

Her hips bucked upwards into the air, indicating that she needed him to touch her. He released a small grunt, one of his palms descending to her ass, pulling her covered core right on his erection. The friction caused her to moan, and she started grinding against him. Miles rutted into her, rolling his hips and meeting her in the middle.

"Huxley," she gasped when his lips wrapped around her pulse point.

"You're going to come just by dry-humping my cock, aren't you?"

Indy's expression full of bliss was almost his undoing. He bucked his hips once again, and when she cried out, he knew he'd hit her clit—the spot where she just needed him to stay.

Miles let go of her and lowered himself on the bench, caressing her thighs as he pushed them apart, guiding her feet to rest on the edge. His jaw tightened at the sight of the swimsuit barely covering her.

"What if someone sees?" she asked, pushing his hair away from his brows.

He pulled the flimsy fabric to the side. "I don't care. Let them see how I make you come so hard. How you only come for me."

"But—"

"If you want me to stop, tell me and we'll go inside. If you give me the signal to keep going, I'm going to eat out your sweet cunt."

Her chest was heaving, pebbled nipples straining against the thin fabric of her swimming suit. She nodded, and that was all he needed to pepper soft kisses on the inside of her thigh.

The thrill of potentially being seen made him even harder,

and he adjusted himself before looking to where Indy was spread out like a feast before him.

"Already soaked." He held the swimsuit aside, then spat on her core. It made her moan, and he raised his brows in warning. "I want you to count out loud."

"What?"

"Count until sixty," he ordered, his thumb finding her clit. She bucked into his touch. "You won't even make it."

"So confident," she purred. When his hand trailed up her abdomen to grab a breast, she started counting. "One."

And that was Miles' cue to latch his lips around her clit, humming.

"Two." She sighed in pleasure.

He licked a flat stripe from her entrance to her clit, flicking at the bud before devouring her with abandon.

Indy grabbed his head, keeping him in place as she moved her hips against his mouth. She was already ten seconds in, her eyes rolling back when the languid strokes of his tongue spread her arousal around.

God, Miles could feast on her every hour of the day. She was sweet, responsive to every flick of his tongue. He looked up at her, mesmerised by the pleasure shattering her expression and the lust darkening her irises.

"Oh, fuck," she whispered. "Sev—seventeen."

He groaned against her, sucking her clit. He felt her legs tremble and knew she was already close. Years of sneaking around, years of studying her body's reactions and the way it responded to his touch, years of listening to her breathy moans like they were music—he'd studied his woman like she was his favourite work of art. Pinching a nipple between his thumb and forefinger, he played with the taut bud until she started shaking.

"Twenty—fuck, Huxley—twenty-eight."

He hummed to encourage her, then kept his tongue flat out against her folds—a thing she loved and made her writhe. Her hips rolled in a frantic rhythm, the sound of his saliva mixed with her arousal filling his ears.

Indy's back arched, her brows pinching together. She crashed her palm to her mouth as her orgasm rippled through her veins, causing her entire body to shudder. She tried closing her legs around his head, but he refused, continuing to lap at her clit until she rode down from her high.

"How many seconds was that, Daisy?"

"Thirty-six." Her chest was rising and falling, her wide eyes full of lust. "Fuck you."

He grinned. "I'd like that. So, what was it that you said about me making you come in less than a minute? Doubtful?"

"Fine," she huffed, pulling him up by the back of the neck. "You win."

Their lips collided, and she hummed at the taste of herself on his tongue.

His cock was throbbing inside his shorts, and as if she'd read his mind, her small hand rubbed its length through the piece of clothing.

"Wait." As much as he loved the thrill of being caught and watched, he still wanted to keep Indy safe. He got out of the tub, helping her out by carrying her. With her legs wrapped around his waist, she kissed him again, and Miles lost his mind. He didn't even know where he was headed to. Sitting down on the lounge chair hidden behind a large sunshade, he kept Indy on his lap.

Their kiss didn't break, his hands sliding to cup her ass as she started grinding on him.

"Fuck, Indy," he said with a grunt. "You're the sexiest woman alive. I swear."

As she dotted light kisses on his jaw and neck, he whimpered. He was guiding her hips as her hands trailed down his chest before reaching the hem of his swimming trunks.

She pulled them down his thighs, just enough to let his shaft spring free. "I want you to fuck me."

He pulled her swimsuit to the side again, collecting her arousal on the tip of two fingers before spreading it around her clit. "I'm going to."

Just the way he liked it, she pumped his erection from base to head, hard. She lifted herself on her knees, bringing the tip to her entrance before stilling and looking into his eyes.

"The condoms are inside," he said, caressing her ribs.

"We don't need them."

He loved how she felt in his hands. Everything about her. "You're on birth control?"

"Yes. Are you—"

"I'm clean," he murmured. Truth was, he hadn't been with anyone since that first time with Indy. She had ruined him for anyone else, and she was the only one he wanted. When he'd sought her out in the past, it was because he was consumed by her—needed to feel her, be with her—but he simply didn't know how to be more than an occasional fuck buddy.

Perhaps he'd needed time to grow, to change and find himself.

Perhaps she, too, needed some time to recenter herself.

And now, they were both ready to cross the line.

"I was going to ask if you were sure," she said with equal softness.

He cupped the back of her head, pulling her in for a soft, lingering kiss. "Yes, I'm sure. You?"

"Obviously."

He chuckled. "Right, you're dripping all over my fingers."

She glided over the head, spreading her wetness around, and he threw his head back. Repeating the movement, Miles looked at where they were connected, at his veiny cock hitting her clit. When she lowered herself, she held in her breath, her lips parting as she found his gaze.

"*Fuuuck*. Yes, Indy," he said hoarsely.

She sank down inch by inch, causing a moan to slip free. She felt absolutely divine—tight, wet, perfectly made for him. He whimpered again, and she leaned forward to kiss his jaw.

He'd never had Indy without any barrier. Never had anyone bare at all. And feeling her wrapped around him like they'd been made for one another was his undoing.

"Quiet, Golden Boy."

Chuckling dryly, he rolled his tongue over the inside of his cheek. "Relax, baby," he murmured when she halted to take a breath. "You're halfway down."

When he was buried to the hilt, he closed his eyes and tried to think of something that wouldn't make him blow in seconds. The intro to a prelude. The buttons adorning his steering wheel of his F1 car he'd come to perfectly memorise. A pastry he wanted to try out.

"Shit, you feel amazing." He brought his thumb to her clit to help her ease the uncomfortable feeling. "Move when you're ready."

She started rolling her hips, her nails digging into his shoulders. "Yes," she hissed.

He tore the straps of her swimsuit down her arms, pulling the fabric to her midriff and exposing perfect, perky breasts. He took a nipple between his lips, giving equal attention to the other by rolling it between his fingers.

Once Indy was adjusted to his size, she picked up her rhythm, switching between rolling forward and backward and bouncing. Miles wrapped an arm around her back, pulling her flush against his chest as he kissed her.

"Yes," she cried out between kisses.

"Ride my cock like you own it. You look so pretty sitting on it."

"Oh, god," she moaned when he pushed his hips into hers, frantic, needy, unapologetic.

"Just Huxley is fine." A jolt of pleasure crashed through him. "Feels good? I can already feel you clenching around me."

She threw her head back, her golden hair falling down her shoulders. "Yes."

He laid back in the chair, looking at her bouncing breasts when she lifted herself up and down. He reached out, unable to keep his hands off of her, to play with her piercings as she found a rhythm that made both of them pant heavily.

She was chanting his name as quietly as she could, soft moans escaping her mouth as she bounced on him.

"Fuck, Indy," he groaned. He was struggling to keep sounds of pleasure from drifting in the open air. "Look at me."

Blue eyes connected with his, and he felt his breath catch. With his hands gripping her waist, he lifted his hips to piston into her.

"Say how powerful you are."

She was breathless, the sun illuminating the sheen of sweat coating her tanned skin. "I'm powerful."

"Good. Again."

Her nails scraped his skin above his heart, her lips parting when his fingers came to circle her clit. "My name's Indigo Bailey and—fuck—right there. I am powerful."

"Good girl."

His cock twitched, and he knew he was about to unravel. He needed her to come with him. Needed to feel her walls tighten. Her legs shake around him. Her breaths stagger as she held her moans in.

"Whose cock makes you feel like this?"

"Yours," she gasped.

"That's right. You're mine."

She was now bouncing, biting her lower lip. He continued playing with her nipples and the barbells across them, grunting when she leaned forward just enough so that her clit hit his pelvis.

"Yours," she agreed, breathless.

He brought his pointer finger to her lips. "Suck."

Sucking on the digit, she swirled her tongue around it, keeping her wild gaze locked onto his.

He smirked then brought the soaked finger to her ass, grazing at the entrance to enhance her pleasure. She held a moan in, and he continued to rub. Her hands grabbed her breasts, pushing them together, before descending down her stomach to touch her clit. Miles groaned. No one could compare to this woman. No one could make him feel like he needed to combust in a matter of seconds.

"You wanna come, Indy?"

She nodded, clenching around him.

He smirked at her desperation. "Work for it, baby."

When her pace picked up, he knew she was close. He held tightly on to her hips, helping her up and down as he tried to meet her in the middle. Her fingers stroked her clit, and her breath hitched.

Forcefully grabbing a breast, her throaty moan music to his ears, he pushed on his heels, rutting into her as she bounced back. Chasing her high, her movements became frantic, and fuck if she wasn't the most beautiful thing he'd ever seen. "That's it," he rasped. "Take what you want."

She called out his name like a worship. A reverence. A prayer she kept on repeating as she convulsed.

Indy fell forward, her walls squeezing him tight as she came with a loud moan. His abdomen and balls tightened, then he spilled into her with such force that he trembled, his vision fading to white.

"Holy fuck," he moaned, holding her in place to release deep inside her, his thrusts sloppy and languid.

His forehead fell into her chest as he chuckled, trying to catch his breath. Her hands passed through his hair, coaxing him as she kissed his forehead.

"I missed you," he whispered, leaving a trail of featherlight kisses on her damp chest.

The haze of lust slowly vanished from her eyes, making way

for a tenderness he came to cherish. "I missed you too. So much."

He kissed her softly, listening to the loud thumping of his heart, feeling the bliss seep through his veins. She pushed herself up on trembling knees, and he pulled out. Then, his fingers gathered their mixed release, pushing it back into her with two fingers.

He thrusted a couple of times, smirking when she watched him with wide eyes. "You've got a fucking breeding kink?!"

"Only with you."

Her laugh was melodious. "I can work with that."

Their lips met again, needy and desperate and full of unreleased passion. He was impressed by the rapidity of his hardening cock nudging the inside of her smooth thigh. "I could fuck you all night long."

"Please do."

"You need to walk around the paddock tomorrow, baby."

She hummed, pushing her breasts into his chest. "I'll be able to."

He chuckled, keeping her legs wrapped around him as he stood up. "Not with the way I'm about to fuck you senseless again."

Her brows rose in defiance. "Let's see if you're a man of your word."

"Doubting me again? Don't forget that you asked for it."

And as they went inside and he threw Indy on the sofa, he realised that she was the reason for his undoing. There had been a time where the thought of being ruined by her terrified him, but he realised there was no one else he'd rather have. In this lifetime and the other ones.

CHAPTER THIRTY-TWO

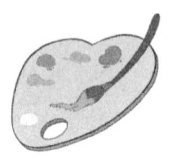

MONTE CARLO, MONACO

"You're glowing this morning," Ava commented as she fell into step between Indy and Kamari, holding onto Rosie's leash. "Is there a particular reason why you look so happy? Maybe involving the broody guy I work for?"

The trio was walking to the paddock whilst Miles, Thiago, and Rowan had taken their bikes to the track. They were probably already there, but Indy was in no rush. Besides, walking through the steep roads of Monte Carlo in high heels wasn't her most brilliant idea.

There was something about the ambiance dancing in the streets of Monaco during race week that she deeply loved. The country filled with people from all around the world that had travelled to watch fast cars race through the streets. The fans wearing their favoured team's colours. The incessant music. The yachts filling the harbour.

Indy looked down at Ava who was already wearing her black

Imperium Racing uniform, her long ebony hair floating down her back. "Why would you say that?"

"She probably got laid last night," Kamari joked, but when Indy beamed, she lifted her brows. "Oh, it finally happened?"

"Yes!" Indy felt her cheeks heat up as flashbacks from last night invaded her mind. He had made her come three times before they fell asleep in her bed. When she had awoken this morning, his tongue was buried between her thighs. "Guys, I missed this man's dick so much."

"It's the only one you've ever had," Kamari pointed out.

"True."

"Really?" asked Ava. "You've never been with another man?"

"I have, but not all the way, if you get me. Huxley was my first..."

"He was?" Evidently baffled, Ava's eyes rounded. "Does he know?"

Indy pressed her lips in a thin line. "No. Until now, Kam was the only one aware."

"Shit. I feel like that would change something in your relationship."

"It's not that big of a deal."

"It is to you," Kamari said. "You always told me you'd sleep with people who mean a lot to you."

"Are you going to tell him?" Ava asked as they crossed the road.

"Should I? I just love the way everything is at the moment, so I don't want to ruin it."

"Why would this ruin anything? He adores you," Kamari softly declared. "We can all see it."

Indy decided that she would eventually confess the secret to Miles, because he deserved to know how much he meant to her.

"He's so in love with you," Ava sighed happily. The words melted Indy's insides, sending her heart into racing mode. "He just doesn't know it yet. But I love the way he's so soft with you, how he's so protective of you and would do anything to make you happy. And the way he looks at you? There's no doubt he's obsessed with you."

Her smile widened. "I know. He's literally everything I've—"

"Excuse me?" a woman interrupted Indy as she stepped before the trio. With her brown hair tied into a loose braid, her body clad in gym gear, Indy thought she looked familiar. The thing was that Indy met new people daily, so she couldn't recall where she'd seen this woman before. "Are you Indigo Bailey?"

Indy beamed. "That would be me. Did you want a photo? I sadly will have to refuse because I need to get to the track, but I'd be more than happy to meet you at the end of the day and—"

"I don't want a photo with you. I don't care about you."

Damn.

Indy reared back.

"Can we help you?" Kamari asked with a chilling calmness, taking a step forward.

The lady blatantly ignored Kamari, keeping her gaze on Indy. She was eyeing her warily, seizing her up and down like she didn't enjoy Indy's outfit or whatever it was that made her lips pull up with disdain.

"Okay, well, have a lovely day." Indy grabbed her two friends' arms, pulling them to the side.

The interaction left a cloud of turmoil brimming her senses, but it was the woman's voice booming again that made her stop short. Made her even more confused. Angered her. Saddened her, even.

"I'm Miles' mother. I need to speak with him."

CHAPTER THIRTY-THREE

MONTE CARLO, MONACO

"THERE'S TWO WEEKS of break after the Monaco Grand Prix. Do you have any plans?"

Miles smiled at Indy who was sitting at the front, notes set on her lap. Seeing her in the press conference room made his chest warm. He was beyond proud of her, and he truly admired her determination and ambition. He was maybe the best in the sport, he was maybe breaking records, but if he could succeed in making her happy, it would undoubtedly be his greatest achievement.

He leaned back on the sofa he was sharing with a couple of other drivers, spreading his legs out. "Do *you?*"

Chuckles reverberated around the room as she lifted a brow, amusement shining in her gaze which seemed to be saying, *Are you flirting with me, Huxley?*

"Let's circle back to this later," she said disinterestedly, like she didn't care for him, which only made his smile widen. "How are you feeling about the weekend? There's been some upgrades on the car."

Placing an ankle atop his opposite knee, he brought the microphone to his mouth. "I'm actually really pumped. Monaco's one of my favourite tracks. It's always tricky and challenging, and the car works well on this circuit."

"Any hopes that we could get a double podium for Imperium Racing?"

Miles glanced at Charlie who was sitting to his right. "We're going to do everything we can to make that possible."

Indy beamed at Charlie. "And any chance you'd let Charlie win?"

Miles shrugged. "You know what, sure. If his car is faster and the strategy works well, it might happen. It's his home race, after all, and he has yet to claim his maiden win. I'd love nothing more than for him to win this Sunday. Maybe we should all light up some candles around Charlie's photo to manifest."

Laughter echoed around again, and he bumped his fist into Charlie's, grinning at his protégé. While most teammates on the grid would see a rivalry between themselves, it wasn't something Miles felt towards Charlie.

"There's an idea." Indy winked. "Thank you for your answers."

He dipped his chin in a polite nod.

"So, Charlie," Franklin Harlow, the head presenter, continued. "Rumour has it that you don't know where you're going next season. Can you tell us more about that?"

As Charlie answered, Miles kept his stare on the stunning blonde sitting across from him. He frowned as she started rubbing the skin between her thumb and forefinger, her absent gaze settled on Franklin.

He needed to find a minute to talk to her between their busy schedules.

What was going through her mind? Why wasn't she her usual bubbly and confident self?

SPEEDING INTO OVERDRIVE

ON FRIDAY MORNING as he entered the paddock, he found Indy standing in front of his motorhome, chatting with Ava.

He hadn't seen Indy last night because he'd come home late after going out for a team dinner. She was already sound asleep in his bed when he came back, and melted into his chest when he draped his arm around her body.

This morning, she had an early meeting, so she had left for the circuit while he was busy sipping on his coffee.

He needed to see her now or else he'd explode. He just *needed* her in order to breathe properly.

"Morning," he quipped as he joined the duo. "How are my two favourite girls doing?"

"Good," Ava answered brightly. "You have a meeting with your strategists in fifteen, and— What the hell are you wearing?"

Miles chuckled as he ran a hand across his chest. "You like it?"

Indy was softly laughing, crimson tinting her freckled cheeks. "You did not."

"Baby, I told you I'd wear merch to the paddock. Tito, Rowan, and Charlie are about to arrive wearing the same shirt."

The words barely left his mouth before Rowan's silhouette caught his eye. He was sporting the *Indy Bailey's #1 Babe* shirt like it was his Primavera Racing suit, grinning smugly like he always did as he entered the paddock.

"Oh my God," Indy mumbled, hiding her smile behind her hands. "This is bat-shit crazy."

"Nah. Just supporting my girl and showing to the world how great of a woman she is."

Her face flushed further, and Miles stepped forward, still chuckling. With his arms wrapped around her shoulders, he pulled her in.

Indy stilled, her hands on his ribs. "What are you doing?"

"Need you in my arms," he mumbled against her temple. "I'm always going to be your number one fan."

He felt the tension evaporate from her body as she exhaled, looping her arms around his waist.

"Everyone's watching us."

"Let them." He kissed her forehead. "Hi, Daisy."

The blue of her eyes was his favourite shade of azure. He smiled down at her, feeling a blush creep up his neck.

"Hi, stud," she whispered.

"You two are adorable." Ava snapped a photo of them, her smile shifting into a serious scowl when she pointed her finger at Miles. "Don't be late."

"I won't, *Mum*."

Indy and Ava exchanged a look before the latter walked away.

"So, what's up with you?" Miles ended up asking when he started walking by Indy's side through the paddock. He was aware of the horde of photographers aiming their cameras at them, but he didn't care. Let them believe all they want. The world already knew that he had a soft spot for her, and her only.

"Nothing," she answered, too quickly for his liking. "Why?" She peered up at him, then sighed. "I'm sorry. It's just a big weekend, and I'm nervous for you."

They stopped in front of the building she was supposed to go in. "You're sweet. But are you really okay? Are we okay? I didn't fuck it up, right?"

"We're perfect." Her fingers found his, entwining, fitting like puzzle pieces. The adoration glinting around her pupils made relief seep through his veins. "I'll see you later? I'm having dinner over at Tito's tonight. Would you like to join us? Rowan and Ava are going to be here. You can ask Charlie to come. I might ask if Aïda's available."

"Is it really a good idea to have them in the same room?"

Indy rolled her eyes. "They need to rekindle their flame, okay?"

"Fine," he chuckled. "We'll be there."

"Good."

"Before you go." He pulled something out of his pocket and slipped it in her palm. When she looked down, she gasped at the sight of the necklace made of white gold, glinting under the beaming sun, the pendant dotted with small diamonds.

"Is this your initial for me to wear on a chain around my neck?"

"Yes." He pulled his own pendant out of his shirt. "I'm wearing yours."

Indy's laugh fed his soul, but he didn't miss the sheer adoration shining around her pupils when he finished securing the piece of jewellery around her neck.

"Thank you."

She took a step to round him, but he caught her elbow, pulling her in to leave a soft, lingering kiss on her mouth. She smiled, and just like that, he felt his heartbeat speed up.

He hummed against her lips. She was an addiction. A drug —the good kind that didn't require a cure. "Have a good day."

"You too, Golden Boy."

As he watched Indy step inside, greeting Carmen and some of her colleagues who were glancing between her and Miles with shocked expressions, he couldn't help but think there was something she wasn't telling him.

※

"This car is shit in quali," he complained to AJ after running his lap.

Miles had easily made it to Q3, but he couldn't manage to make the fastest lap. His car wasn't reactive in corners, and well, Monaco was one of the tightest tracks on the calendar.

His gloved fingers hit the clutch behind the steering wheel, propelling him one gear forward. Driving through the tunnel at over two hundred kilometres per hour was his favourite thing about the circuit. This, and the iconic hairpin.

"Two minutes before the end of Q3," AJ announced. "Let's do one last lap. Give it your all."

In Monaco, the qualifying was more important than the race itself because his result would determine his starting position for the Grand Prix. This track was known for being nearly impossible to overtake on, so that was why Miles needed to be on pole.

His surroundings were a blur as he passed the starting line at full throttle, his gaze focused on the route ahead. Even though he knew the track's shape by heart, roaring off these very streets always made frissons roll down his spine.

The precision, the millimetric accuracy he needed to apply on this circuit wasn't a challenge for him. If anything, having a precise and controlled driving style was one of his strengths. The way he was in charge of his car. The way he knew when to push the vehicle to its limits. The way he could race through the circuit at full speed without so much as breaching the track limits.

Miles' breath was heavy as he passed the hairpin before accelerating again. He flew through the second sector at lightning speed, and soon enough, he was crossing the finish line.

"Great job," AJ praised.

"Tell me we have it," Miles asked, panting. The feeling inside his gut was already telling him that he, in fact, had not secured pole position.

It took a few beats for AJ to respond as Miles drove slowly towards the pit lane's entrance. "You're P3." Which was fine, because the race engineer continued cheerily, "And Charlie's on pole."

CHAPTER THIRTY-FOUR

♟ *MONTE CARLO, MONACO*

MILES TOOK HIS earphones out when Enzo tapped on his shoulder. Standing beside his car under the beaming Monégasque sun, Miles was waiting for the race to start alongside the other nineteen drivers. The starting grid was flooded with car mechanics and engineers, photographers, and journalists.

They had just listened to the national anthem, and Miles had stood behind Charlie who looked so nervous he could've pissed in his racing suit. He'd clapped on his teammate's shoulder, saying *"Prince of Monaco? You've got this, man. This race is yours."* Certainly, Miles always wanted to win, to stand on the highest step after every race, but not today. Today, he would defend Charlie with everything in his possession. His main goal was to overtake Thiago on the first turn to claim P2, and stay there for the seventy-eight-lap race.

Enzo jutted his chin towards the grid, and when Miles turned around, his lips broke into a smile. Indy was talking enthusiastically to the camera pointed at her, one hand holding onto the microphone as the other waved around. She looked so divine, so beautiful like this—in her element.

"Ah, and here's our championship leader! He's currently leading with thirty-eight points ahead of Thiago Valencia." She stepped beside Miles, her smile growing. "Ready? The lights are going out in less than fifteen minutes, and you're starting on the second row."

"Never been more ready," he said, clearing his throat, like her presence had rendered him speechless.

"Talk us through your pre-race ritual."

"Here." Still aware that he was on live TV, he extended an earphone out to her. When the notes rang in her ear, she smiled up at him.

It was U2's *With or Without You* which they had slowed danced to this morning while watching the sun rise on the rooftop.

"Music is really important to Miles," Indy explained to the camera. "If you want to know more about him and his love for music, you can either listen to the most recent episode on *Hitting the Apex* podcast, or check Thunderbolt Sports' YouTube channel to watch the blind date with Miles."

Her fingers grazed his hand, a secret touch of encouragement that set his bloodstream on fire.

Her brows lifted as she glimpsed at the car. One of his car mechanics was readjusting the warming blanket atop the left rear tyre. "You're starting on soft. That's surprising."

He shrugged. "Just trust the process. AJ knows what he's doing, and so do I."

"Well, we can never go wrong with a good strategy. Good luck," she told him, handing back the earphone. Had it not been for the upcoming Grand Prix, the cameras, and the fans all around, he would have shared more music with her. Just because it was *their* thing now—as though a mere string could tether and bind them together.

"Thanks, Indy."

She smiled then walked away, the professionalism not once wavering from her demeanour. "So, this track is a little over three kilometres long. Seventy-eight laps. Charlie Beaumont is starting from pole—third one of his career—and Thiago Valencia is on the front row with him. Who's going to win this Grand Prix?"

※

MILES ADJUSTED his grip around the steering wheel, narrowing his gaze on the five red lights above the starting line. They disappeared, indicating the start of the formation lap.

Following Thiago closely by zig-zagging, switching between accelerating and decelerating, he made sure to warm up the engine, the oil, and the tyres.

Back on the grid, he took a deep, centering breath, waiting for the other drivers to line up in their respective starting position.

Though he stayed focused with his gaze zeroed in on the horizontal lights that would soon light up, his thoughts wandered off to Charlie. He needed his mate to win. He had faith in him, his skills, and his ability to lead the race in its entirety.

The first red light burst to life. Then, all five were lit. Time stood still for six seconds, the sound of engines revving loudly, then the lights went out.

Miles' foot pushed on the gas pedal as he roared off the track, almost racing side by side with Thiago. They went through the first corner wheel to wheel, but Thiago didn't widen his trajectory, forcing Miles to stay behind.

"Good start." AJ's voice came through the radio. "You're less than a second away from Valencia. Full push. You might be able to overtake after the tunnel if you keep up the pace."

Though it was no secret that his car wasn't the best during qualifying this season, it was certainly a rocket ship during races.

He attempted an overtake in the hairpin, but the space was too sinuous to take the risk. He chased after Thiago, wanting to overtake as soon as he could.

Before they could finish the first lap, Miles noticed that Charlie was headed into the pit lane.

"What's wrong with Charlie?" he asked AJ.

Thiago was now leading the race.

"He's got an issue with his gearbox."

His heart dropped. Broke. "No...no, no, man. You're kidding. He's retiring?"

"Yeah," AJ sighed.

Goddamn it. Charlie didn't deserve this.

"Fuck. I'm going to win for him."

※

It was on the eighteenth lap that a yellow flag was announced.

"Safety car is out," AJ said. "Collision in sector one. Be careful, there's some debris scattered on the track."

He slowed down, slight frustration coursing through his veins. He'd been so close to overtaking Thiago. "Is everyone okay?"

"Yes. No one's hurt."

"Good."

The sky darkened, and Miles frowned. "Is it about to rain?"

"Not until tonight. We're keeping an eye on the weather forecast, so we should be good until the end of the Grand Prix. Box on the next lap."

The pit stop lasted for less than three seconds, and Miles grinned in triumph when he exited the pit lane with a fresh set of hard compounds on. He fell back into third place right behind Rowan. The two Primavera Racing drivers were still behind the safety car, and neither of them had pitted yet.

His heart was thumping wildly, his car vibrating against his back as he felt the engine roar like it needed to release its energy.

His grip tightened around the steering wheel, his foot ready to add pressure against the gas pedal just to feel the thrill of the speed.

The smell of burnt rubber invaded his senses, the adrenaline rushing through his veins feeding his soul.

AJ's voice rang through his earbuds a moment later. "Safety car will go in soon, I think. You've got this."

"I know. Let me do my thing."

"Yep. Safety car is going in the next lap. Fifty-five laps afterwards."

Once the burgundy safety car was out of the track and the green flag was waved into the air, Miles accelerated and sought a slipstream, trying to eliminate the distance between him and the red car in front.

ON THE THIRTY-SIXTH LAP, Miles locked up, causing him to nearly drive into a barrier instead of following the trajectory of the track. He grunted, activating the reverse feature as he checked his rear-view mirror. Thankfully, only Rowan managed to overtake, and when he got safely back on track, he was P3.

"You okay?" AJ asked.

"All grand. Rookie mistake."

"Happens to the best. You're four seconds ahead of the McMillan."

Three laps later, there was a red flag.

"What happened?"

"Big incident in sector one again. No one is out of their car yet."

He slowed down, following Thiago and Rowan into the pit lane. "Shit. I hope everyone's okay."

Accidents could be scary and dangerous. Miles hated that twisting sensation inside his stomach whenever a big incident happened.

While he didn't know when the race would resume, he still hoped that he could win. For Charlie.

🏁

THE RACE RESUMED thirty minutes later once the track was clear from the damaged cars and the debris. Three cars had been taken out in the accident, but all three drivers were okay, which was what mattered most.

Having taken advantage of the red flag, Miles' strategist suggested changing his tyres once again. He had another set of hard compounds on as he stopped on the grid. All remaining drivers would start again, but now starting from the position they were in right before the red flag—meaning that Miles was P3 again.

He had a good start, following Rowan closely. Inside multiple corners, he managed to avoid the dirty air and the turbulences caused by it, seeking a slipstream to gain the extra speed he needed in the tunnel—the fastest zone in the circuit.

Even when DRS was enabled a couple of laps later, he still couldn't catch his rival.

But it was on the forty-ninth lap that AJ said, "I think Primavera Racing is about to do a double stack since they didn't do it during the red flag."

"Their loss."

As predicted, the two red cars bolted into the pit lane, giving Miles the title of race leader.

"Say *thank you AJ for being an amazing race engineer.*"

Miles scoffed, yet he smiled as he hit the throttle. "Do you want me to shower you with flowers too?"

"I'd love that."

"Shut up and let me drive in silence."

"Yes, sir."

🏁

"How is it going?" AJ asked just when he passed by the finish line where he'd seen a sign saying *Lap 71.*

"This is boring as fuck. Did you bring your pillow? How many of you are napping in the garage right now?"

AJ chuckled. "They're fighting their yawns."

Nothing interesting had happened since the red flag. Thiago hadn't been able to catch up to Miles. Miles was four seconds ahead of him, but for the public's sake, he hoped some action was happening at the end of the grid.

"Okay, well, hang on. I'm about to win."

Obviously, a lot of things could happen in seven laps, but he was confident that he'd claim the win. For Charlie. His team. His dad. Indy, Kai, Romeo, Ezra. His family.

Panting, sweating, and chuckling to himself, he passed the chequered flag a couple of laps later, lifting his fist high in the air —victorious.

"You did it again!" In the background, he could hear the screams of joy his car mechanics were emitting as AJ congratulated him. "What a man. We don't call you The Lion for nothing."

༺༻

Jumping out of his car, he made a beeline towards his crew standing behind barriers. He crashed into their open arms, smiling when pats of encouragement fell upon his back and helmet.

Miles hugged his father tightly, as always.

He found Charlie, tucking his teammate into his chest and patting his shoulder a couple of times. "You okay?"

"I will be," Charlie answered with a crack in his voice. "But you did so fucking great."

He gave him a squeeze on the shoulder that promised they'd talk later, then went to congratulate Thiago and Rowan.

After checking his weight, taking his helmet and balaclava

off, he looked around the crowd for a stunning blonde. Like a magnet attracted to its other half, he found her standing at the back next to Carmen.

Miles trotted towards Indy, uncaring of the wild roars coming from the crowd or what Kai might think the moment he would see the photos flooding the internet.

"What are you doing?" Her eyes were wide, a small smile tugging at her lips.

He cupped the back of her head to lightly kiss her. Brief yet meaningful.

Indy's smile widened, affecting his heart like a bright ray of sunshine peeking through clouds. She threw her arms around his shoulders, the embrace quick but tight.

"I'm so proud of you," she whispered into his ear.

Pulling away, Miles found utter adoration swimming around her ocean eyes. He grabbed her hand, kissed her palm, and turned around to fulfil his post-race duties.

So this was what it felt like to be loved by Indy? That unyielding feeling of safety. That unwavering support, the unique and exhilarating friendship, and the knowledge that everything was colourful when it had once been grey? If Indy loved him like this, without any condition, then he didn't want it to end.

He'd always thought he was unlovable, undeserving of love, but Indy did it so effortlessly that he understood that it was okay if he let her know he was falling. Because he was safe. Nothing could hurt him. Nothing could break him—not anymore.

MAYBE HE WAS UNBREAKABLE, but Indy wasn't safe, and it made his blood boil.

Folding his arms across his chest, he leaned against the wall, waiting for Tara to speak up. He was ready to leave the track to celebrate his win, but Tara had been waiting for him by the motorhome and had asked for a minute of his time.

"What do you mean?"

"I mean that Indy is no saint," Tara repeated.

"Because you are?"

Tara scoffed, picking at her nails. "She doesn't deserve her job."

Pushing himself off the wall, he tried to take a calming breath in. "You need to stop, Tara. This is getting old. Indy is amazing, kind, and determined. I have no idea of what she's ever done to you, but your one-sided hatred is almost embarrassing."

"A good presenter doesn't send nudes."

He felt time stop. Looking around to see if anyone was listening, he found Ava's gaze from afar. As always, she had his back, but he shook his head, not needing her to be involved in this. But, if things got out of hand, he knew that she would be able to fix everything.

"Sorry?"

Tara smiled viciously. "Your little girlfriend is not as smart as she thinks she is. Leaving her laptop unlocked as she goes to grab a coffee? She should've known someone would find that the pictures on her phone are synced to her laptop."

When Tara slipped her own phone in his trembling hand, he let his blood roar in his ears as he stared at the photos she had taken pictures of. Indy's naked body. Him, taking her from behind, her hair bunched in his fist as she snapped a memory of this heated moment in the mirror. Selfies of himself when they travelled. Private shots, meant for himself and Indy alone.

"You're sick. What do you plan on doing with these? Leak them?" he calmly asked, knowing there was no point in acting on his anger.

"Yep."

"Look." He lifted his phone, keeping Tara's and showing that he'd been recording the entire conversation. She blanched, wide eyes staring back at him. "Delete the pics, and my press officer won't leak this little voice note. You so much as say a thing to Indy about what you saw, you so much as look her way, then everyone will know you've invaded our privacy. Everyone will also know that you sent unsolicited pictures to my friends—"

"I didn't—"

"Let me finish," he snapped. "Charlie told me about the nudes. Enzo too. Tate fucking Richards even got some, but if you must know they were all deleted because your behaviour is disgusting. This is assault, okay? Are you that desperate? What is wrong with you?"

Tara didn't answer, sheer fear painting her face.

"Make the right choice," he said. "You don't want to test me."

Miles deleted the pictures without asking for Tara's consent, because what the fuck? He dropped her phone into her hand, fury still clinging at his chest, his pulse still deafening.

"What was the reason?"

"Indy has everything I want. My job. My fame."

He sighed. "I feel sorry for you, I really do. But please, quit acting like a child. We've got some more important matters in our hands, and if you're jealous of someone who's been nothing but respectful to you, maybe you should get your head checked."

"But—"

"Just apologise, Tara. To me and Indy. Especially Indy. And to be clear, I want nothing to do with you, neither do my friends. You should be fired for what you did."

Tears brimmed her eyes. "No, please don't say anything. Don't tell Indy. She'll report this to HR."

He scoffed. "You bet I fucking will." He turned on his heel, gesturing for Ava to join. He'd let her know everything the moment they'd be safe within walls. "Should've thought about the consequences. Don't talk to me. And apologise to my girl if you want to keep your goddamn job. I'm not afraid of getting my lawyer involved, so be careful with the choices you make."

SPEEDING INTO OVERDRIVE

"Why is Tara apologising?" Indy asked as she slipped a foot in a Jimmy Choo stiletto.

Stopping short, Miles peered at the breathtaking blonde, his shirt halfway buttoned. "Was there any context?"

Indy shrugged. "No."

How fucking dumb of Tara. Hypocrite. Immature and selfish.

Taking a seat on the bed, he faced Indy, tucking a strand of hair behind an ear. "We had an interesting encounter earlier as I was leaving the track."

"You and Tara?" Indy frowned, setting her phone on the nightstand.

Miles nodded, then explained what happened as carefully as he could. He'd already noticed she was lost in her thoughts and didn't want to make her panic any further. By the time he was done, Indy's eyes were flickering between his, obvious distress gleaming in them.

"She—but are you sure the photos were deleted?"

"I did it myself, so yes, they're gone from her phone. Hopefully she doesn't have them backed-up on another device, but my lawyer is already aware of the situation, so if one photo gets out, she's done."

Indy's palm came in contact with her throat, like she wanted to claw at it to find air. "Oh, God. Oh, God. What if the photos get leaked? Both our careers will be ruined."

Gently prying her hand off, Miles cradled her face. "Breathe, baby. We will be okay. She won't do shit, because she's too chicken to actually ruin your life. She knows how powerful you are. She knows that we've got good lawyers. Now all you have to decide is if you want to tell HR about what happened."

"I—"

"You don't have to decide now."

It took a few beats, but as soon as she rolled her shoulders back, determination emanated from her demeanour. Miles loved the sudden ferocity burning around her pupils. "I want her to feel guilty every time she sees me standing in front of the camera. I want her to sit across from me during meetings and see that I don't give a shit that she's seen my tits. I also want her to remember that it's me you're fucking whenever she walks past me, and that she'll never have you."

There she was.

Miles couldn't help but smirk. "You sure?"

"As long as the pictures don't go out, I don't care. But if I see her snooping around my stuff once more, if I see her talk shit about me again, I will not hesitate to destroy her."

Cupping her jaw, he kissed her nose. "You're so strong, Indy."

She kissed him, then moved to straddle his lap. "When did you say we needed to join the guys at the club?"

"Like, fifteen minutes ago," he said, caressing her soft thighs.

"So they won't care if we're even more late." Her mouth found the base of his throat, pressing a light kiss, making him shudder.

A hum rumbled in his chest. "Definitely not. Take off that dress and keep the heels on."

Unzipping the black fabric, their breaths tangled as Miles palmed her ass. Her fingers wove through his hair, her lips moving towards his ear. "Do you think I should send Tara a photo of me riding your cock? Just to remind her who she's dealing with?"

"You're out of your mind," he breathed. "And fuck if I don't find it sexy as hell."

CHAPTER THIRTY-FIVE

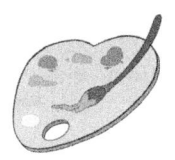

📍 *MONTE CARLO, MONACO*

"Have you told him yet?"

"Sorry?"

Obviously, Indy had heard Ava's question just right. She just needed to pretend she couldn't hear through the loud bass of the music to find a way to tell her friend that she hadn't done what she needed to do.

Ava leaned closer, Rowan still standing behind her with an arm draped across her collarbones. He was swaying to the music, wearing sunglasses—yes, in a damn club—whilst sipping on his drink. "Did you tell Miles about you-know-who?"

Indy winced. "I have not."

"Indy!" Both Ava and Rowan exclaimed in unison.

"You know about this?!" Indy aimed her finger at Rowan's chest.

He shrugged sheepishly. "She's my best friend! We tell each other everything."

"You two are so lucky that you're cute and I love you both."

"We love you too, Ind, but you need to tell Miles. He's noticed you've been acting weird," Ava said. "He's worried that you don't want him anymore or something."

After the mind-blowing sex they'd just had? She frowned. "Is that why he kissed me in front of all the cameras?"

"He thinks he needs to express his love loudly."

But Indy did not need to have cameras aimed at them or the public watching over them to know about the feelings he had for her.

She blew a raspberry and looked around the crowded club to find Miles. He was standing by the bar, surrounded by women begging for his attention, but he was talking to Charlie. When a brunette tapped on his shoulder and leaned in to whisper something in his ear, Indy's chest tightened. He nodded, then her hand brushed his upper arm. He took a step back, and whatever he said next made his interlocutor throw her head back and laugh.

Kamari joined Indy's group, her fingers laced through Thiago's. "Did you and Miles talk yet?"

"God, guys, no! This is not just something I can blurt out like that. He had to focus on his race, and I couldn't just go up to him and say '*hey, baby, did you know your—*'"

"He's coming this way," Rowan warned before kissing Ava's neck.

As if her body had sensed his presence, her skin pebbled when Miles' hands found her hips, pulling her into his chest. His warm breath fanned across her cheek as he leaned in. "Hey. You okay?"

Indy could feel the tension pulling her shoulders taut. She really needed to tell Miles about his mother. It had happened three days ago, and keeping the secret was destroying her.

She turned around, her palms finding his broad neck, sliding upwards to tangle through his hair. He smiled down at her, with tenderness and adoration, and she felt the anxiety evaporate from her veins for a few beats.

"Can we go home? I need to tell you something."

※

THEY WALKED through the streets of Monaco holding hands, doubling over in laughter when Indy reminded him of a childhood memory. They just fitted together perfectly, seamlessly, and there wasn't a shadow of doubt in the back of Indy's mind that Miles was it for her.

When they arrived at the penthouse, Rosie was soundly sleeping by the sofa, and Indy pulled Miles out on the patio.

He didn't flick the lights on, only letting the street lamps illuminate the area. In the distance, thunder rumbled in the sky, and it was a matter of minutes before the city would be engulfed in a downpour.

Miles sat down on a lounge chair, then pulled Indy on his lap when she tried to sit next to him. With her legs dangling to the side, she wrapped her arms around his neck, kicking her high heels off.

"Hi," he whispered, meandering his gaze over her face. The soft smile pulling at his lips made guilt burn through her vessels.

God, she loved him so unconditionally—she always had. So deeply and fiercely. No one had ever made her feel this way, and she hated herself for the pain she would cause. "Hi, Golden Boy."

"I feel like I haven't seen you in a while."

A knot tightened in her throat. "We've been so busy this week. I'm sorry."

"Don't apologise." His calloused palm delicately caressed her thigh. "Are you okay? Did I do something wrong? Is this about the whole Tara thing?"

"No," she whispered, toying with the pendant on his chest—

her initial. "This drama isn't important as long as it stays between us."

"She violated our privacy, Indy. You have to tell me if she makes you uncomfortable."

"I'm okay for now."

The ball in the pit of her stomach started expanding with sorrow, anger, and perhaps fear. Indy took her time to remember every feature of his handsome face—the beautiful green of his eyes, those long and thick lashes, his nose, the shape of his lips she loved so much, that square jaw. He was beautiful, it was no secret, but she loved his kind heart more than anything.

Gently brushing her thumbs over the stubble dusting across his jawline, she exhaled shakily. "Huxley, I want you to know that you've changed my life. You have no idea how happy I am that we finally have this. That we're finally *us*. I love you. I love you beyond measure. I love you so much that I can't breathe, and—"

"Baby," he cut in with a whisper. His eyes were already brimmed with emotion, and it made the ache in her chest deepen further. "You're scaring the crap out of me. Are we—is this over?"

"No, no." Her words were strangled in her throat, but he still exhaled in relief. "I've been in love with you for a decade, I'm not going to let you go that easily."

"That long?" For a beat, his smile took over the worry etched on his expression.

Indy nodded. "I've always been yours."

"You're choosing me?"

"Every minute of every day." Gently, she kissed his lips, and he melted into her. Fell into her. "You're my whole world."

After swallowing deeply, he frowned. It was evident that he was too anxious about the direction this conversation was headed in to react to her confession. "What is it then?"

She took a deep breath, holding his gaze. "On Thursday

morning, a woman came up to me. A woman who claimed to be your mother."

The soft caresses he'd been branding upon her skin ceased. "Sorry?"

At that moment, thunder exploded in the sky. Miles jolted, but kept his focus on her.

"She said she needed to speak with you."

"But—" The confusion and distress were evident in his gaze. "Why?"

"Well—"

"Why didn't you tell me?" The question was barely audible, the words resting on his lips.

"Because you had a big weekend ahead and I didn't want it to distract you. I *know* I shouldn't have kept that from you, but I needed to protect you."

Irritation wove into his words as the muscle in his jaw ticced. "I don't need you to protect me, Indy."

He lifted her off his lap, and she took a step back to give him the space he needed. His chest rose and fell as he passed his fingers through his hair, his brows knitting in confusion.

"You always protect others," Indy whispered. "But there's no one to take care of you."

His shoulders fell—subtle, but there. "Before you, I didn't have anyone taking care of me, and I surely didn't have anyone who would walk through a fire to keep me safe. But baby, what if this woman hurt you? What if—"

"I'm okay. I was with Ava and Kam."

Miles paused. "Ava? Ava knows about this, too?"

Indy nodded. Absentmindedly, she started to rub the skin between her thumb and forefinger— something she hadn't done in a while. "I'm sorry," she whispered. "Please. I need you to understand why I didn't want to tell you yet."

Settling his gaze somewhere behind her shoulder, the absence of emotion in it made her want to reach out and pull him into her. He'd gone from turmoil to shock, and what she needed to do was to give him more space, even if it broke her heart.

"Yeah." He ran his fingers through his hair again, pulling at the roots. "I need to be alone for a while."

CHAPTER THIRTY-SIX

MONTE CARLO, MONACO

Every note echoed in symphony with the anger of the heavens booming overhead. Every note engulfed Miles in an unbreakable bubble, but even confined in his safe space, he was aware that the world was nothing but a dangerous place, filled with people who could still harm him.

He closed his eyes, listening to the loud crack of a thunderbolt that must have illuminated the calamitous sky as it released its sizzling energy. His fingers fled atop the keys like they belonged there, the music consuming him to his very bones.

Words ricocheted against every corner of his mind, more powerful than anything he'd ever heard.

I love you.
I love you.
I love you, Huxley.

The realisation crashed over him, forceful like the downpour, almost sweeping him off his feet any time he'd let those three little words be ingrained into his soul.

He'd never been loved before.

Appreciated. Admired. Worshipped, yes. But not loved to his fullest. Indy loved him fiercely. Not the racing driver. Not the World Champion. Not the famous athlete. Just *him*.

His chest heaved when the song ended, and he opened his eyes to look at his trembling fingers hovering over the piano's keys.

Glancing up, he caught Indy's enthralling silhouette as she leaned against the doorway, her entire attention settled on him. A string of light pouring from the sky had cascaded upon her—she wore moonlight like a tiara, the stars like a halo.

"That was beautiful," she murmured, smiling softly.

How could he miss her when she was mere metres away? Regret clung to his chest as he realised he'd pushed her away, that he had probably hurt her by needing some space.

He cleared his throat. "Thank you. I composed it myself."

She straightened herself, admiration etched on her features. "This is impressive. What did you name it?"

He tilted his head, keeping his eyes on her. "Blue. I named it after you. I wrote it for you."

"When?" she whispered, her hands trembling, her eyes misting over. Fuck if that distance separating them didn't destroy his already fragile heart.

"After our first kiss," he admitted. If she only knew how many songs he'd written about and for her. How his head had been in a constant frenzy, endlessly thinking about her. How his heart had been calling out a name, foreign to him then but clear and logical now. And how a beautiful song had been ingrained inside his mind, spelling out the letters of love for him to write down on a sheet of music. It had always been Indy—the owner of his soul, his heart, his world.

"That was years ago."

"Exactly," he responded with equal softness. "I haven't been able to stop thinking about you. Not for one second."

Indy nodded, crossing her arms over the oversized jumper

she was wearing. He could glimpse a pair of silk shorts beneath it, exposing the legs he thought of at least once a day.

"Did I wake you up?" It was past midnight, after all.

She shook her head. "Couldn't sleep."

"Daisy," he rasped. "Come here."

Indy didn't waste a beat to rush towards him. Sitting down besides him on the piano stool, she sighed with relief as she dropped her head on his shoulder. Miles wrapped his arm around her, pulling her close, now feeling complete and content —like a puzzle finally finding its missing piece. The pull he felt towards her was innate and strong and impossible to resist, like he was a moth to a flame; an ember needing its fuel to spring to life.

"I'm sorry." He kissed her temple multiple times. "I'm so fucking sorry."

Her fingers tightened around the front of his shirt, bunching the fabric. "I'm the one who needs to apologise."

"No. I shouldn't have pushed you away. I do understand why you waited to tell me."

Teary eyes looked up at him, and the fact that she felt guilty, too, made his chest hurt. Like shards bursting through the thick walls preserving his heart.

"Can you tell me how it happened? Tell me everything," he demanded softly, rubbing the spot between her shoulder blades with his thumb.

Her fingers ghosted over the keys, and when she started playing *Au Clair de la Lune,* he chuckled.

"That's all I can do," she said before letting her hands fall down on her lap. "Sorry. I'm deflecting. I just don't get why you're not angry at me."

"I was angry earlier. And I'm sorry for walking away."

"No, your reaction is totally valid."

He loved talking to Indy because no matter what he felt, she never invalidated his feelings, which was something he wasn't used to before becoming friends with her.

"Talk to me," he desperately said. He just needed to know what had happened. Why the demons of his past were trying to crawl back to the surface.

He pivoted to straddle the stool, both legs dangling on either side. Indy followed his lead, but he pulled her closer, draping her legs over his thighs until she locked her feet behind his back.

"Better." He pushed a strand of hair behind her ear. "I need to see those pretty eyes when you talk to me."

"Even when they're puffy and filled with tears?"

"Even then."

Indy took a deep breath, tucking her hands in the sleeves of her jumper. *His* jumper, he finally realised. He almost told her she looked exceptional in his clothes, but now was not the time.

"So," she started, "it happened on Thursday morning when I was walking to the track with the girls and Rosie. A woman came up to me, and I thought she was maybe a fan who wanted a photo. Turns out that one, she didn't like me and did not want a photo, and two, she just wanted to talk to someone who's close to you. She said she was your mother when I tried to leave."

Miles didn't understand why this woman would try to come back into his life after almost twenty years of absence. Didn't *want* her to be back.

"I said it was a bold statement to make," Indy continued. "That she needed to carefully choose her words. That she had no right to come back into your life and ask to see you during one of the biggest weekends of the season. I told her not to come close to you unless *you* chose to speak with her. I told her to leave you alone unless you decided to meet up, *if* and *when* you were ready. I'm sorry if I overstepped. I was really blinded by rage in the moment, and all I wanted was to keep you safe."

Cupping her cheeks, he stared into those eyes he loved so much. "Indy, I know this isn't the right thing to say right now, but goddamn it, you are so sexy when you're angry. When you're protective of me." She chuckled, shaking her head. "In all seriousness, I don't think you overstepped at all. What did she do after that?"

"She looked lost. Maybe high, if I'm being honest with you. She threw me the dirtiest glare and walked away. I asked security at the entrance of the paddock to keep an eye out and warn me if she was lurking around, but luckily no one saw her. She hasn't shown up on any other day, either. It was such a weird encounter."

"High..." Miles scoffed. "Of course she wouldn't have changed."

"But do you think it was really her?"

His hands found her smooth thighs. He didn't even want to ask about her appearance because that would perhaps confirm the doubt. "I don't know. I've had women come up to me trying to tell me I had knocked them up. Tried to get money from me for child support."

Her eyes widened. "What? When?"

"A couple of years ago. But don't worry. I didn't get anyone pregnant, and the only woman I've been with in the past three years is you."

"I still can't believe it," she quietly said, astonished.

He brushed her lower lip with his thumb. "You ruined me for anyone else."

She blushed then blinked, like she remembered what this whole conversation was initially about. "Would you want to have a conversation with..."

"Erica," he filled in. This woman's name left a bitter taste on the tip of his tongue. The thought of ever seeing her, speaking to her, made his stomach churn. He had vomited earlier when he'd gone to hide in his room. For a moment, he felt stuck in his ten-year-old body, panicking and suffering from anxiety because of the words his mother was telling him.

"Right. Do you want to talk to Erica?"

"No," he said without hesitation. "I've already spoken about it with Dad a few years ago, and neither of us would want to reconnect with her. She's hurt us so much. The pain she put us through is not normal. And I still stand by what I said those years ago; I don't want to see her ever again."

"I support your decision. But I have to be honest with you, she tried to ask me for money. She said that she'd never show up again if I paid her."

He frowned. "How much?"

"Fifty grand."

"Fifty—what the fuck? You didn't—"

"I told her to get lost. And not come near me, you, our friends, or else my lawyer would contact her. I was not joking. No one messes with my man."

My man.

Christ, this woman was utterly magnifying. She embodied sunshine, joy, positivity. But it turned out she could turn those golden rays into flames to burn her entourage if her loved ones were so much as threatened. Indigo Bailey was an empowering, loyal, fierce woman. And she was *his*.

"There's a high possibility that she wasn't Erica," he steadily pointed out. "People are crazy. They'd do anything for money. And it's no secret that my mother hasn't been around in a while, so... People know I'm loaded."

"You're annoyingly humble, too."

Regardless, even if this woman was actually his mother, he didn't feel the desire to speak to her, let alone see her.

"You've never told the media about her, right?"

He shook his head. "No, they only know she's not part of my life. It's none of their business, anyway. Besides you, there's only Kai and Ava who know the whole story."

Her cold fingers slipped through his. "Thank you for telling me."

"You deserve to know everything about me. To see every piece of me." The tip of his nose brushed against hers as a shaky breath left his mouth. "Indy, you're it for me. I feel safe with you, and that's all I need. I know I'm broken in a way, but I'm not asking you to fix me."

With a job that required him to travel all year long, it wasn't easy to settle in a place he could call home. Sure, this flat was beautiful, provided him the safety he needed, but it wasn't until Indy had claimed that room at the end of the hall that this flat became a home. Until she'd sprinkled flowers all around, tossed a shoe by the sofa and a lipstick on the kitchen counter. Until she gave him a purpose to come back to Monaco during off-days and feel content to be here.

His home was wherever Indy was.

His home *was* Indy.

"You're not broken. Even if you think you are, I'm going to tell you this: we all are in one way or another. No one's perfect. No one lives a life without being harmed or going through some tough times. That's what life is about—crossing obstacles, battling the climb, reaching the mountain's peak. And through those broken pieces you seem so sure of carrying around, I saw your light. And it's beautiful. It's inspiring. If there's one person who deserves to be successful and happy after all the shit they went through, it's you."

"Indy," he murmured, a thick lump in his throat. "You— fuck, woman. You cannot say those things to me and—" *Not expect me to fall even harder for you.* No one believed in him the way Indy did. He blinked the burning feeling in his eyes away.

Miles' mind was racing. To ground himself, he gently grabbed her face, dusting the smattering of freckles over her cheeks with his thumbs. Softly, his lips fell upon hers, and time stopped. He exhaled shakily, pressing a firm kiss to her mouth before letting his forehead fall onto hers.

But when thunder boomed again, loud and powerful, he startled.

Indy's soft hands stroked the hair at his nape. He closed his eyes, leaning into her touch, lingering in the moment, and listened to the soft patter of rain crashing onto the windows.

Bizarrely, he found a deep serenity within him. Perhaps it was because Indy was here. She was his solace. His calm.

"You don't like thunderstorms, do you?" she asked in a whisper. "Because of your mother?"

Smart woman.

He nodded, opening his eyes to find her attention on him—looking at him like he was a work of art. "The first time she raised her voice at me, there was a thunderstorm. It might sound silly, but for so many years, hearing thunder just reminded me of my mother's angry words. Her cruelty. How she said I was ruining her life. So, whenever there was a thunderstorm, I would go over to Ava's. We'd play board games, watch movies. I felt safe at her place. One morning, after I accidentally fell asleep on her sofa, Zoya—Ava's mum—walked me back to my flat. She wanted to speak to my mother, but all my mother did was look down at me, then at Zoya, and told her she could've kept me forever. Then she left for whatever she had planned that day without so much as saying a word to me."

"What?" Indy's eyes were veiled with unconcealed sorrow. "That isn't okay."

"I now realise it. I just didn't get it then. It was around that time that my nightmares began. They were really bad when I was younger. Now I get them once in a while. They can be bad, like that one time you found me in the middle of the night. But I'm doing okay. I don't let them affect me any longer. Now I know that it was just a dream. That reality is right here, where I am with the people I love. Who love me back."

Indy kissed his forehead. "I'm so proud of you. And your sister? Maya? How did she cope?"

He sighed, gazing at the ceiling. "She was a moody adolescent who acted like an entitled brat. That was how she coped. Mum was her entire world, the way Dad is mine, you know? So when our mum left, Maya was wrecked. She also went to therapy, longer than I did. She was depressed. Grieving. Angry all the time. And then she got into uni, but she hated her classes. So

Dad suggested she went travelling. She travelled with us whilst I was competing in F3. Then she met that guy. Felix. Coolest guy I know working in photography. They fell in love. She was happy, and she just...came back to life. She is happy now, and it's what matters the most to me. She's married. Trying to have kids. I tried protecting her my whole life. Tried to provide her with as much comfort as I could even though it wasn't my job. I don't hear much from her nowadays, but simply knowing that she's okay makes me feel at peace."

She swallowed, a tear rushing down her cheek. "You are such a good man. And you are so loved."

"And I'm going to be okay," he said softly. Mostly to himself.

She hugged him tightly. "You are. I'm going to be there for you. Always cheering you on. Always encouraging you. Always giving you a shoulder to cry on and a hand to hold onto at the end of the day. You're not getting rid of me."

Miles chuckled in the crook of her neck. "That's cool with me. I wasn't planning on letting you go, anyway. I'm always going to be there for you, too, Indy. Always."

"I know."

"Thank you, baby. You have no idea how good it feels to talk about it. How good you make me feel."

Miles was so lucky to be living in the same universe as Indigo Bailey. To be the one she'd given her golden heart to. He would take great care of it—protect it like his most prized possession.

"Let's do something fun?" he suggested. "I need to clear my mind."

Her gaze slipped to the floor-to-ceiling window. "I have an idea."

THE RAIN POURED down on him, his hair sticking to his forehead. He could barely see, but he felt the cold water crashing onto his skin, could hear Indy's soft laughter as she squeezed his fingers, could feel the erratic pulse of his heart as they stepped onto the empty shore only lit by street lamps.

"Your idea was to get soaked under the pouring rain?" he asked, baffled. "In the middle of the night?"

"Not quite."

Thunder still rumbled in the night sky, this time more gently. Indy turned to him, her wide eyes full of joy and her cheeks rosy. "It's okay," she assured softly. "You're safe. Nothing's going to hurt you."

He'd always been one to take care of others, but maybe, just maybe, it was okay to let himself be taken care of.

He swallowed. Braced himself to face his fears. "I know."

When she started running towards the sea where the waves were colliding with each other, and kicked her shoes off, Miles knew what this fearless woman had in mind.

"Indy..." he warned, yet ran after her.

Her socks followed suit, then her pair of shorts fell onto the sand. He watched her with a broad grin, this wild girl having the power of making his life colourful and beautiful.

He glanced at the buildings lined up behind his shoulder, noticing that not a single light was turned on in those flats. Good. This moment was theirs. The universe belonged to them.

"Ever gone skinny dipping, Golden Boy?"

There wasn't a single predictable thing about Indy, and that was exactly why he was so drawn to her. So consumed by her fire. Whilst he was cool and collected, she was vibrant and electric. Indy brought out the best in him, and that was exactly why he knew they'd always been meant to be.

He shook his head in disbelief, pushing the wet strands of hair away from his forehead. "Shit, Indy, I can't even find the words to describe your level of craziness right now."

Her jumper hit the sand, leaving her in a pair of flimsy lavender panties with a matching lacy bralette. She shrugged, a hearty laugh escaping her mouth. "Kam once said I was unhinged. Tito agreed."

Indigo was the portrait of everything that was beautiful and mesmerising in this world—a coalescence of colours, flashes of gold mixed with tangerine and pink, feeling akin to a magnificent canvas that, to some people would look like a mere painting, but to him felt like a work of art only he could read and comprehend.

Indigo was wild, and lively, and full of life.

She was everything.

"You're just perfectly yourself," he said.

Miles pulled his t-shirt off and decided it was finally time to be alive.

Rushing past her, he smacked her ass, causing her to giggle and follow him into the water. They yelped at the cold waves touching their skin, but he still welcomed the sensation. He caught Indy by the waist, then tackled her into the water until they were both soaked to the bones.

"Bastard," she laughed as they recuperated their breath.

He grinned, standing up and pulling Indy with him. He made her twirl, right there under the pouring rain as they stood in the ocean—losing themselves in their own world.

Brushing his nose against her wet one, he let his smile widen. "You love me," he said in a murmur, his heart thundering.

Her gaze softened, her arms winding around his neck. "I do." When her hand grazed his chest, like she was just controlling the drum of his organ, she smiled, and he melted into her touch. "I meant it when I said it earlier. I love you so much, Huxley. I wanted to wait before telling you. Wanted you to realise that you love me too and needed you to say it before I could. But I realised that what you need is to know that you're not alone. That you're loved. That I love you—every part of you."

He swallowed the lump of emotion, cradling her face with his trembling hands. "Thank you." With a soft kiss to her lips, he smiled, a rush of adrenaline racing down his spine. He'd never felt like this before—complete. "You're everything to me. My whole world. Thank you for being patient."

Because of living in a fast-paced universe, he wasn't used to having someone wait on him and welcome him with open arms the way Indy had.

"I'm always going to wait for you."

Miles cradled her to his chest, closing his eyes at the sensation of their heartbeats falling in perfect synchronisation. Miles was going to meet her at the finish line, intent on giving her the world, the galaxy, the universe beyond its infinity.

CHAPTER THIRTY-SEVEN

♟ *MONTREAL, CANADA*

"I LOVE HOW BUSY it gets in the paddock before qualifying," Indy said to the camera as she held the microphone with one hand. "Everyone's running around, and what's most fascinating to me is seeing the drivers focus as they warm up. Look, there's Rowan just finishing with his reflex exercises."

Walking towards the driver dressed in his red racing suit, Scott was in tow with his camera hanging on his shoulder. Rowan grinned at Indy, and Tate, his physiotherapist, waved.

"On a scale from zero to ten, how confident are you feeling about qualifying?" she asked Rowan. "They're predicting heavy rain, especially during Q2 and Q3."

He winked. "But I'm quite the best in the wet. So, I'd say I'm pretty confident. Maybe a twelve out of ten."

A laugh bubbled out of her. "We should all have your confidence. It's great to see."

"Yeah, you know I almost died the last time we raced here, so my plan is to tell the Canadian gods who seem to hate me that I'm going to win this Grand Prix."

"Well, good luck!" She turned to the camera. "Remember to tune in at three-thirty p.m. for a quick debrief before the qualifying starts at four p.m. local time. Who's going to be on pole? Make sure to answer the poll we posted on our social media."

"Sorry to interrupt!" Miles rushed past the pair standing in the middle of the paddock, handing Indy an iced matcha latte before scurrying off.

"I told you to wait until she was done with her interviews!" Ava scolded, running after him.

Indy blinked down at the drink in her hand, then looked up at Rowan who was smiling so broadly that his dimples popped. He gave a dramatic sigh, glancing at the camera. "Isn't Miles Huxley the most romantic man ever?"

Indy couldn't hold the furious blush staining her cheeks. "Okay. Well, good luck, Rowan."

The tattooed driver grinned. "Thanks, Indy. Nice chatting with you."

She chuckled, walking away. "Likewise." She focused on the camera again. "Before we go and find Charlie Beaumont, let's make a quick pit stop in front of Primavera Racing's motorhome because I'm spotting Aïda Romano chatting with her press officer. If you didn't know yet, Aïda is making her debut in a Formula 1 in about an hour during FP3. The first female to ever sit in a Primavera!"

Seeing Aïda dressed in a racing suit, her usually curly hair tied in a loose braid, and determination shining in her gaze, made Indy's chest warm with pride. Sure, Aïda was the daughter of Simon Romano, but she wasn't here because of that. She'd worked hard to earn her place as a reserve driver for the team all the while competing in F2.

"Hello, Miss Romano," Indy greeted breezily as she came to stand beside the brunette. Aïda's blue eyes were always cold as ice, but as she gave a small smile to Indy, her gaze softened. "How are you feeling?"

"Nervous, but excited," Aïda replied.

"A lot of fans are going to tune in to watch you get inside the car for the first time. Do you have any expectations?"

"This is not helping with my nerves," Aïda responded with a nervous chuckle. "But I just want to familiarise myself with the car. Get it to move forward. Have fun."

"You'll do great! Any words you'd like to say to the people watching you today?"

"I do. Especially to the girls and women." Turning to the camera, she said, "Do not give up on your dreams. Do not listen to what the people have got to say about your goals. You want to work in sports? Do it. You want to walk a runway fashion show? Do it. This your life, your dreams, and the only limit is yourself."

"I love this," Indy said, looping her arm through Aïda's. "Life's too short to have regrets. Take the leap, girls."

"Amen."

Indy smiled, hoping that hers and Aïda's message would spread around the world. Would encourage women to grasp their bravery in the palm of their hands and step out of their comfort zone. "This is a message to all the female fans watching all around the world. We, women, belong here. We're going to change the world, and we are here to stay."

॰

WATCHING Miles behind the wheel of his car was completely captivating.

The way he controlled the vehicle with clean precision.

The way he rushed through the track under the pouring rain, sending the drizzle to the cars behind.

The way he managed to regain control if he ever slipped after taking a corner too widely.

Rowan hadn't lied yesterday when he'd said he was the best

in the rain. After making the fastest lap, he secured pole position easily. Miles had qualified second, but Miles was an extraordinary driver and especially during a race start. Within seconds, he was ahead of Rowan.

He'd been leading the race ever since.

Part of Indy was thrilled for a wet race. They were unpredictable. Exciting.

But another part of her was terrified, because crashes often occurred when the rain was this constant and violent.

It was on lap thirty-nine that chaos unravelled for Miles.

I'm losing power, was what he said to his race engineer.

In fact, his car was slowing down.

Indy frowned, uncaring of the wind rustling her hair and the coldness of the air hitting her cheeks. Her grip around the umbrella she was holding tightened, and her heart sank when she read the transcription from the radio exchange.

I'm sorry, AJ said. *You're going to have to retire.*

Bloody hell, Miles commented. *What happened here?*

I'm not sure. We'll talk once you're back in the garage.

Miles' car stopped on the side of the track, a yellow flag instantly brandished in the air at the disturbance. Indy sighed, trying to keep her expression neutral, though the twist of her heart was agonising.

When he got out of the car, taking his gloves off, his shoulders were low, deception emanating from his demeanour.

Indy wanted to rush to him. Hold him. Tell him it was okay. But she kept her journalist mask on and checked the time. Only a few hours until she could find him.

※

IT WAS dark when she stepped outside, shivering as she clutched her laptop to her chest. She walked through the empty paddock, that nostalgic feeling of leaving a Grand Prix behind clinging to her heart.

SPEEDING INTO OVERDRIVE

Frowning, she made a detour and stopped before Imperium Racing's motorhome where Henry Huxley was typing on his phone, leaning against the wall.

"Hi," she said sweetly. "You guys are still here?"

Henry smiled as his gaze collided with Indy's, pocketing his phone. She loved the fact that he was attending most of the races to support Miles. "Miles got out of debrief a couple of minutes ago, so he should be out in a few. I was thinking of taking him out to grab a bite. Maybe you could join us?"

"I'd like that. Thank you." She smiled at the tall man before her. "How are you doing?"

Maybe he hadn't expected her to address this question to him because his brows shot up for a beat. "I'm good. Gutted for Miles, but this is what racing is about. It's going to take a moment for him to understand that, but you know how he is."

She glanced towards the motorhome where she spotted Miles standing with David, his team principal, and Ava. Miles and David exchanged a hug before the latter walked away. "Yeah..."

"He told me about Erica." Henry cleared his throat. "That a woman claiming to be Erica came up to you in Monaco. You okay?"

"I'm alright. I was just scared for him."

Henry glanced away. "She, uh... I saw that woman from afar. I really thought I was dreaming, and all those memories from the past came back, and—anyway, I was really curious so I looked into Erica. Just needed to know where she was at. What she was doing in life. Turns out she passed away two years ago."

Indy's heart stopped. She nearly dropped her belongings to the glistening ground. Nearly let her eyes bulge out.

"What?" she whispered.

Henry blew out a breath. "Overdose. I still don't know who that woman in Monaco was, but all I know is that she did some digging into our past and gathered enough information to know

347

about Erica. I hope she never approaches you or Miles ever again. I don't think she will, though."

"This is so confusing. I'm guessing she came up to me because I wouldn't have recognised her."

"That's what I'm thinking. She probably thought you'd be easy to manipulate."

She shook her head. "Does Huxley know about his mum?"

"I told him the day I found out. I think he's relieved in a way. I know I am. Erica was unhappy. She was depressed and anxious. Had severe bipolar disorder, but she didn't want any help. I just hope she's at peace now."

After all she'd done to him, to Miles and Maya, Henry could still find a good thing to say about her.

"I'm sorry," Indy murmured.

"Don't be. We can all move on now."

"Are you really okay?"

"Totally." His smile was soft. "I'm finally happy, Indy. I never thought I'd feel this way again. I'm seeing someone, and she's wonderful. She's a bit younger, has one kid she's been raising on her own, but she likes me for *me*. I hadn't met someone like her in a while."

Indy blinked, holding her tears in. She'd always been a sensitive person, but after an exhausting day? Tears could come out just at the thought of releasing all the pent-up stress. "I'm happy for you. Both you and Miles deserve the world. Can I give you a hug?"

"Of course. Come here, darling."

Henry's strong arms were a comfort around her. The embrace was quick but filled with gratitude and adoration. She smiled up at the man who'd raised the most wonderful human being she knew, and took a steadying breath in.

"You're an amazing person," he told her, holding her upper arms. "Miles is so lucky to have you. I know he's beyond proud of your achievements. You're all he talks about. You brought him back to life, and you have no idea how much it means to me that you see him for who he truly is. My son loves you very much."

She swallowed the knot in her throat. When she looked over Henry's shoulder, she saw Miles through the window, leaning against the wall and nodding at whatever Ava was saying then laughing heartily. "He hasn't told me yet."

"He's not big with words or gestures. But you, Indy? There's no doubt that he's in love with you. He's not going to let you go."

The door to the motorhome opened, preventing her from speaking. Not that there was much she could have said anyway—the confession had rendered her speechless.

"Ind." It was Ava. "Miles is asking for you."

"Can I go in there?"

"Yes. Most of the team has already left, anyway."

Henry rubbed her arm. "Let's meet in the parking lot when you two are done, okay? No rush. Ave, do you and Rowan want to have dinner with us? Hell, why don't you text Tito and Kam too? Charlie can obviously join. My treat."

Ava beamed. "I'd love that! Let me show Indy to Miles' room and then I'll text the group chat."

"Sounds great."

When Ava stopped in front of Miles' room, mischief glinted in her eyes. "Just a heads-up, Ind, try and be quiet."

Indy's brows knitted together in confusion. "Sorry?"

Ava shrugged and turned on her heel, grinning. "I'll see you in a bit!"

The door opened before she could even knock, and Miles pulled her into his driver's room by the wrist.

"Hi," he said quietly, locking the door.

There was anguish, frustration, and disappointment woven into his tone. Indy deposited her belongings on a nearby chair and embraced Miles tightly. He fell into her touch, into her, exhaling deeply as his grip tightened around her waist.

"Hi, baby," she whispered. He'd changed out of his racing

suit a while ago, his fresh scent swivelling around them like a bubble of solace. "What's up?"

"Why are you still here? I thought we agreed on meeting up at the hotel."

She gestured to her laptop. "I was busy."

Miles sighed, tucking a rogue strand of hair behind her ear. "My hardworking girl. Did you have a good day?"

"I did. And you?"

He shrugged, plopping onto the sofa tucked in the corner of the room. She'd never been inside a driver's room before, but it was exactly how she imagined it to be: a massage table for post-race stretching and exercises, a table where he could eat, a small sofa, and a few photos hung on the wall.

"Can I tell you something?"

Shrugging her coat off and laying it on the back of a chair, she nodded, though he was staring absently at the wall opposite him. "Are we answering questions with questions now?"

The corner of his lips tipped upwards. "I don't know, are we?" He grabbed her hand and pulled her down to sit beside him. His voice was barely above a whisper when he spoke, like he needed this secret to stay confined within these four walls even though the motorhome was empty. "I need to tell you something. Not from a driver to a journalist. Just from me to you. Miles to Indy. Best friend to best friend."

She beamed. "Best friend? Kai is going to make the biggest fuss when he learns about this."

He chuckled, but it was evident that he was disturbed by whatever was rushing through his mind. He slumped back into the sofa, tipping his head back. She studied the strong column of his throat, the way it worked when he swallowed. "I trust you more than anyone. Like, you mean the world to me."

She grabbed his hand, entwining their fingers together. His thumb rubbed her skin in gentle circles. "I trust you, too. What's going on?"

"I was approached by Simon Romano."

Indy let the piece of information run through her mind as her brows shot up. "Why?"

"He's interested in me joining Primavera Racing."

"But—you—Tito and Rowan—what? When?"

Green eyes brimmed with uncertainty found her gaze. "In the next couple of years, or so."

She twisted in her seat to face him. "You're considering taking up his offer."

Miles shook his head. "I don't know. I love Imperium Racing. I feel powerful in the car, with the team. But Primavera Racing is becoming stronger, and their car is almost as fast as ours. Give them another year or two, and one of the two drivers is going to become champion. I can feel Tito winning another championship soon."

"That's true."

"Primavera Racing would offer me sixty million to race for them."

She scoffed. "That's a lot of money."

"I don't care about the money."

"Right. They just need to give you a competitive car."

He nodded subtly.

"Would you sign with them? Leave Imperium Racing?"

He shrugged, as if lost in his world.

Indy cradled his jaw, turning his face so he could look into her eyes. "Do you want to leave?"

"No." There wasn't a single hint of hesitation in the word.

"So what's bothering you?" she asked softly. "I can sense that there's something else. It's because of the race, isn't it?"

Miles swallowed. "Yeah. It's—look, I know it's how racing works. I've been in a car my whole life. But it's not supposed to happen. I'm not allowed to fuck up, Indy. I'm not allowed to fail."

"Hey. No. Don't do this." When she cupped his handsome face between both hands, he grabbed her waist to pull her onto his lap. She was straddling him, both knees on either side of his hips as she held his gaze. Sad. Woven with self-sabotage. Deception. Frustration. "Failing happens to everyone. Even to the best. You cannot blame yourself for an engine failure. For something that was out of your control. You had an excellent weekend until you had to retire from the race. You're allowed to be angry and sad about DNFing, but it doesn't mean you're going to feel this way for the rest of the season. You're the championship leader. You're the best driver. You're going to get back in that car in two weeks for the Spanish GP and show the world that you're still here. The Lion is unbeatable, isn't he? But he's also a human being who's allowed to fail from time to time."

"But I'm just an F1 driver. It's my job to stay consistent and—"

"You're so much more than just a Formula 1 driver," she cut in firmly. "This is Indy speaking to Miles. By the way, I hate saying your first name." He laughed heartily at that. "Not Indy the F1 journalist trying to cheer up the driver. You are a wonderful man, Huxley. You're driven and naturally talented. You're selfless, caring, loving even if you don't necessarily see it. You're a phenomenal person, even outside of racing. Don't let anyone make you feel less than that."

His forehead fell on her collarbone, his exhale warm against her skin. "How do you always find the right words to say?"

"I just don't want you to think that you're alone. Because you're not." She threaded her fingers through his hair, soft from the shower he'd recently taken. "I think you've been focusing on the negativity, and I know it's inevitable when you make a mistake. But this wasn't your fault. Sure, there's always going to be people who want their favourite driver to beat Miles Huxley. Sure, there are some who are going to lash out on you and tell you that you deserved to DNF. But fuck them. You need to look on the other side, at the people who are certain that you're going to be back in two weeks. That it's not an engine failure that's going to take the championship away from you."

He sighed shakily and nodded. "You're right."

"I know I am. And honestly? People are always going to talk behind our backs no matter what we do. But here's the thing, just walk forward and let them stay where they are, which is behind you, because their opinion doesn't matter, okay? Let them talk about you. Let them have something to say."

He sighed, nodding. "Thank you, baby. Your way of thinking is so sexy. I'm not going to let what happened today destroy me."

Their foreheads gently collided, their noses brushing in a featherlight way that made her heart thunder. "I love you. And I'm so, so proud of you."

Miles kissed her. "Say it again."

"I love you," she whispered against his mouth.

Regardless of her desperation to hear those exact words coming from him, Indy believed his devotion was equally strong with the way he kissed her. Softly. Languidly. As if he had all the time in the world. The way he touched her, his fingertips digging into the skin of her thighs like he needed to realise she was real.

The kiss turned more feverish, more passionate, when his tongue brushed against hers. When she pulled herself closer, feeling his hard bulge press the inside of her thigh. His rough hands brushed her legs, slipping beneath the hem of her dress that had ridden up, then cupped her ass.

"Huxley."

"I love it when you say my name like that," he rasped.

She tipped her head back when his lips skimmed her jaw and throat. "Your dad—"

"Fucking hell. I know some of you find my father attractive but can you please not talk about him when you're grinding on me?"

She hadn't even noticed that her body had started moving of its own volition. His teeth grazed the swell of her breasts, and she rolled her hips against his erection. "He's taking us out to dinner. He's waiting for us."

Miles stood up, keeping Indy pressed to his chest as she

locked her legs around his waist. He marched until her back was against a wall, his eyes dark with lust. "Then we better be quick. And quiet. I need to fuck you because you in that dress? Had a semi all day by just looking at your legs. You ever been fucked by a driver in his room, baby?"

Indy shook her head, already grabbing the hem of his shirt, her breath staggered.

"Good. You're about to be."

CHAPTER THIRTY-EIGHT

MONTREAL, CANADA

"ARE YOU OKAY with this?" Indy asked as he yanked his t-shirt off to throw it on the floor. She felt absolutely divine in the palm of his hands. Perfectly made for him.

Letting her down on her feet, he looked at her blood-rushed lips. Her heaving chest. That casual yet classy black dress that hugged her curves. "Yes. Are you? We can stop if you're scared of—"

"I'm not scared of getting caught. We fucked in public spaces before. I just—you're not doing okay, and I don't want you to think I'm disregarding your feelings or anything."

His heart was about to burst at the seams. Her selflessness was the most attractive thing about her. "I know you're not. I'm going to be just fine. But we can stop here and wait until we get to the hotel later. I just need to fuck you so hard that you'll forget your own name."

Her smile weakened his knees. "Then fuck me, Huxley.

Now." In the next breath, his lips crashed on her own, a moan escaping her throat. But before he could even get lost in her touch, her desire, Indy paused. He leaned forward to capture her mouth, but she pressed her palm to his chest. "Wait, wait, wait."

"What is it?" His brows knitted together.

She sighed, shaking her head. "I can't believe I forgot to ask, but your dad told me about Erica... How are you feeling?"

Was it inconsiderate of him to not feel anything at all? That no guilt or regret or sadness flooded his senses? That part of himself felt relieved for her because maybe now she was at peace? "I'm not particularly sad."

A delicate caress was pressed to his cheek. "That's okay."

"I grieved for her for way too long. She's been dead to me for a while, but I guess that I've always wanted nothing more but for her to be happy, and maybe she is now."

Indy nodded, searching his gaze for a moment. "Okay. Good."

"Can we get back to business now? Time's ticking."

The instant she nodded, he was stealing her breath away, his tongue moving in a fiery tango with hers. He cupped her face, as though he was anchoring himself to her, because his knees felt like giving up on him at the way she brazenly kissed him.

"Quiet," he commanded when she moaned again.

"I know." Her hands caressed his shoulders as he unzipped her dress. "Ava warned me."

Miles frowned. "Ava? Jesus. How often does she and Rowan fuck in his room?"

"I don't know. I don't care right now." She pushed on his chest to make him step back, then let the dress pool at her feet.

Miles felt his jaw going slack as he passed his fingers through his hair. "Holy fuck. This red on you... You are so sexy."

"Thank you."

"I love that you own so many nice things. But I'm going to spoil the shit out of you with new lingerie when we get back to Monaco."

She grabbed him by the back of the neck, those addicting lips finding his and stealing the breath straight from his lungs. He palmed her breasts, smirking when he felt her nipples pebbling, and braced a hand around her throat, applying enough pressure around her windpipe to make her gasp.

"You're going to be a good girl and be quiet?"

Indy nodded, unbuttoning his jeans. When her knuckles brushed over his erection, he whimpered. "Yes. And you? Gonna be a good boy for me and not make a sound?"

Miles dropped to his knees, unable to resist her sultry voice, letting his lips skim over her thigh before hooking her leg over his shoulder.

"Let me see how much of a pretty boy you are when you're on your knees." Tilting his chin upwards with the tip of her forefinger, the salacious smile she gave him made his pulse thunder. "So handsome."

Knowing they needed to hurry, Miles pulled her lace underwear to the side despite wanting to take his sweet, sweet time with her. At the sight before him, his fingers dug into her thigh —claiming. Branding. Embedding one word: *mine*. "You're drenched, baby."

Indy unclasped her bra, letting it fall beside his discarded shirt, and toyed with her piercings. Miles groaned, keeping his gaze locked to hers as he licked a flat line from her entrance to her clit.

She tipped her head back, a sigh escaping her nose. His tongue lapped at her clit, her sweet taste making him lose his mind. His left hand cupped her ass, kneading, as his right one slipped inside his briefs to take his erection out.

He pumped himself whilst devouring Indy. She was rolling her hips, spreading her wetness all around. A hand shielded her mouth, her brows pinched with pleasure as she kept playing with her nipples.

He emitted another grunt when her fingers tangled with his

hair, tugging at the roots, holding his mouth where she needed him the most.

"Oh, fuck," she whispered, her body convulsing.

She unravelled with the sexiest silent cry, her head tipped back, perky breasts pushed out. He kept licking her clit until she stopped trembling, then rose to his full height and pushed his briefs and jeans down just enough to free his cock.

Her pupils were blown wide, a blush coating her cheekbones. He kissed her, and she moaned softly at the taste of herself on his tongue. Tugging her scrap of lace down, he brought his cock between her legs, rubbing the tip over her arousal.

"You're always soaked for me."

"Huxley." She arched off the wall, but he pushed her back into it, hooking one of her legs around his hip. He circled her clit with the tip of his cock then brought it to her entrance, teasing her by leaving it there. "I need you."

"Beg for it."

Her nails dug in his shoulders, a soft cry sticking in her throat when he brought his mouth around a nipple. He pushed inside her—barely an inch—then retreated, and repeated the action. Feeling how wet she was, how ready she was, made his mind go into a frenzy.

"Come on," he whispered before sucking the swell of her breast, leaving a reddish mark. "You're the prettiest when you beg. Let me hear you say it."

Her hands travelled down to his biceps, up towards his shoulders before drifting down his back until she bracketed his ass. "Please. Please, Huxley."

"Beautiful." He entered her in a swift motion, covering her mouth with his palm, though he didn't manage to control the grunt rumbling in his throat. "So desperate for my cock."

Bringing both her legs around his waist, he rutted into her restlessly, burying his face in the crook of her neck. She tried to contain her moans to herself, failing miserably when he slammed roughly into her.

Miles also wanted to be loud. To make her understand how she made him feel, but his voice was only a gravelly whisper. "Fuck. You're so tight. So soaked that you're drenching my cock. But I need you to be quiet. Or else I won't make you come."

Indy threw her head back, her eyes rolling when he pulled out to the tip and thrust back in. Her nails were probably leaving crescent marks on his shoulders, but he loved the slight pain.

His fingertips dug into her ass as he continued to piston into her, hard, fast. Their bated breaths echoed in the room, a bead of sweat rolling down his chest when his rhythm picked up.

"Or maybe it's what you want, right? Moan my name to let everyone know you're being fucked so hard that you won't walk straight tomorrow. That you'll walk out of here with my cum dripping down your thighs. Do you want that?"

Indy whimpered. Miles watched her expression full of ecstasy, full of pleasure—those glazed eyes holding his gaze, those flushed cheeks, those enticing lips he couldn't stay away from.

He kissed her again, then pulled out, putting her down. He made her spin around, pressing her chest into the wall, then entered her again. He kept her pressed to his damp torso, looping an arm around her front to grab her breast.

"Yes," she hissed, tipping her head on his shoulder.

Holding a groan in, Miles watched as she brought a hand to her clit. "You're doing so well. Taking my cock like a good girl. Touching yourself to get there faster."

He slammed into her, rough and unrestrained, pinching her nipples to make her writhe. "Huxley," she whispered.

"I know, baby. You're doing so well." He peppered kisses to the side of her neck, his bated breaths fanning across her skin. "I've never wanted someone the way I want you, Indy. It's never been like this for me. Ever."

Her free hand tangled with his hair, tugging as her legs trembled. She closed her thighs, a moan catching in her throat when his palm found her hip. "For me, too."

He felt his abdomen tighten, a blinding white light flashing in his eyes when his cock twitched. He sped up, fingers plucking her taut nipple.

Miles braced her throat with his hand, bringing his lips to her ear. "I'm fucking obsessed with you. You're mine. I'm yours. I've always been yours. And I'm going to show the world that there's only you for me."

Those words seemed to bring her on the edge of the precipice. Indy fell apart, her cry muffled by his hand, her body shaking so hard that Miles couldn't help but unravel, too. He groaned and gasped into her shoulder, shaking when she clenched around him.

With a few sloppy thrusts, he made sure to ride them through their high, coaxing Indy with soft kisses on the side of her neck.

He chuckled, then turned her face to peck her lips. "Holy shit. I can cross something off my bucket list now."

Indy laughed softly, her back heaving against his damp chest. "How many girls have you wanted to bring in here to shag after a race?"

Miles pulled out, but made sure to gather his release on the tip of his fingers to push it back into her. "Just one. You."

Her body shuddered. "I'm flattered."

He made her spin around, planting a soft kiss on her lips. "Hi," he whispered.

Indy giggled softly. "Hi."

Laying his forehead onto hers, he sighed, feeling his smile widen. His heartbeat still erratic. His fingers shake. "I'm going to tell Kai about us. I think it's time we have this conversation, and if it's okay with you, I want to be the one to talk to him."

Indy nodded, her thumbs caressing his jaw. "Are you sure?"

"Am I sure about you? Us? Yes. I'm telling your brother first.

Then I'll call your parents. I'm sure everyone's already suspecting that we're a thing anyway."

Her cheeks turned redder. "It's not like you came running over to me and kissed me in front of cameras, or anything."

Chuckling, he pecked her nose. "Right."

"Okay, Golden Boy. Let's do this."

When they were freshened up and she tried to put her panties on, Miles swatted her hand away, balled the lace, and put it in his jeans pocket. "You're going to walk out there with my cum dripping down your thighs. You so much as complain, and I'll have to fuck you all over again at the hotel against the window to show everyone who you belong to."

"God, who are you?" She feigned shock, though the heat blazing around her pupils made his cock harden once more. "Such a gentleman behind closed doors."

⁂

"So, what did you want to talk to me about?"

Miles sat down in the chair beside Kai, allowing himself a moment to stare at the setting sun reflecting a golden hue on the lake. When he turned to look at his best friend, the latter was holding a beer between both hands, a peaceful expression on his features as he soaked in the warmth of the evening sun.

With two weeks of break between two races, Miles had rented a small cabin near Montreal and invited his closest friends to spend a few days disconnected from the real world.

Miles then looked over his shoulder to where Indy stood next to the barbecue Thiago was managing. She was chuckling at something Romeo had said. Ezra was here, too, doubling over in laughter with Ava who wiped the corner of her eye. Kamari and Rowan were setting the table, and whatever Rowan had said made Kamari roll her eyes, though Miles didn't miss her smile. Charlie was joining Thiago at the barbecue, a cheeky grin on his lips.

Nothing made him happier than spending quality time with his favourite people.

"Miles?"

He looked back to Kai. "Yeah. Sorry. Got distracted for a sec."

"Oh, yeah? By my sister?"

Miles leaned his elbows atop his thighs and rubbed the back of his neck. He stared at the still water, knowing that Kai was looking at him with that shit-eating grin of his. As his heart started beating faster, he was aware that he was about to confess to Kai that he had broken the only rule they had set. That he'd fallen so hard for Indy that he couldn't imagine a life where she wasn't part of it. That he'd take a bullet for her.

He found his friend's gaze, then straightened himself. "Look. I'm going to be honest with you, okay? And I just need you to listen to me before you say anything."

Kai nodded and took a sip of his beer.

Miles took a deep breath. "I'm head over heels in love with Indy."

Kai paused, pressing his lips in a thin line. "What?"

"I love your sister, man. She's everything to me. I've never felt that way about anyone, and I just—" He laughed, perhaps nervously, raking fingers through his hair. "You know I've met a shit ton of girls before. But the way I feel about Indy... She's the first woman I've wanted to marry from the first kiss. I look at her, and I just see a lifetime with her by my side, you know? She makes me feel good. She makes me happy, and I think I make her happy, too. She makes me want to be a better man. I also know that she's going to be successful—more than you and me—and I just want to cheer her on for the rest of our lives. This isn't a fling, or a simple crush. I think I've loved Indy for a while, and now I know that I want to marry this girl. I mean, she's it for me."

Kai's brows were high with surprise, but the emotion swamping his eyes didn't go unnoticed. He cleared his throat, exhaled, and took another drink of his beer, smiling behind the rim. "Miles. My guy. Took you long enough."

"And I—what?"

Kai laughed. "I know I can be clueless sometimes, but I've known that you were obsessed with my sister for years. You kissed her on live TV for fuck's sake. I was just waiting for you to tell me. To realise it."

Miles' brows pinched together in a confused frown. "How?"

"The way you look at her. Come to her defence. Break down your fucking ice walls just for her. You don't just let anyone in, and to be honest, I've been waiting my whole damn life for you two to fall in love."

"But you—"

"I was messing with you when I told you to stay away. If there's one guy who deserves Indy's goodness, it's you. And if there's one man who's going to treat her right, it's you. She's been with idiots who didn't care about her, or wanted her to find a connection to our parents, or belittled her for being a woman working in motorsports and having a better future than any of them. You, my guy, you let her shine. Support her. Love her. You're all she needs."

Miles swallowed the heavy knot in his throat. "Kai."

"Does she know yet?"

Why was his heart still in racing mode? He cast a glance to where Indy was, dancing to the beat of the music and chanting the lyrics. She truly had given him something to look forward to outside of winning a championship. "No. I'm going to tell her soon."

Kai set his bottle down and stood up. "Come here, man."

Their embrace was full of brotherly love as Miles tried to keep his emotions at bay.

"Thank you," was the only thing Kai said when they parted ways.

"You're not pissed off?"

"Nah. I knew you'd make a move on her."

"I think she was the one to make a move on *me*."

Kai turned to look at his sister. "I'm not surprised. But wait... What about the chick you've been hooking up with for the past couple of years? She took that well?"

Only a weighted glance was thrown at Kai.

Slowly, realisation flashed in his eyes as he tipped his head back and groaned. "Bro. You've been fucking my sister behind my back for so long and I can't believe it took you years to fall for her."

"Trust me, it was a challenge not to let feelings get in the way."

Kai shook his head in disbelief then waved to their friends, his voice booming louder when he shouted, "Yo! Romeo and Ezra, you both owe me two hundred bucks each."

Romeo and Ezra exchanged a glance, everything stilling around them.

"Why the fuck would we do that?" Romeo asked. Then his eyes rounded as he turned to Indy. "Oooh shit, no way! Indy, I truly had faith in you."

Indy, who was still standing next to Thiago, frowned. "I'm so confused right now."

But Miles hit the back of Kai's head. "You did not make a fucking bet with those two motherfuckers."

Kai looked proud of himself. "I did. And I won."

Barking out a laugh, Miles shook his head at his friends' recklessness. His gaze locked to Indy's, and the world ceased to exist. Yeah, that girl right there? She was the love of his life, and it was all that mattered. No amount of trophies or championships could level up to the power of her love.

CHAPTER THIRTY-NINE

📍 BARCELONA, SPAIN

IT HAD RAINED the entire day, and Miles was certain they'd delay the race start with how wet the track was. Fortunately, everything went according to plan, and the formation lap had started at three p.m. on the dot.

Miles loved wet races for the sole reason they were always chaotic. Exhilarating. Unpredictable.

Back on the grid after getting his engine and tyres warm, he quickly glanced at Rowan who was starting on pole.

"How wet is the track?" AJ asked while the other cars lined up in the respective starting position.

Miles hated it when AJ talked to him seconds before the race start. Still, he answered, "Like a goddamn pool."

"Maybe we should've put wet tyres on."

"No. Intermediates are fine. The track is going to dry out in a couple of laps."

"Understood."

Miles flexed his fingers around the steering wheel, his foot hovering above the gas pedal. His stare was zeroed in on the five horizontal lights, his breath catching when the first one lit up. When all five of them went out, he pushed on the throttle and roared off the track.

Rivulets of water were being sprayed towards him as he followed Rowan's trajectory. Good thing he knew the circuit's shape by heart. This track was one of Miles' favourites—a track filled with high and low-speed corners, a long, straight line at the start to push at full throttle, and a corner in turn three where he knew his car had a great balance to favour overtaking.

"I can't see shit," he told AJ. "I can't even imagine how it is at the end of the grid."

Just as he said those words, a yellow flag was brandished in the air.

"We can barely see anything on the monitor, either."

"What happened back there?"

"Just a little collision, but it's all good now. Green flag. You're a second away from Emerson. Catch him."

❦

Ten laps later, the track had finally dried out. Despite always racing less than a second away from Rowan, Miles hadn't been able to find a gap to overtake and was waiting for DRS to be enabled.

"No rain for the next fifteen minutes," AJ announced. "McMillans are about to do a double stack to put slicks on."

Miles frowned and hit the left paddle to downshift as he took turn fourteen. He then sped up through the straight line, staying lined up behind Rowan to seek a slipstream to gain extra speed. Rowan slipped away after the first turn, and Miles continued to follow his trajectory and the dry line.

"Risky, but okay. Is it supposed to downpour or just drizzle?"

"Heavy rain."

"Then we're keeping inters on."
"You sure?"
"I'm the one driving the car. Let me do my thing."

༄

IT TOOK twenty-two laps for DRS to be enabled. By staying lined up behind the race leader, Miles had managed to gain extra speed. He was less than a second away from Rowan, and in the DRS zone, he hit the button that made the upper part of his rear wing flap open, and his top speed was finally increased.

He overtook Rowan on the inside of turn three whilst the latter locked up and slightly drifted off the track limits before regaining composure and chasing Miles down the circuit.

"Yes, baby!" AJ shouted, excitement blending into his tone. "That's what I'm talking about."

༄

THERE WAS a yellow flag on lap forty-one, right after the rain had stopped pouring. Heavy rain was actually drizzle, and Miles had pitted to put another set of intermediate compounds on. He was still leading the race.

"This race is chaotic. So many yellow flags."

Miles had predicted it—the thrill this Grand Prix would bring him. Despite loving a wet race, he still prayed no one would get injured. He'd witnessed too many accidents in the past whilst driving in the rain.

"Yeah, but it's Charlie this time, so..."

Panic flared inside his chest. "What happened?"

"Bauer spun around, taking Charlie with him. Front wing damaged. There's debris on the track, so the safety car is arriving. It was inevitable for Charlie, so he's out. But he's okay."

"Damn it, Charlie."

TWENTY-FIVE LAPS LATER, Miles was zipping through the track, flat out. His suit was damp with both perspiration and rain, his breathing staggered.

"Last lap," AJ announced. "You can set the fastest lap time."

If he did, he'd gain an extra point. "Damn right, I will."

A little over a minute later, Miles passed the chequered flag, claiming the win after a challenging race.

"Mega race," AJ said cheerily. "Nice fight with the guys."

He waved to the full grandstands, then gave a thumbs-up to Rowan and Thiago who drove past him. "Yeah. It was fun. Every GP should be like this."

"Agreed."

When his car was parked, his engine turned off, and his steering wheel plucked out, Miles pulled himself out of the car and stood on the halo, pumping both fists in the air. He ran towards his pit-crew, his car mechanics, and his dad who were all chanting his name behind barriers. Jumping into their arms, he accepted the congratulatory pats and laughed.

He embraced both Rowan and Thiago, then unbuckled his helmet and tore off his balaclava. Passing his fingers through his hair, he sighed in contentment and searched the crowd. He spotted Indy in a heartbeat—his agonising heart finding its other half, the desperation to be complete fading away as he was met with sapphire eyes—then rushed towards her despite Ava telling him he needed to head into the cool-down room.

The trophy didn't matter at that moment. The post-race interview he needed to attend didn't matter. All he could see was Indy beaming at him from where she stood. He knew that she was working, knew he shouldn't make a beeline for her like this, but he couldn't help himself.

He swept her off the ground, one hand wrapped around her waist, then kissed her.

"What are you doing?" She laughed, her wide eyes staring at him.

He put her down, leaving a lingering caress on her hip. He was aware of the world's attention set on them, of the cheers that had erupted in the crowd, and that Ava was about to scold him, but he didn't care. He simply grinned, marched backwards, and winked. "Just saying hi to my girl."

༺༻

"Stop looking at me like that," he muttered to Ava as he walked out of his room with her on his heels.

"Like what?"

"I don't know. Your little smile. Why are you smiling like that?"

A laugh bubbled out of her mouth, and they stepped outside of the motorhome. Miles was exhausted from the weekend, but he knew that his friends were about to head out to celebrate, so he decided that instead of being anti-social, he'd accompany them.

"I like seeing you happy," Ava confessed softly.

"Because I won?"

She glowered at him. "Miles. I've always liked your passion for racing, and you've worked so hard to get where you are today. But you know I'm talking about you and Indy. You just look so... carefree. Relieved. I love this for you."

He wrapped an arm around Ava's shoulders, pulling her in. "Thanks, Ave. It means a lot."

Her big, brown eyes stared up at him, glinting with emotions. "You deserve to be happy."

God, how far they'd come—the both of them. Ava had seen his bad days like the good ones. Had always cheered him on, no matter what. Even when they had distanced themselves from one another when she'd worked for Primavera Racing during a couple of years.

"So do you. Rowan, he treats you well?"

Her smile grew at the mention of her boyfriend. "Like a queen. Why? You're going to threaten to kill him if he hurts me?"

"Yeah," he said seriously. "You're like my sister. No one harms you."

Ava rolled her eyes. "Men." She hugged him tightly. "You're insufferable."

He kissed the crown of her head, chuckling. "Love you, too.

"Besides, your behaviour with the media has really improved. Sure, your answers are still short and cold, but you're more open in a way. You've attended more events than ever this season, and you've participated in a lot of activities for PR. I'm really proud of you."

Before he could express yet again his gratitude towards her, Rowan came running over to her, wrapping his arms around her waist and planting his chin atop her head. "Why are we being sappy?"

Miles exchanged a glance with Ava, and smiled.

When Indy reached them, she looked up at Miles. The adoration and longing in her eyes couldn't be mistaken, and he just loved that look she only kept for him. Loved the way her features brightened when one of her colleagues called out her name to say goodbye. Loved the way she hooked her arm under Ava's to pull her towards the paddock's exit. Loved her laugh as it boomed. Loved the way she stopped, letting Ava join Rowan, and turned around with her palm extended towards him—like an invitation to spend an eternity together.

He loved her.

He loved her.

He loved her, and it was about time he let her know.

"All good?" she asked.

He kissed her temple. "All perfect."

CHAPTER FORTY

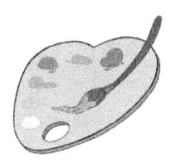

♀ *SPIELBERG, AUSTRIA*

THIS WAS THE best way to wake up. Legs tangled with Miles'. His cheek resting on her chest, his steady breathing fanning across her bare skin. His body pressed into hers like he needed her to be as close as possible. Like he needed her to be able to breathe.

Indy basked in the warmth and utter comfort of his embrace, keeping her eyes closed and letting her fingers tangle through his messy locks.

She sighed happily.

The golden boy of Formula 1 was finally hers.

The man that the world had deemed unworthy of good things outside of racing.

The man the public had claimed as untouchable, unattainable, uncaring.

The man who'd been abandoned when he was just a boy and who simply needed someone to hold him.

And she would love him his entire life. Would love him

enough for the both of them, until he'd catch up with his feelings and the way he felt about her. But deep to her core, she knew that Miles loved her fiercely—his actions had always spoken louder than words.

He stirred, interrupting her thoughts. "Good morning," he rasped, snuggling closer. His hoarse voice made a shiver roll down her spine. "Man, I love waking up next to you."

"Morning," she whispered, her smile uncontrollably spreading across her lips.

His gruff voice tickled her ear, then she felt his lips skim over her jawline. "Wanted you to be asleep."

She frowned, watching him prop himself on an elbow. His eyes were still glazed with sleep, but there was something shining around his pupils that made her pulse thunder. Lust. Desire.

"Why?"

He crawled under the blankets, pushing her legs apart as he peppered kisses inside her thigh. "I wanted to wake you up with my tongue buried inside you."

A silent gasp brushed against her lips, but she opened her legs further for him. "Huxley—"

"Unless you don't want this, you better keep your moans quiet or else you'll wake the whole damn hotel." His fingers were already collecting her arousal, coating her clit with lazy strokes.

She nodded eagerly, pushing a rebellious strand of hair away from his brow. "I want this."

His smirk was a thing of savage beauty. "Thought so."

Then, he went to work, and this was *definitely* the best way to start the day.

"THANK YOU, CHARLIE." Indy beamed at the driver, completing the post-free practice interviews. He'd set the fastest lap, his car having a good pace during both sessions of practice. Miles had finished in second place, and it seemed like Imperium

Racing would dominate all weekend long again. "Best of luck for tomorrow."

Charlie winked. "Thanks."

This had been the last interview of the day. Wrapping up with Scott and carrying her microphone along with her notes to the office, she soaked in the warmth of the late afternoon sun, enjoying how busy it was in the paddock.

She truly felt in her element.

Like she belonged here.

Like she was meant for this.

And nothing in the whole wide world could compare to the joy this job provided.

Learning to believe in herself again had been a challenge, but having friends—family—who kept reminding her how deserving she was and how great she was doing, had helped her forge her confidence into something unbreakable.

She smiled at Thiago who was rushing after his physical trainer and Alex.

Returned the fist-bump Rowan aimed at her when they crossed paths.

Winked at Ava who managed to catch her eye between walking through the paddock and typing on her phone.

Then brushed her fingers to Miles when he passed by her whilst he was chatting with Enzo.

The moment their skin touched, it felt like the entire world came to halt. All that mattered was him. All there was was *them*. In a world alone. In a world where, despite the challenges and obstacles, they knew they could rely on each other to find light. Solace. Love.

Miles smiled at her—broad and unrestrained—then disappeared into his motorhome.

"So you're really dating Miles Huxley? Finally secured your spot in motorsports and got what you wanted?"

Indy halted, brows slowly rising as she turned to look at Tara. The latter was sitting down at a table in front of the building dedicated for media, not even meeting Indy's gaze as she pretended to type on her laptop.

Indy had managed to avoid her coworker the best she could, save for team meetings and mandatory interactions at the office. It was obvious that Tara was ashamed of what she'd done as her general behaviour had improved, but Indy hadn't forgotten about the way she and Miles had been treated.

Indy took a calming breath and sat across from her colleague. "Look, I don't know what your problem is, and not that I should justify myself, but I landed this job long before Huxley and I were a thing."

Tara glared at her.

"If you still think that I'm dating him just to make sure I'm keeping my job, then you need to look around, Tara. I hate to brag, but I'm appreciated around here. I do a damn good job at what I do. I'm a woman working in motorsports. You are, too. You know how hard it is for us to forge a place in this industry, how much we want to be seen as an equal to a man walking through this very paddock. If you think that we're here to look at the drivers or try to get them between our bed sheets, then I'd suggest you sort out your priorities."

"All I did was ask if you and Miles are a thing."

"And all I heard was jealousy. It's unnecessary. I don't know what I did to you, but ever since the season has started, you've just been downright rude to me. But I get it. You want my job. You want my man. And look, I want you to achieve your dreams and become a presenter one day, but with your mindset? I'm sorry, honey, but it won't happen. We're a team. Not enemies."

There was a beat of silence, but when Tara didn't seize the opportunity to say anything, Indy continued. "Also, it's really bold of you to talk to me, knowing I hold evidence of what you did. I wouldn't try to mess with me if I were you. I should have gone to HR, and you should definitely be fired for violating my privacy, but guess what? You deserve a second chance, and I'm not going to hold grudges. Just don't talk to me, all right?"

Indy stood up.

It was only when she was almost inside that Tara's wavering voice echoed. "I'm jealous of you because it's so easy for you. You have everything you want with the snap of your fingers."

"I don't think you get the point. I don't have it easy—I never have. I just work hard and I don't give up, and I certainly don't try to hate those who don't struggle. Everyone's journey is different."

She entered the building, a certain weight being lifted off her chest.

People had told her she couldn't do it. That she wasn't capable. That she wasn't enough. But slowly, yet surely, she was proving everyone wrong.

Slowly, yet surely, she was reaching the mountain's peak.

CHAPTER FORTY-ONE

SILVERSTONE, ENGLAND

"So, what was that about?"

Miles finished drying his hair with a towel as his father entered his room. It had been a good Saturday. What better than setting the fastest lap on one of his favourite tracks and starting the British Grand Prix on pole position? After qualifying under the beaming sun, attending numerous interviews, and participating in the debrief, he was looking forward to tomorrow's race, but also to head home and relax.

He loved racing at Silverstone because it was his home Grand Prix and because the track was iconic. He'd always spend a couple of days at his dad's townhouse after the race—to catch up, disconnect.

"The booing?" he asked, tossing the towel aside. "It's not the first time."

"Yeah, but it's not okay, man." Henry sat down at the small desk. "Just because you and Valencia did the same lap time, but you finished your lap first meaning you got pole, doesn't make it okay to just boo in your face."

"Let it go, Dad. You know that the hate doesn't get to me."

"Don't do this. Not to me."

Miles sighed and sat across from him. "The hate is just going to push me to do better. Prove them wrong. And to be honest, I just feel numb. Like, I don't even care anymore."

Henry observed Miles for a few beats, then nodded. "It takes a lot of strength to be able to shrug off this kind of behaviour towards you. I've always admired your resilience."

"Learned from the best," Miles quipped.

Henry tutted. "I had nothing to do with the man you've become."

Miles threw his head back. "Come on, Dad. Didn't you raise me? You're the strongest man I know. That shit you went through? It taught me not to let the bad things tear me down."

Emotion swamped at Henry's eyes as he released a shaky breath. He simply nodded, blinking. He cleared his throat, then said, "Indy defended you on live TV."

Miles swore he could feel his heart expanding at the thought. This fierce girl who always had his back. This lively girl who wasn't afraid of anything or anyone. This sensational woman who was his. As a kid, he loved watching her from afar, admiring and wishing for a future by her side. Today, he was insanely in awe of the woman she'd become—a queen claiming her throne in this high octane world. He couldn't be more proud to be hers.

"Well, she said 'and remember, booing isn't the way to do it. Please respect every driver. Make this a safe space for them, too.'"

"She said that? On live TV?"

"Verbatim." He glanced at the wall closest to them where three photos were displayed: one of Miles and Henry after his maiden win; one of Miles standing with Kai, Romeo, and Ezra in skiing gear; and one of Indy and him grinning at the camera under the setting sun. "Are you happy?"

Miles smiled, nodding, his racing heart solely beating for the blonde beauty. "Yeah. Yeah. I really am. I've never been happier."

"Good. You deserve it. You and Indy deserve each other. I always knew you two were meant to be."

"Really?"

"First day you met at that karting race? You were so mesmerised by the fact that she liked cars. By *her*. You two just made sense from the moment you met."

He'd once thought happiness came with trophies and a maximum of wins under his belt, but true happiness was finding love with Indigo Bailey.

📍 MONTE CARLO, MONACO

THE PENTHOUSE WAS ANNOYINGLY empty without Indy.

Without her contagious laugh, her infectious, good spirit.

Hell, Miles even missed her goddamn mess, the shoes she'd leave in the foyer and the purse she'd throw on the sofa. He missed seeing her snuggled in blankets while watching reruns of her favourite show. Making her a matcha latte every morning. Eating dinner with her on the patio. Taking her to the closest French town to spend a morning at the farmers market.

And instead of tidying the flat and cleaning up the scattered chaos, he had left everything as it was. Because this place was only lively because of Indy. Because she had turned a dull house into a vibrant home.

Miles felt incomplete without her. Like he'd been thrown into shallow waters and was drowning, unable to swim to the surface and catch a breath.

Whilst Miles had gone back to Monaco after spending a few days with his father in London, Indy had decided to stay to catch up with Kamari and her own family.

It had been a week without her.

And Miles felt like dying.

Obviously, he'd called her everyday. But he just *missed* her.

"Fucking hell. I'm pathetic," he muttered under his breath. Rosie's ears perked as she peered up at him from the carpet. "Stop judging me, Rosie. You miss your mama, too."

For the fourth time, he replayed the video Indy had posted on her social media this afternoon. A compilation of little videos of them dancing in the kitchen, painting, cooking. Videos of him playing the guitar, or holding onto Rosie's leash as they strode on the windy shore, smiling at her. She'd captioned the post with *"to the love of my life, thank you for making me the happiest."*, and the video had already generated over one million likes.

His phone rang, and his pulse quickened as he saw Indy's caller ID flash on the screen. "Hey, baby," he said softly. "Everything okay?"

"Yes. I'm boarding the plane in a few. Are you ready for me to be back home?"

"Fuck, no," he mocked, smiling widely. He looked around, nerves starting to rattle through his body. He'd spent hours on her homecoming surprise. "I love how quiet it is when you're not here."

She laughed, knowing damn well that it was a lie. "I don't blame you. I'm such a mess."

"You're my mess."

Indy chuckled. "Stop hitting on me."

"What are you going to do about it?" A grin took over as he imagined the challenging gleam in her eyes. "Get some rest because I have something fun planned for us tonight."

"Is that so? Aren't you full of surprises?"

Tonight was the night he'd show Indy how deep his affection for her was. If this didn't seal his promise to wanting to spend his life with her, then he didn't know anything about love.

CHAPTER FORTY-TWO

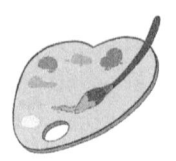

MONTE CARLO, MONACO

Indy dropped her bag to the floor as soon as she stepped into the penthouse. A gasp brushed her lips, her heart stopping for a moment before going back to thumping wildly.

"Hi," Miles greeted with a soft smile, a bouquet of daisies in his hands.

She didn't know what to say. What to do except look around the flat he'd flooded with tons of daisies. Music was blasting from the speakers, candles were lit on the dining table, and the smell of her favourite meal was lingering in the air.

"Huxley," she whispered, looking around with awe. Tears were prickling her eyes, burning and uncontrollable. "Are you trying to seduce me?"

He stepped forward, smiling so beautifully that she felt weak in the knees. "Please tell me it's working."

"Shit, you can't make me cry," she said, falling into him with her arms wrapped around his middle. "My makeup looks so nice today."

Miles grabbed her hand, lifting it above her head to make her spin around. "You look beautiful." Then he cupped her chin, gently placing his lips upon hers. She melted into the kiss, her heart thundering as butterflies erupted inside her chest. "Hi. I missed you."

She smiled, cupping the side of his neck and feeling his wild pulse drum beneath her palm. "Hello, stud. This is a lovely surprise."

He handed her the bouquet, the tops of his cheeks rosy. That was when she noticed Polaroid photos of them had been included amongst the flowers. "I would hope so. Took me days to organise and prep everything."

She beamed, grazing a petal and the closest photo: a shot of Indy kissing his cheek as he grinned at the camera. This was so thoughtful, so sweet of him.

It all made sense now. When she'd asked him if he was going to pick her up at Nice Airport, he told her that something had come up and that he couldn't be there, which had piqued her curiosity about his whereabouts. Indy wasn't disappointed at all because Thiago had picked her up, and she loved catching up with her friend.

Indy lingered her gaze on the photos, but Miles interrupted her thoughts. "Dinner will be ready in a few. Do you want to change?"

She nodded and deposited the bouquet on the coffee table before following Miles who had taken her luggage. He passed by her room without stopping, and Indy frowned when he entered his own bedroom.

"Moving me in?" she teased.

"Yes," he answered seriously.

She stopped short, staring at him utterly dumbfounded. "Really?"

"Does it look like I'm joking?"

"What happened to my old room?"

He gestured behind her shoulder. "See for yourself."

As soon as she opened the door, a small gasp fled her mouth. He had turned what once had been a bedroom full of clothes and high heels scattered around, piles of books on the floor, and a bed far too big for just herself, into a room dedicated for her passions—art, books, and motorsports.

The bed was gone, so were all her belongings. A large bookshelf was lined up against the wall to her right, her novels sorted by colour. A reading chair was placed by the window, the blanket she loved cuddling up with neatly folded atop it. To her left, a simple armoire on which he'd put all her painting and pottery equipment. Above it, a shelf where he had deposited two plants and some of her handmade ceramics. Her pottery wheel was sitting in the corner of the room, and the desk he had set up by the window was adorned with the set of microphones she used to record her podcast.

"You—Huxley." Her fingers were trembling by her side. "What is this?"

"This is your room," he murmured from where he stood by the doorway. "To paint. Read. Spend some time doing whatever you want. This room is way bigger than the one you used to work in, so I figured you'd love to have more space."

She walked to the bookshelf, swallowing the knot inside her throat. "Organised by colour?"

"Ava's suggestion. Bought you a couple of new books as well."

"When did you start doing this?" She looked at him as he stepped towards her, a soft smile on his lips. Tender, unbound adoration shining in his eyes.

"The moment I got back home from London. Ava, Rowan, Tito, and Charlie came to help."

"And my clothes?"

"All moved into the walk-in closet attached to our room."

Our room. "I saved a couple of drawers for myself. The rest is yours."

"What happened to the junk room?" For months, most of her belongings had stayed in boxes, but now they were all displayed and ready to be used.

"I'm planning on turning it into a music room. It's kind of a mess in there, but I'm having some recording equipment delivered soon. A drum set, too, because I missed playing them."

"I can't wait to hear you play." She wanted to cry at the thought of Miles finding his way back to his roots—music—and finally understanding he was free to play any instrument if he wanted to. "Drummers are so hot."

"I thought you were more into guitarists."

"I'm just into you, Golden Boy."

This man. Who had stolen her heart from the first corrupting kiss. Who had gone above and beyond to make her happy with small actions that spoke louder than words. Who had broken all his rules just for her.

"I have bad news," she said with dramatised suspense, letting her words hang into emptiness for a beat.

Miles narrowed his gaze. "Do tell."

"You're not getting rid of me now."

A laugh erupted from his chest. "That's terrible news," he deadpanned. "I'm devastated."

"I bet you are."

When Miles lowered himself on a knee, she felt a thorough skip in her heart. Was he— No. No. He couldn't be.

The quiver in her fingers worsened. "Huxley..."

"Wait. I'm not proposing. Yet." He held up a key, smiling softly. "But I want you to move in with me. Officially. I don't care if we're moving too fast. If we're skipping some steps or whatever. There's nothing I'm more sure of than what I feel for you, and I want it all with you. Your mess. Falling asleep after watching a hockey game and waking up next to you on the sofa with my neck sore as hell. Have dinner together and watch romcoms afterwards. Invite our friends over and have chaotic evenings. Dance on the rooftop. Go in the hot tub at midnight."

Indy fell to her knees, cradling his handsome face. He was grinning broadly, and she couldn't contain her chuckle as she pulled him into a tight embrace.

"Took you long enough."

"Is that a yes?" he asked against her neck before leaving a soft kiss on it.

"Obviously." Relief flooded his body as he exhaled, and she smiled into the crook of his neck. "I want this with you, too."

⸙

"And Kam's new café looks absolutely incredible. She's done such a good job."

"I'm really happy for her," Miles said after swallowing his bite of lasagna.

"Me too. She really deserves this. She's worked so hard."

His gaze softened, pride glinting in it. There was something about making Miles proud that was more special than making her parents or brother or friends happy. "So did you, to become one of the lead presenters at Thunderbolt Sports."

She set her cutlery down, wiping her mouth with a napkin. "Speaking about that. I have some good news."

His brows were lifted in slight surprise. "Yeah?"

The wide smile spreading across her lips was out of her control. "I got a call this morning. Guess who's now an F1 Ambassador?"

Miles' eyes widened, then he dropped his fork, but instead of landing it on his plate, it stumbled onto his shirt and lap. "Oh, fuck." After putting the fork back onto the plate, standing up and shrugging his stained shirt off, he pulled her up and wrapped his arms around her shoulders. "You're kidding me."

Indy chuckled, caressing his toned, bare back. "I'm not."

"Indy. This is phenomenal." He cupped her cheeks, his

bright gaze gleaming with so many emotions. "I'm so proud of you. Do you know how many presenters become ambassadors? And in such a short amount of time after starting the job?"

"Thank you. It was so unexpected, but I'm really proud of myself."

She'd come so far. Had gone through so many critiques that had helped her grow. Had faced many obstacles, and despite it all, she kept pushing to live her dreams.

Being proud of herself wasn't something that seamlessly came to her. It had always been a struggle. But for the first time in years, she could finally look at her reflection and see the efforts she had made to get where she was at today.

"You should," he murmured, caressing her cheekbone with his thumb. She sank into his touch, his love. "This is amazing. There's no one else who can fit this role better than you."

"You think so?"

He nodded. "You're positive. Outgoing. Uplifting and encouraging. You know what you're doing, you know about the various motorsports disciplines. Your platform keeps on growing, so yes, I really do think you're perfect for this."

Winding her arms around his waist, she tightly crushed him to her chest. "Thank you for always supporting me."

He kissed the crown of her head, and she felt his chest rise and fall. "Always. Ready for the next part of the surprise?"

"There's still more?"

Gently, he tilted her chin upwards with the help of his forefinger, compelling her to hold his devastating gaze. "Oh, baby. I'm nowhere near done with you."

And there was absolutely nothing gentle about the way Miles uttered those words. About the way he looked at her.

Indy lifted herself on her tiptoes and brushed her lips to his. "You spoil me."

He hummed, the low sound sending a jolt of electricity through her bones. "And if you keep on being a good girl, you'll be rewarded."

"Are you joining me, or what?"

The sound of water filling the bathtub was overpowering the music softly resonating through the room, the scent of jasmine swivelling in the air. Miles had scattered rose petals from their bedroom floor to the en-suite bathroom, then had brought her a cup of herbal infusion along with a bowl of her favourite chocolate.

Indy tilted her head, observing Miles' ethereal frame take up the whole space in the doorway as he leaned against it, his torso still bare.

"This is for you," he said, his gravelly voice making a shiver roll down her spine.

She took her top off, exposing a pastel blue lace bra. "And if I ask you nicely to join me? The bathtub is big enough for both of us."

His jaw tightened, but his fingers found the button of his jeans. "Fine."

"I'm really convincing, aren't I?"

His gaze dropped to her cleavage. "So good at it."

She grinned. "Thanks."

Once they were both undressed and lowered into the warm water, facing each other with bubbles floating on the surface, Indy sighed in contentment. She closed her eyes, smiling. "Best evening ever. I could do this for the rest of my life."

Before Miles came into her life and flipped her orbit onto its axis, she thought happiness came with good liquor, parties, and friends. It turned out that genuine happiness came with this man who had taught her that love was calm, peaceful, and exhilarating without needing spotlights shining upon them. That love was slow, and good, and alive if they let it bloom like a flower in the spring.

When she opened her eyes, she felt her pulse quicken at the way he was watching her. With his arms draped over the edge of the tub, a strand of hair toppling over his forehead, and that soft smile he only kept for her, it was evident that Miles Huxley was hers.

"What?" She felt her cheeks heat up under his scrutiny.

"I can't believe you love me."

She frowned, sitting up.

"I can't believe you fought for me even after I pushed you away time after time," he continued. "How you deemed me worthy of love, worthy of *you*, when I shut myself off."

Was it possible to feel her heart shatter even though it felt full? "Huxley," she whispered. "I know it's been hard for you to realise this, but you are worth fighting for. I would've waited for you if you needed more time to be ready. Because you deserve someone who's willing to fight for you, no matter how hard the battle is. You deserve someone who's going to stick by your side, during your best and worst moments. Someone who's going to hold you when you're at your lowest, but also to cheer you on any time you're successful. I've wanted you my whole life. You, Miles Huxley, the man who goes above and beyond to make your friends and family happy. The man who's so caring, gentle, and loving. The man who always makes sure I'm okay. I love *you*. Not the talented F1 driver who brings a trophy home after each race, not the man who breaks records and drives at full speed. I do love him; how relentless he can be and how passionate he is about racing. But he doesn't compare to the man I've fallen in love with."

His throat bobbed when he swallowed, his eyes veiled by a layer of unshed tears. "Come here."

She scooted forward until she was kneeling between his parted legs. He cradled her face, gently placing his forehead against hers. "Thank you, Daisy."

She smiled at the nickname. "We've been through this. You don't have to thank me. Never for loving you, because it's the easiest thing I've ever had to do."

The kiss was gentle, full of devotion. He smiled against her mouth, then asked her to turn the other way so that her back was facing him. He pulled her into his chest, kissing her cheek.

His fingers danced across her ribs and trailed down to her hip. She told him more about the days she spent in London. Her plans for the summer break she had made with the girls to spend a few days in Spain. Then silence fell—the kind that made her linger in the moment, the kind that made her close her eyes and feel everything: his touch, his body caging her, his soft lips peppering kisses on her shoulder.

"What are you thinking of?" she asked.

His hands caressed the outside of her thighs, the rise and fall of his chest steady against her back. "I thought of you every single day for the past three and a half years, Indy. I was just too scared to seek you out because I was messed up in my head. I was so focused on racing and I was terrified of pushing you away. Of hurting and losing you. But I couldn't get you out of my head. Every time I looked at you, all I wanted was to *have* you. And every moment I got to have with you were the best minutes of my life. There's nothing in this world that compares to you. To the way you make me feel."

Indy felt her chest tighten at the confession. She turned her head to look up into his eyes. "Huxley?"

"Yeah, baby?"

"I need to tell you something. Please don't freak out."

He frowned as she sat up, shifting to face him. Their fingers entwined, confusion etched on his handsome features. "Are you pregnant?"

She shook her head, eyes widening. "No. No."

"Oh. Okay." His expression was unreadable, which made panic flare through her for a beat.

"But do you want kids?" He'd told her once that women had tried to trap him with lies. Besides, even though being a mother was a dream, she wasn't ready for this. There was still a world to explore. A life to live with Miles.

"With you, yeah. But not right now. In a couple of years."

She smiled softly. "Really?"

"Yes. When I look at you, I see a future with you. I always did. And I don't want to scare you away, but I truly want to marry you someday. Have kids. Buy a big country house somewhere, raise our children there and teach them about racing, art, music."

Planting a kiss in the palm of his hand, she murmured, "Sounds like a plan."

"Good." With his wet fingers, he tucked a strand of her hair behind an ear. "What is it then?"

She inhaled, flicking her gaze between his. She'd wanted to confess this secret a while ago, but she hadn't known how to say it until now. "You were my first."

It felt as though time stood still as Miles blinked. "Sorry?"

"You were my first time," she repeated in a whisper.

Shock skittered across his eyes as his jaw went slack. "I—you—me? In Abu Dhabi?"

She nodded.

"Fuck." He ran his hands over his face. "Are you serious?"

"Yes."

"But—" Something like regret misted over his eyes, and she felt her heart sink. "I was so brutal with you. We fucked on the desk. I didn't even—and you—"

She cupped his face. "It's okay."

"But—did I hurt you?"

"No. You were perfect. I promise."

He shook his head, the divot between his brows deepening. "How—"

"I practised a lot with vibrators," she confessed, her cheeks reddening. "There's no one I wanted more than you to be my first."

Miles brushed his hand over his mouth, then stood up.

"What are you doing?" she asked as he stepped out of the tub to grab a towel.

"Making it up to you. Come here."

She rapidly pulled the plug out, then stood to join Miles. He wrapped a towel around her, his soft lips instantly falling onto hers. She melted into him, her hands finding his chest where his heart was hammering beneath her palm.

"I'm sorry," he whispered. "I'm sorry. I wish I had known."

"You would've treated me differently."

"I—"

"You would've said no. Would've been too gentle. I didn't want that."

Against her eyebrows, his own knitted together. He exhaled tremulously, "Indy."

"Look at me." Gently, she took hold of his face, forcing him to look at her. Those crestfallen eyes made the crack in her chest widen, but when she kissed him again, the anguish dissipated. "It's okay. I promise."

He searched her gaze for the lie, and ended up nodding. "Okay."

His mouth found hers again, kissing and claiming every breath she released. His hands found the back of her thighs, hoisting her up until she sat on the bathroom counter, the towel loosening its hold and pooling at her waist.

She didn't care though. Didn't try to understand if the shivers racking her skin were caused by the air colliding with her flesh or the way he kissed her so firmly yet gently, like he was terrified to shatter her. Her fingers tangled with the wet hair at his nape, scraping his scalp, which made him groan.

With her legs locked around his hips, his hands drifting towards her backside and her nipples grazing at his chest, she couldn't contain her pleasured sighs when his tongue started to explore her mouth.

"I'm sorry, baby," he repeated. "Let me make it up to you."

"You don't have to." She pulled away just enough to watch the lust take over his gaze. "I told you that because I want you to know how special you are to me."

He gulped. "Did I make you come?"

Indy blushed. "You know you did."

"Good." A smug smirk touched his lips. "Tonight you're going to come at least six times."

Her brows shot up with disbelief, her pulse quickening with anticipation. "Six?"

Peppering her jaw with light kisses, he hummed. Her fingers tightened around his biceps when he sucked at the spot below her ear. "Have you been a good girl lately?"

"I believe so."

"Then like I said earlier, good girls get rewarded."

His mouth wrapped around a peaked nipple, and Indy threw her head back. Miles pushed her legs apart, and she bucked her hips into the air in search of friction. Anything to make the ache fade away.

He used his free hand to palm her other breast, toying with the taut bud before giving it some attention by licking at it.

"I need you," she whimpered. "Don't act like I'm made of porcelain."

Miles smirked against her skin, his teeth firmly tugging at her nipple and his tongue lapping against the barbell.

"Tell me what to do," she said, desperate.

"You're just going to come on my fingers now." Then, his middle finger found her clit, and he groaned at the feel of her wetness. "Already soaked."

She quirked a brow. "Sounds like a complaint."

"On the contrary. I love that you get drenched just for me."

He circled her clit with three fingers as he kissed her—urgently, messily. Indy pulled him towards her, needing more friction as she tried to push her breasts against his torso. He smirked again at her desperation, his pace picking up.

"Have you touched yourself this past week?"

"Yes," she admitted, throwing her head back. "So many times."

"Yeah? Did you listen to every audio we've recorded to get yourself off?"

"Yes," she panted. "You?"

"What do you think? Can't spend a goddamn night without fisting my cock when you're not around."

He inserted two fingers at once, his thumb finding her clit. "Do your fingers satisfy you as much as mine?"

His thrusts were controlled, rapid, digits angled upwards and brushing the spot that made her writhe and tremble.

"No."

"Do they make you come as hard as my cock does?"

"No," she said in a breathy exhale.

"Do you always imagine it's my cock filling your tight cunt?"

She nodded, lips parting when she felt her core clench. "Always."

The moment his tongue flicked her nipple, she reached her high whilst whispering his name. She had barely caught her breath when Miles picked her up, locking her legs around his middle to walk them out of the bathroom.

"That was one." He laid her down on the mattress, planting both hands on either side of her head.

"There's no way you're making me come six times," she bit out, though the mere thought of it made her shake with anticipation.

"You don't want to test me right now, Indy. If you think you're going to be able to walk tomorrow, then you might want to change your plans."

She propped herself on her elbows, spreading her legs apart. "I dare you."

He smiled, like he'd been waiting for her to say this. Trailed open-mouthed kisses from the column of her throat to the valley of her breasts to her navel. Licked one flat stripe from her entrance to her clit, making her breath hitch.

"We're going to use a safe word, okay? Use it if you want me to stop."

She cupped her breasts. "Can we use colours? Green, orange, and red?"

"Like a traffic light? Yeah, I like that." Miles moved to the nightstand on her side of the bed. "So, you said you like vibrators."

"Love them."

He opened the first drawer. "Which one do you want to use today?"

He had moved her collection of toys to his room, too. She hoped their friends hadn't seen it, but even if they did, Indy wasn't embarrassed. Pleasuring herself was something she enjoyed.

"You choose."

Miles arched a brow, then tossed a purple toy at her. "Show me what this one does."

She grabbed the silicone cock, already knowing she would come in a matter of seconds with this one. "Only if you sit in that armchair and watch me."

"Easy." He went to sit down, his hard cock standing tall and begging for her attention.

She tutted, turning on the toy. "You just watch. You can't touch me or yourself."

Miles licked his lips, then balled his hands atop the armrests. "So bossy."

"Don't you like it?"

He took a deep breath in. "I love it."

"Thought so."

Sitting back against a pillow, Indy kept her legs spread out, offering him a full view of herself. His nostrils flared, his jaw tightening. He shifted in his seat, his knuckles whitening for a beat as it was evident that he was controlling himself not to pump his cock which was already leaking with pre-cum.

Indy brought the tip of the vibrating toy to her slit, moaning when she pushed it into her. "This one is my current favourite. The tip curls upwards to graze at my G-spot." She pushed it in until it was buried to the hilt, her breathing already staggering. "And this—oh, fuck. This little thing vibrates against my clit."

She watched how Miles observed the way she pulled the toy out and pushed it back in, her hips rolling when the vibrating tip brushed her clit.

"You are so sexy." His voice was hoarse, husky. His scrutiny as burning as ignited sparks.

"You have no idea how many times I used it when you were right down the hall."

He wet his lips. "Fucking hell."

With her free hand, she played with her nipples. The toy was being thrusted into her, rapidly so, making her feel like she was on the brink of climaxing again.

She opened her eyes to look at Miles. His stare was on the toy, his chest rising and falling, his laboured breaths echoing.

"It feels so good," she murmured, pinching her nipple.

"Indy," he huskily said, his hips absently bucking in the air. "Please."

"Please what?"

"Please let me play with you. Touch you. I'm dying here."

Her back arched off the mattress, her legs shaking. "Get down on your knees and show me how badly you want this."

Miles obeyed in a heartbeat. Falling to his knees, the despair in his eyes was as evident as the lust. She watched his cock, a bead of pre-cum leaking from the slit, the angry veins throbbing. His name fled her mouth when she felt her walls tighten.

"Please," he repeated. "I need to touch you."

"Crawl to me like a good boy." Moaning at the sight of his obedience, she smiled.

Miles was kneeling between her legs the next second. "Can I?"

"Yes."

Lying down on his stomach, he pushed her legs to her chest, then took control of the toy. He groaned, thrusting the purple cock in and out of her, and spat on her clit. The angle made her whimper. "I bet this is not enough for you, though. My cock fills your cunt way more fully."

"Definitely." She threw her head back, using both hands to play with her nipples—tug, pinch, roll.

"I'm going to do something," he said. "Tell me to stop if you don't like it."

Then, his tongue was flat out against her back entrance. Indy moaned loudly at the sensation.

"Okay with you?"

She nodded. "Keep going. I'm already close."

Miles licked at the puckered hole all the while fucking her with the vibrating toy. Indy gripped the bed sheets tightly, her eyes squeezing shut when a euphoric haze started to blind her. "Oh, God."

"It's Huxley for you, baby. Come on. Let me see how pretty you look when you come on this toy."

And it was all it took for Indy to fall apart. The intensity of this orgasm couldn't compare to the previous one as she cried out loud, shaking and letting white stars blind her.

"Beautiful," he praised. "How many was that, Daisy?"

Her legs were trembling, the cloud of pure bliss still controlling her body. "Two."

Miles tossed the toy aside, and he pushed her knees further against her chest. With his darkened eyes locked to hers, he licked a teasing, slow, flat line along her folds. The vibration of his groan against her flesh made her spasm again.

"I can't," she said breathlessly.

"Yes, you can." He flicked her clit with the tip of his tongue, dragging a finger along her arousal. "You're soaked. Making a mess all over my face."

"Just marking my territory."

He grinned devilishly. "That's my girl. Colour?"

"Green."

When his lips suctioned on her clit, she shuddered. Miles' green eyes stayed locked to hers as he devoured her, and soon enough, Indy came with a cry.

"Three," he whispered against her thigh, which he peppered with light kisses.

Indy's fingers found his hair, pulling at the roots when she found the strength to catch her breath. "I need you."

Rising to his knees, he wrapped his fist around his rock-hard erection, giving it a pump whilst trailing his regard over her. He rubbed the tip to her entrance and collected her wetness, then entered in one swift motion.

"Oh, fuck," she murmured, feeling him stretch her out.

"God, Indy." He pecked her lips once, moaning. "You feel so good."

The angle made Indy lose her mind. With her knees still pressed to her chest, he could rut into her deep and hard. Which he did the moment she started pleading for him to ruin her.

They shared a messy kiss, their ragged breaths becoming one as his balls slapped her skin. He rammed into her with abandon, moans and whimpers rising from the back of his throat.

Miles let out a low grunt as he forcefully kneaded her bouncing breasts. "Fuck. Whose cock makes you scream like this?"

"Yours," she gasped.

"Who do you belong to?"

"You." She brought her fingers to her clit, drawing rapid circles. "It's always been you."

His breathing was heavy, a bead of sweat trickling down his temple. "And it's always been you for me, too."

Indy was losing herself into a blissful pleasure, and the moment she felt her walls clench around him, he pulled out and rolled her onto her stomach. With his hands on her hips, he dragged her ass upwards, keeping her chest pressed into the mattress.

He entered her from behind, and Indy screamed his name at the way he torturously plunged in and out, his hand holding her head in place against the pillow, fingers pulling at her hair. His thrusts were frantic, and through the noises of skin slapping, arousal mixing, and moans echoing, she couldn't think straight. Indy felt her legs shake, her eyes screwing shut.

Miles pulled out, and she whined at the empty sensation.

He spat on her sensitive clit, then his tongue was on her again. "I can't come yet," he said. "I know I won't be able to control myself when I feel your greedy cunt squeeze me."

He devoured her eagerly, like he couldn't get enough. Entering two fingers, he curled them just so that they could graze her sweet spot, his tongue flicking her clit. "One more." He added a third finger, groaning. Indy's fingers tightened around the bed sheets, nearly bringing her to the cusp of ripping the fabric to shreds.

"Please. Please. Huxley."

His tongue found her back entrance just as she brought her own fingers to her clit, circling desperately to find release. Falling onto the mattress, she came hard, letting her scream of pleasure be muffled by the pillow.

"I love the way you come." Miles peppered her back with soft kisses, then brought his cock to her entrance. "Four. You okay, baby?"

Indy blinked the stars away. "Yes. Still green."

That was all he needed to thrust into her.

Indy was still shaking from her four orgasms, but Miles was now fucking her slowly yet deeply. He leaned forward to kiss the back of her neck and shoulder blade, breathing heavily. "You're perfect," he whispered. "I love the way you take my cock. I love how you aren't afraid of challenging me. I love how we fit so perfectly."

She turned her head to kiss him, and that was when he picked up his pace. His right hand travelled from her breasts to her clit, his fingers applying the perfect amount of pressure.

"Fuck," she cried. "I can't."

"You can, baby." A harsh slap to her ass. "I can feel how desperate you are to come again. Just two more for me."

He sat back, pulling her with him so that her back was in contact with his damp chest.

"Ride my cock. It's yours. Use it."

As she started switching between bouncing and undulating her hips, she tipped her head back, sinking into his touch as he played with her nipple and circled her clit. The sounds of skin slapping with the feeling of her wetness dripping down her thigh onto the mattress made her entire body shake.

"Good girl. Taking it so well. I wish you could see how beautiful you look right now."

"Huxley." She repeated his name over and over, finding a rhythm that made his cock twitch.

His hand slid towards her throat, baring it, his hot breath fanning across her jaw. "Yes," he hissed. "Don't stop. Just like that."

Indy could feel the climax crash over her, building up like flames nourished by gasoline, ready to shatter her into a haze of blinding, white stars.

"Indy," he moaned. He held her close, pounding into her. "You're so wet."

She came for the fifth time. She was spent. But Miles was a man of his word, so he rolled them over, laying her down on her back. Draping an ankle atop his shoulder. Entering swiftly, pounding restlessly. She could feel every single inch of him throbbing, filling her up. Crying out as his fingers found her sensitive clit, she repeated his name when his sweat-slicked forehead crashed against hers. His damp breath fanned across her opened mouth. His brows knitted in pleasure as a loud moan broke free. He slammed into Indy, murmuring her name like it was a worship, then everything exploded into pure ecstasy.

In perfect sync, they came together. Hard. Blinding. Blissful. He whimpered loudly, shaking uncontrollably before stilling as he spilled into her all the while she lost sense of everything. The orgasm made her collapse into emptiness, her chest rapidly rising and falling.

Her entire body was trembling, so was his. Coaxing her with tender kisses on her temple, his fingers caressing her sweaty hip as he tried to catch his breath.

Then, he pulled out without making her move, his fingers gathering their mixture of release to plunge it back inside her.

He kissed her jaw. "That's six."

⚜

THE VERY LAST part of the surprise was so unexpected that Indy thought she was dreaming.

After taking another bath, lying for an hour in her bathrobe and listening to Miles play the piano, he'd asked if she was able to stand. Obviously, she had thrown him a dirty look before promising that she was more than fine. Though she felt sore, she didn't complain—because she didn't want to give him the satisfaction of being right. But yes, her legs had felt like jelly for far too long.

He took her to the beach whilst holding her hand. There, set up under the moonlight's glow and basking beneath the starry sky, was a blanket and pillows atop it.

"You did all of this?" she asked as she took a seat on the blanket.

"With Ava's help."

"This is the sweetest thing someone's done for me."

He cupped her chin. "You deserve the world, Indy. You deserve the best in every situation. Do you realise how amazing you are? How extraordinary and fun you are?"

She shook her head. "You make me feel like it."

"Because you are. I've never met anyone like you before."

The cord securing her heart to his was everlasting. And his hold over her soul was unwavering. She was his until the stars no longer shone and the universe was mere dust.

He extended a thick jumper for her to shrug on, and after lying down, he gestured for her to come closer.

With her ear pressed to his chest, she could hear the even beat of his heart. Miles was observing the Milky Way, absently tracing her back with intricate shapes.

"Orion's belt," he pointed out.

She smiled. "I didn't know you were into astronomy."

"It was something that Ava and I found interest in when we were bored."

"I love that. Which one is your favourite?"

"I like Cassiopeia," he confessed in a soft murmur. "It resembles an M from a certain angle. Sirius is one of my favourites too. It's shaped like a dog."

She chuckled. "And Ava's?"

"She's always had a thing for Draco. I'm not sure why, but it's her favourite along with Orion."

She could fall asleep right here in his arms with the cool breeze brushing against her cheekbones. With the sound of waves gently crawling to the shore. With the feel of his heartbeat matching hers as they stared at the night sky.

But his gentle voice kept her up. "Remember when you asked if I had a dream?"

She nodded. "You said you wanted to be happy."

"And I am." He shifted to prop himself on an elbow as she rested her head down on a pillow. His fingers delicately brushed her temple to push wild strands of hair away, his gaze tender and loving. "*You* make me happy. You make me feel loved. You're the girl of my dreams, Indy. I think you always were, but I always thought you were out of my league. Having you love me... It's like a dream come true."

Looking into his eyes, she could see the sincerity, and the love, and the vulnerability he only kept for her. She reached up, toying with the initial hanging from his neck.

Miles took a breath in, smiling down at her. "I love you, Indy."

Searching his adoring, tender gaze, she felt the tremble in her fingers as a smile touched her lips. She couldn't believe it.

Couldn't begin to fathom how the universe had brought them together, intent on sealing their once desperate souls to make one.

"Say that again," she whispered. She'd waited years to hear those words that felt like spun-sugar—bringing her a euphoric feeling—and needed to hear them over and over again so that she could replay them inside her mind like her favourite melody.

He leaned in, his nose grazing hers. "I love you, Indigo Bailey. I love your spirit. Your wildness and how carefree you are. I love how passionate you are about life. How fierce you are. How intelligent and bright and down to earth you are. I love everything about you."

She pulled him into her, and he laughed heartily as he crushed her down into the blanket. He left multiple kisses on her jaw and cheek, repeating how much he adored her.

"I love you," she told him.

He smiled. He was handsome. He was *hers*. "I love you. Always."

"Always."

And finally, Indy had everything she'd wished for.

Some people would have told her to give up, to stop running after someone who'd made her run in circles. But in the back of her mind, Indy knew that she belonged with Miles. In every lifetime.

Being persistent and not giving up had brought her the brightest star, the most beautiful flower, the entire world—*him*.

CHAPTER FORTY-THREE

ABU DHABI, UNITED ARAB EMIRATES

Four months later

"How does it feel to take pole for the last race of the season?"

"Feels good. Especially after the struggles we faced during FP2 yesterday," he answered. Gripping the railing, he offered a soft smile to Indy. She was evidently destabilised by his gesture, and he enjoyed seeing the power he held over her.

She returned a devastating beam, and he felt his cheeks heat up. Screw that. She always knew how to weaken him. "You're only two points ahead of Thiago in the drivers' ranking. Do you feel confident? Think you can be a four-time World Champion?"

He nodded, determined. "I do. The car works well on this track."

"Are you having flashbacks from 2021?"

He chuckled. "I will definitely have them during the last couple of laps. But you know what, Thiago's performance was amazing this season. I went up to him this morning to congratulate him. He was consistent all season long and his skills have improved a lot. I'm really impressed."

"This is very nice of you to say," Indy pointed out.

Beside him, Ava was holding the recorder, but her smile was as full of pride as Indy's.

"It's just the truth."

"Well, thank you for your time. Good luck for tomorrow's race."

"Thank you." He winked, and as he was ready to turn on his heel, he stopped short. "I forgot to ask. What are your plans for the winter break?"

A laugh bubbled out of Indy's mouth, its sound akin to his favourite song blasting from a stereo. "We're still live."

Miles feigned shock. "My bad. See you, then."

Walking away with Ava, he simply exhaled happily, and draped an arm around his press officer's shoulders.

"What's up with you?" Ava amusedly inquired while typing on her phone.

"I don't know. Just happy. Life's good."

Miles peered behind his shoulder to watch Indy conduct her last interview of the day with Thiago. She threw her head back and laughed, a hand on her stomach, and Miles stopped in his tracks to simply stare at her. Ingrain this image in the back of his mind. With the evening sun streaming down her face, she looked absolutely angelic, and he wondered if she knew that she effortlessly attracted light. If she knew that, when the universe was on the brink of welcoming nightfall, she was still radiant.

Indy, this beautiful woman who'd achieved her goals and inspired others not to be afraid and chase after their dreams.

Indy, this bright person who had held his hand when he was basking in darkness.

Indy, the love of his life, who had guided him towards light —his own personal star.

※

"Update me," Miles breathlessly demanded to AJ. "How far am I from Valencia?"

"The gap between you two is eight-thousandths of a second. It looks like Valencia's front end isn't as reactive as it was a couple of laps earlier. Especially in corners."

Interesting. "Okay."

Miles' gloved fingers tightened around the steering wheel as he panted, keeping his focus zeroed in on the red car before him. The heat coming off the circuit blending with the high temperature of the engine made beads of sweat cascade down the bridge of his nose and temple, dampening his balaclava.

"My water system is broken," he indicated as he braked before taking a tight corner.

He was so close to Thiago.

So close to overtaking.

He'd had a good start and led the race for twenty-two laps until he had to pit and change his tyres. With now a fresh set of compounds on, he could reclaim his position and win the race. Especially with a distance so minimal between the two cars, and knowing that his engine was powerful on this track.

"Copy," AJ responded. "There are thirty-one laps left. Think you can hang in there until the end of the race?"

"I don't have a choice. It's fine."

"Seven-thousandths of a second between you and Valencia. C'mon, baby. DRS is activated."

The front wing of his car nearly grazed the side pod of the red car as they drove through turn six before twisting into turn seven. The engine roared in his ears when he accelerated, his fingers pushing at the clutch to move gears forward. He pushed at full throttle down the straight line, staying behind Thiago to seek a slipstream. Gaining the extra speed he needed right before the corner, he slipped on the inside, finally overtaking Thiago.

He zipped through the circuit, watching his rival chase after him.

"That's what I'm talking about!" AJ shouted. "Get us that win."

༶

FIREWORKS STILL EXPLODED in the night sky when he parked the car before the "1" sign. He fell back against his seat, tipping his head back as he shut his eyes all the while sounds of cheers resonated around him. He lifted the visor of his helmet, pressed his fingers to his eyelids, and released an exhale full of relief.

Just because it was the fourth championship he secured under his belt didn't mean that the feeling of winning wasn't thrilling anymore. On the contrary, it was sensational and exciting. Phenomenal. Incomparable.

He'd broken another record, and he was proud of himself for doing so.

Savouring this blissful feeling, he laughed, then looked up to see Thiago and Rowan hover above him. They had already taken their helmets off, their grins wide and full of happiness.

When he pulled himself out of the car, he stood on the halo, raising both fists skywards, roars of joy exploding in the crowd. He then stumbled in his friends' arms, patting their backs.

"You're fucking incredible," Rowan told Miles, squeezing his nape.

"You really deserve it," Thiago said, engulfing him in another embrace.

He winked, swallowing his emotions. "Congrats to you two."

Charlie hugged him tightly, whispering how proud he was to have Miles as a mentor, a friend, and the brother he never had.

After taking his helmet and balaclava off, he ran into the wall of car mechanics screaming his name, laughing heartily when they lifted him over their heads. All the pats he received on his back were full of delight and pride. This was his team, his family, the people who worked their asses off to build him the perfect car.

Miles pulled AJ in. "Thanks, man."

AJ smacked his back. "Thank *you*."

He was congratulated by Enzo, his team principal, Kamari and Ava who were waiting for their boyfriends, and even Kai, Romeo, and Ezra were there. How the two hockey players had managed to find the time to travel while still in the season was beyond him, but having his friends cheer him on meant the world.

He fell into the arms of his father, the hug lasting longer than the ones before. Henry cupped the back of Miles' head, a sob racking his chest. "That's my son! You're incredible."

Miles sniffed, firmly gripping his Dad's shoulder. "I love you, Dad."

"I love you too, man. Go find Indy. She's a crying mess."

He chuckled. "Of course, she is."

Miles jumped over a barrier, making a beeline for the woman who had been holding his heart in the palm of her hand since the moment they met.

She was standing at the back with Scott, looking all serious and professional, but her rosy cheeks were stained with tears, her eyes still glassy as she followed him with her gaze.

She cast a quick glance to Scott. He nodded, smiling. "Go."

Indy ran over to him, in her Louboutins and pretty, off-shoulder burgundy dress, falling into his embrace.

When he swept her off her feet, arms around her waist as he made them spin around, it seemed as though the entire world became a blur.

SPEEDING INTO OVERDRIVE

She cradled his damp face, her forehead falling against his as her laughter blended in with his own.

"You did it," she murmured. "You did it again."

His chest rumbled with laughter and emotion as he set her down. With the pads of his thumbs, he dried off her face. "How badly did you want to jump and scream and tell me to win?"

"So badly. I couldn't help but sob when you crossed the line, though. Carmen might have a word with me about that later. You're worth the trouble."

Softly, he kissed her, his heart exploding in sync with fireworks. "I love you. I love you so fucking much."

That was all he could say in this moment. All he could think of.

He just needed to hold her for a while. Needed to anchor himself to her after this stressful race, so he simply tucked her into his chest, aware of the photographers surrounding them. Threading his fingers through her hair, he leaned down, his mouth finding hers in a sealing promise—to always support her the way she continuously showed up for him. Tears blended together, heartbeats syncing, and just like that, everything made complete sense.

"The man that you are," she said, shaking her head in disbelief. Another tear rushed down her cheek, and he wiped it away with his thumb. "Remarkable."

"And the woman you are... Absolutely breathtaking, amazing, and stellar."

"Stellar? Are you flirting with me?"

He barked out a laugh, delicately brushing her cheekbone. "Thanks for only noticing now."

Indy pecked his jaw, then took a step away. "Go do your thing."

"One last thing." He caught her hip, needing her as close as he could to murmur the next words into her ear. "Truth or dare, Indigo?"

Emotion swamped her mesmerising gaze. "Dare."

"I dare you to spend the rest of your life with me."

Sapphire eyes bore into his, her smile matching his wide one. "Challenge accepted, Golden Boy."

FIN.

EPILOGUE

LAKE COMO, ITALY

Two years later

"Yo, Miles. Would it be okay if I married your soon-to-be wife?"

Miles whirled at the sound of Romeo's baffling question, his fingers hovering over the bow-tie loosely hanging around his neck. "Say that again?"

Romeo whistled, closing the door behind him. "Indy, man, she looks beautiful in her bridal gown. Like an actual goddess."

Narrowing his gaze on the tall hockey player, Miles didn't miss his red-rimmed eyes. "There's so much info I need to process," he mumbled, ignoring the way his heart rate had picked up at the thought of Indy dressed in white. "The question is: would Isla be okay with that?"

At the mention of his beautiful date he'd been pining after

for years, a furious blush heated Romeo's face. He simply shrugged to answer Miles' question, then turned to look at his reflection in a mirror and fix his dark hair.

"Next question, please."

"Okay. When are you going to stop pretending you're not obsessed with your fake girlfriend?"

Romeo glared at him. "Next question."

"When and *why* did you see my fiancée?"

Yes, you read that right. Indy was Miles' fiancée, and had been for over a year now. It happened one summer night in Monaco as he had taken her to paint on the beach. While she had drawn his portrait, he'd written *"May I be your husband?"* on a canvas which he ended up showing to her when she least expected it.

She hadn't hesitated, and he still could remember the feeling of completeness as he knelt before her and brought the diamond ring to her finger. Then, she'd tackled him to the blanket, spilling paint all over it and over himself. The night had ended up with paint stains all over her art room when they'd decided to continue making art in there—the floor, the door, the wall. Like the colours were screaming of love, too.

Romeo's signature shit-eating grin spread across his face. "Thought I'd just go and say hi to my favourite person. I made her cry."

"Of course, you did. Bet you cried like a little bitch, too."

He raised his hands. "Hey, in my defence, my words were really, really emotional. So yeah, I cried. What's wrong with men embracing their sensitivity?"

The door opened and Ezra strolled in, his untied bow hanging around his neck. "Your speech was shit. Indy cried because she's just sensitive."

Romeo scoffed. "Yeah, right. I can't wait to hear your stupid speech later. I bet it's bland like your fucking ass."

Kai stepped into the room with a grin, Rowan in tow as he tightly held Ava's hand.

"Pregnant lady coming in. Make room. Don't touch her. Be careful. Give her food. ASAP!" Rowan bellowed as he led his own fiancée to an armchair.

Ava swatted Rowan's hand away, rolling her eyes. "I'm fine."

"Yeah, but—"

She gently cupped his face, pecking his jaw. "I'm all good for now."

"What about baby g—" Rowan stopped himself, pressing his lips in a thin line, which made Ava sigh in exasperation.

Miles' eyes bulged. "Were you about to say girl?"

"Goat," Rowan said. "Baby goat."

"You're such an idiot," Ava muttered, though she smiled when she met Miles' bewildered gaze.

"I'm sorry, sunflower."

"Are you having a girl?" Miles asked slowly.

Ava and Rowan exchanged a glance, then nodded, beaming.

"Fuck yes! I knew it!" Ezra laid his palm flat out. "Huxley, Bailey, Quinn. You each owe me one hundred bucks."

Kai groaned. "Damn it! I wanted baby Emerson to be a dude."

Miles shook his head then fished his wallet out, throwing a bill at Ezra's proud face. He then walked over to Ava and Rowan, throwing his arms around them.

"I'm so happy for you two," he whispered, emotion rising in his throat. "You're going to be the best parents ever."

"Damn right, we are," Rowan quipped.

Ava took a seat on a chair after accepting the hugs and congratulations. "Why is everyone betting on my baby's gender?"

"Because it's the most exciting thing that's happening right now," Ezra answered breezily. "Aside from the wedding. And Kai getting back together with Amara after being apart for ten years. And Romeo being here with the girl he's been in love with his whole—"

"Okay we get it," Romeo cut in, shaking his head.

Ever since Ava had announced her pregnancy to her friends and family a couple of weeks ago, her bump looked more defined. And ever since she'd told Rowan about it, he was overprotective of her, but in the best way possible.

Miles thought his best friend looked absolutely exquisite with her pregnancy glow and small bump. And seeing her in a terracotta silk dress made his eyes water. She was not only his best friend, but also one of Indy's bridesmaids.

"I can't believe you're getting married," she murmured when it was just the two of them whilst the rest of the boys were chatting amongst themselves.

Miles smiled as she fixed his bow. "Please don't make me cry. I can't believe *you're* engaged and about to have a kid."

"Miles," Ava whispered. "I know it's not the time, so you can think about it, okay? But we'd love for you to be our daughter's second godfather."

"Who's the first one?"

"Tate." Rowan's best friend.

"Makes sense." He grinned broadly, taking her shaking hands in his. "I'm honoured. I would love to be her godfather. You three are very special to me, and I promise I'll take good care of you all."

"You have some real nerve to say that to a pregnant lady. Now I'm getting emotional."

"My apologies." He chuckled, then pecked the crown of her head. "Love you, Ave. Would a doughnut make you happy?"

She nodded, sniffing. "You know me so well."

"He's stressing me out."

"He's nervous. Let him be."

"But why is he pacing like a mad man?"

"Because he's nervous? You blokes are so insensitive. He's about to get married, for fuck's sake."

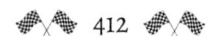

Miles took a deep breath, then turned to his friends—his groomsmen. Before him, all dressed in regal tuxedos, they all gaped at him with admiration and emotion. Kai, Romeo, Ezra, Thiago, Rowan, and Charlie. The men he'd grown up with, and the ones he raced against on Sundays, but became family on other days.

"I'm nervous," he admitted.

"No shit, Sherlock," Rowan commented with a soft scoff.

"I hadn't noticed," Romeo deadpanned.

"Okay, none of us are helping with the situation," Kai said. "How about we take a shot? Oh, wait. No, this won't help our groom here."

"We already took one," Thiago said. "Let's save the liquor for the party."

"Tito always being the responsible one," Charlie remarked wryly, which earned a grin from Thiago.

A knock on the door resonated, and when it cracked open, Lisa Bailey popped her head inside. "Hi, gentlemen. Mind if I catch a moment with Miles and Malakai?"

When everyone was out of the room save for Lisa, Kai, and Miles, he felt the tension rattling through his bones vanish. Lisa's eyes shone, and emotion started to grip at Miles' heart again.

He could still remember the day he'd taken the Bailey's out for lunch when he and Indy were visiting in London. While Indy had been busy catching up with friends, Miles had grabbed the opportunity to ask her family, in secret, if he could take Indy's hand in marriage. Lisa had cried, so had Zach, and so had Kai.

"You look handsome," Lisa murmured, taking his hands in hers.

"And you look ravishing." Indy had inherited her father's blonde hair, but her stunning crystal eyes were the exact copy of Lisa's. "How are you?"

"I should be asking you this question," she countered. "How are you feeling, love?"

"He's about to piss his pants," Kai said.

"*Malakai.*"

"I'm really nervous," Miles answered, ignoring his best friend pretending to be annoyed with his mother. "What if Indy changes her mind?"

Lisa's fingers tightened around his own. "That will never happen. She's going to say yes the moment she walks down the aisle. Miles, Indy loves you so much. She's loved you her entire life. There's no doubt you two are meant for each other. You told me once that you thought you two were moving too fast, but there's no such thing as rushing when you know she's the one. My daughter is happy, and I'm so, so thankful that you're the one who makes her life so beautiful and exciting."

Swallowing the tight lump that had built in the back of his throat, Miles nodded, unable to find his voice.

"Are you happy?" Lisa continued softly.

"Never been happier."

Miles looked over to Kai as the latter wiped a tear off his cheek. "I'm not crying."

Lisa and Miles laughed. "Sure."

Kai's hand came to firmly grip Miles' shoulder. "You've always been part of the family, but I still think I need to say this to you. Welcome to the family, mate. I love you, but if you so much as make my sister cry—except for when you exchange your vows—I will strangle you."

⁂

THE DISTANT RUMBLE in the grey, brooding sky was not a good sign. Despite the warm, summer air, Miles had a feeling the downpour would come to disturb his plans soon. He fixed his vest, standing at the altar, and watched over the guests who were calmly chatting amongst each other.

He cast a quick glance to the front row where his father and his girlfriend were sitting. Both tenderly smiled at him, a gesture he returned earnestly. Next to them was Lisa fanning herself with a hand, Rosie lying at her feet, Andrew and Zoya (Ava's parents) on her other side and smiling proudly back at Miles. Maya was chuckling with her husband, but when her gaze found her brother's, tears brimmed her already-puffy eyes.

He could see some of his favourite car mechanics he'd been working with for years sitting at the back, AJ and Enzo amongst them. Even Tate Richards (who held his daughter, Nora, on his lap), Callahan Langdon, and Alex Myers were here.

It wasn't a big wedding despite the fact that Indy was terrifically popular. They had invited the people closest to them to Italy to celebrate this big day.

When the pianist and violinist started to play one of his original pieces, Miles felt the ball in his throat grow and grow, the knot in his stomach twist and turn. First, Kai appeared with Kamari—his best man and Indy's maid of honour. Kamari was a beautiful, devastating woman who stole everyone's breath away. When they reached him, Kamari squeezed Miles' forearm before going to stand opposite him as Kai stood by his side.

Next, it was Romeo and Diana, Indy's other best friend with snark for days and coppery hair floating down her back. Ava was holding Ezra's arm as they marched steadily towards the altar, one hand hugging a bouquet as the other rested on her bump. Behind them, Rowan was glaring at Ezra. He was walking in the company of Amara, Kai's girlfriend. Thiago appeared next, Isla St James on his arm, winking to Kamari when he passed in front of her. And finally, Charlie and Aïda came into view. The sight of them together made Miles' heart swell with both pride and happiness.

Then, the music shifted.

Nothing surrounded him.

Nothing mattered or existed.

There was only Indy. *His* Indy.

Instant tears started to blur his vision when she came into

view, one hand tightly clutching her father's arm and the other holding a beautiful bouquet.

But her…

There were no words that could describe her beauty and how she managed to steal the breath away from his lungs. Her ivory dress was breathtaking, but her smile was even more mesmerising.

Miles couldn't help but sob when all the sounds around him buzzed to life, his hands shaking and tears streaming down his face. He caught his breath, accepting the handkerchief Kai slipped to him.

So, this was real, right? He wasn't dreaming.

Indy and Zach stopped in front of him, and it took every sliver of strength he possessed to look away from the love of his life. Whispering something in Indy's ear, Zach finally let go of his daughter and pulled Miles in for a tight hug.

"Take care of her," Zach whispered.

"Always."

The next moment, he extended his hand and invited Indy to step into his cosmos.

"Hi, stud." Indy's fingers entwined with his, and just like that, his body sparked to life. "Fancy seeing you here."

"Hi." He swallowed and let out a shaky breath. "You look stunning."

She smiled, weakening him in the knees. "You're not too bad yourself."

As she stood across from him, admiring him and letting awe draw upon her expression, Miles couldn't believe she was his. Couldn't believe they were about to bind themselves to an eternity together and let that invisible string tethering them together become stronger and unwavering.

He couldn't look away from her. Couldn't do anything except let himself fall further, waiting to be hers for life.

The moment it was time to exchange their vows, he inhaled deeply, his eyes looking from the little note held between his fingers and the lovely woman who was about to have his last name.

"Indigo," he softly said, his voice trembling. He chuckled, staring into her ocean eyes swamped with tears. "How could I ever find the right words to thank you for loving me? I've kept everyone at arm's length my entire life, not wanting to let anyone in or close to me, but then there was you. You've always known how to tear my armour down, and it terrified me for years because how could someone as extraordinary as you could want someone like me?

"We met when we were just kids, and even then, I knew that you were special. If there's one person who's always been able to see right through me and break my walls down, it's you. Life with you is simply beautiful. It's filled with laughter, joy, art, music, racing. It's filled with moments I will always cherish, even the tougher ones. You saw something in me—something I sometimes wonder what is—and never once looked back. You are the greatest woman I've ever met, and I will always be in awe of you. Of your dedication, your passion, and your selflessness. I am so incredibly lucky to be yours. Thank you for loving me, Indy. Thank you for loving every part of me, even the ones that are harder to love, and for seeing my scars and cherishing them. I've never felt as loved and appreciated as when you're with me. I love you. Always. Loving you is the easiest thing I've had to do, and I promise I'll do it every day. And in every lifetime, I will be yours."

A tear rolled down Indy's cheek, and Miles reached over to delicately wipe it away. She leaned into his touch, causing fireworks to burst inside his chest. He gasped for air, feeling a tear of his own crash down his cheekbone.

Sounds of sobs and sniffles resonated around the space, mixing with the thunder rumbling overhead. All that mattered, though, was Indy who accepted the note Kamari slipped into her hand.

Her chest rose and fell, and the moment she inhaled, rain

came pouring down. A laugh bubbled out of Indy's mouth whilst some guests gasped. He looked around, seeing umbrellas opening and other guests taking in the rain just like he was.

"Huxley," she started, emotion woven into her tone. "You'll always be Huxley to me. Because Miles belongs to the world, but Huxley is the one who stole my heart when I was three and plucked a daisy out of my crown to tuck it into the pocket of his racing suit." He smiled at that memory, and in the distance, his dad's chuckle echoed. "I always knew that you were the one for me. From the moment I met you, I just knew there was something strangely amazing that kept pulling me towards you.

"You're an amazing man, who deemed me, a chaotic girl with pieces that needed to be mended, worthy of your love. I will always be grateful for that. You delicately helped me put myself back together. You taught me that love doesn't need to be rushed, that it is calm and peaceful. Thank you for choosing me, for loving me, every single day. Thank you for being my biggest supporter and for always swimming by my side when I find myself drowning. You always know how to pull me up and show me how great I'm doing. Thank you for holding my hand and wanting to spend the rest of your life with me. I can't wait to see how the rest of our married life unfolds. I know it's going to be amazing beyond measure. I promise that I will cherish and love you for the rest of our lives, and even when death does us part, I will find you in every lifetime and claim myself as yours."

Miles couldn't see through the tears blinding his vision. His lungs were craving for oxygen, his fingers trembling from anticipation.

Golden bands adorned their ring fingers a moment later, and when he finally heard *"you may kiss the bride"*, Miles caught Indy's waist, dipping her to kiss her soft, pink lips. The cheers erupting from around were drowned out by the heavy rain beating down on them—like the downpour had engulfed them in a cosmos of pure, eternal happiness.

Indy smiled against his mouth, her shaking fingers cupping

his jaw. He kissed her softly, gently, sealing the promise of his love through the entwine of their breaths.

Their foreheads touched, and Miles breathed in the scent of the rain, the fresh air, her perfume. He chuckled as rain crashed down on them, brushing her cheekbones with the pad of his thumbs. "Hi, wife." God, didn't that sound right.

As always, Indy's smile was akin to warm sunlight. She kissed him again, whispering words he'd dreamed of once. "Hi, husband. Are you ready to be sick of me?"

He laughed. "So ready. And you?"

He almost collapsed at the sight of her dilated pupils, her beautiful eyes flickering between his. "I've been waiting for this my entire life."

"Good." Weaving his fingers through hers, he grinned at the way they perfectly fitted together. "Let's do this then."

With yet another powerful kiss binding their souls and hearts together, Miles finally felt happy and alive and complete. He knew then, that this was the beginning of a beautiful story—a story he'd, one day, tell his kids about a fierce, intelligent, captivating woman who had made his heart speed into overdrive, claiming it and never giving it back to him.

WHAT'S NEXT?

Enchanted by Kai, Romeo, and Ezra? Their books are next! To see more updates about them, find me on Instagram @kanitha.author — I will be announcing the series *Alpine Valley* soon.

Charlie's story is next (and last) in the Full Throttle Series. Will he rekindle his flame with his long-lost love, Aïda? And what happens when she becomes a Formula 1 driver, too? On-track, they'll be competing against each other, but off-track? He's trying to win her back. Coming soon!

In the meantime, you can read Thiago and Kamari's fake dating story in *Falling Off the Cliff*, and Rowan and Ava's workplace romance and secret relationship in *Chasing the Slipstream*!

ACKNOWLEDGMENTS

This book was such a delight to write. Indy and Miles were so loveable and easy to relate to, and I hope you had the best time falling in love with them! If either of their stories/backgrounds hit close to home, I'm sending you lots of love. Remember to leave a review on Amazon to give my book a chance to be seen by other readers—it would mean a lot.

Starting as always by thanking the best cover designer, Ivy. Thank you infinitely for creating the most beautiful, mesmerising covers, and for being such a good friend.

Nyla, I know I sound like a broken record, but I seriously couldn't do this without your support. You're the best hype-woman ever, and your encouragement is always what I need when times are tough. Thank you for everything.

E, you're my rock! Thank you for always cheering me on and giving me some love when I can't find the energy to love myself or my work. You're the best friend an author could have.

Jessica Rita Rampersad, Casey, Phoebe, and B, I love having you on my team!

Sarah—Thank you for being such a sweet, loving soul. You're probably my biggest cheerleader and I'll never find the right words to say how much I appreciate you.

Hannah—it's always a joy to work with you. If this manuscript is polished to perfection, it's all thanks to you.

Also a quick thanks to Sam and Mel at Ink & Velvet Designs for creating the cutest heading images!

And to all my readers, no word will ever express the sheer

love and appreciation I have for each one of you—especially the ones who've been there since the first book was published and constantly give me some love. I could never do this without your support.

Last but not least, thank you to the love of my life, Jeremy, for always showing me how worthy of great accomplishments I am. The past year was rough, but you were always there to pull me up, or just hold me when I needed it.